Praise for *USA* [obscured]
Ch[obscured]

"Equally passionate and emotional, this tale will quicken pulses and firmly tug on the heartstrings... An excellent story that you hope won't ever end!"
—*RT Book Reviews* (Top Pick) on *Can't Fight This Feeling*

"[E]verything romance readers love."
—*BookPage* on *Can't Fight This Feeling*

"Ridgway's writing is impeccable."
—*RT Book Reviews* on *Make Me Lose Control*

"This sexy page-turner [is] a stellar kick-off to Ridgway's latest humor-drenched series."
—*Library Journal* on *Take My Breath Away*

"Emotional and powerful...everything a romance reader could hope for."
—*Publishers Weekly* on *Bungalow Nights* (starred review)

"Kick off your shoes and escape to endless summer. This is romance at its best."
—Emily March, *New York Times* bestselling author of *Nightingale Way*, on *Bungalow Nights*

"Sexy and addictive—Ridgway will keep you up all night!"
—*New York Times* bestselling author Susan Andersen on *Beach House No. 9*

"Pure romance, delightfully warm and funny."
—*New York Times* bestselling author Jennifer Crusie

"Christie Ridgway writes with the perfect combination of humor and heart. This funny, sexy story is as fresh and breezy as its Southern California setting. An irresistible read!"
—*New York Times* bestselling author Susan Wiggs on *How to Knit a Wild Bikini*

Also available from Christie Ridgway and HQN Books

The Beach House No. 9

Turn Up the Heat
(anthology featuring "Beach House Beginnings")
Beach House No. 9
Bungalow Nights
The Love Shack

Cabin Fever

Take My Breath Away
Make Me Lose Control
Can't Fight This Feeling
Keep On Loving You

CHRISTIE RIDGWAY

keep on loving you

ISBN-13: 978-0-373-78911-5

Keep On Loving You

This edition published by arrangement with Harlequin Books S.A.

For questions and comments about the quality of this book, please contact us at CustomerService@Harlequin.com.

www.HQNBooks.com

Printed in U.S.A.

For my readers. Thanks for enjoying the books—
I keep on loving you!

Dear Reader,

We're returning to Blue Arrow Lake, where high peaks, tall evergreens and deep waters are in great contrast to the Southern California cities and beaches just a couple of hours away. Mackenzie "Mac" Walker, the second of the mountain-born-and-bred Walker siblings, is the last of them single, too...and it's starting to wear a little. Everybody believes she's still hung up on her first love, but he's been incommunicado for a decade, except for postcards that have continually arrived from all over the world.

And then one night, a familiar stranger shows up at a family celebration...

Zan Elliott returns to the place of his childhood that never quite felt like home. He has a job to do—handle his grandfather's estate—and then he presumes he'll return to his globe-trotting lifestyle. But the girl he's never forgotten has now grown up, and their connection is as strong as ever. Can he risk attaching himself to this woman when he knows how tenuous life and love can be?

I've been excited about telling the story of Mac and Zan from the beginning of the Cabin Fever series. Their young love is a legend around the region—I hope you find their second take just as epic. Grab your ticket and join me on another emotional, sexy journey. Destination...romance!

Christie

People don't notice whether it's winter or summer
when they're happy.

—Anton Chekhov

CHAPTER ONE

THAT CRISP JANUARY night Mackenzie Walker couldn't help but notice the beauty of the bride and the handsomeness of the groom. All the family and friends at the reception glowed, too, reveling in the couple's obvious happiness.

The whole lot of them was giddy with gladness, with just one exception.

The maid of honor—Mac herself—was miserable.

Not that she'd allow anyone to guess that. Instead, she smiled and laughed and responded gaily to every question thrown her way.

Wasn't her new sister-in-law's gown lovely? Of course it was, Mac agreed. Who would deny it? The ivory-colored dress clung to Angelica's figure, her golden skin showing through spangled chiffon sleeves that began just off the shoulder and ended at her wrists.

Didn't Brett Walker appear just as comfortable in his charcoal suit and silvery-gray tie as he did in his usual uniform of jeans and work boots? No doubt, Mac responded. Her big brother rocked the formal wear.

And what a bridesmaid dress! one of Mac's cousins exclaimed. Everybody knew those could be dreadful. Hers was not, Mac had to concur. The pale blue was the color of her eyes and it had a flattering, sweetheart neckline with sheer sleeves dotted with crystals just like the bride's.

Yes, her attire was lovely. That wasn't the source of Mac's low mood.

On that thought, she made her way to the bar at Mr. Frank's, an old-fashioned restaurant and bar with red vinyl booths and dark paneling in the village of Blue Arrow Lake. The lake itself was private and the surrounding lavish homes beyond pricey, because Southern Californians could find stupendous mountain scenery and four real seasons just a couple of hours away from urban centers and sand and surf.

This was a vacation spot for them, but locals lived—much more modestly, of course—in the area, too. Mac's family, the Walkers, had been here for over one hundred and fifty years, part of the first wave of pioneers who labored up the mountain with their oxen for lumber opportunities and stayed because they fell in love with the land.

She slid onto a bar stool and sketched a wave at the bartender. "Hey, Jim." His white shirt was starched and his red vest well pressed. "Looking good."

He beamed, his fiftysomething face lighting up. "Nothing but the best for your brother and his bride. We were only too happy to close the place for the reception."

Though Brett and Angelica had actually run off to Vegas and done the deed in October, they'd decided to celebrate the tying of the knot with all the trimmings once the holidays had passed. It had been a bit of trouble getting the dresses in a timely fashion, but the rest had fallen into place.

"What can I get you?" Jim asked.

"Um…"

While she pondered, his gaze wandered over her shoulder. “They sure are a picture.”

Mac glanced back and took in the sight of the bride and groom surrounded by the rest of the bridal party: her two sisters, their fiancés and five-year-old Mason, Mac’s nephew, who had also stood up with the groom. When her stomach tightened, she told herself it was wrong of her to let her own feelings darken even a moment of these happy hours.

“You’re the last single Walker now, eh?”

Except there was that unavoidable truth. Of her four siblings, Mac alone was single.

Single. Alone.

Suppressing a sigh, she decided on her order. “A tequila shot, please.”

Jim didn’t remark on the out-of-character request, though Mac rarely took her spirits straight. Instead, he plunked down a napkin and then a shot glass filled to the brim with a golden liquid. “Top shelf for you,” he said.

Because he was sorry for her, just as she feared everybody she knew was sorry for her, just as she was a little bit sorry for herself.

Single. Alone.

She threw back the liquor, choked, coughed, then slammed the empty glass back on the bar. Heat coursed through her, hot enough, she hoped, to burn off the uncomfortable sense of being the odd woman out in her own family. Just months ago, the Walker siblings had been hardworking singletons. Now three of the four were still hardworking, yet exuberantly happy people paired off, leaving Mac the odd wheel.

Honestly, that wouldn’t be so bad if—

"There you are!"

She slid her gaze to the side, taking in her date for the evening, Kent Valdez. "I'll have what she just gulped down," he said to Jim.

Mac showed the bartender two fingers, indicating another tequila shot was in order for herself. "Having fun, Kent?" she asked, forcing herself to sound pleasant. Not that there was anything wrong with the man or anything wrong with the obvious good time he'd been having. But she'd invited him to be her date and he'd been whooping it up with the other guests instead of hanging at her elbow, doing his part to assure everyone that Mac had a full and very satisfying romantic life.

Because the other downer she'd been dealing with lately was the astonishing and irritating revelation that her entire community still believed her to be hung up on her first love.

Who had left her and the mountains ten years before.

In order to correct that group delusion, she'd hit upon the scheme to attend each of the Walker matrimonial events—all happening in the next few weeks—with a different eligible bachelor.

She'd show everyone in the vicinity of Blue Arrow Lake that the last single Walker standing was happy and heart-whole.

The recollection of that goal plus the burn of the second tequila shot got her off the bar stool. Tugging on Kent's hand, she towed him toward the dance floor, just as a line dance was forming. Thrusting both arms in the air, she let out a loud "Woo-hoo!" and took her place beside Angelica, who shared a grin. Then the bride stuck out her tongue at the groom, who stood on the sidelines, arms crossed over his chest and a smug half smile curving his mouth, his gaze never leaving his beautiful new wife. She laughed and blew him a kiss that he pretended to catch. Then Brett clapped his hand to his heart.

Mac froze, stricken by the romantic gesture coming from her usually reserved older brother. But when the music ramped up, she drove off the melancholy by throwing herself into the moves, hoping the old fake-it-until-you-make-it adage would blow away her doldrums.

And it worked.

Not for one instant did she leave the dance floor, finding partners for the slower dances and gyrating with her girlfriends during the fast numbers. Kent did his part, and when he begged for a breather she waved him off with her blessing and a smile. When the DJ segued into another romantic ballad, Ed Sheeran's "Thinking Out Loud," she sidled into a shadowy corner to enjoy the song and the sight of Brett and Angelica wrapped in each other's arms, their foreheads touching, their mouths a millimeter apart.

Closing her eyes, she tried ignoring the pang in her heart.

But the sudden sensation of a male body behind her and muscled arms crossing her waist couldn't be disregarded. She started, but his hold tightened and a hard jaw pressed against her temple as a low voice whispered in her ear. "Just enjoy the moment."

Only slightly swaying to the beat, he drew her closer to his solid warmth.

Goose bumps rolled down Mac's body, hot chills of sexual response. Her breath caught in her throat. Who…?

Not Kent, because through the dancers she could glimpse him at the bar talking to Jim. Anyway, she already knew he didn't draw this kind of reaction from her. As the sweet notes of the song wrapped around them, curiosity prodded her to turn and confront her partner, but another part of her didn't want to disturb the strange and strangely compelling bindings that seemed to be lashing their bodies together.

His heart beat against her back.

Hers sent an urgent message to her brain. *This is something special.*

Mac didn't dare disturb the magic created by the sensation of his exhalations stirring her hair. Breathing deep of his scent, she felt both bold and safe enough to lean into his strength, going so far as to wrap her fingers around his forearms covered in the fine wool of an expensive jacket.

Enjoy the moment.

She couldn't recall the last time she'd done that. Walkers worked hard to keep their place on the mountain and she was no exception, doing everything from washing windows to sending out invoices as the proprietor of Maids by Mac. Housework wasn't a glamorous career, but she'd never wanted anything more than to be her own woman.

Except when you longed to be Zan's woman, a devil whispered in her head.

She kicked away the thought of Alexander Elliott. He didn't belong in this sweet bubble of possibility. Closing her eyes again, she allowed herself to bask in the man's scent and in the man's heat and mused that maybe Mac Walker wasn't destined to be single and alone, after all.

Lost in that, she missed the ending of the song until the loud shriek of the mic yanked her out of her reverie. The DJ began speaking and she dropped her hold on the stranger behind her. But just as she turned to look at him, her sister Shay's stepdaughter-to-be, London, grabbed Mac's hand and hauled her onto the dance floor.

"Wait!" Mac glanced around, trying to find her partner, but she was already surrounded by a bevy of other women. "What's going on?"

"The bouquet toss, silly," London said in an excited voice, having lost her usual teenage insouciance somewhere after the I do's.

Mac groaned. The tradition was embarrassing and one she did her best to avoid. But London had begged Angelica to include the custom and the kid had Mac's wrist in a viselike grip. She tried tugging free. "Why don't I get Shay and Poppy out here," she suggested, naming her two engaged sisters. Once away from the teenager, she'd actually go on the hunt for her sexy stranger.

"They already have rings on their fingers," London said. "This is for us."

"You're too young to get married," Mac replied. "And I'm too..."

Hung up on Zan Elliott, the devil murmured again.

Instead of shrieking in frustration, Mac gave up. The absurd ritual couldn't take long, right? Then she'd find the stranger and do...what?

Throw herself at him?

Maybe, she decided, reliving the sensation of him surrounding her. Reliving that so unusual—for her—trust she'd felt leaning against his larger body.

The women around her were chattering and the DJ

was making noises into the mic, but Mac ignored the sounds, her thoughts focused on that man. Movement in her peripheral vision caught her attention and she turned her head.

Her breath caught in her throat. Her eyes widened in complete surprise.

There, beyond the tight clutch of women, a figure stood in profile. A figure she hadn't seen in ten years and who was more muscled than when he'd left, but one she'd recognize anywhere.

And one she should have known when he stepped up behind her to whisper in her ear.

Just enjoy the moment.

Heat rose from her chest and flamed up her throat to her face as she recalled how quickly she'd relaxed in his hold. What did he think of that? And why would he have…have ambushed her in that way at this important event?

As if sensing her regard, his head turned, too, and their gazes met. His mouth quirked, stopping somewhere between a smirk and a smile.

Her temper kindled. What gall! What gall to show up so suddenly and without even a word of warning.

Just as she made to break out of the female circle in order to challenge her unexpected and unwelcome blast from the past, something soft and fragrant struck the side of her face. Instinct had her putting up her hands as a cheer sounded throughout the room.

Mac looked down at what was now cradled in her arms, trying to come to terms with the fact that she'd caught the bridal bouquet—and that Zan Elliott was back in town.

THE FRAGRANCE OF roses and lavender wafted up from the flowers. She gulped in a breath of it, then peered over the women gathered around her in congratulation, once again seeking out Zan.

He'd moved from where he'd been moments before… if he'd really been there moments before. It was as if he'd vanished into thin air. Could it be possible she'd imagined him?

Angelica broke through the ring of celebrants and beamed at Mac. Really, she was breathtakingly beautiful with her shiny brunette hair and dark eyes. She and Brett were going to make beautiful babies, and proud Auntie Mac would dote on them from her comfortable spinsterhood, unless Zan—

"I'm so glad you caught the flowers!" Angelica said, leaning in to kiss Mac's cheek. "I know you consider the tradition barbaric, but I thought it was fun."

She pretended to scowl at her new sister-in-law. "How come there's no garter toss if you find tradition so great?"

"That's because your brother's a caveman. He said he didn't want me baring my legs for all the wedding guests to see."

Speaking of wedding guests… Mac took a quick look around the room, then leaned in to whisper in her sister-in-law's ear. "Have you seen Zan?"

Angelica pulled back, her eyes going wide. "Zan? *Your* Zan?"

"He's not *my* Zan," Mac said quickly. "But I…I thought I caught a glimpse of him a minute ago." *I thought I felt his arms around me. I thought maybe my heart would beat out of my chest as we swayed to the music.* "Did he call Brett or something and say he was coming back to town?"

The bride shook her head. "Not that I know of."

"But did you see—"

"I wouldn't recognize him, right? We've never met."

"Oh." Mac felt another flush climb up her neck. The man—whoever he was—had her so flustered she wasn't thinking clearly. "Never mind, then. I'll just, uh, go put the bouquet down at my place at the table."

Then she hurried off the dance floor, keeping a lookout for a dark-haired, hazel-eyed ten-year-gone guy. But when she didn't see him, she began to wonder about her sanity. Perhaps the night before she'd stayed up too late boxing the chocolates that were going to the guests as party favors. Maybe she needed to gulp down a large cup of hot coffee and get her wits back in place.

"There you are!" Her sisters, Poppy and Shay, approached, their long skirts swishing about their legs. They wore gowns identical to Mac's, only different in color. Poppy's was pink, while Shay's was a subtle peach.

"Nice catch," Poppy said, nodding to the bouquet.

Mac rolled her eyes. "You saw what happened. It hit me in the head."

"Maybe you'll be better prepared when I throw mine at my reception in two weeks," Shay said.

"No," Mac groaned the word. "Not you, too?"

"London is insisting."

"I'll hide out in the bathroom, then," Mac said. "Promise you'll give me the high sign?"

"Absolutely," her youngest sister said.

Mac narrowed her gaze. "You're a terrible liar."

"I'm not even going to pretend I won't make you be in the gaggle of bachelorettes when it's my turn," Poppy put in. "But, anyway, did you see—"

"I did." Mac's heart jumped, then started to race. "I thought maybe I imagined it, but if you saw Zan, too…" She broke off at the puzzlement on her sister's face.

"Zan?" Poppy said. "I was going to ask if you'd seen Mason dancing with the little McDonald girl."

"Um, no, I didn't," Mac mumbled, feeling stupid. "Never mind—"

"Zan is here?" Shay asked. "Zan Elliott?"

"I don't know. Probably not. It was just a glimpse," Mac said.

Her two sisters exchanged glances. "How much have you had to drink?" Poppy asked.

No way would Mac mention the two tequila shots. "Never mind. I'm sure I was mistaken."

Her sisters looked at each other again. "Oh, Mac," Poppy said in a concerned voice.

Mac winced. Poppy had the gooiest heart of any of the Walkers, and right now she was clearly oozing pity for her poor, unattached sister who had delusions about the return of her very first boyfriend, her very first love. "It's nothing," she told her sister in a firm voice. "Like I said, a mistake."

"But—"

"Look, they're about to cut the cake." Mac pointed toward the other end of the room. "We'd better get over there."

Thankfully, that distracted her sisters, and Mac followed slowly in their wake. Could she really have mistaken some stranger for Zan?

In her mind's eye, she saw him as he'd looked his

second-to-last day in the mountains. She'd been eighteen, he'd just turned twenty-one, and they'd been a couple for two years. That afternoon they'd taken his boat to a secluded cove, where they'd spread a blanket and a picnic. Her intention had been to tough it out and not allow her belly-hollowing longing for him and her aching sadness at his imminent departure to ruin those final warm, sunny hours.

They'd made love for the last time, the wide shoulders of his rangy body blocking the sun so that she couldn't read the expression in his hazel eyes as he'd entered her. But her legs had wound around his hips, tight, like two vines that could bind him to her forever.

He'd cupped her face in his hands. One hot tear had leaked from her eye and he'd brushed it away with his thumb, the stroke slow and tender. "Mackenzie Walker," he'd whispered. Just that, as if memorizing her name.

Maybe he no longer even remembered it. Maybe he'd never thought of that girl again, who'd given him her body and who'd wanted to give him everything else: her heart, her soul, her whole life.

She grimaced, thinking of that green and unguarded young woman. Likely Zan had headed down the mountains and never thought of her again.

Except that didn't explain the postcards that had come to her regularly over the past decade. On their fronts were photos of places like Oslo and Algiers and Singapore. On the other side, a single-letter message, three bold strokes that made up the letter *Z*.

No other thought. No return address. Just a pointed reminder of the young man who'd left her behind.

Mac was older now, but maybe no wiser if she truly

thought for even a second that Zan might return to the place he'd always sworn to leave.

Standing near the table at the far end of the room, she watched Angelica and Brett feed each other bites of cake with the tidiest of manners. When her brother brushed an errant crumb from his bride's bottom lip, a hot press of tears burned at the back of Mac's eyes, which she ruthlessly held back.

God, how was she going to make it through two more of these darn events?

Poppy was the family crier, but Mac was on perilous ground herself and thanked God she was recruited to pass out slices of cake. A diversion was necessary. Moving among the guests wasn't as much of a reprieve as she'd hoped, however. It was easy to agree about the bride's beaming smile and the groom's clear dedication to his new wife. But other comments weren't so simple to smile through.

When will we see you married, Mac?

Why hasn't some man finally put a wedding band on your finger?

Whatever happened to that boy of yours...that Zan Elliott?

At this last, she stopped short, staring down at tiny Carmen Lind, who had to be closing in on ninety and wore her silver hair braided in a crown on top of her head. "What made you think of him, Mrs. Lind?" Mac asked, through a suddenly tight throat.

The little lady dug into her cake with relish. "Who, dear?"

"You mentioned Zan."

"Who?"

Mac smiled a little. "Zan Elliott. You just brought up his name."

"Oh, yes. Such a good-looking young man. But he got into a lot of trouble, I recall. Those bad boys always catch a girl's eye, don't they?"

At nine years old, Mac's big brother had brought Zan around one day, and she'd tagged after the two boys until Brett knocked her down into a pile of pine needles. Already she'd been too stubborn to cry or complain. Instead, she'd thrown a pinecone at Brett in retaliation and her bad aim meant it nailed Zan in the butt. He'd whirled, laughter glittering in his eyes, then leaped on her to "shampoo" her hair with a handful of dusty needles.

Red-faced and sneezing, she'd handed her heart over to him.

It had been that fast. That simple.

Mrs. Lind glanced around, her fork in midair. "You know, I thought I saw him a few minutes ago. Did he come to congratulate your brother?"

Brett. Mac whipped her head around, searching out the groom. If Zan *had* returned, surely he would have spoken with Brett.

It wasn't easy getting a quiet moment with the groom, though. The reception was wrapping up and it seemed that each guest needed to pause on their way out the door for a short word with the new couple. She hung in their periphery, intent upon swooping in as soon as her brother was free.

Finally, the only people left in Mr. Frank's were the bridal party and the bartender. While her sisters went to a back room to help Angelica out of her gown and into something warmer for the ride home, Mac snagged her brother by the sleeve.

"Hey, I've got to ask you something."

"Me first," Brett said. "I'm going to drive the car around. In about five minutes, when you hear me honk the horn, bring my bride outside, okay?"

"Okay. But—"

"No time, Mac. I want this to go perfectly." Then he strode away.

Vexed, Mac huffed out a sigh. But then Angelica came back into the main room, still managing to look bridal in a pair of leggings and an off-white winter coat, the hood lined in pale pink fleece. Her cheeks matched the color and her obvious happiness couldn't help but spill over on everyone within ten feet.

Mac exchanged smiles with her sisters. "Lucky brother," she said, then hooked her arm in Angelica's. "Lucky us to get such a wonderful new sister."

Tears swam in the bride's eyes.

"None of that now," Mac admonished. "I'm determined to keep my composure."

Poppy's fiancé, Ryan, had already handed Poppy his handkerchief. Shay was digging through her man Jace's suit pocket for his.

"C'mon, guys," Mac scolded. "This is a celebration." Then she heard the sound of a car horn. "That's our cue."

Angelica didn't resist as Mac pulled her toward the front door. When Mac threw it open, they stood in the doorway, silenced by the sight in front of them.

A sturdy SUV stood angled at the curb, a vehicle made for the mountains with its heavy-duty snow tires. But instead of being the usual black or silver or white, the paint job was a profusion of flowers in pink and green and yellow and blue.

Jace cleared his throat. "Check out the license plate."

Mac redirected her attention. Seven letters spelled out *WLKRWIF.*

"Walker wife," Angelica whispered, then hiccuped a sob.

"Oh, jeez," Mac said, even though her heart was being squeezed like a sponge. "You've turned sappy, bro."

But Brett only grinned as he pulled his bride into his arms. "You're a real mountain girl now," he told her.

"I'm your mountain wife," Angelica said, pressing her cheek to his chest. She let out her breath in a shuddering sigh. "You know what I need."

"I do." He kissed the top of her hair. "And I'll always do my very best to give it to you."

Angelica looked back at the car, smiled. "What made you think of spring on four wheels?"

"Because you're every season of my heart."

On the brink of losing control of her own sentiments, Mac walked away, pushing past Shay and Jace and Poppy and Ryan, both couples moved by the moment into their own hugs and kisses. The closeness of the pairs was cutting her to the bone and another moment witnessing their happiness might have her bawling like a baby. *Single. Alone.*

Who would have thought Brett had such a grand gesture in him? The SUV symbolized that Angelica had carved her place as a Walker in their mountains. But he'd made it all her own by painting it to please his bride's very feminine side.

"Mom always said," she murmured to the empty

room, as she went in to collect her belongings, "there's something irresistible and utterly grand about a grand gesture."

Reaching her place at the long table where the bridal party had sat, she snatched up her coat from the back of the chair and tucked her tiny evening purse in the outside pocket. Then she looked at the bouquet. Maybe she'd leave it there.

But that might hurt Angelica's feelings. So she scooped it up and brought the cool petals of the roses to her nose. As she drew in their sweet fragrance, her gaze landed on the cocktail napkin that had been tucked beneath them.

Emotions bombarded her. Elation. Anticipation. Thrill. Then the lessons learned through heartache had her locking down on those feelings. The older and wiser Mac was no longer the naive girl who'd been left behind. Experience had taught her to protect herself by curbing flights of fancy and avoiding bouts of what-could-have-been.

Still, that didn't stop her from dropping her hand to the soft paper surface, where she ran a fingertip over the three distinctive ink slashes that etched a single letter.

Z.

CHAPTER TWO

ZAN ELLIOTT PUSHED open the door of Oscar's Coffee, situated smack-dab in the middle of the village of Blue Arrow Lake. Already chilled by the short walk from his car, the inside heat hit him like a slap, and a shudder racked his body. He clutched the jamb as the world tilted for a moment. When it righted again, he shrugged off the brief disorientation.

A caffeine deficit, most likely. Or it could be that the altitude was getting to him. Though he'd traveled to higher elevations in the past ten years, it had been that long since he'd visited these particular mountains.

He was surprised by how…not odd it was to be back.

That befuddled him, too. He'd never considered the environs of Blue Arrow Lake truly home—that had been the beach house where he'd lived with his parents and siblings until he was nine—yet coming back four days ago he'd experienced an unexpected settling of his restless soul.

It should worry him a little, he thought, as he stepped up to the register and gave the order for his drink. Christ, did it mean he was getting old?

Then he moved toward the pickup counter, his gaze landing on the man standing directly in front of him—and suddenly he was a boy again.

Aware of the grin stretching his mouth, he clapped

his hand on Brett Walker's shoulder. "So you're a husband now. It boggles the mind."

Brett turned, and his familiar gray eyes widened, then narrowed. "Zan."

"In the flesh." He rocked back on his heels, studying his old friend. While he'd seen Brett at a distance when he'd crashed the wedding reception, he hadn't been near enough to completely register the changes the years had wrought. The other man's hair was shorter now, and scars slashed his eyebrow and across the bridge of his nose. He'd probably gained thirty pounds of pure muscle. "I'm not sure I'd beat you at arm wrestling like I used to."

"That's revisionist memory, pal," Brett said, then turned back when the barista called his name. Swiping up his drink, he didn't give Zan a second glance before strolling around a corner to the seating area.

"Well," Zan said to the empty space around him, "thanks for the effusive welcome. It's great to see you again, too." Not sure if he should be amused or affronted, Zan shoved his hands in the pockets of his jeans. Apparently Brett wasn't interested in hashing over old times.

Not that Zan mulled over them very often himself. He wasn't a person who liked to look back, and it didn't take a genius to understand it stemmed from the family tragedy he wanted to forget. Still, he'd had many good times with Brett. He'd been living with his grandfather just a few weeks when after school one day the towheaded oldest Walker had casually asked him, "You fish?"

Zan had lied, of course, and said yes. Little time passed before they were fishing buddies, and biking buddies, and, later, chasing-after-girls buddies. Nearly inseparable, though their temperaments were not completely aligned. When Zan had proposed trouble, Brett had counseled caution. Zan ran red lights, Brett took note of stale yellows. During the execution of Zan's wildest pranks, Brett had participated only as lookout.

But they'd both had a dogged determination, so when his own tall Americano was ready, he took the same path as his old friend. He really wanted to have a conversation with the other man. What was the story about his wife and marriage? How were the rest of the Walkers faring?

Sue him, but he was curious about what Poppy and Shay had been up to during the past ten years.

Not to mention their older sister.

Turning the corner into the seating area, he caught sight of Brett in the far corner at one of the brightly painted picnic tables set on the scarred cement floor. Across from him sat dark-haired, blue-eyed Mackenzie Walker.

Zan's world spun again as a thousand memories assaulted him.

Cheeky little-girl Mac, with her gamine grin and her resolve to do anything and everything along with her big brother and his best friend. Like Brett, he'd ignored her, teased her and even went to great lengths to ditch her until her pouting lower lip would melt his will.

Coltish preteen Mac, all skinny arms and legs and big eyes that followed his every movement. She'd had dark mutterings about every high school girl who caught his and Brett's attention freshman year.

Then she'd been in high school, too, and other boys were fixating on *her*. For a time, he'd fooled himself that his own interest in Mac was merely brotherly—and that the eye daggers he threw at the guys who hit on her were because he only had her best interests at heart. Then one summer afternoon, a playful wrestling match rocked his world when he flipped her to her back and found himself hovering over her, his hips between her spread legs.

This is Mac, he'd tried telling himself. Mac, who in winter had a habit of shoving snow down the back collar of his jacket. Mac, who'd once pretended to have a leg cramp while swimming in the lake so he'd jump in to save her—wearing his favorite leather boots. Mac, who'd hidden his car keys when he was sixteen so he was late to pick up Hot Body Harmonie Ross the night he was her date to her senior prom.

Mac, he'd thought, as he'd lowered his head and kissed her.

She'd tasted like cinnamon candy and paradise. Sweet, burning heaven.

He and Brett had gone a round or two about the change in circumstances until Mac herself waded in and made clear—with a fist to her big brother's gut—that being with Zan was *her* choice. And no one was fiercer about getting what she wanted than Mackenzie Marie Walker.

They'd been together as a couple for two years while he finished up his college degree. After fulfilling that promise to his grandfather, he'd left town, hell-bent on quenching his wanderlust.

A decade had passed since he'd held her in his arms…until the night of the wedding reception. Impulse had directed him to slip behind her and pull her against him. He'd breathed in her scent and enjoyed the slight weight of her against the frame of his bigger body.

But he'd resisted allowing her to look at him then.

And now, as if she sensed his presence and his thoughts, her head shifted slightly and her gaze left her brother's face for his.

He went dizzy and for a moment she wavered in his line of sight like a mirage.

When his vision cleared, his pulse was going too fast and there was a clammy sweat on the back of his neck. He hauled in a steadying breath and reminded himself that this beautiful woman was the same old Mac of his youth.

At the wedding, she'd naturally looked different in her bridesmaid getup and her hair in a fancy twist. But he hadn't taken the opportunity to notice other changes. Now they were all he could see.

Without thinking, he walked slowly toward her, drawn to the fine-boned elegance of a face that, in the past decade, had lost all remnants of childhood. Her cheekbones were etched, her nose straight and small, her lashes and her mouth lush. Her blue eyes, he saw, were the icy shade of water beneath the thin frozen surface of a mountain lake.

And he didn't remember them ever looking so cold.

Brett must have noticed his sister's switch in attention, because he glanced over his shoulder as Zan approached their table. When Zan put his cup on the table, the other man didn't say anything, but he did slide along the bench to allow Zan space beside him.

The movement was begrudging and Mac's stare still so very chilly.

"Is this any way to greet the guy who knows your deepest, darkest secret?" he joked, settling into place.

When they didn't answer, he tried out a smile. "The hollowed-out log near the cabins? The secret compartment to keep hidden treasures?"

Brett's mouth twitched. "God, what must be in there? Mac, didn't you stash that unicorn Beanie Baby in the hole, sure it would be worth a mint in a few years?"

She made a face.

Brett pointed at Zan. "And it's where you hid your Molotov-cocktail supplies, so they'd escape your grandfather's detection." His expression turned serious. "Hey, about that. Condolences on his passing."

"Yeah. Thanks." Zan stared into his cup of dark brew. "And the same to you for the loss of your mother." Though Dell Walker had passed about two years before Zan left, his wife hadn't died until after Zan had been gone from the mountains. It was the Walker parents who had provided the warm influence an orphan needed in the earliest years, though to be fair, his grandfather had never complained about the kid foisted on him late in life.

When he'd left the mountains he hadn't parted harshly from the elderly man, but they'd kept in touch only on a semiregular basis. While they'd actually met up a few times, twice in London, and then in Prague and Lisbon as well, Zan hadn't been at his side when he'd died.

Nor had he returned directly upon the man's passing, when he might have managed to stop his cousin from running amok. "You heard about Vaughn?"

Brett flicked a glance at his sister. "Actually, my wife and I were involved in his capture."

His attorney had shared that the old man's will had left a lot of furniture and memorabilia to the Mountain Historical Society, which had auctioned off the items in a very successful fund-raising effort. But Vaughn Elliott, bitter that he hadn't been named in the document, had taken it upon himself to recoup the "lost" objects by stealing them from the winning bidders.

Zan frowned, thinking that over. "God, I'm sorry. Grandfather left his entire estate to me, and Vaughn didn't take it well." He cleared his throat. "I hope you won't be offended that I've retained good defense counsel for him."

"Out of your own pocket, I suppose," Brett said.

"It appears Vaughn ran through his own monies a few years back."

His old friend shrugged. "I understand. Angelica and I weren't injured in the incident… As a matter of fact, you could say it brought us together."

"Your Angelica?"

"That's right," Brett said, his mouth curving in a satisfied smile. "Angelica Walker."

Zan glanced over at the silent Mac. "What about you? Husband?" At that wedding reception, had he cuddled close to a married person? The nights since, had he been spinning little fantasies—and he had, no point in pretending otherwise—about some other man's woman? His stomach churned at the thought and a chill rolled over him. He pushed his coffee away, no longer interested in it. "Well?"

Mac held up both bare hands, clearly showing she wore no rings, wedding or otherwise.

His world tilted again… Christ, was that really *relief*? Before he could convince himself otherwise, Brett had his own question. "So, back in town, huh?"

"Yeah. And I'd sure like to spend a little time with my favorite mountain family. Not to mention meet your wife." He glanced over at Mac. "I confess I crashed your wedding reception for a few minutes."

"What? You should have spoken to me."

"I didn't want to draw attention to myself on someone else's special day. But I'm surprised Mac didn't mention it to you. We, uh, had a moment."

Brett's brows rose. "I'm surprised she didn't mention it to me, either."

"I forgot all about it," the woman said. "I was there with Kent Valdez, remember? He occupied my thoughts."

"Kent Valdez?" Zan could remember the guy. "Wasn't he president of the Future Pig Farmers of America or something in high school?"

Color washed up Mac's beautiful face, and for the first time her blue eyes looked heated. "Are you really going there?"

Zan felt woozy again, but that didn't stop him from running his mouth. "C'mon. He was a head shorter than you and harassed all of us as the self-appointed hall monitor."

Mac glared. "The only one who is small right now is you."

Had they ever argued when they were together? Maybe she was mad about that little surprise move he'd made on her at the wedding. "Take it easy," he muttered. Why was his head pounding so?

Mac's spine straightened. "Take it easy? Pl—"

"Maybe we should save this for another day," Brett put in hastily.

"I don't know why." Zan pressed his fingers to his temple. "I'm only trying to catch up with old friends, for God's sake."

"That's why you're back, to catch up?" Mac asked.

Her image was wavering again. "I'm here to manage some details of Grandfather's estate. It should take a week or two. Then I'll be gone again."

"Of course you will."

There was subtext to the four words that couldn't penetrate the throbbing in his head. His skin flashed hot then cold and the roots of his hair began to hurt. He rose to his feet, one hand on the tabletop to keep him steady.

"Zan?" Brett questioned. "Are you all right? You don't look so good."

He didn't feel so good, either. "Uh..." The room was revolving around him.

"Do you need—"

"Just some fresh air," he said, trying to shake off the dizziness. "I'll see you later."

Then he began to walk away, all the pleasure he'd felt in seeing the Walkers again tarnished, but he couldn't figure out why.

He glanced back at Mac. She was watching him leave, but the expression on her lovely face didn't exactly shout warm welcome, that was sure.

They said a person could never go home again... Apparently he couldn't even go back to the place that had been the next best thing.

Or to the girl who had once been the first in his heart.

ONE MOMENT MAC was watching Zan thread his way through the tables toward the exit and the next she found herself on her feet.

"What are you doing?" her brother asked.

"I'm not going to miss this opportunity to give him a piece of my mind," she said. "You heard him. He doesn't plan to be around long."

"Now, Mac, is this about him crashing the reception? Because—"

"Don't 'Now, Mac' me," she said. She wasn't going to share with her brother about that "moment" they'd had on his big night, but it still embarrassed her to recall how readily she'd responded to Zan's encircling arms. Not that she intended to get into that with Zan—but she had other things to say to the confounding man. "Have you forgotten on his way down the hill ten years ago he warned other guys to stay away from me?"

Brett rubbed his hand over his mouth as if to wipe away a sudden grin. "Who would take that seriously?"

"Maybe my perfect man!"

This time her brother laughed out loud. "How would he be perfect for you, then?"

She ignored his logic. "And what about those postcards? Ten years of finding reminders of him in my mail, with that *Z* as the only message. Don't I deserve an explanation for *that*?"

Now she looked toward Zan, noting he'd been stopped by a middle-aged couple at a table on the other side of the room. The Robbinses had recently began living full-time in the mountains and were clients of her Maids by Mac business.

Without another word to her brother, she headed in that direction, prepared to engage Zan when he wrapped up his conversation with the pair. And she didn't feel the least bit guilty over eavesdropping in the meantime.

"Ash came home exhausted but exhilarated from his experience with your documentary crew," Veronica Robbins was saying.

Documentary crew? Ash was the Robbinses' twenty-something son, and she'd heard the woman mention him spending time traveling since an internship ended in the fall.

"When will we get to see *Earth Unfiltered*?" she asked.

"It's in postproduction now, but the IMAX theater dates should be nailed down fairly soon."

"Nine years in the making," Veronica gushed. "Footage from the remotest locations in the world."

"I've been lucky to be a part of it," Zan said.

From the corner of her eye, Mac studied him. Was he a documentary filmmaker? Really? That would mean that while she'd stayed home and cleaned up other people's messes, he'd been traveling the world, gaining sophistication and savoir faire.

Not that he looked all that urbane at the moment. He was paler than he'd appeared when he first arrived. Her brother was right, Zan didn't look so good. Was he sick?

Not that she should care. And she didn't care that building a business in Blue Arrow Lake likely wouldn't impress one of the creators of some IMAX theater-bound film called *Earth Unfiltered.* Zan had been born to a world of privilege but she'd been born to the mountains and considered that the best advantage of all.

She wasn't afraid of hard work and she wasn't impressed by material wealth. As a matter of fact, the Walkers and other longtime locals were quite suspicious of the moneyed flatlanders who moved up the hill. Zan's grandfather had turned his vacation place into his permanent retirement home, but even though the luxury estate had been in the Elliott family since the early 1900s, he'd never achieved homegrown status in the eyes of the full-time mountain residents.

"I'll see you later," she heard Zan say to the couple, and then he was again on his way to the exit.

She hurried after him, frowning when he bumped into a table and then into the newspaper stand. Its metal frame rocked back and forth and Zan himself seemed ready to topple. Her hand shot out reflexively, and she grabbed his arm to steady him.

Slowly, he swung about, then stared down at her, blinking as if surprised to see her.

He wore dark jeans and a cashmere sweater that clung to his wide shoulders and broad chest. How had he gotten so big? Maybe he'd grown taller after leaving Blue Arrow Lake. She couldn't remember his exact height then, but surely he hadn't made her feel so… feminine. So fragile.

She shook off the thought. Feminine and fragile sounded like weak and wussy, and no man was going to make Mackenzie Walker that way. Especially not the guy who had left her—and left a warning behind for the other guys in town. "I have a few things to say to you, Zan."

"God, you're beautiful. More beautiful than ever."

The words instantly flustered her. "Well…" She rubbed her hands down the legs of her ancient jeans, suddenly aware she was dressed for work in threadbare denim and a sweatshirt with pilled ribbing around her hips and at the bottom of the sleeves.

"You were gorgeous as a girl and took my breath away dressed as a bridesmaid," he said. "But now, like this…" His hand waved to indicate her figure.

Mac gaped, supremely aware she was dressed like a ragamuffin. "Are you blind or are you making fun of me?"

He blinked again. "Remember that day at the hot springs?"

She barely resisted squirming. "The time I had to come get you and Brett because the both of you had downed too many beers and weren't sober enough to drive? When Missy Waters puked out the car window on the way home and I threatened to make you clean it up with your tongue?"

He winced. "Not that time. *Our* time. Your first time."

"Shh!" She glanced around. "We're not talking about *that*."

"I dream about it sometimes. Do you?"

Gah! The man was making it hard to hold on to her mad. "I never think of it," she said. Oh, but she did. Wouldn't every woman remember her first time? Summer again, both of them in bathing suits at the remote hot springs that could only be reached by starting from the Walkers' private land.

Upon becoming a couple, they hadn't discussed the day, or if there ever would be a day, when she'd give him her virginity. But the knowledge that she wanted to be with him like that had hovered over her for weeks.

Months. Years. Even when he'd seen her only as his best friend's pesky younger sister.

Maybe she'd not had all the details of that kind of intimacy quite worked out when she was a girl, but anything she'd had then, she'd wanted to be Zan's.

She'd been so gone for him.

Just as she'd been that lazy afternoon at the hot springs when she was seventeen. They'd had a cooler containing green grapes, a plastic container of chocolate chip cookies she'd baked from scratch and a thermos of iced tea. They'd immersed themselves in a spring, and then, when they were too hot to stay in a second more, they'd stretched out on double-wide-striped beach towels and let the afternoon breeze cool their skin.

Propped on an elbow, she'd fed him grapes, her breast pressing against his bronzed biceps, her nipple pebbled to a tight bead at the contact. He'd let his fingertip drift over the bumps of her spine until it touched the bow of her bikini strap at the middle of her back.

His gaze never left hers as he slowly picked up the end of one damp string and pulled it free. Her breath ragged, she'd sat up and loosened the top bow herself. The scraps of fabric had fallen into her lap.

Second base, as she'd still referred to it then, hadn't been new to them. But it was the first time he'd played with her breasts when the only other item she wore was a tiny pair of bottoms. Even now, she could remember the brush of his wet hair on her skin as he sucked on her nipples. She'd clutched the heavy bone of his shoulders, her breath shuddering in her lungs.

There didn't seem to be any air to pull into them right now. Shoving the memory away, she folded her arms across her chest and tried to get a handle on the conversation. "Are you really a documentary filmmaker?" she heard herself ask. "Never mind," she added hastily. "I want you to know that—"

"I wish I had that moment on film," he said, his voice low and whisper-rough. "But I can close my eyes and see it in Technicolor. You had a sunburn on your nose and you bit your bottom lip when I—"

"Zan!" She felt her whole body flush. "Please. Stop."

He smiled. "That's not what you said then. Well, not the 'stop' part, anyway."

"You're a beast," she whispered. "Now quit embarrassing me. I already have a bone to pick with you."

"Yeah?" He seemed unconcerned as he reached out a hand to tuck a strand of her hair behind her ear. The gesture was too familiar and even more so when he stroked his fingertips slowly down her cheek.

Chills tumbled across her skin and she batted his hand away, but his fingers tangled with hers and he lifted them toward his face, rubbing her knuckles against the rasp of his whiskered jaw.

She tried tugging free, but he tightened his hold. "Zan Elliott, what are you doing?" she said through her teeth.

There was a feverish light in his eyes. "Remembering how good we were together."

She tried gathering her mad again. "Well, I'm remembering that you rode out of town, but not before apparently informing the male half of our community that I was still somehow yours."

The corners of his mouth curled up. "But you were."

"Zan! You left."

He stroked the back of her hand against his face once again. He was hot, she realized. His skin burning up.

She frowned. "Are you feeling all right?"

"Better seeing you. Always better around you. It's been a long ten years."

Something definitely wasn't okay with him. Where he'd been pale before, now he had a definite flush and his lips looked too dry. As she watched, a fine tremor racked his body.

"Maybe you should sit down."

"I—"

"Oh. My. God. Zan Elliott," someone called.

Mac closed her eyes. *Hell.*

"And with Mac Walker." There was glee in the voice of the biggest gossip in the mountains. Missy Waters, she of the puking incident, who had never forgiven Mac for having "stolen" Zan—when the other woman had never had him to begin with.

"Hey, Missy," Mac said, resigned to be the star of a story for the rest of the week.

"Missy…" Zan said, as if trying to place the name.

Irritation flashed across the woman's face, then smoothed out. "I'd not heard you'd come back to town," she said to him, her gaze dropping to their hands, still joined. "Or that you two have picked up right where you left off."

Crap. "That hasn't happened. That's never going to happen," Mac said, trying to free herself from him.

He had a grip like an octopus. "Missy!" he said, his memory obviously clearing. "Didn't your hair used to be dark?"

It was platinum now, and Missy's pride and joy. She fluffed it with her fingers and beamed at him. "Thank you for noticing. I went blond and have never looked back. Unlike Mac, I should say, who everyone knows is stuck in the past."

"What?" He shifted his glance from Missy to Mac. "What's that mean?"

"Nothing," Mac said firmly. Desperately. "Missy, did you hear about Angelica's new car? Brett gave her the sweetest ride as a wedding gift."

"Really?" For a moment she was diverted. Then her attention went back to Zan's fingers, still wrapped around Mac's. "Zan, you haven't let go of Mac."

He followed her gaze, executed one of those odd blinks that seemed to suggest he was having trouble focusing. "No, I haven't let go of Mac."

This was getting out of control. At this point, she was willing to give up on the big tell-off she'd had planned for the man if only she could end this odd conversation. "I've got to get to work."

When he didn't release her, she jiggled their joined hands. "Work, do you hear me? That thing I do that allows me to put gas in my car and food in my belly."

"I'll do that," Zan said. "Go out to dinner with me tonight."

"I will not."

Missy was following the exchange with unconcealed curiosity. "You should, Mac. It's not like you have a steady guy or anything. Nobody thinks you'll ever stick with anyone because—"

"Do you *mind*, Missy?" Mac asked, done with politeness. "This is a private conversation."

"In Oscar's?" she questioned. "I'm not the only one watching Zan stake his claim."

"Good God." Mac felt as if the walls were closing

in on her. "That's not happening. I'll never be his to *claim*."

"Wrong, Mackenzie Marie." Zan's cheeks were flushed even redder, and his eyes glittered feverishly. "You'll always be mine."

That was it. *I'm done with this.*

As she lifted her free hand to slap some sense into him, however, he collapsed. Catching him in her arms, she staggered, the two of them crashing into the nearby wall before sliding to the floor.

CHAPTER THREE

MAC HAD LOST the round of rock-paper-scissors. She tried convincing Brett to make it two out of three, but he squeezed his "paper" hand over her "rock" fist and promised to call later to see if she needed him to spell her at the end of his workday. However, she knew he had an evening meeting scheduled with a client who wanted him to design a landscape—something her brother was now finally seriously pursuing after years building up a mowing-and-blowing business. She wouldn't allow him to put that off, nor did she want to compromise her pride by admitting she was the least bit anxious about being left alone with Zan Elliott.

Which meant Mac was on her own dealing with the one sick puppy that he seemed to be.

At Oscar's she and her brother had wrestled Zan into her car—with little help from him and with a lot of senseless, feverish mumbling. Brett had followed her to the Elliott estate and fished for the keys from his buddy's pocket himself. Then they'd propelled him to the master bedroom, where he was obviously staying.

Spotting the bed, Zan had stumbled to it and then fallen on it face-first.

She'd gnawed her bottom lip. "Are you sure we shouldn't take him to see a doctor?" she said, voicing the same concern she had at Oscar's before they decided to bring him here.

At that, Zan had roused a little. "Don't want a doctor," he'd muttered, turning over to look at them. "Just wanna sleep."

"Zan..." she'd started.

"Just wanna sleep," he'd repeated.

At that, Brett had advised a wait-and-see approach, and she'd reluctantly agreed, even though Zan resembled a giant sugar pine felled in the forest. So her brother had gone off to work and she'd reached for her cell phone to rearrange her day.

It took only two calls. One, to ensure it was okay to clean her afternoon house the next day. The second was to her most reliable employee, Tilda Smith, who was happy to up her hours for the week by doing the windows and floors at the home Mac had planned to work at that morning.

Then she phoned her sister Poppy.

"What's going on?" the younger woman asked, cheery as always.

"Are you alone?" Mac asked in a low voice.

Automatically, Poppy's went quieter, too. "Yeah. Ryan dropped off Mason at school and then had to go down the hill for a meeting in LA. Is there a problem?"

"I'm in the Elliott mansion."

Poppy gasped. "We've wanted to get inside there for years! How did you do it? *Why* did you do it? Does this have something to do with your supposed sighting of Zan at the wedding reception?"

"No 'supposed' about it," Mac said. "Guess who showed up at Oscar's this morning while Brett and I were having coffee?"

Another audible gasp sounded through the phone. "No!"

"Yes."

"And he brought you home with him?" Poppy's voice filled with glee. "Mac, have you already gone to bed with Zan Elliott?"

Pulling the phone away from her ear, Mac frowned at it, then put it back. "Of course not. I'm never going to bed with Zan Elliott."

Her sister snorted.

"I'm serious!"

"I'll believe you if you tell me he hasn't aged well. Is there a bald spot? A paunch? Did he turn out to be one of those men who rejects personal hygiene?"

"He looks gorgeous, you ninny, and he seems freshly showered to me…but he's sick."

Poppy went quiet. "Oh, I'm so sorry to hear that. Did he come home to die?"

Mac rolled her eyes. "My God. You've got too active an imagination. No, he didn't come home to die. He came down with a flu bug or something, and Brett and I had to drive him here. I'm, uh, staying awhile just to make sure he doesn't need medical attention."

"Oh. That's nice of you." She paused. "Can I come over and snoop around the house?"

"Poppy—"

"Please? You know we've always wanted to get in there."

"Zan never invited us."

"Which only made it all the more enticing. Say yes."

Maybe she'd called her sister for just that reason. But it seemed a little sneaky. "What if Zan wakes up, suddenly better, and finds us wandering around his house?"

"Pfft," Poppy said, dismissing the objection. "Let's cross that bridge when we come to it. I'll be there before you know it."

Mac tiptoed back to the master, pulled a throw over Zan's unmoving figure and shut the bedroom door. By the time she went back down the stairs, her sister was trucking up the walkway, all big eyes and flushed cheeks.

"Have you seen any ghosts?" Poppy asked. "You know, the kind with knives dripping blood, who hold their severed heads under their arms?"

That had always been rumor when they were kids. That the French château–inspired Elliott manse was peopled with specters and spooks. Mac held open the door and gestured her sister inside. "Have a look."

Poppy's shoulders slumped as she ventured into the foyer. "What? No suits of armor?"

"Maybe they were auctioned off by the Mountain Historical Society." Many items from the house had been bequeathed to the organization and then sold for fund-raising purposes at a black-tie event the summer before. Mac hadn't attended, but her sister and her fiancé had bought a few antiques.

"No, I didn't see anything like that," Poppy said, now moving into the large living area with its slate floors, paneled walls and huge marble-wrapped fireplace. "The views of the lake are spectacular."

"Your windows open onto the same thing."

"On the other side of the lake," Poppy said, running her hand over the moss green velvet of the massive couch. "This place has been here forever, too—I heard it's on the National Register of Historic Places."

Mac trailed her sister into the kitchen. "Doesn't look historic in here."

"No." Poppy turned a circle. "It's completely updated."

They wandered together from room to room, admiring the details of the massive staircase, the ridgeline or water views from every window, the carefully detailed bathrooms. Even the smallest bedroom had a fireplace.

"Oh, I do love it in here," Poppy said, peeking into a room with built-in floor-to-ceiling bookcases that included a ladder that rolled along rails. Her hand trailed along the spines of old books that smelled like leather and lavender. "Maybe there are ghost *stories*."

"Pretty different than where we grew up," Mac said, recalling the ramshackle house where she'd lived with her brother and sisters. Their father had been terrible with money, causing problems in the marriage when Brett, Mac and Poppy were small. Dell Walker had even left for a time, during which his wife had an affair and became pregnant with Shay.

But he'd returned and patched things up with Lorna, which included embracing Shay as his own. From then on, the Walkers had lived rich in family and love for the mountains, despite the meager state of their bank accounts.

Walking back into the hallway with its plush Oriental carpet, Mac's younger sister made a face. "No headless ghouls. I'm so disappointed," she said, crossing to another door and reaching for the knob.

Mac lunged for her sister's hand. "Wait—"

But she was too late. Poppy stood, framed by the

jamb. "Oh," she said. "Maybe not so disappointed, after all."

Mac peeked around her shoulder and into the master bedroom, then swallowed her groan.

Zan still lay on the mattress of the massive four-poster bed, but sometime since she'd checked on him last, he'd shed his shoes. And his clothes.

All of them.

Facedown once again, he was naked, a pillow clutched in his arms like a lover.

"I'm going all tingly," Poppy whispered.

"You're engaged!" Mac said, elbowing her ribs.

"That doesn't mean I'm blind. And I definitely can't unsee *that*." She pointed. "I don't *want* to unsee that."

Mac didn't, either. Her gaze meandered over the wealth of skin on display, from the heavy bulges of his biceps, to the intriguing contours of his back on either side of the long furrow of his spine, to the muscled rise of his ass. "Um…"

"He's aged well," Poppy offered.

"Really, really well." Mac's skin prickled beneath her clothes and even her eyeballs felt hot. "This is bad." *Bad for me.*

Poppy nodded. "We should leave."

They both didn't move. Then he did, in a restless stretch drawing up one knee to reveal—

Poppy yanked Mac back into the hall and shut the door.

"Hey," Mac protested.

"If you're never going to sleep with him again," her sister said, suddenly all prim and proper, "then ogling's inappropriate."

"Fine," Mac said, hoping it didn't sound as if she

was sulking. She glanced around the hall. "Looks like there's one more chance to find us something spooky." Nodding her head, she indicated the final closed door on the second floor.

Poppy didn't hesitate to throw it open. Then she froze. "Speaking of ghosts..."

It was a young man's room. Ratty sports equipment on a bookshelf along with tattered copies of mystery novels. A fishing pole propped in a nearby corner. A king-size bed covered with a navy blue duvet. On the bedside table...

Pain ripped through Mac's chest as her heart gave a vicious twist.

"Didn't you give him that photo?" Poppy asked.

Speech was beyond Mac. She nodded. It was taken the last summer he'd been in the mountains. They were sunburned and barefoot, her back to his chest. How young they looked. Her neck was twisted so she could smile up at him. His eyes were on her face and alight with...

Whatever feelings he'd had for her that had allowed him to walk away—and leave the keepsake behind.

Swallowing hard, she drew her sister away and shut the bedroom door, dismissing the sharp jab of disappointment. It was silly of her to have even for a second imagined he would have carried it—her, them—with him on his travels. He'd moved on.

And so had she.

Poppy was staring at her, her expression concerned. "Do you want me to take over nursemaid duties?"

Mac moved toward the stairs. "Of course not. I can do this."

"But—"

She glanced back at her sister. "I'm over him. I have been since the minute he left here and drove down the hill."

"Um…I remember it differently."

Squeezing shut her eyes, Mac stopped. The truth was, she'd been a lovelorn mess after he'd gone. For the first weeks she'd wandered around aimlessly like one of the ghosts they'd expected to find at the Elliott estate, causing everyone around her to wring their hands and utter helpless noises. But then she'd realized the sympathy they offered only served to make her softer—powerless and weak.

Not to mention that her family had also been suffering, not only from their own loss of Zan, but also because their dad had died less than two years before. Her unhappiness, she'd realized, was only doubling down their own.

So she'd straightened her spine and elected to stop her wallowing. Tossing out the used tissues cluttering her room, she'd decided to get on with her life—which became the impetus to begin building a business instead of drowning in the misery of lost love.

"But I did get over him eventually," she said, striding for the stairs again. "You know I did."

"Okay." Poppy followed on her heels as she sped down the steps. "Still, it might bother—"

"Nothing bothers me," Mac declared, wanting the discussion to end. "Now, don't you have to go home and make Mason an after-school snack or something?"

Poppy sighed. "If you're sure…"

"I'm sure. Thanks for the offer, but I've got it." Her nod was decisive. "Absolutely."

Once she heard her sister motor off, she breathed a

little easier. Poppy was so damn sentimental, thinking it might hurt Mac to see Zan through this sickness.

She didn't need to shirk this task she'd taken on—especially when doing so would only underscore her sister's mistaken idea that she'd never gotten the man out of her heart. Sure, walking away from him now might have proved her indifference, too, but there was more to Zan than the man who'd left her.

Being able to remember that was part of the proof that she was over the guy.

Before that time as her lover, he'd been the boy who'd fixed the chain on her bike innumerable times. The guy who'd helped her with her Spanish homework in middle school—he was aces with languages. The very same person who'd jollied her out of her doldrums when the boy she'd liked between eighth grade and high school had left her for some summer girl.

She could safely perform a favor for someone who was no longer anything more to her than an old family friend, right?

With that still at the forefront of her mind, she made her way back into the master bedroom as evening darkened the sky. Upon a little exploring, she figured out how to start the gas fireplace across from the bed. Then she managed to get Zan under the covers…keeping her gaze trained away from anyplace intimate.

Soup and crackers didn't interest him, but though he at first batted away her hands she was able to get some water and pain relievers down his throat. His eyes were half-open and dull through the process. If he knew who tended to him, or had an opinion about it, he didn't comment.

When she tired of watching TV downstairs, she

headed back to his room. The gas fireplace was simple enough to turn on and made her spot on the couch beneath the windows even more cozy. She was plenty comfortable with the blanket and pillow she'd spied on a shelf in the closet and wearing a flannel shirt she'd found hanging there as a nightgown.

With light from the flames in the fireplace flickering against the plaster walls, she snuggled into the cushions. Unused to a day without much physical activity, she thought she might have trouble finding sleep, but with Zan's breathing as her lullaby, she drifted off.

To jerk awake at the sound of his strangled voice.

"No. God, no." Zan thrashed, fighting with the covers.

Mac jackknifed up and struggled out of the blanket wrapped around her legs. The wool rug was soft against her bare feet as she made for the bed.

"Simone," he said, stopping Mac's headlong rush. "Please, baby. *Simone.*"

Simone? She ignored the new twist of her heart. "Zan," she said, keeping her voice soft. "You're having a dream."

"Don't leave me," he begged.

Licking her lips, she crept closer to the bed. "It's me, Mac," she said. "You're at the lake house. In the mountains."

"Noo," he moaned again.

In the light from the fireplace, she could see that his eyes were pinched tightly shut. "Zan." She reached out a tentative hand, brushed his hair from his warm forehead. "It's all right."

"Simone." He sounded urgent, anxious, and his head turned in her direction. His eyes opened, but they stared at Mac, unseeing. "Come back, baby. You've got to come back."

"Shh." She stroked his hair again. "You're having a dream."

"Didn't happen?" His eyes closed again and his body seemed to relax.

"Didn't happen," she whispered.

When he seemed to slip back into slumber, she leaned over the bed to straighten the sheets and duvet around him. In a quick movement, he snatched her off her feet and yanked her into his body.

"Zan—"

"Shh," he said, echoing her from moments before. Tucking himself around her, he pinned her to him with a heavy arm across her waist. "Sleep now," he muttered. "Go to sleep."

Wriggling away was futile. Every time she tried to move, he mumbled into her hair and tightened his grip. Just a few minutes, she told herself, relaxing into his hold, even as she registered the dangerous sense of rightness she felt with his body curled around hers. Once he returned to deep sleep, she'd slide away.

Leave him alone with his memories of Simone.

Simone, *baby.* Had Mac stiffened? Because he nuzzled her hair now. "Shh, shh, shh," he said, his voice low, slumberous.

The sound of it was mesmerizing, yet there was still that alertness inside of her, her guarded heart keeping its barriers high and strong. But as time passed and he breathed deeply and slowly behind her, it was impossible not to melt a little against his heat.

His mind is on another woman, she reminded herself, which sent her wiggling again.

Zan's arm hitched her closer and his breath tickled her ear, raising goose bumps along her neck. "Rest, Mackenzie Marie," he said. "Rest."

Mackenzie Marie? Zan knew it was *her* he held?

He knew it was her. But the thought didn't give her any ease at all. Because as she lay wrapped in his arms, a new, uncomfortable awareness grew. Someone else was most definitely sharing the bed with them—and it wasn't Simone.

Instead, it was the ghost of her past love for him.

Her breath caught. Oh, how she wished it wasn't true, but there was something here beyond the tepid remains of a former friendship. Though she had recovered from his leaving her ten years before, though she was sure she was telling the truth when she asserted she was over Zan, with him pressed close to her back and his arm tucked under her breasts, her heart beat in an erratic rhythm and her skin felt both tender and much too warm.

What they'd once had no longer could be dismissed from her mind and memory. With his return, it was resurrected as a renewed, palpable presence in her life.

She swallowed a humorless chuckle. It turned out the Elliott mansion—or perhaps just Mac herself?—was haunted, after all.

She could only hope the ghost would disappear when Zan once again went away.

ZAN CAME AWAKE by degrees, with each passing moment a new muscle screaming at him, protesting that he was conscious, that he was breathing. Had he been hit by a truck? He'd seen the aftermath of such an accident, but—

Something stirred in his arms.

He blinked, wincing at the pain in his eyelids, and took in the back of a woman's head. Her dark hair. Inhaling, he breathed in her scent.

Mac.

What the hell?

Snippets came back to him. Running into her and Brett at Oscar's. His own pleasure at the meeting. Her frosty attitude.

The antagonism had disappointed him. The only good thing he'd considered about coming back to Blue Arrow Lake under the circumstances was the chance to reconnect with the Walkers. If he had to be bound to someplace for a couple of weeks, at least it was where the companions of his childhood were firmly rooted.

But Brett, and then Mac, hadn't been particularly welcoming.

Yeah, it had stung.

So he'd stood to leave, and then… It went blurry after that. He remembered the dizziness, the sudden heat followed by the sudden cold. Mac again, grabbing him before he could get out the door.

I have a few things to say to you.

But it went mostly blank after that, so he could only suppose he'd looked sick enough that even a hostile Mac took pity on him…and somehow ended up in bed with him.

Now, at the thought, another muscle was making itself known. A morning erection was nothing new, of course, but this one was starting to ache like a sore tooth. With his body curved around Mac's, if he didn't take a stern stand with himself he'd be grinding into her most excellent ass at any moment.

A fine way to reestablish a friendship with her…not.

Willing himself not to move, he shifted his gaze out the window, where he could see the blue sky and an even bluer lake, surrounded by peaks bristling with dark evergreens. In his mind's eye he saw the day he'd first arrived here, a boy trudging up the steps beside the grandfather he knew, but not well. In a just-the-facts style, the man had pointed out the amenities—the billiards room, the in-home theater, the Olympic-size pool in its glass capsule a few steps from the main house. Then there'd been the boathouse and docks. The speedboat he'd be able to drive at twelve, the small sailboat he could learn to maneuver straightaway, the paddleboat they could buy if Zan wanted one.

He'd wanted nothing but to return to the house at the beach. It had been spacious but not showy. The ocean views grand, as had been the life he'd led as the youngest of three kids. He'd skateboarded with his big sister and boogie-boarded with his older brother, and his mother had made cookies and his father had good-naturedly cursed the grill that seemed to burn everything he'd laid upon it.

The community of Blue Arrow Lake had seemed as alien as the moon to him, as void of warmth, until that boy in his class at school had said, "You fish?" and Zan had found a way to hang on.

And people to hang on to until he finally surrendered to his itchy feet and restless soul and turned his truck down the mountain.

The woman in his arms stirred now.

Zan kept himself completely still, though he was supremely aware of the softness of her breasts just above the band of the arm he'd flung over her.

Then she froze, too, as if suddenly aware of their positions. He was naked and she looked as if she was wearing his flannel shirt, but their bare legs were tangled and their position was almost as intimate as two lovers' could be.

"Zan?" she whispered, her head still turned away from his.

"You crawl into other ill men's beds often enough that you don't know?"

In an instant, she'd flipped over to face him, her expression indignant. "I didn't crawl, I'll have you know! You manhandled me onto the mattress."

His smile even hurt, but that didn't stop it from spreading. "Sorry. I hope I'm not contagious. But if so, I promise to take off all your clothes and—"

"You did that yourself, too!" she said, scowling at him. Then she put her cool hand against his forehead. "Fever's gone."

He caught her fingers in his, kissed the back of her hand. "Yeah. Thanks. I'm not a hundred percent, but I know where I am now. Who I'm with."

Her gaze shifting away from him, she tugged her hand from his clasp. "Um…"

"This is a first," he said. "We never woke up beside each other, did we?" While they'd made love dozens of times, they'd never had the luxury of spending an entire night together. Maybe he should have coaxed her down the hill at some point and booked a hotel room, he thought, frowning. Why hadn't he done that?

"I beg to differ," Mac said now. "I recall several times waking up with you in that old tent we pitched in our backyard."

He nodded, conceding the point. "When we were

kids. All of us packed in there, Brett, you, Poppy, Shay and me. It smelled like mildew and Poppy screeched at every critter scurry."

"Our scaredy-cat."

"When we finally stumbled into your kitchen in the morning your mom would make cheesy scrambled eggs and bacon. I've had some good meals in my life, but those breakfasts were the best."

"Yeah," Mac said, reaching out to brush his hair back. Then her eyes went wide, as if bothered by her own offhand, clearly unplanned intimacy. "Um...why don't I make those for you now? Could you eat?"

His stomach growled in response. "What do you think?" And he watched her roll off the bed. He was sad to see her go, but happy to have one of his oldest friends heading down to the kitchen, where they would share a meal.

By the time he got down there himself, however, freshly showered and shaved and feeling somewhat close to human, Mac had that chip squarely rebalanced on her shoulder; he could tell by the wary way she eyed him as he entered the room, her cell phone to her ear. "He's here now, Brett. We'll eat some breakfast, and then I'll be off to work."

After ending the call, she slid her phone into her pocket and turned toward the pan on the stove. "Cheesy eggs," she said, spooning them onto plates. "OJ and bacon out already."

He glanced over to see the small breakfast table in the nook had been set. Taking both plates from her, he carried them over himself. Once they were settled on the place mats, he pulled out her chair for her.

Mac's brows shot up in surprise. "Manners?"

Showing her he had them might dull her at-the-ready thorns and render her a little more approachable. He was serious about wanting to reconnect with the Walkers, if only for his short time in their mountains.

Noting the two pain reliever tablets set by one of the glasses of orange juice, he smiled a little. "Taking care of me some more?" he asked, scooping them up. "Is that what you do—nursing?"

She made a face. "Hardly."

Odd that she didn't elaborate. "Well? Should I guess?" He cast his mind back to her childhood ambitions. "Snake charmer? Fortune-teller?"

At her snort, he tilted his head, considered the lovely angles of her face and the crystalline quality of her blue eyes. "Fashion model?"

She rolled them. "No."

He waggled his brows. "*Lingerie* model?"

A flush pinkened her face. "I clean houses."

"Clean houses."

"Yes! There's nothing wrong with honest work, you know."

"I never said there was." Jeez, she was so touchy now. "You clean houses. Good for you."

"I run my own business," she mumbled, gaze on her plate. "Maids by Mac."

"I'm not surprised, Mackenzie Marie."

Her head came up, her eyes narrowed. "What? That I clean up other people's messes for a living?"

"That you're a businessperson. That you're in charge."

"Oh," she said, her expression evening out.

"You always were a bossy little thing," he added.

"Oh!" She tossed her balled-up paper napkin at him.

He laughed. "Tell me everything about everyone.

About Brett and Poppy and Shay. And anyone else I used to know."

"Does that mean you've missed us?"

"I…" Christ, had he?

Instead of waiting for him to answer, she began to talk. It was grudging at first, he decided, but soon her voice warmed as she filled him in on her brother and sisters. In a few minutes he knew about Brett's landscape business and his wife, Angelica, about Shay with a stepdaughter-to-be and the builder she was about to marry. Finally, he heard about Poppy, her little boy, Mason, and Ryan Hamilton, former actor-turned-producer whose bride she would become in a few weeks.

"How could all this have happened?" he wondered aloud.

"Ten years," Mac said, her demeanor cooling again. "It's been ten years. Maybe if you'd bothered to stay in contact, none of this would come as such a shock."

He hadn't wanted to stay in contact. At the time, it had seemed smartest to leave without backward glances.

"So…you?" Mac gathered up their plates and took them to the sink.

"Let me do that," he protested, but she ignored him.

"Pay me back," she said. "Your last ten years?"

Exciting. Challenging. Wearying.

"Something about a documentary?"

At his puzzled glance, she explained. "I heard you talking to Mr. and Mrs. Robbins at Oscar's yesterday. *Earth Unfiltered*?"

"Oh. Yeah. In my travels, I stumbled upon the crew in their early days. Joined them. Learned a hell of a lot, at first from just humping shit from place to place, then I did more. Research, camera work, a little writing."

"Wow."

It had been wow so much of the time. But there'd been arduous treks, long delays, bad reactions to strange foods…and, finally, a pervasive sense of dissatisfaction. "Traveling to remote corners of the world has a way of making one feel small. And unconnected."

Mac was looking at him funny. He tried to make a joke of it. "Did I just say that out loud?"

"A person can feel alone anywhere," she said, then turned her back to put the plates and utensils in the dishwasher.

A weird vibe entered the room. Zan rubbed at the back of his neck, trying to dissipate the sense of needle-toed fairies dancing over his skin. Christ, he'd thought conversation would get him comfortable with Mac, bring them back to friendly footing. But so far…

"Who's Simone?" she suddenly asked.

"What?" It came out like a squawk.

"Simone. You talked about her in your sleep last night."

Simone. Zan squeezed shut his eyes, saw her golden tan, her wild, streaky hair, heard her throaty laugh. They'd been two of a kind, each recognizing the other instantly. Wanderers. Adventurers. Nomads.

People tied to no one.

"Zan?"

He cleared his throat. "She was part of the documentary crew the last couple of years. We were…coworkers."

"Lovers." She didn't say it like a question.

"For a time we shared a bed on occasion." He glanced up at Mac, but her back was still to him. "For a very short time. Neither one of us was interested in anything remotely permanent."

Mac's head bobbed in a nod. "Where is she now?"

He hesitated.

"You wanted her to come back." She shut the dishwasher door with a clack. "That's what you said last night, anyway."

Oh, shit.

"She can't. She died." He winced, hearing the bald way he'd said the words when Mac stiffened. "I'm sorry to put it like that. It's just..."

Mac turned and leaned back against the counter, regarding him with serious eyes. "It's just...what?"

"It was such a random thing. The act of a moment." Zan scrubbed his hand over his face. "We'd been to the Russian steppes and the Sahara Desert and the Solomon Islands. Cozied up to tribal warlords and run from violent warthogs. Scaled slippery waterfalls and explored deep, bat-filled caves. We ate things that make my belly cringe thinking about, not wanting to offend our hosts. Any one of those things could have ended in death."

Mac reached for a fresh glass, filled it with water, then brought it over to him. Grateful, he took a long swallow. "It was in Berlin. We were walking to lunch, the lot of us. Simone was trailing behind, looking at her phone, checking the weather for our next day's flight. As mundane as that."

"And?"

"And she stepped off a curb without looking. A truck took her out. The driver couldn't stop in time—there was no time." He closed his eyes. "No time left for Simone."

"I'm sorry." Mac's voice was low. "I'm so sorry for your loss."

He was sorry that Simone was gone, too. Sorry, sorry, sorry.

And how sorry was it that he wanted to turn into Mac's body so badly. Bury his head between her breasts and bury his sadness in the familiarity of her body. Lose himself in his lust for her that apparently hadn't dissipated in ten years.

Hold her as if she was more than just an old, old friend.

CHAPTER FOUR

AS SHE CLIMBED out of her shabby sedan, Tilda Smith glared up at the gathering clouds, hoping a challenging stare would stave off the predicted rain…at least for the time it would take her to collect the groceries stored in the backseat and cart them up the walkway and steps that led to the fancy house.

She took another quick peek at the place, exhorting herself not to be intimidated by its amazing lakefront location, its immense size, the wealth that it testified to. The area surrounding Blue Arrow Lake had been home her entire life and the divide between the haves and have-nots something she'd breathed in like the clean mountain air.

Most locals didn't resent the rich who had homes on the choicest coves or the most stupendous mountainsides. Without them, what jobs would they have? The way things were, there was a need for grocers and Realtors and restaurateurs to serve the needs of the affluent who came up the hill with their inherited fortunes or with the money they made from TV or tech or investing other loaded peoples' dollars.

Most locals didn't feel the least bit used by the well-heeled whose lawns they tended, whose food they prepared, whose houses they cleaned.

A few locals, though, ended up providing services

of an entirely different nature. And to Tilda's mind, they *were* used.

She pushed that thought away, along with the pang of grief that accompanied it. Neither were productive and she didn't have the time or energy for anything beyond what would keep her solvent—making her rent, filling her gas tank, filling her belly and paying for the online courses that were her only way of getting an education beyond her high school diploma.

At twenty-one, she was on track for getting her degree in biology in another six years.

Shoving a long swathe of her wavy brown hair off her shoulder, she bent to scoop up the grocery bags. Her boss at Maids by Mac, Mackenzie Walker—whom Tilda also counted as a friend—had passed over a list and the cash to pay for the items. She understood that Tilda didn't have the extra to float the purchases until getting back to the office and handing over the receipt.

She shut the back door of her car with her hip and gave a cursory glance at the upscale vehicle she'd parked beside. Only two things interested her about automobiles: Did they run or didn't they? But it was hard not to admire the gleaming black finish and tinted, smoky windows of the luxury ride. By comparison, her dented two-door with its faded paint looked like something that had been abandoned in a weedy, empty lot for an untold number of years.

Exactly what Roger Roper had claimed when he sold it to her, as a way to account for the astonishingly low mileage.

Tilda had known he was lying—she figured he'd fooled with the odometer—but the price had been right, and so far it had been kind to her.

Unlike the weather. As she moved toward the front door, big, cold drops shook out of the overhead clouds, leaving fat dots on her ragged jeans and on her faded green long-sleeved T-shirt. It read Blue Arrow Lake down one arm and the hem was unraveling, but it was good enough for her work as a maid.

Sometimes, if the homeowner was present, or if she took on a side job for a local caterer, she wore black pants and a white blouse as a "uniform." But her helping with food service was irregular and the places she cleaned for Mac were usually empty during the week and used only on the weekends. So most often when working, Tilda dressed just one stage above rags, to prevent an errant product spill or a particularly grungy task from ruining a choicer piece of her meager wardrobe.

Now rain found the hole in her right sneaker, the one over her big toe.

An expert at ignoring things that caused her discomfort—from mere nuisances to actual anguish—she continued on, not even wishing she'd selected her other pair of work shoes for the day.

At the front door, she juggled the bags to free a finger and press the bell. It started up an intricate set of bonging notes, a classical tune, she supposed, that someone might learn to recognize in a college music appreciation class or even through the speakers in an elevator.

But Tilda would never register for a course so impractical.

And she'd never been in an elevator in her life.

It was weird, that, but true. She tried not to think it was because she wasn't born to rise above her station.

Then the door swung open and her mind fogged.

Her expectation was to find on the other side an old friend of Mac's who also was a former flame. He was recovering from the flu, she'd said. His cupboards were nearly bare. Tilda's job had been to do a bit of marketing and to deliver it to the man—whose name was Zan Elliott.

But the person on the other side of the threshold wasn't him.

Ash Robbins, her inner voice spoke in an appalled whisper. *You weren't ever supposed to see him again.*

In her head, the fog cleared and playing cards—each an image of their one night together—were dealt across its surface. But she ruthlessly swept them away even as her skin flashed hot-cold-hot. It would be almost a relief to imagine she might be getting the flu, as well.

But what she was really getting was another look at Ash Robbins. *Oh, God.* A tidal wave of shame washed over her.

"Tilda!" He said her name and his handsome face split into a wide, white, perfect smile. As if he was happy to see her. How could he be happy to see her? "My God, this is amazing."

Amazing? It was awful.

And so surprising that she stood like a stone, just staring.

His smile died. A faint pink stain spread across his cheeks. "Uh…" He swallowed. "Remember me? From that night, um, last May? Ash Robbins."

Wow. She'd rattled golden-boy Ash Robbins, who was twenty-two and the apple of his filthy-rich parents' eyes. They'd met right after his college graduation and the night before he left for an impressive summer internship in international banking.

She bobbed her head and said, "Ash," as if he were, like his name, nothing more than a smudge of gray dust on her memory banks. Then she glanced down at the groceries, back up at him. "Can I come in for a moment?"

"Of course, of course. God, you must think I'm a moron."

No, only the most attractive guy I've ever seen. That's what had caught her attention at first, the night of her twenty-first birthday. His good looks. Only later, when he'd had the waitress deliver a drink and she'd smiled in return had he wandered to her table and introduced himself. His name had let loose her worst impulses.

"Let me take those," he said now, bending a bit at the knees so he could get his arms under hers. His wrists brushed the undersides of her breasts and an answering shiver rolled down her back.

His gaze jumped to hers. "Sorry."

"About what?" she asked vaguely, releasing the bags. Let him think his touch was nothing she remembered. That it didn't affect her in the least.

Ash turned and she shut the door behind them, then followed him across gleaming floors to a state-of-the-art kitchen. Her apartment had a microwave and a single burner she and her roommates plugged into an electrical outlet. But thanks to the job that took her into many of the priciest homes in the area, she recognized the upmarket appliances and their functions.

He set the bags on the island and peered into them. "Uh…"

"I'll put the things away," she offered. His privilege probably meant he didn't know if canned soup belonged in the pantry or the refrigerator. "I am at the correct house, right? This is Zan Elliott's place?"

"Yeah." Ash ran his hand through his hair, rumpling the golden-blond waves. "He's taking a shower. But he knows his friend—Mac, isn't it?—was sending someone by with groceries."

"That's me…not Mac, but the someone with the groceries."

He smiled, a dimple digging deep in his cheek. Outside, the rain began in earnest, coming down in sheets.

Ash's dimple. Heavy rain.

It only needed a flat tire to cap out a really crappy day.

"How have you been?" Ash said, as she moved toward the pantry, the soup and a box of crackers in her hands.

"Um, fine." Small talk? After what had happened that night he wanted to chat?

"I've been fine, too—though I've thought about you again and again, hoping I didn't leave you with a bad impression."

Her head whipped around. "What?"

"I didn't even wake up to say goodbye."

It was actually she who'd left without a word while he was sleeping, sneaking out to do the Walk of Shame at dawn—and boy, had she been ashamed. Of course, there had been no getting away from her own conscience, but once the hotel door had locked behind her, second thoughts had been useless.

"No big deal," she said.

"I wished I'd found a minute to make contact before I left."

"You had a plane to catch that morning."

"Yeah." Once she returned to the bags, he spoke again. "But I also wasn't my best the night before."

As if she'd been a saint.

"I don't..." He cleared his throat. "After a certain point I don't really remember too much about it."

Now she turned her head to stare at him. Could it be true?

His hands dived into his pockets and he hunched his shoulders, appearing as uncomfortable as a rich, handsome young man with the world at his feet could look. "Possibly it was that last bottle of champagne I ordered from room service."

As she continued staring, he shrugged.

"I don't recall paying for it. I only know I must have seriously overtipped the server who delivered it."

A new surge of heat rushed up her neck. "I should have—"

"Nothing's your fault," he said quickly. "It's just... it was a great night and I feel like I let it end on a sour note."

Swallowing, Tilda made herself return her attention to the items in the bags. Her hand found the carton of eggs. "It doesn't matter. That was a long time ago."

And then Ash was at her back. She turned, to see that all the awkwardness had fallen away. He looked rich and smart and...confident. Smiling, he tucked a strand of hair behind her ear.

The touch pierced skin, bone, marrow. She froze.

"I planned to find you, you know," he said. "It's a

good omen that you appeared on the doorstep my first full day back in Blue Arrow Lake."

Her eyes rounded. "You're staying here?"

"For a few weeks. Then I'm off to England."

"You were in Europe before."

He nodded. "All over it, all over everywhere, actually. After my internship ended, I caught up with Zan Elliott and worked with him and a documentary crew for a couple months. But I've got a job in London waiting for me."

He had a job in London waiting for him.

There were some toilets waiting for her and a scrub brush.

She decided to abandon the rest of the groceries and get on with her life. Ash or this Zan character could figure out what to do with the rest. "I've got to go."

"Not yet."

She was bound by his words, by her memories, by guilt over what she'd done and why she'd done it. Her mouth dried. "What?"

"You've got to let me make it up to you."

Him make it up to *her*? She'd wronged him in ways she hoped he'd never discover. "I don't know what you mean."

"Another night together." His smile flashed, so disarming it was dangerous. "Just a date, Tilda. To get to know you better."

Meaning, *I'm not expecting you to jump back into the sack with me.*

Yeah, that dangerous, because didn't every woman—particularly one like Tilda—hope to find a man just like Ash Robbins who wanted to get to know her better… and not just get her into bed?

But truly, he wouldn't at all appreciate what he'd find out about Tilda.

He had a job in London. She had a job cleaning litter boxes and kitchen sinks.

Even if they could forget about that one night they'd already shared—and she could not—the divide between them was much too wide.

MAC LOVED HER small office situated on a side street just off the main road that bisected the village of Blue Arrow Lake. It wasn't much, primarily a main room divided by a counter between the entry door and her desk. Behind the central space was a large closet that held supplies, a small restroom and a back door that led to a tiny courtyard. That was a fine place to grab some lunch in good weather.

Sometimes she felt a bit embarrassed by the pride she felt sitting at the secondhand desk she'd found at a local thrift shop. But growing up, on rainy and snowy days her sister Shay had played school, Poppy had played with dolls and Mac had imagined herself in command of schedules and a staff.

You always were a bossy little thing.

What Zan had said was true, but her drive to own her own business was likely less to do with her temperament than to an early memory. When she was little, she'd been in line at the bank with her mother when Miss Cherie, the owner of the local beauty shop, had come in to stand behind them.

"A good week?" her mom had said, nodding at the money pouch the other woman carried.

"Very good," Miss Cherie had said, hefting the bulging zippered bag.

When Miss Cherie had stepped up to the teller beside the one helping her mother, Mac's eyes had gone wide at the stacks of money and checks she withdrew from the pouch. How much could the total have been? she wondered now. A few hundred dollars, she supposed.

It had looked like the contents of a leprechaun's pot of gold to one of the Walker family, whose finances had always been precarious.

So she loved being in charge of her own bottom line as well as being in charge of herself.

On the one hand, she was single and alone. On the other, she had her well-valued independence.

The front door pushed open and Tilda Smith came inside. You had to love the girl—not just because she was an eager employee, never saying no to extra hours or extras tasks, but also because she was a by-her-bootstraps kind of person. She'd been raised by a single mom who'd scraped by as a barmaid at various establishments—a single mom who hadn't always made the best emotional choices for herself. At the woman's sudden death several months before, Tilda had kept on marching, though, moving into a tiny apartment with two other girls and working for Mac and occasionally for one of the caterers in town as well as picking up any other odd job that she could.

Like dropping off groceries for Zan Elliott.

"Hey, Tilda," she called out in greeting. "I've got the cleaning caddy all ready for you." One day a week Mac devoted to paperwork, so the young woman was going to be cleaning a four-bedroom luxury lake-view condo on her own.

"Thanks." The girl seemed a little distracted as she approached, binding her wealth of long, wavy hair in a rubber band at the same time. Shadows beneath her green eyes only made them appear more jewel-toned. Ah, youth.

"Are you okay?" Mac asked, studying her with new concern.

Their relationship went beyond employer-employee. Not just because she recognized a like soul—they both were tough-skinned survivors—but they'd shared a lot about themselves when they worked together. Polishing two dozen place settings of silver or scrubbing a kitchen sized for an army turned out to be natural times to trade confidences.

They began with how best to stretch a dollar and which bank had the most generous overdraft protection, then moved on to the more personal.

Tilda had revealed her mother's history of affairs with married men as well as her own lackluster attempts at romance.

Mac had talked about the three times she'd attempted commitment in her early twenties—all awkward failures that had left her believing she was better off being alone. She'd even explained about the postcards that arrived at the office from around the world… and about what their sender had once been to her.

"I'm okay," Tilda said now. "Fine." She pushed through the swinging door cut into the counter. "Any special instructions?" she asked, first snatching up the keys to one of two small sedans with the Maids by Mac signage on the side. Second, she scooped up the plastic holder that contained gloves, cloths and their preferred cleaning products. It would take another trip for her to retrieve the vacuum cleaner and mops and stow them into the car's trunk.

Mac narrowed her gaze, taking a closer look at the younger woman's face. "You're not coming down with something, are you? Did Zan pass along the same flu that flattened him when you delivered the groceries?" That had been two days ago, long enough for illness to incubate.

"I didn't even see him then," Tilda said.

"Really?" Mac frowned. "But he sent me a text, thanking me for the delivery. How did you get into the house?"

"Ash Robbins was there."

"Ah. John and Veronica Robbins' kid." The couple's home was on a regular rotation for Mac's cleaning service now that they'd retired to the mountains. While she didn't know them well, it was clear they loved their son. "According to his mother and father, the boy can do no wrong."

Tilda flushed. "He's not a boy. He's a man."

O-kay. Mac knew Tilda didn't have much to do with boys—uh, men. Keeping oneself financially afloat took a lot of time and energy—at least that had been Mac's excuse the past several years. "I didn't realize you two knew each other."

"We don't, not really." The girl lifted a shoulder. "We ran across each other last May. But we're not in the same league."

"What?" Mac bristled. "Is that what he said?"

She shrugged again. "Imagine what his father's opinion of me would be."

His father? What would his father have to do with anything? She frowned. "Til—"

"I need to get going," the girl said, spinning around to head out.

Mac bustled into the back room to grab up the mops and wheel the vacuum toward the street. Before she reached the front door, Tilda had returned. "I've got this," she said, taking over.

Frowning again, Mac put her hands on her hips. "I can help."

The girl shook her head. "I don't want to get used to that."

Mac let her go but continued to watch as she exited. Clearly Tilda valued her autonomy, and her boss could appreciate that, but as a friend it worried her.

Then the door reopened, letting in a blast of winter air and someone she'd been thinking about since the moment she left him alone at his house two days before. She allowed herself a single assessing glance at Zan, then deciding he looked back in good health—and as handsome as always—she turned and pushed through the swinging panel to put the countertop between them.

Stacking the papers on her desk, she threw him a polite smile. "Hey, there."

"Hey back," Zan said, looking curiously about the room. "This is nice."

"It's small." Truthfully, she could have run Maids by Mac from her duplex, but it seemed more…businesslike to have a dedicated office space. The rent didn't kill because the office was, indeed, Lilliputian-sized. And with Zan's broad shoulders and long legs between the four walls, it felt just that much more crowded.

No wonder she could hardly breathe.

Mac took another peek at him. He wore dark denim and a high-end, high-tech-looking winter jacket with a wealth of pockets that probably cost more than her monthly profit margin. "Did you need something?"

"To say thanks for the groceries. They kept me fed and indoors for another twenty-four hours, which allowed me to kick the bug for good."

"Awesome." She rubbed at the touch pad of her laptop, bringing the screen to life so she could focus on the spreadsheet there instead of the man and his big… presence.

"I also hoped to talk you into coffee with me."

"I'm too busy to go…" she began, the words automatic, but they trailed off as he placed two paper cups on the counter. So eager to avoid looking at him too long, she'd neglected to notice what he'd carried.

"From Oscar's," he said, pushing one of the beverages her way. "They told me your favorite order."

"I…" She was forced to leave the desk to retrieve it. Refusing seemed too rude, even though she'd decided the safest way to deal with Zan and all the memories his presence invoked was to keep her distance. Instead of rattling those bones she wanted to pick with him, she'd decided to let them settle. That would, she figured, keep the unwelcome Ghost of Love Gone By as undisturbed and inactive as possible. "Uh, thanks."

Watching her, he shook his head as she took her first sip. "I can't get over the fact that you drink coffee. When I left you wouldn't touch the stuff."

"People change." Some traveled the world. Took lovers named *Simone*. "I learned to like coffee."

He leaned against the counter as he picked up his own beverage. "The village and the mountains are much the same, though."

"Still beautiful."

With a smile, he toasted her with his coffee. "Present company included."

She ignored the stupid flutter in her middle. "Well, see, you're much the same, too. Still a charmer."

He only smiled again at that, so she moved back to her desk and fiddled with a pencil. "This is my paper-work day, so…"

"Oh, you won't get rid of me so easily."

Well, that didn't seem fair when he'd left the mountains so easily before, she thought, frowning at her cup. Not to mention that he'd left without even taking the photo of them she'd presented him with before he'd packed his truck and driven it down the hill. That knowledge, she had to admit, still rankled.

She had a matching picture herself, now relegated to the dark corner in her chest of drawers under the single socks she was too cheap to throw away.

Hey, you never knew when their partner might show up again.

After all, hadn't Zan returned?

Not that they were parts of a pair or anything.

Annoyed at her train of thought, she squared her shoulders, took a bracing swallow of espresso and steamed milk, and told herself, rude or not, it was time to show him out.

Of her office.

Of her could-have-been file, too.

Clearing her throat, she met his gaze. "Zan—"

"I brought you something else."

The expression on his face gave her sudden pause. It was half guarded and half pleased. Exactly how he'd looked when he'd presented her with her eighteenth birthday present—the receipt for four brand-new tires for her battered baby SUV.

I know it's not romantic, he'd said.

Then she'd thrown herself into his arms, grateful, touched to the bone because those tires would keep her safe on the mountain roads for years to come. He'd known pride would never have allowed her to accept them as charity, but as a birthday gift…yes.

She thought of what Angelica had said to Brett the night of their wedding reception. *You know what I need.*

But the way of those memories lay danger and not the distance she'd decided upon, so she returned to the moment at hand. "A croissant? One of Oscar's cinnamon buns? I warn you, I don't like the lemon cake."

He grinned. "I recall your aversion to citrus paired with sweets."

It took effort to pretend that didn't stab. He remembered? "That's right. No lemon bars. No key lime tarts."

"But you indulged my love of peach pie."

Mac's body froze. Had he really said that? *Peach pie?* Um, sexual innuendo, much?

But before she could think of how to respond, he pulled something out of one of his many coat pockets and set it on the counter. The item was about the size of a large baked potato. Which turned out to be a very weird first impression of the actual object.

Her gaze glued to it, she moved forward, unable to stifle her curiosity.

"It's a Russian nesting doll."

Her fingertip stroked the smooth surface. More than that, it was a work of art. On the carved hourglass shape, a woman's face and figure decorated the pale wood. Dark-haired, blue-eyed, she was delicate and so, so lovely.

"I watched the artist paint her," Zan said. He cleared his throat. "She, uh, makes them by request."

Her head shot up. It didn't take a genius to realize the rendered woman had her coloring...even, perhaps, her features. Mac put her hands behind her back. "It's wonderful."

His mouth quirked. "I thought so." Then he picked it up and twisted.

A bleat of protest escaped her mouth.

He laughed. "Watch."

It was a work of moments. Inside, were five other figurines, each one opening to reveal a smaller figure, similarly painted, until the smallest was revealed, the size of a thimble.

Mac stared at them, noting that each had the same features and each wore a beautiful blue gown, highlighted with what looked like gold leaf. So exquisite. Inhaling a breath, she shifted her gaze to Zan again. "For me? Really?"

One of his long fingers brushed the painted hair of the largest of the dolls and his gaze tracked the stroke. "Yeah. I'll miss her, though. She's been with me a long time."

Like the long time he'd been gone. Ignoring the hot pressure behind her eyes, she watched him renest the dolls into one.

Then he cradled it in his hands like a kitten, bringing it close to his face. "We had many the long, dark-night conversations, didn't we, girl?" he asked, addressing the piece.

Oh, man. That burn intensified behind Mac's eyes and she felt a traitorous twinge in her chest. On long dark nights, had he needed a friend? During those lonely hours, had he been talking to a surrogate for her?

She curled her hands into fists to keep herself from reaching out to him. *You need to keep your distance*, she reminded herself. *You need to keep up your guard.*

But when he offered the object to Mac, she couldn't help but lean closer to take it from him. As her fingers neared, he lifted it just out of reach. "Now, what am I going to get in return for this little pretty?" he asked with a roguish glint in his eye.

It was charming as heck, so the look she sent him was stern. "A simple 'thank you' won't do?"

"Surely you can do better than that. Think of the miles I've traveled to bring her to you. The terrain I've overcome! The dangers I've braved!"

"The bullshit you've dished out along the way," she said drily.

His lips twitched. It drew her attention, reminding her of kisses, hours of them, that mouth on hers, taking her to new and heated places. That mouth, exploring new and heated places.

Peach pie. She felt a blush rush up her neck and cursed the persistent memories.

"I think you've turned into a cruel and cold woman," Zan declared.

She latched on to that. "And don't you forget it."

"But still," he said, in that teasing tone, "one small kiss doesn't seem too much to ask." His fingertip tapped the edge of his jaw. "And then I'll be on my way."

And then she'd be safe from him, her space once more her own. And yet… "Zan…"

He wiggled the doll back and forth. "Please?" His smile was boyish and friendly. "With sugar on top?"

"Good God," she muttered but found herself giving in to his ridiculous request. Bellying up to the counter, she closed the gap between them. Then she fisted her hand in the lapel of his jacket, drew his face close and rose onto her tiptoes. "Thank you," she grumbled.

And moved her lips to his cheek.

At the same instant that he turned his mouth to meet hers.

CHAPTER FIVE

WHEN THE DOOR to the lakefront, Mediterranean-style villa swung open, Zan's gaze dropped to find a smiling, gap-toothed little kid, and Zan's already good mood bobbed even higher. "You must be Poppy's boy," he said. The family resemblance was strong.

"Mason Walker. Almost Mason Walker Hamilton." The boy talked as if he was fifteen instead of five or so. "I'm a best man."

"Yep," Zan agreed. "You strike me as a good kind of guy."

"He means he's my best man…when I marry Poppy." A dark-haired grown person strode up behind the kid and held out his hand. "Ryan Hamilton."

"Zan Elliott." He cocked his head, taking in the other man's famous face as he passed him a bottle of wine. "I heard it through the grapevine, but it's hard to believe Poppy Walker snagged one of Hollywood's most entrenched bachelors."

"Has me wrapped around her little finger." He looked cheerful about it.

Then Poppy herself crowded into the doorway, and Zan was reminded of how wrapped around her finger *he* used to be. "Hah," she said to Ryan. "You knew I was behind you when you said that."

"Doesn't mean it isn't true."

She sent her fiancé an indulgent look, then grabbed Zan's arm and tugged him into the foyer. "Come in, it's cold out there." His hands were in her small ones as she took a long look at him. Her brilliant smile was as warm as the hug that ensued after.

"I'm so glad you could come to dinner," she said against his chest, squeezing hard.

He returned the embrace, charmed by her all over again. "Not mad that I practically invited myself?"

"Practically?" She leaned back and grinned at him. "You *did* invite yourself."

A big dog pushed between them. "Who's this?" he asked.

Mason ran his hand over the canine's big head. "Our dog, Grimm."

"So domesticated, Pop," Zan said, his gaze lingering on her. When he'd left she'd been a teenager, coltish and sweet as candy. "It looks good on you. Beautiful, actually."

Ryan's brows rose. "Uh-oh. Do I have to take you out?"

"Oh, you," she said to her man, then grabbed Zan's hand again and began towing him forward. "Though I did have a wild crush on him when I was a girl."

"You did?" he asked, as she pushed him onto a stool drawn up to the granite island in a spacious kitchen with views of the lake. "How come I didn't see that?"

"Because you only had eyes for Mac, of course."

What could he say? But he was glad he was spared from answering when Ryan pressed a cold bottle of beer in his hand. "Thanks, man."

"No problem—"

The peal of the front doorbell interrupted him.

Grimm barked and the Walker-Hamilton household inhabitants rushed for the foyer again. Zan slugged down a mouthful of beer before they came back, ushering people in front of them.

Zan got to his feet, prepared for more introductions and greetings.

Shay Walker, who had turned chic on him, squealed like the young girl she used to be when she caught sight of him. He caught her up, whirled her around, and then they grinned at each other. "Wow, you grew up good," she said.

"Back atcha." Then he turned and held out his hand to a big man with wide shoulders and a sturdy build. "Jace, right?"

The other man's grip was strong. "Nice to meet you." He indicated a teenager a step behind him. "My daughter, London."

She sketched a wave. Zan followed suit.

Then Brett was in his face. "You live. And you're here, once again mooching a Walker meal."

"Some things never change." Except others did, because then he was meeting the man's *wife*, Angelica, an exotic brunette with a smile that could melt steel. He glanced at his old friend. "I'm speechless."

Brett smiled, slow, his gaze resting on his bride's face. "I'm a lucky SOB."

But Zan would swear that was him as the chatter rose around him. When he'd called Poppy to say hello, she'd mentioned a family dinner and, as she'd said, he'd invited himself. So once again he was in the midst of chatter and laughter and teasing, just as if he'd never left. Their warmth and camaraderie had always been on loan, of course; he wasn't really part of their clan, but he fell right into the comfort of it, like a big feather bed.

Okay, he might have experienced a brief pang of melancholy when he compared this convivial atmosphere to the mausoleum-ish air of his grandfather's house, knowing he'd have to return to it at evening's end, but then somebody handed him another beer. Following that, Poppy passed him a small plate of appetizers—including little tiny hot dogs covered in puff pastry that a man would have to be dead not to appreciate—and then another presence strode into the kitchen.

Mackenzie.

Mason claimed her attention first, followed by Grimm. She bent to kiss the boy's head and followed up by petting the dog. Then she straightened, and he swallowed, hard. For some reason his throat felt tight.

A big, ivory-colored sweater swallowed her slim frame. It had a lace inset at the neck, making it nearly transparent from her collarbone to her cleavage. Ruffles of the stuff hung from the knitted hem. Denim clung to her legs and she wore tall leather boots that strode across the floor as she moved among her family members, dispensing hugs and kisses.

Then she turned toward the island, where he sat, and the crowd shifted.

Their eyes met.

A chill washed over his skin as her gaze turned icy.

Whoops. She was still mad about that kiss. He popped off the stool and reached for the open wine bottle nearby. A free glass sat beside it and he poured out a healthy dose, then took it to Mac like a peace offering. “How was your day?” he asked, pressing the stem into her hand.

“Why are you here?”

“To eat dinner,” Poppy called out, fortunately leaving out the part where he’d invited himself. “And it’s time.” She removed a huge casserole dish from the oven.

The exodus from the kitchen to the dining room and its long table covered over any further Zan-Mac awkwardness. She ended up across from him and a couple of seats down, but that was all right. If she and her temper needed space after their lip-lock in her office a couple of days before, so be it.

Okay, maybe he was a little ticked that *she* was ticked. It wasn’t as if it had been intentional.

Lie.

But he hadn’t intended it to happen, that was true. The opportunity had just presented itself as she moved her lips toward him, coming in for a cheek-swipe. Instead of offering up the side of his face, he’d cheated just a little and provided his mouth instead.

Sue him.

He hadn’t even tried any tongue.

But still, the kiss had been electric. Zing. Hiss. Wowza.

Mac had panicked, jerking away and staring at him through accusatory eyes. *That won’t happen again*, she’d said.

He’d responded with a shrug and left as he’d promised, happy enough that it had happened once. Not that he’d explained any of that. But why wouldn’t he be pleased that the old black magic had set off a spark? It only went to prove that his memory had not overelaborated all the sputter and steam that had been kissing Mac.

The flames and the burn that had been bedding Mac.

Best not to think about that now, though. He applied himself instead to helpings of an excellent lasagna, green salad and garlic bread. As the meal wound down, he tuned into the talk around the table. Then he had to turn to the woman on his right, Angelica, Brett's wife.

"What cabins?" he asked in an undertone.

"Do you know about the mountain, the fire?"

He nodded. The Walkers owned a tract of land, the last from what their ancestors had purchased when they'd first arrived to log the mountains 150 years before. A small ski resort had been situated there, run by the family, which had burned to the ground when they were kids. "They're rebuilding?"

"Can't," Angelica reported. "Their dad sold off the top of the mountain—"

"To a man who refuses to speak with us," her husband said from the other side of the table. He must have caught the drift of Zan's conversation with Angelica. "Victor Fremont."

"No spitting," Ryan put in, holding up a hand.

While no actual saliva was involved, the siblings turned their heads to the side and pretended to spit on the rug at their feet. Four shoes rubbed there and then four fingers made crosses over their respective hearts.

"May his days be cursed," Poppy muttered.

Zan didn't bother to suppress a grin. This was such a Walker thing. They were a ferocious band, and he'd reveled being associated with them when he'd lived here. Still, the explanation wasn't completely clear. "Cabins?"

From her place at the end of the table, Poppy—hostess, mother, almost-wife, it still boggled the mind—leaned his way. "Don't you remember? There are a dozen of them—now eleven—that have been sitting empty all these years. I came up with the brilliant idea to refurbish them and rent them out."

High-end seclusion, she went on to explain. No Wi-Fi. Rustic surroundings with luxury bedding. Gourmet food and drink available for delivery.

"Sounds good to me," Zan said.

"I know." Poppy beamed. "We're all on board—and excited."

Near the other end of the table, Mac raised her hand. "Voice of reason calling."

Poppy groaned and Shay and Brett frowned at her.

"Voice of pessimism," Poppy grumbled.

Which was weird, Zan thought, as Mac talked about advertising and discoverability and maintenance costs—all communicating her clear doubts. Truly, as Poppy said, very pessimistic, which wasn't like the old Mac at all. The old Mac had been full-speed-ahead, we-can-do-anything, let's-put-on-a-show.

This Mac was… Maybe it was just maturity.

Angelica leaned close, speaking under the general conversation. "I wish they could find a way to regain the mountaintop property and rebuild the ski resort," she said. "Let me show you the drawing that Brett did in college for a lodge."

Pulling out her phone, she called up a photo on the screen, then passed the device over. Zan gazed down at the image, his fingers tightening on the pink plastic case. It brought him back. The three amigos—Brett, Mac and himself—lying in the grasses on the mountain peak, dreaming up a vacation destination from which families could hike or bike in the summer, spring and fall, and ski and sled in the winter months. They'd argued and debated and refined their idea time after time.

Brett had drawn it just as Zan remembered.

Maybe better than he'd imagined.

Pain radiated from his chest, and his throat felt strangled again. Shit, was he getting sentimental in his old age?

Feeling eyes on him, he looked up to see Mac was staring.

She abruptly stood, stacking a few plates, and headed to the kitchen with them. Without thinking, Zan followed with more dishes. There was some protest around the table, Poppy telling him he was a guest, but he just announced that he and Mac had the dishes.

Her back to him, she was already rinsing and putting items in the dishwasher. He saw her spine stiffen as he came up behind her.

Sheesh. So damn prickly, he thought, feeling another echo of that earlier pain. Where had his Mac gone, that fun-loving girl full of enthusiasm and zest for life? He wanted to find her inside this new hard shell.

As he put his dishes onto the counter, an idea came to him on the fly. "Hey, I have a proposition for you."

"No."

"A *business* proposition." Which he immediately realized was how he should have couched it. And it was a sensible idea, really. If she complied, then he'd be able to dispatch his obligations here that much more quickly and get on with…whatever he was going to do next.

"No," she said again.

Brat. "You don't even know what it is yet." And the more he considered it, the more necessary it was to him.

In the distance, he could hear the Walkers still talking around the dining room table. Arguing, really, and the kids were even getting into it. The sound of the good-natured squabble made him grin. He couldn't let go of these people quite yet.

Walking out of here tonight might mean not seeing them again. But if he could get to Mac, that would get him a small toehold into their lives. Temporarily, yes, but he'd take it.

"I need some help at my grandfather's place," he said to her. "Clearing out belongings, sorting things, cleaning up so the house is ready to be put on the market."

She'd gone still. "I suppose I could send over Tilda or one of my other employees…"

"Oh, it has to be you."

Over her shoulder, she sent him a narrow-eyed glance.

He hoped he looked innocent. "I need your good advice on what should stay, what should go. You'd be good at that, since you're in and out of other people's homes around here all the time."

She'd yet to reply when Shay came into the room, followed by teenager London. They halted, their gazes going between him and Mac, as if they sensed the tension between them.

"Um, everything okay?" Shay asked.

"Sure," Zan said, all casual attitude. "I just presented

a business opportunity to your sister and she's mulling it over."

"Mac's mulling over a chance to make money?" Shay asked, in obvious surprise.

"It involves my grandfather's house. I think she's afraid—"

"I'm not afraid of anything!" Mac retorted.

"Then I guess that means yes," Zan said, on a smile.

It didn't die until Shay brushed past him. "Dude," she murmured. "You should be careful what you wish for."

ASH ROBBINS HAD a few terms he liked to think described himself. *Well educated* was one, and he believed just about anyone would agree it fit, thanks to his parents' money and his own pride in achievement. His name and *hardworking* had been mentioned in tandem more than once, and he'd also been taught to never stand on others to get ahead. He strove to be kind to everyone, small children and animals in particular.

His parents, successful and respectable John and Veronica Robbins, for twenty-two years by word and through example had raised their only son to become an upstanding, decent man.

He could only imagine their disappointment if they knew he was also a latent stalker.

Still, Ash's gaze stayed glued to the back of Tilda Smith's hair. Its waves bounced against her thin jacket. He frowned at that. While it was sunny today and the last weather event here in Blue Arrow Lake had been rain, there was snow on the higher peaks. It glistened between the evergreens on the mountainsides, and the breeze wafted like frosty breath across his face.

Tilda should be dressed more warmly.

She turned a corner and he hurried, instinct pushing him to keep her in sight while still maintaining distance. Something about the girl was like floating dandelion fluff, a rainbow-hued bubble passing in the air, that great idea hovering at the edge of your mind that you'd lose if you reached for it too quickly or grasped too greedily once your fingers closed around it.

If he wanted her, he had to take great care.

And yeah, he wanted her.

Again.

From across the street, he saw her slip inside a little hole-in-the wall eatery. The place looked to be nothing more than a counter and a few molded plastic tables, chairs bolted to their metal legs like student desks in a classroom. Aware too much aggression might spook her, he didn't follow her in immediately. Instead, he shoved his hands in his pockets and watched as she ordered, then passed a couple of bills to a ponytailed girl.

Next she took a seat at one of the tables, her back to the window. After a few minutes she stood to retrieve what appeared to be a cup of soup and a few packets of crackers.

"You need something, pal?"

Ash jerked his attention from Tilda. Another guy, about his age, was giving him a suspicious stare. His unremarkable jeans, navy watch cap and battered boots proclaimed him a local. Vacationers and the day-pass boarders who visited the area dressed in garishly colored winter resort gear and footwear that looked right out of the box.

"I'm thinking about lunch," Ash lied. He tilted his head to indicate the eatery. "That place any good?"

"No sushi, no sweet potato fries, nothing made with kale," the stranger said. "For that you need the cafés on the main drag."

"Burger? Shake?"

The other guy's gaze flicked over Ash, clearly skeptical that he was after something so prosaic. He stood his ground under the scrutiny. Until he'd wandered into an old-school restaurant in the village last May, he hadn't been aware of the decided separation between the mountain visitors and the mountain natives. That night, he'd caught the raised eyebrows and the distrustful glances and realized he'd crossed a gulch without an invitation. He might have gotten the shit kicked out of him by a knot of young drunks, but he'd sent a drink to Tilda before he'd fully realized the danger.

Then she'd taken a shine to him. Once he'd slipped into a chair at the table with her and her girl pals, he'd been safe.

The man taking stock of him now might well have been one of the toughs who'd wanted to kick his ass from their hangout. "You had your eyes on Tilda," the guy said now.

Ash shrugged. What was the point of denying it? "You know her?"

"Only since kindergarten."

"I met her last May," Ash said.

"Yeah? That was a rough time for her. Lost her mom in April."

Hell. Ash frowned. She hadn't told him that. She hadn't told him much of anything about herself, except it was her twenty-first birthday. That had prompted him to order the first bottle of champagne. And then another, later, when they were alone.

He'd thought perhaps she considered him a birthday present to herself.

But maybe it had been something else altogether. A way to numb her pain?

Then he'd gone all smooth operator on her—ha—by passing out in bed so that she'd left him without a goodbye.

"Order the patty melt," the stranger said, then touched his cap with two fingers in a goodbye salute.

Leaving Ash alone with his second thoughts.

After all, she'd not exactly thrown herself into his arms at Zan's the other day. When he'd asked her out, she hadn't said yes.

She'd told him she was running late and had to be on her way.

But that meant she hadn't refused him, either.

It was enough to get him on the move again, and he slowly crossed the street. It gave him time to consider why he was so bent on taking that night they'd shared out of the serendipitous column.

One answer: he hadn't felt right about the single shag aspect. His father always emphasized treating the opposite sex with the utmost respect, and buying a girl some birthday drinks, then sweet-talking her into a hotel room, and *then* basically going near-cadaver on her after the deed was done didn't feel very honorable.

Another answer: because something told him any subsequent nights with her might just be stupendous.

It was that simple.

Or not. Because when he opened the diner's door, Tilda stood in the frame, clearly on her way out. God, their timing sucked.

They both sidestepped to avoid a collision of their

bodies—but they sidestepped in the same direction, their actions becoming a dance move.

That night, back in May, she'd taught him how to two-step.

In sixth grade his mother had sent him to Mr. Preston's School of Manners. Honest to God, they called it that. Boys and girls had to put on fancy clothes and learn to address each other as if they were people from the era of *Mad Men*. Boys wore stiff shoes. The girls wore gloves.

There, he'd learned to fox-trot and waltz, keeping his body a precise number of inches from his partner—and his elbow ached just remembering the required angle necessary to keep that precise distance. The music had come out of an old-fashioned boom box and not once after that sixteen-week experience had he ever danced again. At the dances after football games in high school he'd lounged at the back of the gym with his buddies.

In college, on Friday nights he'd hung in his dorm room or apartment and got buzzed on beer like every other normal student.

So last May, when she'd pulled him onto the dance floor he'd been two left feet and very little rhythm.

But her laugh had distracted him—delighted him—and it hadn't taken him long to get the hang of quick-quick, slow slow. They'd moved together counterclockwise around the dance floor and he'd not thought about his feet or the hokey country ballad or his odd outsider status.

He'd only thought about getting closer to Tilda.

The same urge overtook him now.

As he moved closer, she moved back—dancing again!—and the door swung shut behind him.

Ash stared into her beautiful face, her cheeks just the slightest bit pink, making her green eyes stand out all the more. Her lashes were long and curly and her mouth… Oh, God, he remembered how soft and sweet it was to kiss.

The memory muddled his good sense.

All his life he'd been taught to use his head by the man he esteemed above all others. *Think things through, Ash!* his father always warned. *Consider first, talk second* had been drummed into him from an early age.

Strategizing had become second nature. But when it came to Tilda, he wanted only to obey his instincts.

Be with me. The words were on the tip of his tongue. *Be mine.*

But he curled his fingers into fists and exhorted himself to take it slow and not overwhelm the girl. *Go out with me.* He'd start with that.

"Tilda—"

"I never expected to see you again," she said in a rush, preempting him. "Especially not now—in winter. Guys like you…they're summer guys."

"Summer guys?"

She shrugged. "Temporary. Vacationers."

"My parents had a place here they primarily used in the warmer months. But upon retiring, last spring they bought a new house, and they've moved here permanently. My mom loves the mountains."

Tilda crossed her arms over her body, hugging herself as if she were cold. "And your dad?"

"Loves my mom and will do anything that makes her happy." It was his turn to shrug. "They still have a place in Palm Springs so snow doesn't get in the way of his golf game, though." Ash didn't know why the hell they were discussing his family, but then he remembered what the stranger on the street had said. "Tilda..."

She glanced up at him, glanced away.

"I didn't realize you'd lost your mom right before we met. I'm really sorry about that."

"You had nothing to do with it."

"Well, no, of course not. But I..." This was going all wrong. Frustrated, he shoved his hand through his hair. "I'm usually much smoother than this."

"I'll bet," she said, the two words laced with cynicism.

Ash closed his eyes. What an ass he must seem in her eyes. Out-of-towner who'd tried to impress her by ordering fancy bottles of champagne and sweeping her into a luxury hotel room, only to pass out like a teenager after downing a couple of wine coolers.

"I snored, didn't I?"

She blinked. "What?"

"Drooled?"

Her lips twitched.

If his heart could give a fist pump, it would. "That night... I'd come off five days of cramming for finals followed by a graduation ceremony that had me broiling in the sun for seventeen hours or so. I wasn't at my best."

"Is that right?"

He nodded, trying to look pitiful. "Then we came up to the mountains to find my parents' new house had sprung a major plumbing leak, so we had to take hotel rooms in the village. I was so wired I couldn't sleep, so then I took a walk and..."

"Found Mr. Frank's."

"…found you." He lowered his voice. "And you know what I thought when I saw you?"

She shook her head, her green eyes big and trained on his face. "Don't, Ash—"

"I saw you with that paper crown on your beautiful hair and I thought, 'I've got to get to know this girl.'" He leaned close. "You want to hear my darkest secret?"

"No."

Another thing he'd been taught by his dad was not to give up easily. So he didn't let those two letters deter him. "I've never felt that way about anyone before, Tilda. With anyone."

Her eyes widened and her face colored more. "I…I don't know what to say."

"Tell me what you thought about me."

She swallowed. "You don't want to know that."

"Sure I do." He smiled. "Let me help you get started. When I held out my hand and said, 'My name is Ash Robbins,' you thought…"

"This is a really bad idea."

Okay, tough nut to crack. "Tilda…"

"I'm being truthful. I knew it wasn't a good idea but I…I went ahead and invited you to sit at our table and asked you to dance and then I left with you."

He winced. "You consider it a mistake?" God, that hurt.

Her expression softened. "No, I… It wasn't about you, Ash." She caught one of his hands with hers.

He didn't hesitate to wrap his fingers around hers and the current of buzzing heat that shot up his arm was welcome. Fucking wonderful.

She was staring at their joined hands, her color

high, her expression anxious. Impulse urged him to pull her close, to put his mouth to hers, to end this confusion and awkwardness by communication of the carnal kind.

Be with me. Be mine.

He'd say it with kisses. Caresses. With their bodies aligned and their hearts beating against each other.

But he listened to a saner voice. Go slow. Strategize.

Don't scare her off.

So he called her name, in a soft but insistent tone. "Tilda."

Her head came up and she met his gaze. God, another thrill.

Ash cleared his throat. "Tilda, go out with me."

Her lashes dropped, her hand slid free of his. "No," she said, and then she scooted around him and was gone.

Again.

Maybe for always.

CHAPTER SIX

ZAN WAS LATE. Mac checked her phone for the dozenth time, confirming that he was fifteen minutes past their designated meeting hour of 11:00 a.m. and that he'd neither called nor texted. "I've waited long enough," she muttered and moved her hand to the ignition just as a car pulled behind hers in the driveway of the Elliott mansion.

Poppy jumped out of the fancy SUV she was driving these days and let herself into the passenger side of the company sedan that was Mac's ride that morning. "Why are you sitting here?" she asked.

Mac's gaze took in her little sister, dressed in dark jeans, an oversize yellow sweater that met her knees and a pair of warm suede boots. A knitted stocking cap in goldenrod was pulled over her honey hair. "You look like a ray of sunshine." It made her smile.

Poppy returned the assessing glance. "Ball cap, check. One of Brett's old flannel shirts, check. Denim that's about to split at the knees. You look like you're on your way to the county dump."

Mac's smile died. "Gee, thanks."

"Well, why are you dressing like that?"

"I'm only meeting Zan," she said, gesturing toward the house. "Or I *was* meeting Zan, but he's stood me up apparently."

Poppy pressed her lips together, causing Mac to narrow her gaze. "What's that expression mean?"

"I only think it's high-larious that you were shooting eye daggers at him over dinner and the next minute you agreed to do a job for him."

"High-larious," Mac muttered. "It was that lasagna you made. The carbs made my brain muzzy." The fact was, she'd been goaded into agreeing when he accused her of being afraid. Pride sometimes sucked.

"Still—"

"Anyway, I'm reneging. He's not here now, and I don't have time to reschedule." Noting her sister was about to make another comment, she took control of the conversation. "What about you? Why are you on this side of the lake?"

"Cabin business."

At Mac's arched eyebrow, Poppy continued. "I have a friend who's going to show me some ins and outs of website design."

"I thought London and Shay put together a prototype for you that some techie at Ryan's production company was going to polish."

"I decided to do it myself. I've got the time."

"With a wedding coming up? And a kindergartener, not to mention a fiancé and an overfriendly dog?"

"I'm not at the front desk of the lodge anymore. There's a free hour here and there."

Poppy's work for several years had been at a lakeside inn, which she brought up time and again when anyone questioned the success of the cabin venture given the Walkers' lack of experience in the hospitality industry. *Anyone*, of course, coming down to only Mac these days.

She sighed. "Are you ever—"

"Never," Poppy said cheerfully, "if you're wondering if I'll ever give up on making something of that land. It's our legacy, and we're so close, Mac!"

Close to investing their hearts into something that could very well fail.

"You know, you used to be a lot more fun." Poppy poked her in the shoulder. "When did you turn so gloomy?"

It began the day my childhood dreams drove down the hill. Though Zan had talked about leaving the mountains forever, as a girl she'd never imagined that day would come, especially not once they were together as a couple. For a while she'd wondered if she would have gone with him if he'd asked…but since he hadn't, she'd never nailed down an answer to the question.

"I have a practical nature," Mac said now. "And that practical nature thinks it's time I boot you out of my car so I can get on with my day."

My Zan-less day, just like so many before it.

Hadn't she known not to count on him? Experience predicted it.

"Too late," Poppy said, glancing over her shoulder. "Here comes your appointment now."

Which meant Mac could only gnash her teeth as her sister exited her car and Zan pulled up alongside. Poppy gave him a wave before motoring off, and when he approached Mac's door, she only cranked her window down a few inches.

"You're late," she told him.

"What?" He looked distracted. His big hands clutched a zippered leather portfolio.

"I tried calling you. If you had picked up, I could have explained then that you lost me. I can't stay."

After a long moment, he blinked. "We arranged to meet." He seemed to be reminding himself of that fact.

"At your insistence." He also appeared impervious to her glare and a little niggle of worry tickled her neck. "Are you all right?"

Without answering, he began wandering to the front entry.

Mac jumped out of her car to follow him into the foyer. "Zan? Are you feeling sick again?"

He shut the door behind them both and headed for the thermostat. "It's a little cold in here."

"This house is big."

"Yeah." Dropping his head back, he appeared to inspect the soaring walls of the entry that rose an impressive three stories. "There's so much of it. So much of everything."

Instead of the jeans she'd expected to see him wear, this morning he was in dark charcoal wool slacks, a blue dress shirt without a tie and a gray sports jacket. She shoved her hands in the pockets of her threadbare jeans, painfully aware of the ragged state of her clothing. Obviously she'd done her very best to demonstrate how little he meant to her.

Embarrassed, she glanced over her shoulder to the door. "I really should go."

He looked at her now. "I…" His hand forked through his hair. "Maybe you should stay."

Her instincts started chattering at her now. *Get out. Go away. Something not good is up.*

But her stupid feet wouldn't move. Instead, she stared at him, remembering another helpless moment.

When his lips had touched hers in her office.

Her muscles had seized then, her whole body transfixed by the familiar taste of him, the delicious sensation of his mouth once more on hers. Years of longing plus even more of loneliness coupled with the knowledge of how good they had once been together had struck her dumb.

No had fled from her vocabulary. *Stop* had gone on hiatus.

Tears had burned hot behind her eyes. But Mac Walker didn't cry, and she'd jerked free of the spell.

Then found her voice. *That won't happen again!*

But the truth was, she'd wanted it to happen once more, right that moment. Right this moment. Blame it on the Ghost of Love Gone By.

Or her own fickle foolishness.

"Let me make us some coffee," Zan said now and started for the kitchen.

And yes, her fool-status was confirmed, because once again she followed him.

Upon reaching his destination, he removed the jacket and hung it over one of the ladder-back bar stools drawn up to the granite island. While he folded back the cuffs of his shirt, Mac self-consciously pulled off her ball cap and tried fluffing out her hat hair.

"I, uh, have a house to clean this afternoon," she said by way of excusing her attire. "I'm dressed for dirty work."

He crossed to the pantry without glancing her way. "You look great," he said in an absent voice. Then he stood at the mouth of the cavernous space kitted out with multiple shelves and bins, sparsely populated.

"Do you need help finding the coffee?" she asked, coming up behind him.

"Shit, yeah." His fingers pushed through his hair again. "I need help."

Unsure exactly what he meant, she brushed past him to enter the space, turning until she found the grounds that she knew Tilda had shopped for and delivered. "Here we are."

She carried the bag to the maker on the countertop that seemed, to her, as long as the number of years they'd been apart. "It's a very big house," she said, reiterating her earlier comment to break the weird silence.

"Scared the hell out of me when I first moved in."

Interesting, she thought, glancing over at Zan, then proceeding to dump grounds into the filter. She'd never suspect he was scared of anything. "We've always thought it was haunted—and, uh, confession time. The other day when you were sick I let Poppy in to look around." She slid him another look. "You mad?"

He shook his head. "Nah."

"Why didn't you ever invite us over?" she ventured now, adult enough to broach the subject. "When we were kids, I mean. I don't think you were ashamed of us—"

"Hell, no!" He reached into a cupboard and brought down two mugs. "It was nothing like that."

Mac pressed the on button, then turned toward him, her curiosity aroused. "What was it like, then? Brett was your best friend. I was your…"

"Teen lover?" He waggled his eyebrows and a small grin made him appear more relaxed.

She shot a finger at him. "Don't try to distract me.

Did your grandfather disapprove of the Walkers or something?"

"He wasn't a snob," Zan said.

"Sorry. I guess I don't know what to think."

He busied himself filling the mugs. "The shame was on my side, I suppose."

"Huh?"

"Your family was so…normal. Like a TV family—"

She snorted. "You know we had our share of soap opera drama, anyway, with my dad taking off and my mom getting pregnant with Shay by someone else before Dad returned and they patched it back together."

"That's when I knew you all. When it was patched back together. And I didn't want you to see how…empty it was here, in this place. It needed more footsteps and more voices than an old man and a kid could create to make it a home. I was just sort of…warehoused here."

Mac clutched the mug he handed to her. "Oh, Zan." To her, he'd always seemed to be the person who had everything. Clothes, the toy of the day. Later, cars and money.

As she watched, he crossed to the windows overlooking the lake and stared through the glass at the expanse of wintry blue water and the surrounding peaks covered by pines and snow.

She joined him there. "I didn't know how it was for you. How you felt…"

"Solitary." Then he turned slightly to brush her hair off her shoulders. "Except for when I was with you Walkers. Later, except for when I was with you, specifically."

His eyes were a dangerous place to stare. When they were together years ago, they'd lie on the grass, or on a beach at a lake, or they'd stretch out on the rug in her family room and just gaze upon each other, their hands entwined. *How can one person make me so happy?* she'd think. *How can one person feel so right to me?*

Now it was too easy to be sucked back to those feelings, that mixed sense of familiarity and fate.

But clearly, they had not been destined to be together as the naive and dreamy girl she'd been had once imagined.

Shaking her head, she redirected her attention out the window. "I'm sorry," she said.

"Now I feel like an ass. I wasn't begging for your pity, Mac."

"It's not pity." Though there was a couple of inches between them, his body's heat seemed to seep into hers, the warmth melting her bones and finding the cold place deep, deep in her chest. The barren tundra that was the surface of her heart. "It's more like understanding."

When she was a young girl and especially at sixteen, seventeen, eighteen, he'd seemed so put-together to her. Confident. Fearless. Complete.

And now she saw that maybe he'd been driven away because he was searching for something he was lacking—and not because she wasn't enough, the anxiety that had nagged her when he'd first left.

Tucking her hands beneath her elbows, sadness trickled through her—and maybe the very smallest beginnings of forgiveness for the young man who'd broken her heart.

"You've become a mystery to me, Mac. I don't know what to make of this quiet, contemplative girl."

"It's because I'm a woman now," she said, glancing

over at him. "All grown up, Zan, with ten years of my own experiences."

He was shaking his head. "Is it wrong of me to miss that eager young thing?"

With a roll of her eyes, she grimaced. "You mean *worshipful* young thing."

"I worshipped you right back."

Yeah, because every guy left behind the girl to whom he gave his devotion. That thought only made her sad again. "Maybe we should leave the past alone."

"I don't know if we can do that, Mac."

She gave him a sharp look. The tension she'd felt when he'd arrived was back. "What are you talking about?"

"We're still all tangled up." He sighed. "God, Mac. It's so effing messy."

Mac frowned, her instincts once more on high alert. How she wished she'd driven away when he'd been five minutes late. But fifteen minutes in, Poppy had shown up, and she was the most stubborn Walker of them all. There was no way Mac could have kicked her out of her car, because her sister was unmovable when she wanted to be. Plus, doing anything that rained on the Poppy parade always made Mac feel like shit.

Her little sister was getting married in just weeks and deserved the world to be kittens and puppies. With a side order of cotton candy.

Yeah, Mac knew her sister had a spine of steel, but you just couldn't help wanting to make her world beautiful.

Steeling her own spine, she met Zan's gaze. "What's going on?"

Looking away from her, he cleared his throat. "I have some news. Uh, bad news."

ZAN CURSED HIMSELF the moment he heard "bad news" come out of his mouth. But that damn thing had been flapping its lips without his permission since Mac had followed him into the house. Still reeling from the meeting he'd had with his grandfather's attorney, he'd had no rein on it.

"What kind of bad news?" Mac asked, narrowing her eyes until they were slits of icy blue.

The gaze was sharp enough to jab some sense into him. Coming clean, right here, right now, wasn't the thing to do. More thinking time was necessary. And perhaps he should first divulge the issue to a different Walker altogether.

"The bad news is also the actual mess," he lied, hoping she'd buy it. "Three stories of dust and furniture and other stuff that needs to be dealt with."

"Zan—"

"Let me show you what I mean," he said, heading out of the kitchen and toward the staircase. "I know you said you'd looked around, but surely you didn't see all of it."

He could feel her and her suspicions trailing behind him.

"Zan…" she began, and then a distinctive melody intoned—the bell.

He continued toward the front door, ready to kiss whoever it was on the other side. A gray-haired, middle-aged man stood there, in dark pants and a white shirt with the embroidered logo of a courier service.

His eyes went wide as his gaze shifted behind Zan. "Mackenzie?"

Glancing over his shoulder, Zan saw a strange look—discomfort? embarrassment?—cross her face. He turned back to the delivery person. "Yes?"

It took moments to sign for the package and to guess it was more materials pertaining to his grandfather's estate. Through the manila envelope it felt like paperwork, anyway. Most likely proof of things he owned that he'd never wanted.

The courier was lingering on the front step, his gaze once again shifting to Mac. "Jeff's doing fine," he told her.

"That's, um, great," Mac said, hunching her shoulders and shoving her hands in her jeans pockets. "I'm glad to hear that."

"Jeff's dating a woman who works for the county," the man added. Before she could respond to that, he switched his gaze to Zan. "Alexander Elliott, huh?"

"Yes." Zan sent a questioning glance to Mac, who was staring at the toes of her sneakers.

"I've heard about you."

Still puzzled, Zan nodded. "Okay."

"I didn't move my family here until about eight years ago, but everybody's heard of Zan. Of Zan and Mac. Mac and Zan. The two of you…legend."

"Uh, okay." It was true that their community had taken an interest in their young romance from the very start.

"My son, Jeff, he knew about the Zan and Mac legend, but that didn't stop him from—"

"Isn't it time you get on with your deliveries?" Mac

said, halting the flow of the man's words. "You have some sort of time guarantee, right, Wes?"

The older man was silent a moment, then gave Zan a once-over before opening his mouth again. "Mac's a good woman, you know. Hardworking. Loyal to family. Could have any unmarried man in a hundred-mile radius. And nobody really blamed her, not me and Jeff's mother, not even Jeff himself, when—"

"Let me just walk you back to your van, Wes," Mac said, interrupting again and bustling past Zan to link arms with the older guy. She chattered away at him as she drew him off the porch and back to his vehicle.

Bemused, Zan watched the show, wondering just what had prompted her need to hurry the courier on his way. When she jogged back up the steps as the van drove off, he studied her face. Once upon a time he would have known every expression. Or, more likely, once upon a time she'd been much easier to read.

He sighed. "You really did grow up, didn't you?"

"We haven't all been here, in stasis, just waiting for your return, Zan."

God, had that been his expectation? "That would make me an arrogant SOB, wouldn't it?" Then he held up a hand. "Don't answer—instead, tell me more about the adult Mackenzie Marie."

"She still hates when you call her that," she said with a little smile.

He tugged on the ends of her hair as if she were ten. "Tough."

"What about that tour?" she asked.

Remembering that had been his earlier intent, he led the way up the stairs, opening doors of unused rooms and pointing out the shelves of books that would have to be packed up, the closets that were jammed with who-knew-what, the neglected baseboards and the cobwebs taking over the corners.

In a third-floor space, they passed a narrow mattress set on an iron bed and covered with a faded quilt on their way to the set of mullioned windows that provided light and a spectacular view of distant mountains.

Mac stared through them for a long moment. "This is a room for daydreams," she mused and drew a fingertip over the glass, tracing a design in the accumulated dust.

"What are yours?" Zan asked, studying her profile. God, she was beautiful. That hadn't changed.

"You remember my snake charmer ambitions."

He shook his head. "I mean now."

She continued to draw designs. "I don't have any."

"No?" He tucked her hair around her ear so she couldn't hide behind it. "I find that hard to believe."

At his touch, she'd stilled. Now she dropped her hand, though her gaze continued to focus on the distance. "Poppy's our dreamer these days. Not that she wasn't always, of course, but she's got this vision for the cabins, and one by one Shay and then Brett have adopted it as their own."

Oh, hell. Zan sucked in a deep breath. "You don't see it as they do?"

She shrugged. "It's hard to make a go of any business. But Poppy is really bent on this new income stream for the family."

"Excuse me..." He cleared his throat. "But, um, I get the impression that Poppy and Shay... Well, the men they're marrying look to have plenty of money."

She turned her head and just stared at him.

"I don't mean to imply they're *marrying* for money—"

"This is about the *Walkers.* A *Walker* business on the last of the *Walker* land."

A Walker *business on the last of the* Walker *land.* Zan was hip-deep in muck now. There was no way he couldn't tell her. Putting it off another moment would only submerge him completely in shit.

Reaching out, he took her hands in his and turned her toward him. "Mac, honey."

She tried tugging free. "Show me the rest of the house."

"Not yet," he said, then hesitated. "Mac, we need to talk."

Her face took on a pinched expression. "The last time you said that to me, you told me you were leaving the very next day."

He looked away, closing his eyes as he remembered making that decision. Until there was less than twenty-four hours left for them to be together, he hadn't let her know his flight was booked, his plans ironclad.

At the time, he'd told himself it would make leaving easier on her if it wasn't drawn out. Now he wondered if it hadn't been for him. If given more time to look into her tear-drenched eyes, he would never have left at all.

But going…that had seemed an imperative.

As was this conversation.

Unwilling to put it off even as long as it would take to get downstairs, he guided her over to the small bed and pulled her down to sit beside him.

"You're scaring me, Zan," she said and yanked her hands from his to twist her fingers together in her lap. "Did you…" Her throat moved as she swallowed, hard. "Did you come home to die?"

"What?" He stared at her. "*No.* Where'd you get that idea?"

Her laugh was shaky. "Sorry. It was just something ridiculous that Poppy said. I guess it stuck in my head."

"About Poppy…"

Mac's brows came together over her small, straight nose. "About Poppy…?"

Crap. Was there any way to soften this? "I met with my grandfather's attorney this morning. We went over everything."

She was still frowning. "Everything?"

"It was all left to me. His estate. His holdings. The whole wad, including cash and properties."

"You told us that at Oscar's the other morning."

"Yeah. Right." He grabbed her entwined hands and cupped them in his. "God, Mac, how I wish I didn't have to tell you this."

"All those years ago…" Her voice lowered to a whisper. "You said those exact words, too."

Then, the color had drained from her cheeks, leaving her mouth pink and her eyes a blue that was drowned in tears. His gut tightening, he brought her fingers to his mouth and brushed his lips over her knuckles. "Here's the thing, Mac. My grandfather…it turns out he owns the Walker land."

She blinked at him. "What?"

"I found out today my grandfather owns the Walker land," he said, looking her straight in the eyes.

She blinked again. "The mountaintop? Well, I guess I'm not unhappy about that. It's good to know it's no longer in Victor Fremont's evil clutches."

Zan nodded. "The mountaintop he did get from Fremont. Apparently he gave him an offer he couldn't refuse." Then he pulled in a long breath. "But…but my grandfather also ended up with the rest of it, Mac. It started with an agreement your dad made with him years ago."

Her body froze. "An agreement…?"

"The other parcel, Mac." He squeezed her cold hands in his. "The cabins parcel."

"The cabins parcel," she repeated, as if she needed to say it to absorb the truth.

"I can lay it all out for you," Zan said. "Show you the paperwork."

"Dad was terrible about that kind of thing—paperwork." Her voice sounded wooden and her words came out slowly. "Brett's been complaining about it for years. So many things we couldn't find."

"I suspect some of what came about was because my grandfather was actually trying to do your family a favor—at least that's what the lawyer believes. To be honest, it's complicated and intentions have been lost in the fog of time and because the principals have all now passed on—including the original attorney. I'm working with his grandson."

She frowned. "This isn't making sense. I know we've been paying the property taxes."

"Yes," Zan said. "Originally, my grandfather loaned your father money, using that land as collateral on the loan. Your family held on to the deed and your dad paid the annual property taxes as well as a small amount against the loan to my grandfather each month."

"A small amount," Mac repeated.

"It wasn't very much," he admitted. "And before your dad died—what was it, about eleven, twelve years ago?—he'd already missed a big balloon payment that was part of the deal. The loan was a couple of years in arrears at the time of his death."

She rubbed at her forehead. "Why didn't we know about this?"

"My grandfather either forgot about the loan or opted not to call the note—and I'm guessing the latter—maybe because your father and then your mother passed away and also maybe because of my longstanding friendship with your family. I think he might very well have considered that money a gift and didn't mean there to ever be a transfer of the property."

"But we hardly knew him."

Zan shrugged again. "Anyway, it boils down to this. Because he didn't clear up the situation before he died, we don't have any choices. The estate must be settled. Due to that missed balloon payment, the property rights have legally been reverted and will be recorded at the county to show that the parcel… belongs to me."

"To you." She pulled her hands from his again. "Really? *Really?* The last of the Walker land belongs to *you*?"

Watching her closely, he nodded.

A beat passed, and then she fell back on the mattress, threw her forearm over her eyes and…

Laughed.

Right away, Zan knew there was no humor in the sound. It was a wretched noise, as miserable as the sobs she'd let loose all those years ago when he'd told her he was going down the hill.

Feeling like shit, he could only watch as her shoulders shook with more bleak laughter. When it finally petered out, however, he only found the ensuing silence more unnerving.

"Mac…" he started, wondering what the hell he could say.

Her body jerked back to a sitting position and she looked at him, dry-eyed and lioness-fierce. "This is how it's going to go."

"How?" he asked, cautious.

"You can't tell anyone else."

"Mac—"

"Not yet, I mean." She bit her lower lip so hard it flooded with color and she grabbed his forearm in a tight grip. "Poppy… We have Shay's wedding and then hers in less than a month. The cabins have been Poppy's project for so long, and it would take some shine out of her if she finds out before she marries."

"Mac—"

"Poppy's got to shine, Zan," Mac insisted, her fingers clutching him harder and shaking him a little. "On her wedding day, *Poppy's got to shine.*"

"Okay." The frantic note in her voice stabbed at him. He'd talked to the lawyer. Surely that particular red tape could be left untended for a few more weeks. "Okay."

"You mean it?"

He swept her hair from her forehead with his free hand. "Yes, baby. Yes." Mac's urgency bothered him, but he had no trouble agreeing. It would have to be sorted out sooner than later, but no way wouldn't he give her this.

"You promise?" she asked, her gaze roaming his face as if to assess his truthfulness.

It killed that she'd doubt him for a second. "I promise, sweetheart. Of course I promise."

Then she dropped his arm and flopped back to the mattress, as if emotion had wrung the bones and muscle right out of her. His heart moved in his chest. Lying down beside her, he tried gathering her in his arms.

She resisted, pushing him away, which reminded him again of that day he'd told her he was leaving and how she'd fought against his offer of comfort. Now, like then, he brought her back, three times, until her energy seemed depleted. Her head dropped to his chest and he palmed the back of her silky hair. They breathed together.

Her arms suddenly came around him, clinging. "You promise?" she asked again, her voice hoarse. "You really promise?"

"I do, Mac," he said, and then he shifted her up to seal it with a kiss.

It was supposed to be an act of reassurance, a physical symbol of his pledge.

But with their bodies so close together, when his mouth touched hers, all intentions fled. What flooded in was impulse, imperative, immense waves of sensation. Heat. The softness of Mac's lips. Her fresh, sweet taste.

His head spun as he hitched her closer and touched his tongue to her bottom lip.

On an instant she opened for him and his head revolved again, but he didn't let the dizzy feeling prevent him from surging inside the heated cavern of her mouth. Her hands slid into his hair and her body pressed closer—or maybe that was his doing, because he drew one hand down to her ass and pushed her hips against his.

It felt like no time at all and also forever since he'd been like that with Mac. Relief and regret and lust coalesced into a molten ball that formed in his belly and traveled toward his chest. He was burning all over and greedy for more of her. So he pushed her to her back, taking them from their sides in order to press into the cradle of her pelvis. She instantly made room for him there, parting her legs so he could tuck his erection against the warm center of her.

She moaned, and his hand slid up her side to cup her breast. Her hips tilted and she ground herself against him as he thumbed the nipple that went hard beneath his touch.

His tongue dived deeper into her mouth. She sucked on it, shooting his lust even higher and taking the last of his air. He tore his lips from hers to pull more in, then lifted his head to look at her flushed face. The pink made her half-closed eyes a brighter blue.

Struck by her sweet beauty, he toyed with her nipple, loving the little catch to her breath. "God, Mac. I've missed you."

Which he discovered were the exact wrong words to say, because they were barely uttered before she was pushing on his shoulders, shoving him off her so she could jump from the bed. Her feet landed with a *thunk* on the floor. Her finger shook as she pointed it at him. He stared, still horny and totally unable to think straight.

"I told you," she said, her color high and her eyes glittering. "Not happening again."

Then she was gone, leaving him with the echo of

her footsteps racing down the stairs as if she wanted to outrun an enemy.

And, considering he now owned her family's most prized possession, that's probably exactly what she considered him to be.

CHAPTER SEVEN

TILDA SLOWLY APPROACHED a huge wooden front door and told herself she wasn't the least bit intimidated. After all, for months, as one of Mac's employees, she'd been in and out of many of the most impressive homes in the area. Looking up, and up again, she acknowledged this one wasn't even as posh as some others surrounding the lake. It had more of a lodge feel, the exterior walls half rock and half stained wood.

Her fist looked small and pale as she lifted it from her side, but she made herself knock anyway—and pretended her knees weren't doing the same as she waited for a response.

Then the door swung open and a tall woman with a perfect platinum bob and Ash's dark blue eyes looked down at her.

Tilda swallowed. "I'm sorry. I'm part of the catering help. I didn't see a way to get to the back entrance..."

The woman smiled and it looked as expensive as her hairstyle. "Come in, come in. We don't expect you to use a service entry, I promise you."

"I'm Tilda," she said, stepping over the threshold. When the woman didn't react to her name, the knot in Tilda's stomach loosened a little.

"And I'm Veronica Robbins. Let me show you to the kitchen."

She followed behind Ash's mother, noting her dark gray slacks and the deep violet sweater she wore with them. Cashmere, Tilda supposed. She'd considered not taking the job the caterer had offered—to act as server during a bridge luncheon—but she'd never been in any position to turn down extra cash.

Not so different from her mother, she realized, and the thought made her a little ill. She rubbed her queasy stomach but let her hand drop when Mrs. Robbins glanced behind her. "Tilda, did you say?"

Did she know of her, then? Had Ash mentioned her before? Or was it for some other reason? Shame set her cheeks flaming and Tilda tried ignoring the edge of panic. "Short for Matilda."

"Such a charming, old-fashioned name," the woman said.

"My grandmother's." Tilda took strength in that. Until the day she died, the practical old lady had encouraged her granddaughter at every opportunity. *You have backbone and brains, girl—which means you don't bow your head to anyone!*

So Tilda kept her chin lifted now until she was ushered into the kitchen. There, she could breathe a sigh of relief. She might not need to bow her head during this job, but she had every intention of fading into the woodwork. Ash was an unlikely guest to his mother's luncheon, so she could do her work, collect her pay and get on her way without any close contact with any of the Robbins family.

Later, when the dozen guests were gathered at a long table in the dining room, Tilda perfected her silent act by moving about the table like a ghost, serving plates, filling glasses, bringing in more courses.

The food smelled delicious and she prayed her stomach wouldn't grumble. The good thing about these gigs for the caterer, after the guests were finished, there would usually be leftovers offered to the servers. They'd sit in the kitchen, resting their feet while chatting about the party.

The camaraderie came in near second place to the food. A little patience and she'd get her taste of linguine and shrimp, the crunchy rolls and possibly some of the delicious cheesecake for dessert.

She was half dreaming about the creaminess of her first bite of the stuff when she tuned into the conversation at one end of the table. Mrs. Robbins was responding to a question about her son. "Oh, Ashton." She beamed just saying her son's name. "Yes, he has that six-month job in London starting in a few weeks. It's far, but that just means we'll make many opportunities to visit him there."

"Then it's just a hop and skip to Paris," the woman to her right added.

London, Tilda thought. Hop and skip to Paris. Ah well, she still had cheesecake.

"Is there a girl in his life?" another of the guests asked.

Tilda bobbled the stacked plates in her hand, causing a minor clatter that caused several of the guests to glance around. Her face heated and she wondered if letters were scrolling across her forehead. I HAD A NIGHT WITH ASH ROBBINS! I'D LOVE TO HAVE ANOTHER!

Except, of course, she really wouldn't love to have another.

Because of the way the first one had ended.

Because of the reason why the first one had even happened.

And especially because another night might cause her to want yet another and then yet another and her grandmother hadn't raised any fool. A girl with backbone and brains didn't believe there ever could be a future between a Smith and a Robbins.

Though as these thoughts wound through her head, that didn't mean her ears didn't pick up Ash's mother's response to the question. "No one special. Ash is too young to make any kind of commitment, even if the right kind of girl came into his life."

Tilda was definitely not "the right kind of girl."

After the dessert had been offered, then cleared, and after she ate a plate with the other servers, she expected to be released from duty. Instead, the caterer and operator of Fare by Fanny, Fanny herself, turned to Tilda as she performed the final tidy of a countertop. "Could you do me a favor, honey?"

The older woman was motherly and friendly and now passed her another piece of leftover cheesecake. Double desserts! "Um, sure?" she said.

"It means more money for you."

Tilda smiled. "Absolutely sure, then."

"I was going to stay another two hours or so, put the remainders in the fridge and then serve coffee and tea a bit later, along with some nuts and candies. But I just got a call that one of my ovens is acting up. I need to go sweet-talk the thing immediately. Can you take over for me here and put out the beverages and sweets? She wants them on the small buffet in the card room. Ninety minutes, two hours max."

Tilda hesitated. She had the time, and there had

been neither sight nor sound of Ash, but she didn't want to push her luck. Yet what could she say? "Of course, Fanny."

After helping the caterer carry her now-clean pots and pans to her van, Tilda stayed busy stretching plastic wrap over the leftovers and rearranging the Robbinses' refrigerator to hold the new items. While she had it open, she took an inventory of its contents, and it served as yet another reminder of the Tilda-Ash divide. The teeny fridge in her apartment that she shared with two roommates contained generic condiments, a couple of store-brand yogurts and some questionable lunch meat that no one claimed, so everyone declined to throw out.

On the other hand, the Robbinses had a drawer of gourmet cheeses alongside butcher-paper-wrapped packages with adhesive tags that proclaimed them to be different kinds of ham, turkey and pastrami. Bottles of European sparkling water and organic milk sat next to juices that were labeled Fresh-Squeezed. There were five different kinds of mayonnaise and three of mustard, and none of them were the white and yellow kind with which Tilda was familiar.

We don't even eat in the same universe, she thought.

Then she checked the time and turned away from the refrigerator in order to prepare a tray to take to the card room. This part of the afternoon turned out to be a little trickier than she'd expected, because Mrs. Robbins asked her to fetch teacups and tiny plates from the immense breakfront in the dining room.

But she didn't break any of the china and enjoyed admiring the pieces as she carried them carefully to each of the guests. It was a little like playing tea party.

When she was little, she'd had a set of thin plastic dishware about the size and colors of Necco wafers. There'd been three plates and two cups—her grandmother had found the partial set at a garage sale—and Tilda had shared imaginary meals with many a princess before she'd understood that only in a Cinderella story did a scullery maid ever get to dine with royalty.

Finally, the guests began to leave, which was Tilda's sign to begin clearing the dishes and remaining food. It was all put away and she was glancing around the kitchen to make sure everything was in place when Mrs. Robbins strolled through the door, one of the delicate cups and saucers in her hand.

"Oh," Tilda said, hurrying forward. "I'm sorry. I missed one."

The older woman held it aloft. "No, no. This was mine and I'm just finishing it up. After an afternoon like that it's either more caffeine or open a bottle of wine early."

"I understand," Tilda said. "Would you like me to put on the kettle? Make an espresso for you?" There was a gleaming machine on the counter and she hoped she could figure out how to use it if Veronica Robbins said yes.

"I'm fine." She smiled. "How old are you, Tilda? Eighteen?"

"Twenty-one."

"You'll be glad to look younger than your years when you get to be my age," Mrs. Robbins said, smiling. "Husbands get more distinguished while their wives just get older."

Tilda fumbled with the apron bow at the small of her back. Talking about husbands and wives, particularly with this woman, was not a discussion she wanted to have. "I should be going."

Mrs. Robbins tilted her head. "Is this what you do?" she asked. "Work for Fanny?"

"Mmm," she said, trying to sound noncommittal.

"Fanny," the older woman said again and slapped her free hand to her forehead. "I completely forgot to hand her a check."

"She'll invoice you," Tilda said.

"No, I better get it now. We're going to the Palm Springs house for a few days. If I give it to you, will you be seeing her soon?"

"I can drop it off on my way home," Tilda offered. "No problem."

"Excellent." Veronica Robbins beamed. "You wait right here. I won't be long."

That's why, when she heard footsteps approaching, Tilda felt no alarm. But instead of Ash's mother entering the kitchen, it was Ash himself.

He stopped short, staring at her.

"Um, I helped with your mother's luncheon." She backed up a step. "I'm leaving in just a minute…"

Why did he have to be so gorgeous? That rumpled golden hair, the lean body, the way his mouth curled at the corners—the entire package was just. So. Hot.

As if he read her mind, he came closer.

Tilda retreated. "Your mom will be back any second."

"Don't look so scared, Tilda. I'm not going to bite you."

Her laugh came out weak. "Of course I don't think that."

"I took you at your word," Ash said, still moving forward. "I've left you alone."

She'd said "no." She hadn't said anything about him leaving her alone. Not that she was going to make that distinction, because of course she wanted him to leave her alone.

Except now, when he was closer than he'd been since that night in May, she couldn't leave *him* alone. She couldn't move, except to breathe in the soapy scent of him.

"Go out with me," Ash whispered.

She should speak. At least shake her head. In some way indicate refusal.

"Your mom will be back any second," she repeated. The idea of Veronica Robbins walking in on them standing so close caused Tilda to panic. Her throat squeezed and the back of her neck flashed hot. "You don't want her to catch us, um, you know…flirting."

"Flirting?" One of Ash's eyebrows winged up and his mouth quirked. "Is that what we should call this?"

"What, um, else would it be?" Damn! She sounded breathless and helpless and spineless.

"Let's call it kissing," Ash said. Then he leaned down and brushed his lips against hers.

The floor went unsteady beneath her feet. To keep upright, she curled her hand around Ash's biceps, feeling the flex of his muscle in reaction to her touch.

"Go out with me," Ash said against her mouth.

In the distance she could hear footsteps and his mother's voice. She was on the phone, it sounded like, and on her way to the kitchen.

With Ash's lips still soft on hers, Tilda tried marshaling her thoughts. But only one was crystal clear: *I like his mouth on mine.* Her common sense had completely left the premises or was wrapped in the honey sweetness that was Ash's hand now in her hair and the fingers of Ash's other hand stroking her cheek.

Shivers rolled down Tilda's body as that voice and those footsteps got closer and closer.

"Go out with me," Ash said a third time.

And it was the charm. Because Tilda said, "Okay, okay, but please, get out of here."

Flashing a triumphant smile, Ash departed, leaving Tilda vaguely recalling her vow to fade into the woodwork and definitely worrying about what trouble "Go out with me" could cause.

For them all, including Ash's mother and his father.

MAC RETURNED TO Zan's the day after he dropped the bombshell about owning the cabin property. She'd had twenty-four hours to get her head on straight and her emotions locked down and now she was prepared to do the grown-up thing. An adult would be able to look her old flame in the eye, get down to business—he had a job for her, she always needed money—and proceed in a professional manner.

Hot kisses be damned.

He pulled open the door and the surprise on his face kind of pissed her off. She frowned at him. "What? You thought I'd run away for good? I'm no quitter."

"But you hold grudges damn well," Zan said.

Narrowing her eyes, she tried not to absorb how mouthwatering he looked in battered jeans and an off-white chambray shirt, cuffs rolled up, tails out. No way would she recall the weight of his body on hers the day before, the solid heat of him all around her, and especially against that pulsing place between her legs.

Blame those moments on her weak will following his

announcement. She'd been flabbergasted and beyond anxious about how the rest of the family would take the news—especially Poppy. Her mind reeling, she'd succumbed to the warmth of his arms and of his body, and after breathing in his scent she'd temporarily lost all her good sense.

"I remember getting the deep freeze," Zan continued now, "for at least two days when I hid Curly."

"I was *twelve*, Zan."

Faintly smiling, he shrugged. "It was a teddy bear, Mac."

She ignored his crack about the favorite stuffed animal of her childhood. "Aren't you going to invite me in? We have a job to negotiate."

His expression turned serious. "You don't have to do anything for me to ensure I keep that promise I made you."

Instead of waiting to be asked in, she pushed past him. "I'm not 'doing anything' for you. I'm going to help you clear out this place and in return you're going to pay me a fair wage. Feel free to throw in a big tip."

"Mac—"

She glanced over her shoulder at him. "I know you'll keep your promise." Though she might not know what the Walkers would ultimately do about this new turn of events—was there anything *to* do?—she was certain Zan wouldn't break his word.

"Thanks."

He followed her into the kitchen, where he poured her some coffee, and she laid out the hours she had to offer and they negotiated her rate. She allowed him to be generous without being ridiculous. They exchanged a heated word or two about that. "You're a prideful woman," he finally concluded.

She thanked him for the compliment and he only shook his head.

"Are we ready to go upstairs and do a thorough survey?" she asked, getting to her feet.

He was staring at her. "What?" she said, alarmed. Looking down, she brushed at her jeans. They were her good black pair, which she'd worn with dressy-ish half boots and a V-necked lightweight knit top with an asymmetrical hem that swung about her hips. Okay, so she'd not gone the driving-to-the-dump route this time, but she also hadn't intended to do anything grimy today, so—

So she'd wanted to look nice for her ex. It wasn't a crime.

"That sweater…it makes your eyes look like blue ice."

Her whole body warmed.

"Thanks," she said, working to sound offhand. "I stole it from Poppy." For just the exact reason he'd said, and—though she'd never admit it out loud—she'd worn it today in hopes that he'd notice. Then she cleared her throat. "Ready for that survey?"

"Almost," he said, then hesitated. "Do we need to talk about what happened on the bed?"

This time her body flashed hot. "I think we shouldn't." There was nothing to say. It had been a short loss of control. A brief aberration.

"Mac—"

"Actually, I *insist* we shouldn't," she said, then started striding out of the room. When the faint *bock, bock, bock* of a chicken cluck sounded behind her, she pretended she was hearing things and stomped up the staircase. "Let's work from the top down."

The third floor had the most number of empty rooms, but what was in them primarily appeared not worth saving or selling. "I'll come with boxes next time and we can dump this stuff in, cart it downstairs. The old pots and pans, those mismatched sets of dishes and the lamps we found we can deliver to the charity thrift store."

On the second floor, they both contemplated the room with the floor-to-ceiling bookcases. Mac pulled out a heavy, embossed volume. "I'm not sure anyone will want the *Encyclopedia Britannica* set published in—" she checked "—1955."

Zan was perusing the tomes on the other side of the room. "Here's a paperback version of *The Lord of the Rings* trilogy that I think I borrowed from Brett, like, fifteen years ago." When he pulled a book out, the pages separated from the cover and fell to the Oriental carpet. "Oops. I won't be able to return it in this condition."

Mac strolled over to him. "What else is there? Are those graphic novels? Now, they could be worth something." As she pulled a few free, the action loosened another item farther down the row and it fell from its spot, nearly landing at Zan's feet.

They both stared a moment, then dived for it at the same time. Zan won. Mac tried to wrestle the scrapbook away from him, but he forcefully yanked it out of her grip and held it over his head. She hated that grin of his.

"I want that back," she demanded. "Give it to me."

"Forget about it," he said, still wearing that triumphant smile. "This was a gift to me."

"That you clearly cherished so much you left it here stuffed between your *Archie Comics* and your—" she pointed at them "—*Sports Illustrated* swimsuit issues."

"Those were my grandfather's."

"Right." She rolled her eyes, then held out her hand, trying to appear calm and mature and not as if she was one second away from a teenage tantrum. "Please, Zan."

Stepping away, he brought the book down to eye level. She'd made the whole damn thing, Mac remembered. From the pages cut from construction paper to the binding, which was cardboard that she'd wrapped in material cut from her old jeans. On the front cover she'd managed to place a back pocket and even without looking she knew inside there was a key she'd found at a flea market. With a red ribbon she'd tied a piece of tagboard to it that read, "The key to Mac's heart."

How young, how trusting she'd been.

No less worse was the fact that in permanent pen she'd titled the scrapbook, *Mac and Zan: The Early Years.*

Their only years.

As he opened it, her heartbeat went crazy. Pasted to the first page was a photo of them before they'd become an item. Zan was mugging for the camera, all teen hotness, while she was looking at his face, yearning written all over it. Why the hell had she put that front and center? she thought, mortified by it now.

Because, secure in his feelings for her, deep in sticky, sticky love, she hadn't been afraid to let him know how she'd always felt about him. Mac had felt it safe to love Zan.

Looking away, she could hear him turning pages and it felt as if he was peeling layers from her heart. She remembered attaching more photos of them and gluing pictures from magazines that reminded her of things they did together as well as lyrics from music that communicated all that Zan had meant to her.

Country songs. Rock ballads. Top 100 singles from the top boy bands.

Yeah. How young, how trusting she'd been.

She was gearing up to attempt another snatch-and-grab, when he spoke again. "I'd forgotten about the poem."

Kill me now, came the silent whisper straight from her raw heart as she squeezed shut her eyes. *Kill me right now.*

Unfortunately, she was still alive when he decided to share once more. "How could I have failed to remember that *Zan* rhymes with *lamb*?"

"Don't do that," she said in a low whisper.

"What?"

"Don't do that." She opened her eyes, met his. "Don't laugh at that scrapbook or that poem. Especially, don't laugh at *me*."

His eyebrows rose and she could see there wasn't a hint of humor left on his face. "Mac…"

"That girl—" she gestured toward the book in his hand "—can't we just let her be?"

Slowly, he folded the cover over the pages. "Sure, Mac. No problem."

The way he was watching her so carefully made her want to kick herself. The mature Mac had almost come to begging and tears over a stupid scrapbook she'd poured her emotions into when she was seventeen years old! Great. Such a professional.

Shoving her hands in her pockets, she addressed the toes of her boots. "Maybe I should go."

"Or maybe we should take a different trip down memory lane," Zan said in a casual tone. "I could really go for a chocolate malt from the Shake Hut. Is it still there?"

Yeah, it was still there, and she was not a fan of running from him again. She reminded herself she was tough. Mature. No longer that heart-open-wide, defenseless young girl. "A malt sounds good."

The Shake Hut was off the main road that ran through the tiny town of Cedar Creek, a few miles from Blue Arrow Lake. As she had dozens of times before, she rode shotgun with Zan driving, her nose nearly pressed to the glass as she took in the snowy woods on her side of the car.

It calmed her to look at the pristine white and suddenly she had a different idea. "Shake Hut second," she said, then pointed. "Turn off here first."

He glanced at her and she knew he understood the place she wanted to visit. So there was no further need to provide directions, and she sat back as he drove along smaller and smaller roads. Finally, they were at the bottom of the long steep drive that led to the cabins and surrounding property.

Zan slowed. "It's plowed."

"Brett keeps it that way. He and Angelica live in one of the cabins."

When he grimaced, she put her hand on his arm,

squeezing it briefly. "Don't worry about kicking them out—"

"I wouldn't."

"They bought a cozy bungalow house closer to the village. The move-in date is coming up."

At that, he directed the car up the driveway and gave it gas. The powerful vehicle had no trouble making the steep grade and in no time they reached the main cluster of cabins. The rest were scattered in the surrounding forest. Above them rose the mountain, its slopes cleared of trees long ago. It had been a sweet little place to ski, a favorite of families.

"Cabins look in good shape," Zan said.

"It's been a group effort," Mac said, then admitted, "except for me." She felt a little ashamed about that now, especially when they did appear in good shape, thanks to the many hands that had contributed to refurbishing them over the past months.

She pointed to the nearest, with wood stacked high on the porch. "Brett and Angelica live there. They'll be at work now, though."

"I don't think we should pay newlyweds an impromptu visit, anyway."

Mac shot him a quelling look. "My brother, remember? Don't put that in my head."

But other things found their way in as they remained in the warm car, gazing upon the fruit of her siblings' labors. Making the cabins a retreat for visitors wasn't something Mac had cottoned to when Poppy came up with the idea. In her mind, the place had carried a curse. There'd been the fire that had swept through years ago. And she'd been sitting right on the porch of the cabin that now housed her brother and his wife when Zan broke the news that he was leaving the very next evening.

As if that memory had the power to affect the weather, at that moment it began to snow. The flakes drifted down, large fluffy ones, and they brought with them other remembrances of the past, those, too, falling softly into her consciousness.

Running through the trees playing hide-and-seek with her siblings.

Riding high on her father's shoulders on a tramp through the woods, as she spoke to the curious squirrels and the scolding blue jays.

Sledding and skiing and making snow angels.

Hiking to the top of the Walker mountain with Brett and Zan in the summer season to lie in the dry grasses and dream up a spectacular lodge. Brett would talk about teaching snow sports and leading hikes. Mac would be in charge of the day-to-day doings at the lodge. They picked out other tasks for their two little sisters.

Zan had added his bit to the design of the place, but he'd never assigned himself a job. Even then, she realized now, he'd mentally had one foot out of the mountains.

Really, she shouldn't have been so staggered that day, perched on those porch steps, when he'd opened his mouth and released the words that had struck her heart like a steel-headed mallet. *I'm leaving, Mac. It's time for me to go.*

The pain of that memory on top of the other, happier ones was why coming back to this land had been bittersweet to her all these years. Mostly bitter.

She'd been bitter, she saw now.

And blind.

Because, though she might have lost her first love here, she'd never lost her love for this place. It was so beautiful. But now this legacy was lost, too.

"Mac," Zan called softly.

She looked over at him. There was concern on his face and an undeniable tenderness in his eyes. Squirming on her seat, she had the uncomfortable sense that he was reading her mind.

"I'll sell it to you," he said, proving what she imagined was true. "I should have said that right away. I intend to make sure you get repaid for the property taxes and insurance as well, but I'll get the lawyer to draw up a bill of sale—"

"No." Mac shook her head. It was worth a fortune. "The Walkers don't have near the cash—"

"I'll sell it to you for a dollar."

"No."

"Fifty cents. Fifty dollars. Whatever works."

"No."

His hand shoved through his hair, a frustrated gesture. "Why not?"

"Because that's absurd." Fifty cents! She wanted to get angry with him for even suggesting something so outrageous, but she didn't have the energy. "Because—"

She broke off and dropped her head to the back of the seat. Couldn't he see?

Life had moved on. Times and people had moved on. Changed.

The child in her remembered how good it had all once been. The adult in her had to accept things could never be that way again.

CHAPTER EIGHT

TILDA HAD A HABIT of bracing for the worst...something that came naturally when the worst had a habit of turning up in her life. No father, beloved grandmother gone too soon, mother taken out fast and furious by an infection of unknown origin.

Never any spare money.

But when it came to the date she had made with Ash Robbins, she'd made a complete mental turnaround. Instead of dreading it, she'd come to her senses and decided to view it as an opportunity, not a mistake. Over the past several months she'd built him into something much greater than reality warranted. Yeah, he was good-looking. His smile could make her belly flutter.

But he was just a guy, one with whom she didn't have any particularly special connection. He'd appeared at her elbow on her twenty-first birthday, when she'd been a little low over the recent loss of her mom, and she'd gone to bed with him for that and other reasons. Okay, for one big, hairy reason.

Still, it didn't have to be such a major deal.

And neither was he.

So their late-afternoon meet-up—her idea, because it was too early for drinks and shouldn't last as long as dinner—would give her the chance to see that he wasn't anyone she needed to avoid.

Or anyone she was interested in, either.

Though she did do her best with the looks and the clothes she had to work with—because that was only polite, right?

The dark jeans she'd bought on deep discount at the village boutique where she was usually only a lookie loo. A green sweater with a deep V neck that had been her mom's, but that matched Tilda's eyes. One of her roommates lent her a scarf in greens and blues hand-knit by the girl's crafty mother. The other roomie let her borrow her black medium-heeled boots. They'd taken a Sharpie pen to the scuffs on the toes and the "leather" appeared near-perfect now.

Flat-ironing her hair had been considered, then abandoned as trying too hard.

So it had been her usual waves and a little heavier eye makeup plus a swipe of pretty gloss a scant shade darker than her natural lips.

She'd even walked through a spritz of perfume that had been her mother's also—and Tilda didn't let herself think about who had bought her mother the stuff as a present—that was part of the big, hairy reason. No matter what, it smelled nice.

Ash had agreed to meet in the village and so she climbed into her car and headed in that direction, leaving plenty of time to arrive but not so much that it would appear she was overeager for the date.

But she was eager. Eager to be over the way he'd been hovering in her consciousness. And her conscience.

While her mother had often made bad choices when it came to her relationships with men, in May it was Tilda who had been the wicked one, which wasn't usually her way. If Ash ever found out, she was afraid he'd think—know?—she'd used him.

The day was bright and cold and she hummed because Roger Roper's miraculously low-miled car had a big hole where the sound system was supposed to sit. But the heater kind of worked and its low rattle combined with her wordless singing couldn't completely cover up the first sputters of her vehicle's engine.

Familiar with the adrenaline spike of potential impending disaster, Tilda breathed through the quick moment of panic and silently encouraged the tires to keep rolling. But then the engine hiccuped again and at the subsequent loss of power she directed the nose of the car to the side of the road.

For a moment, she allowed misery to wash over her as she continued to grip the steering wheel and stare straight ahead through the cracked windshield. "Buck up, Tilda," she muttered, then reached for the lever to pop the hood.

Once outside the car, she huddled in her coat, boots to the asphalt as she stared into the mysterious inner workings. She knew a little something about living organisms, thanks to her biology courses, but clearly her car was dead, dead, dead.

She glanced around at the deserted side road. Her apartment's rent was cheap because the building was tucked in an out-of-the-way location. Pulling her phone from her pocket, she wasn't surprised to see she was without cell coverage. The out-of-the-way location also meant shoddy reception.

Her only choice, since she was now closer to town than to home, was to hike in that direction. Once she could make a call, the first would be to cancel her date with Ash. The second would be to a car mechanic buddy. Since she couldn't afford a tow, she could only hope he was free at some point to drive her back to her car, where she could also only hope that he could fix it on the spot.

If he couldn't…

She decided not to brace for the worst until she had to.

Five minutes later, her trudge turned onto one of the more trafficked access roads to the village. Three minutes after that, a car passed her, braked, then reversed.

The passenger window slid down and through it she saw Ash.

Her heart leaped, then dropped to the pit of her belly. "Oh, hey," she said, raising a hand.

"You're walking to our date?"

Tilda grimaced. "I was planning to call you about that once I had some reception," she said, pulling out her phone. It still lacked bars. "I, um, have to cancel."

He beckoned her closer. "Get in."

She got near enough to hold on to the window frame. Bending a little, she breathed in the scent of expensive leather seats and the faint whiff of an aftershave that smelled subtle and salty and fresh. A shiver overtook her body.

Ash frowned. "You're cold. Get in."

No way would she tell him it wasn't the January breeze that made her tremble. "I can't. I have to track down a buddy instead of having a late lunch with you."

"Will you consider me an insufferable, spoiled prig if I tell you how unhappy that makes me? I've been looking forward to this ever since coercing you into saying yes."

She ignored the little thrill that wiggled through her when he said he'd been looking forward to seeing her again. "You didn't coerce me."

"It feels like I twisted your arm." His expression turned serious. "Did I push too hard?"

"I don't know," she said, teasing him a little. "You only asked me three times."

"Four. Once at that diner, then three times in my mother's kitchen." He frowned. "I *did* push you."

"Ash..." She was supposed to be losing interest in him, not interested enough to set him at ease. "I don't say yes when I mean no."

He seemed to relax. "Good to know. Now, get in the car."

It would get her faster to Lee's garage, she supposed and yanked on the door handle to slide in. "Just drop me off by the coffee place."

"You want caffeine? We can go to Oscar's before the café."

"Ash, I mean it. I have to cancel." She glanced out the window. "I have a car issue."

"A what?"

It embarrassed her to share when problems came up. How could a wealthy guy like Ash understand that having transportation problems in her life was like losing one leg of a three-legged stool?

"Car issue." She squared her shoulders. "As in, it stopped on the way here."

Instantly, Ash braked. "What? Where is it?"

"On the side of the road back there." Her gesture was vague. "I'm hoping my buddy Lee—he's a mechanic—can give me a hand."

Ash spun the wheel to make a quick U-turn. "*I* can give you a hand."

She stared at him. "It's a car." If she had to guess, he didn't even lift a hand to wash his.

But she didn't say so, figuring there was no need to shame the guy during the last few minutes they'd ever be together. That didn't stop her from feeling shamed for *herself* when she caught sight of her car on the side of the road and took a look at it through his eyes.

It was a total beater. The silver paint was oxidized, every corner had been crumpled by previous drivers—or just one, if Roger Roper was to be believed, which he wasn't—and hanging from the rearview mirror was a small stuffed squirrel wearing a glittery scarf, which she'd thought was cute when a friend gave it to her, but now just appeared tacky.

Ash parked his fancy sedan nose to nose with the beater. "Did you run out of gas?"

"No." She'd put nine bucks in just the day before.

"Did the battery die?"

"Uh…I don't know?"

He grinned at her, then hopped out of his car when she handed over the keys. Moving more slowly, she climbed out as well and stood there while he studied the engine.

Tilda studied Ash.

Dark wash jeans sat just right on his lean hips. His shoulders and wide chest were encased in a thin, soft-looking knit. A steel-colored watch was strapped to his wrist and he wore loafers. Honest-to-God black loafers that did not call attention to themselves in any way except in the way that they didn't call attention to themselves.

Like his subtle aftershave.

His perfectly cut hair.

And it struck her, actually struck her like a real blow that took her breath away, that Ash Robbins had got up that morning and dressed himself like this—beautifully—knowing he was going to meet her.

Meet Tilda Smith.

She was still not breathing when she came to the swift conclusion it didn't look right that luxury denim and sumptuous wool and those sleek, elegant loafers should be anywhere near her crappy car. To be anywhere near *her*, in her discount clothes and her borrowed boots, polished by their best efforts with an indelible ink marker.

Sometimes her life made her just so…tired.

"We should go," she said, her voice weary. "You can drop me at Oscar's. I'll find Lee."

"We don't need Lee," Ash said, turning his head to send her a grin. "I've got just what you need."

With a screwdriver he pulled from his glove box, he proved he was not just a pretty face by scraping some crud off her battery terminals—she learned that's what they were called—which seemed to solve her car issue. Sooner than later, he was following her into town. Ash had insisted that she lead, so he'd know first thing if she had any further trouble.

The last time anyone had so thoughtfully taken care of her was when she was five years old and there'd been an outbreak of lice in kindergarten. Her grandmother, doubting her mother would take the proper precautions—and she'd been right—had combed through Tilda's long hair every day with a special comb, looking for signs of the pests.

Of course, she didn't share that personal story with her afternoon date. Instead, overwhelmed by relief that she'd dodged a bullet and her car was running again as well as being more than a bit intimidated by the elegant beauty of the guy sitting across the table from her, she'd gone quiet.

Until Ash had made her laugh.

This time, it wasn't over his first, clumsy attempts at the two-step. Instead, he told her about his initial days at his internship in England and how he'd been bewildered by British slang.

She found herself laughing with *Ash Robbins*, so hard that she had to hold it back with the palm of her hand, because he'd discovered telling a coworker some assigned task was a "biggie" didn't mean it was monumental or important. *Biggie* was a child's term for poo.

Or Brit lingo for an erection.

After that, his coworkers—and later, friends—loved to toss out any Britishism they knew would throw him for a loop.

If he wore a new tie to work, he was dressed like "dog's dinner," aka nicely.

They'd invite him to a wild "knee's up"—dance party—on the weekend, where they planned to get "legless"—meaning drunk.

They'd hand over a tissue and claim he had a "crusty dragon"—a booger.

When he'd figure out the meaning of one of those foreign phrases on his own, they'd crow, "Bob's your uncle!"

She had to smile at him. She had to say, "You liked them very much."

And he responded, "Bob's your uncle!" which only

made her start laughing again, so hard she didn't remember her car or her crappy shoes or the million years it would take to finish her bio degree or that she so often felt alone in this big, big world.

And he was smiling at her as if he was glad to make her laugh, as if that was the only thing on the agenda for the day of rich, smart, great-looking Ash Robbins.

Then he caught her hand in his. His eyes turned serious, even though his beautiful mouth was still smiling. "Say you like me, Tilda."

But she wasn't supposed to! She was supposed to be proving she had no interest in him!

The truth slipped out instead. "I like you, Ash," she whispered.

Probably too much.

ZAN HUNCHED OVER his beer in the darkest corner of the bar at Mr. Frank's, occasionally checking out the football game playing on the TV. The place wasn't busy—it was a weeknight—so he wasn't terribly surprised when the mostly idle bartender wandered his way not long after delivering his cold draft.

"So," the young man said, using a rag to wipe the bar top. "What're you doing here?"

"Drinking?"

"I mean in Blue Arrow." He stepped back, his gaze assessing. "Doesn't look like you're here for the snow."

Zan thought he might hit the local slopes one of these days, but he hadn't gotten around to it yet. "I lived here as a kid. With my grandfather. He passed, so I'm here to sort out things."

"Oh, sorry, man."

"Appreciate it."

The bartender wasn't done with him, however. The night, apparently, was that slow. "Then you're going back to...what?" he asked, swiping at the bar again.

What *was* he going to do after this? Zan had come back to town sick, which had taken a few days to clear. Then he'd been caught up in his grandfather's business, but that wasn't going to last forever.

Maybe it was time to do a little thinking.

Where would he go next?

What did he want next? After graduating high school, he'd promised his grandfather he'd stick around until getting his bachelors in anthropology. At a college he'd commuted to down the hill, he'd managed to finish in three years. Since that time he'd wandered, and then wandered with the *Earth Unfiltered* crew, and now he didn't have a plan.

Or a clue.

A commotion at the entrance to the bar caught his attention. A knot of young women were laughing and jostling each other on their way to a couple of round tables they shoved together in one corner of the room. Under their arms were gifts wrapped in silver and white and each of the women had a poufy bit of transparent white fabric pinned to her hair.

It was the Walker sisters, with a posse of their girl pals, all wearing veil-like things on their heads.

Most settled into chairs. Two separated themselves from the group and approached the bar. The guy manning it moved to greet them.

"Hey, Sean," a redhead called.

"Hiya," he answered. "You ladies celebrating tonight?"

"Yes, we are. And we have a designated driver and everything, so no watering down our drinks."

"As if I'd do that, especially with brides-to-be in the party."

"Then we want two pitchers of beer and two pitchers of margaritas."

"Coming up."

The ladies seemed content to wait for them, as there was no server on duty that night. Zan watched them through the mirror as they chatted with each other.

He slightly turned his shoulder when he heard them mention Mac, and he kept his ears open. They were talking about the woman who'd once written him a poem rhyming *Zan* with *lamb*. The woman who'd pasted that poem into a scrapbook she'd made for him when she was seventeen. He'd pored over it the night before, memories flooding in, memories of the woman he'd traveled as far from as he could.

But she'd been in his arms not long before and he'd seen the lost expression on her face when they'd visited the cabins. So he was going to eavesdrop and not even feel guilty about it.

Though guilt—or something like it—sliced through him every time he recalled her whispering to him, *That girl? Can't we just let her be?*

"She's quiet," the redhead was saying now to her blonde friend. "Weird-quiet."

"Yeah," the other woman said. "Do you think it's because we saw Jeff at the last bar?"

Jeff? Wasn't that the name the courier had mentioned to her on Zan's doorstep? Who the hell was Jeff?

"And Adam."

"Adam?" the blonde squeaked out the name. "Adam was there? I didn't see him."

Adam?

"He was at a table behind you, with a woman wearing a dress that was way, way too short."

The blonde shook her head. "Mac wouldn't care about Adam seeing someone, not even someone wearing a too-short dress."

"Maybe not before," the other one said. "But now… now with her two sisters getting married and Brett having already tied the knot… I don't blame her for feeling a little, well, left behind. For acting a bit removed, maybe?"

Removed? Not Mac Walker, who was rooted to her mountains and to her family, no matter what their marital status.

But he thought again of that expression on her face as she stared at the cabins and his gut tightened, wishing like hell he hadn't been forced to tell her that one of those very roots that were so much a part of her character was now severed.

Pitchers in each hand, the women returned to their friends. Zan swallowed more beer, but it didn't relax that knot in his belly. What crap news to deliver to an old friend. If he thought for a second she'd give in and let him sell her the place—hell, he'd *gift* her the property—he could feel more settled. But he could tell—at least for now—she wasn't budging on the issue.

With business in the bar slowing down again, the bartender wandered back. "I saw the way you were checking out those ladies," he said. "They're lookers."

Zan hadn't noticed. He'd been focused on their conversation, not anything else. Laughter came from the bridal corner and he studied the party in the mirror. Mac's back was to him, so he couldn't judge whether she was quiet, weird-quiet or otherwise.

But he couldn't get the women's words out of his head.

Feeling left behind. Acting a bit removed. He didn't like the sound of either, not at all, because he well knew the feeling and he never wanted that for the woman who'd once rhymed *Zan* with *lamb.*

He continued keeping an eye on the celebration, so he was aware of the moment when Mac abruptly rose from her chair and wandered away from the tables. No one else seemed to be aware of her leaving…nor should they, he supposed. Likely she'd left to freshen up.

But she didn't turn in the direction of the restrooms.

With no coat over her little dress, she opened the front door and slipped out.

It was nothing, he told himself. She'd forgotten something in her car. She was dashing outside for better reception on her cell.

But when five minutes passed and she hadn't returned, he threw some cash down on the bar and followed. They might have been over long ago, but that didn't mean his need to watch out for her had died. Hadn't she helped him through the flu just days ago?

The heavy door squeaked as he stepped out, the area dimly lit by a few canned lights built into the restaurant's overhang. Glancing around, he saw her by one corner of the building, her body half-turned, her shoulders by her ears, her hands clutching her elbows.

He made for her, going slowly to give himself a chance to suss out her mood. But his steps quickened when he saw her shiver. He took his leather jacket from over his arm and draped it across her shoulders.

She started, glanced around, her eyes wide.

"Just me," he said, studying her face in the half shadow. "You okay?"

"Awesome."

"Yeah? You always venture into temps below twenty degrees when you're awesome?"

"Don't worry. Everything's cool."

He watched a tremor run through her and clamped down on his temper. "Cool enough you'll get frostbite out here, dressed like that." The material of her dress was thin and clung to her curves. She wore it with tall boots, but they couldn't provide nearly enough warmth on a night like this.

"I've got a coat inside."

"You're standing *out*side, Mac." And it bugged him, that she'd felt the need to get away from her sisters and her friends.

He stepped closer, hoping some of his body warmth would transfer through the chilly inches between them. He was in jeans, a T-shirt and a wool sweater, much better dressed for the weather. "Do you want to go somewhere else?"

Her gaze slid away from his. "I should probably return to the party." She didn't move.

He used a single finger to tuck a lock of hair behind her ear. The strands felt cool and he had to bank the piercing need to pull her close and warm her with his body. "Feel like talking?" he asked again, intentionally softening his voice.

"To you?"

"Why not?" He wouldn't let her wariness put him off. "I'm here."

She still hesitated.

"And I'm interested," he added. Then, frustrated by her continued lack of response, he took her by the arm and practically hauled her to his SUV. At his urging, she hopped into the passenger seat and he considered it a win that she didn't climb back out as he made his way to the driver's side. Once there, he started the engine and nudged up the heat.

Turning to her, he found she was texting. Maybe her escape really had been a search for cell reception.

"Mac?"

She shut down the phone. "I texted Shay I ran into someone so they won't worry."

"Why did you run in the first place?"

"Well..." In the glow of the dashboard he saw her gaze slide right.

Thinking she might be more forthcoming without that light on her face, he dimmed the dash, plunging the car into an intimate darkness. Then he touched her cheek with the back of his knuckles.

She jumped.

He stroked her cheek again.

Reaching up, Mac pushed his hand away.

He let it fall but asked his question again. "Why'd you run?"

"If you really must know..."

"I must."

"Fine." There was an unfamiliar note in her voice. Embarrassment? "I was getting a little sniffly."

"Sniffly?" Zan figured at times bridal celebrations

might naturally bring out a few tears between sisters and friends. "So?"

"It would diminish my rep."

He frowned. "What rep is that?"

"My tough-girl, unsentimental rep. The reputation of Mac Walker being untouched and unaffected by mawkish sentiment."

How he wished he'd left the dash light on, he thought, staring at her, trying to figure her out. On a night like this, the Mac he'd left behind would have written a poem rhyming *bride* and *sigh* and she would have been mopping up weepy tears with that fluffy veil still pinned in her hair.

"That girl…" he murmured.

"What girl?" Mac asked.

"You asked me to let her be." He couldn't help it, he touched Mac again, drawing his fingers through her hair. "But I want to know… God, I want to know where she went."

In the darkness, he sensed the shrug of her shoulders. "I'm not entirely sure. Maybe she disappeared when you did."

Taking with her Mac's old exuberance, her optimism, the shine that she insisted on for Poppy.

He didn't want to think it was his fault, and she wasn't placing the blame squarely in his corner. But still, the loss of the old Mac stung. It made his chest ache like a bitch. For a second he wanted to shake both fists at the night sky.

"I sense you don't care much for the new Mac," she continued, her tone nonchalant. "But—" The word ended in a yelp when he took hold of her shoulders and yanked her forward.

For a kiss. A hot, demanding, message-filled kiss that arose out of that sting, that ache, the frustration he felt about not understanding where this change in her had come from.

Don't think for a moment I don't care for you, he was trying to tell her.

Don't think for a moment I can't see through that tough exterior you show to the world.

Don't think...

And then he wasn't, his entire focus only on sinking into another taste of Mac. There was the tart lime flavor of margarita on her tongue, but beneath that, it was Mac, his Mac. The female half of Mac and Zan, the yin of their young-lovers legend.

For a moment she was stiff in his hold, unresponsive, and then her hands shot into his hair and she gave herself to the kiss, gave herself to him. He wanted closer, more, the weight of her against him, and though it had been years since he'd made out in a car, flipping his seat to lie it flat was the work of a moment and then he was lifting her over the console.

His jacket fell from her as she allowed him to pull her on top of him.

Their mouths broke contact for a breath, but then they were back at it. Her knees were on either side of his hips, and he ran his hand down her spine, encouraging her to settle on him as their tongues tangled and their hearts beat like mad against each other.

He groaned, his hands wandering everywhere, taking in every inch of her slim body. His palm slid below her booty and he realized the hem of her slinky dress had ridden up and his bare flesh found her bare flesh.

She moaned, lifting a little into the contact, and he didn't contemplate his next move.

His next move was dictated entirely by that sweet sound coming from her throat.

As they continued devouring each other's mouths, he drew his touch up the naked back of her thigh…all the way until he found the edge of a silky pair of panties and his fingertips delved under. Her head shot up and she pulled in a ragged breath of air. He took the opportunity to find her throat with his lips, and he felt the shudder of pleasure run through her at his exploration of this new territory. Her hands clutched his shoulders as he tongued and sucked on her tender skin, not hard enough to mark, and not hard enough to satisfy that growling voice inside of him.

Mine, mine, mine.

His name came out on another of her breathy moans. He couldn't chance she'd question any of this; if she asked what the hell they were doing he had no good answer, so he silenced her again by tipping her head back down to his and clamping his teeth around her full bottom lip.

She jolted, and his fingertips tucked just beneath the elastic moved, sliding a few inches toward her soft center.

Her body froze.

But all Zan felt was heat.

There was no stopping him…unless she said the word, and she didn't. Instead, she thrust her tongue deep in his mouth and Zan slid his fingers just a few more inches.

The danger zone.

When they'd first got together, that's what he'd

called it in his mind. It had been Mac, new in his arms, his best friend's little sister. Hell, she was one of *Zan's* best friends, and he had never wanted to scare her off by pushing too hard, too fast. For a long time he'd kept them on a strict course of wet kisses and full-body hugs. Then it was touching over clothes.

And ultimately it was everything.

He was glad to know that what hadn't changed about Mac was the way she responded to him. Just kissing—okay, deep kissing—and she was soft and wet and searing-hot between her legs. With her knees on either side of him, her position allowed him to take full advantage of the danger zone. And he did, delving deeper beneath her panties to caress the soft folds, then sliding one finger into the wet grip of her body, then two. She had her weight on her knees and her hips tilted to allow him that access and his muscles tightened as he played...keeping his touch intentionally away from the small knot of nerves he knew from experience was pulsing in anticipation.

"You rat," she said against his mouth.

He smiled against hers. Then he pushed his two fingers deeper into the tight clutch of her, and then he gave in and brushed his thumb against her takeoff button.

Seconds later, she flew.

God, he loved sending Mac on a thrill ride.

When she finally stopped shaking, she buried her face in his neck and he stroked the back of her hair as her breathing slowed. He felt her lips move against him. "I...I don't know what to say, Zan."

He stroked her hair again and made his decision. "I do. I'm saying I don't have a condom and, anyway, I think I'm too old to get any more adventurous in the parking lot at Mr. Frank's."

Her head shot up. "We're in the parking lot at Mr. Frank's!"

He winced at her near-shriek. "Nobody's around us. Nobody saw anything."

She let her forehead fall to his shoulder, where she bumped it lightly, over and over. "Why did this happen again? What the heck are we doing?"

It happened because the chemistry between them was so damn strong. Because they'd always combusted when they were together...and he suspected that wasn't ever going to change.

But he guessed that wasn't what she wanted to hear, and he didn't feel like arguing now, when his dick was hard as a pole and his brain was still smoky with lust.

"For now," he said, "what we're doing is ending our little reunion so you can get back to your other party. I'm going to watch you go inside and then I'm going to head to my grandfather's."

Where he'd take the fucking coldest shower in the universe.

And that's how it went. But as he drove the mountain roads, cold air blasting in from his open window cleared his head and realization rushed in. He had found at least one answer.

What he wanted? In the short term, that was easy.

Mac.

This Mac. He wanted this maddening, prickly, tough-girl Mac in his arms, in his bed, her scent in his head, her taste in his mouth.

CHAPTER NINE

AS TILDA APPROACHED the door to the Maids by Mac office, a cup of Oscar's coffee in each hand, it suddenly swung open and she was jerked inside. Then Mac locked the door and towed her quickly to the privacy of the back storeroom.

"There," she said on a sigh of relief.

Tilda eyed her friend and boss. "Um, hi?" She handed over one of the paper cups.

"Thanks," Mac said, swallowing down some of the beverage immediately. "I need this. I didn't sleep last night."

"Are you going to explain?" Tilda asked. "I noticed the front room lights aren't on and now we're crowded in with the Pledge and the Windex. I assume we're hiding?"

"You don't have sisters," Mac said. "If you did, you'd know it was necessary. They're relentless and nosy and they've been leaving texts about wanting to talk with me ASAP."

Tilda had been struggling with her own nagging worries after her date with Ash, but seeing the usually unflappable Mac so agitated was proving an interesting distraction. "Does this have something to do with your visit to Mr. Frank's last night and how you abruptly disappeared?"

Her boss and friend stared.

"Followed by your reappearance in a decidedly disheveled state?"

Wincing, Mac half closed her eyes. "You heard about that?"

"Mountain grapevine," Tilda reminded her. "It flourishes at our favorite coffee place."

Mac groaned. "It would be nice to be an idiot without a thousand people talking about it the very next day."

"Idiot? You?"

The other woman waved her free hand. "Not using my head."

Word was, she and her old flame might be taking up again. "Do you want to tell me about it?"

"I wouldn't even know where to start," Mac admitted.

Tilda sipped from her own cup. "I hear this Zan is all kinds of gorgeous."

Mac sighed again. "Hence, the idiocy."

Ash flashed in Tilda's mind, his perfect features, his golden hair, his expensive loafers. The way he'd made her laugh and for a little while forget all her troubles. Was it so very bad for her to have enjoyed herself? Was it really such a terrible thing?

She released her own sigh. "Why can't a woman spend time with gorgeous?" she asked Mac.

Her friend leaned one shoulder against the shelving and sifted her free hand through her sleek dark hair. "Because it's asking for trouble, right? Because we work too damn hard to turn around and self-sabotage."

"Self-sabotage?" Tilda thought of the way Ash made her feel beautiful, interesting, worth knowing. A spark of rebellion fired her blood. Perhaps she'd been looking at this all wrong. "Maybe we work hard enough that we deserve a nice time with a good-looking guy. Some… I don't know. Recreation."

"Recreation," Mac repeated, gazing at her over the rim of her coffee. "Hmm. That's an idea, you have. Recreation." She took a sip, her eyes narrowing in obvious thought. "A nice time. Nothing serious."

"Right." Tilda nodded, optimism growing. "Amusement. Diversion. Plain old fun."

"Fun…" Mac seemed to mull over the word, almost like it was unfamiliar. "You know, it's possible we might have been taking ourselves a tad too seriously."

Yes, they'd been taking themselves too seriously, Tilda decided, feeling her own jangled nerves smoothing out. A date with Ash, with a man who made her laugh and feel good about life, about herself, wasn't a disaster at all! There was no need to blow the circumstances out of proportion.

Then Mac's voice lowered. "On the other hand, we just might be fooling ourselves."

She looked so gloomy, and so weary, too, Tilda had to do something to lift her spirits. "You're my hero, did you know that, Mac?"

Her boss's blue eyes went wide. "Tilda…"

"After my mom died, when I told you my situation, you managed to give me more hours. But better than that, you gave me faith in myself. I was feeling pretty low, pretty rocky—"

"I know."

"—but you assured me I could keep going. Remember? You said I was from strong mountain stock, just like you."

Mac smiled. "We are. We're strong mountain women. Smart, strong mountain women."

"You believed in me, and I believe in you, too. As a smart, strong mountain woman, I know you'll figure out the right thing to do for yourself."

Her friend's smile brightened further and she tilted her head. "Yeah?"

"Yeah." Tilda gave a sharp nod. "As a matter of fact, I believe that good things are coming. Good things are coming to us both."

She didn't know how long she'd hold on to that belief, though, because this was a first for her. All her life, even when her mother was alive, she'd been merely getting through, scraping by, making it only to the next day but not looking beyond that.

Sure, she was taking those online courses, but the truth was, she still had been looking only as far as the next footstep on the dark road. Not once had she glanced up toward the horizon.

But now she could swear she sensed the glimmer of dawn ahead.

Tilda tapped her cup against Mac's. "To us."

Grinning, Mac tapped right back. "And to good things."

MAC BOUNDED UP the steps to Zan's grandfather's house, ignoring any craven impulse to scuttle back to her car and call in sick for the day. When they'd settled her schedule, she'd promised to show this morning. The fact that the night before she'd allowed Zan to kiss and caress her to climax was no excuse to skip out. As Tilda's pep talk had reminded her half an hour ago, she was strong. Tough. She'd suffered through more difficult things than meeting the eyes of a man who'd taken her to heaven after an absence of ten years.

That didn't mean she didn't snatch the note he'd left on the front door with a surge of hope. Hope that stayed high when she read he'd had to go out, he'd left the door unlocked for her, and she should let herself in and get started sorting and packing.

A reprieve from his company—however brief—wasn't unwelcome.

He'd probably texted her the very same message, but she hadn't read the two he'd sent. Not because she wasn't tough…but because she'd yet to figure out exactly what she wanted to do about the Zan situation.

Ignoring him was impossible, since she'd committed to working for him. Slapping him silly was not a valid option, either, as she could have stopped things before they'd gone that far the night before. That left… See? She just didn't know.

Dropping her purse and coat in the kitchen, she glanced around, noting the unwashed dishes, the open cupboards, the cereal box out and the cereal inside getting staler by the second. Mess was her business, and walking away without doing something about it was impossible.

So before heading upstairs, where they'd decided to begin, she moved about the large, bright kitchen. Plates and bowls were stacked in the dishwasher, the cold coffee dumped out of the carafe and the carafe itself cleaned, and boxes of food were returned to the pantry.

She touched a cabinet door with her elbow and watched it quiet-close, then snatched up one of Zan's sweaters half falling off a chair at the kitchen table. It struck her, hard, that this wasn't unlike moments she'd fantasized about all those years ago. Mac picking up after her man. Mac picking up after Zan and the family they'd one day make. Without thinking, she brought his sweater to her nose and breathed in the same delicious scent of him that she'd been so close to in his car.

In Mr. Frank's parking lot!

That still astounded her.

But one touch from his lips and she'd been lost in passion. Their hands had been all over each other and she'd shut off her brain and allowed herself to revel in him instead. He'd been heavy and hard and all-man beneath her, an intoxicating feeling, especially because it was Zan, his low groan, his sure touch, her response not measured or considered.

With Zan, she'd been wild.

That was the worry. When a person went wild, they weren't thinking what could go wrong. They weren't remembering unhappy endings. They were living in the moment, which sounded great, until the moment passed and the big crash came.

Mac liked to look ahead these days. Proceed with caution after considering all the consequences.

Leaving the kitchen, she mounted the staircase and hoped that Zan had gathered the cardboard boxes as he'd promised. On the second-floor landing, her gaze caught on the open door to the master bedroom, the room he was using. Then she glanced down, realizing she still held his sweater in her arms, clutched tight to her chest.

Gah. Time to get rid of it.

So she strode into the room. *Set it down on the bureau, Mac*, she told herself. *Then back away.*

But it was a mess in there, too. Clothes on the floor,

drawers open. Through another door she could see a pile of used towels on the tile in the attached bathroom. On a sigh, she tucked the sweater away, closed all the drawers and moved to pick up the strewn garments, gathering them for a trip to the hamper she could also see in the bathroom.

Naturally, it was full.

"Time for a trip to the laundry room," she told the wad of boxers and jeans and T-shirts. It had wheels—ingenius!—so she rolled it in the direction of the washer and dryer that she'd seen on this floor. There was another set on the main floor, too. Nice, not having to lug items up and down the staircase.

Another woman might have worried it was presumptuous to tackle the laundry. Another woman didn't know Zan Elliott, or, for that matter, any of the male species. The day a man objected to someone running a load of wash for him was the day she turned in her business license and her membership in the Men-Love-Being-Taken-Care-Of Club.

To the low hum of the washing machine, she made her way back to Zan's room, where she tackled the unmade bed. She tried not thinking about his long, muscled body on the sheets or his handsome head on the bunched pillow. When she picked it up to fluff it smooth, her eye caught on the item beneath its neighbor.

Mac and Zan: The Early Years.

He'd been reading the old scrapbook in bed?

Unwilling to think about that, with quick movements she finished tidying the room. Then she set the scrapbook on his night table and hightailed it to the next floor and the room with all the bookshelves. As promised, empty cartons were stacked in the space.

The encyclopedias would go first.

They were dusty and she wished she'd brought gloves with her, but she ignored the grime on her hands and dropped the first load into an empty box. She was ass-up adjusting them for the best fit when she felt a tingle at the base of her spine. Her face heating, she rose and spun.

As she'd suspected, Zan had returned. He stood in the doorway, leaning against the jamb, one ankle crossed over the other. A half smile tilted the corners of his lips as his gaze lifted to meet hers.

Oh, boy.

Her mouth remembered the hard press of his and all that came after, which made her nipples contract to tight beads and a spasm occur between her thighs. She wiped her hands on her jeans, hoping he didn't see her press her legs together to try to ease the ache at their center.

"Zan," she said.

"Morning, Mac." His smile widened. "You cleaned the kitchen. You made my bed. You put my clothes in the wash."

She hung her head. "It's a compulsion. Comes in handy in my line of work, but the sisterhood might boot me out for straightening up a mess of your own creation."

"I'll wash your car later," he offered.

"So we're dividing up work on gender-based lines?"

"You started it, honey, and as it turns out—" he grinned "—I like things that are gender-based."

He said that to tease her, of course. To get her remembering that other gender-based activity of the night before.

The heated confines of the car. His fingers sliding beneath her panties. Her melting response as he stroked her, his sure touch knowing all the places and all the ways to please her. Her skin prickled beneath her clothes and she felt her face flush again. Try as she might, she couldn't look away from him or stop the desire that flooded her blood and coursed through her body.

Oh, Zan.

There was something about him in that moment, his eyes warm, his pose relaxed, that grin all male and oh so confident that compelled her heated, needy response.

And she knew, then, what she wanted to do about Zan.

Good things are coming.

The truth was, she wanted to go to bed with him. For recreation. For fun. Because she worked hard and deserved to spend some time with gorgeous. A woman had needs and wasn't she allowed to seek their fulfillment?

But Mac also was smart, which meant she needed to protect herself by defining the situation for them both up front. As any mature person would, who had learned to be tough and frank and who might want pleasure but not at the expense of future pain.

That meant eyes wide-open and expectations clearly laid out.

With all that firmly in mind, she strolled forward. "So...I have an idea."

"Yeah?" He still gazed upon her, all lazy male grace.

"Maybe we should do something about all this—" she spun a finger in the air "—heat."

His brows lifted. "Yeah?"

"Yeah." Mac hauled in a breath, then let the words fly. "Want to be sex buddies?"

He shot up, his brows slamming straight, his grin dying. "Huh?" he said.

Sue her, she enjoyed his look of surprise at her blunt question. He'd trampled the heart of that defenseless girl she'd been. Now he'd learn that she'd matured into a smarter, stronger, wiser version of Mackenzie Walker. Mac was a woman now who could reach for what she wanted on her own terms.

"Sex buddies," she repeated, liking the idea better by the moment. "Are you familiar with the concept?"

It took him just seconds to recover. His smile shone white again as he once again leaned into the doorjamb. "Familiar…and quite fond, as a matter of fact."

Of course he'd be quite fond of no strings, she thought, wanting to frown. But she forced herself to let go of her quick resentment.

"I just wasn't sure about you," he continued.

She shrugged and spun a finger between the two of them again. "This…you know. Thing. Force. It's not going away."

"True." He continued to study her face as if assessing her seriousness.

"You don't have a girlfriend or a wife anywhere, do you?"

"No."

"And you're not planning on becoming a permanent fixture in Blue Arrow, right?"

"I'm temporary, you know that."

"Thus the perfect sex buddy," she said, with the air of someone reaching a logical conclusion.

His gaze narrowed now. “Is this something you do a lot?”

Again, she stifled her resentment. She was a grown woman, with needs, thank you very much. “Is that any of your business?”

Zan didn’t seem too happy about her counter question.

In the distance, came the ding of an appliance. “I’ll just start another load and give you a chance to think about my proposition,” she said in a nonchalant tone as she breezed past him on the way to the laundry room.

While descending the staircase, she heard the doorbell’s distinctive melody. “I’ll get that,” she called over her shoulder and jogged toward the entry.

It wasn’t the courier Wes on the porch, but a regular mail carrier who needed a signature, and hers would do. She signed for the parcel, then was handed it, along with a short stack of envelopes.

One being a very familiar envelope.

Oh, no. Oh, no, no, no.

Quickly, she ducked into the kitchen and dropped all the mail but that one piece on the counter, the one piece that could screw the pooch on her whole casual and uncomplicated sex buddies solution to the Zan problem.

Looking around, she tried deciding how best to get rid of the envelope.

The one containing the invitation to her sister Shay’s wedding.

Zan was to be a temporary amusement. Her potential gorgeous-in-bed. And if that happened, it would be no strings, all surface. Having him on hand at a family event, a very emotional and romantic family event, could cause trouble for her.

Remembering Brett and Angelica's celebration, she was aware such an occasion could chisel a chink in the very hardest of hearts, creating the means for a man to find his way in.

Zan was never getting into hers again.

Suddenly, he loomed large in the room. "What do you have there?"

Mac gave a guilty jump, then whipped the invitation behind her and stuffed it into her jeans at the small of her back. The same place a PI shoved his gun in detective shows when he went out on a mission. This situation might be just as dangerous.

"A pile of mail came for you," she said, nodding to where she'd set it down. Then she sidled in the direction of the staircase. "I'll just get back to work."

He stepped in front of her, blocking her easy escape.

Then, without thinking, she feinted in the other direction. He shifted that way, too, and his move gave her enough space to make it between him and the door frame. Then she took off running.

There was no grand plan forming in her mind. But when she heard footsteps at her back, the most insane urge to giggle crawled up her throat.

She gave in to it as she raced into the living room. Despite being dead serious about keeping him from the wedding, a giddy playfulness welled up inside her. For a moment she felt like a girl again.

The new space was wide and rectangular, with big pieces of furniture and a grand piano in one corner. Skirting a low, heavy-legged coffee table, Mac took refuge behind a massive couch upholstered in dark gold.

Her breath heaved in and out as Zan entered the

room. His gaze trained on her face, he stalked toward her. "Now, what's all this running away about, honey?" His croon was deceptively sweet, because his eyes were narrowed and intent.

Mac moved along the back of the couch, putting more distance between them as she stifled another wild urge to laugh. Maybe she needed this, too. Hardworking Mac getting a sex buddy and a chance to explore her mischievous side, too. "Why, I don't know what you're talking about, darling."

A feral smile overtook his face. "I know that look, Mac. It's the exact same one you wore when you'd hidden my keys before my big date with Harmonie."

She used to do things like that, Mac remembered, then gave an exaggerated sniff. "She was too old for you."

"It's the same age difference between you and me." He prowled closer.

Eyes on him, she began sidling again.

Then he pounced. It didn't seem possible, because he appeared to be half the room away, but in one leap he had his hands on her and was lifting her over the couch. She let out a very unadult shriek—half gleeful, half alarmed—and twisted from his grasp just to make another mad dash…

Only to have him corner her in the room, beside an ornate desk. *Gah! Trapped!* Laughter bubbled again, and she felt alive as she hadn't in years.

"Well, well, well," he said with a mock leer, palms on either side of the wall, caging her in with his body.

Then, while she was still struggling to keep a straight face, he dived his hand behind her back and found paper. She gasped but then he had it in his hold and stepped back to stare down at it.

"What the heck?" he asked, glancing up at Mac's face. "I thought Publishers Clearing House had finally delivered my check and you were attempting to steal it."

Now she did laugh. "It's an invitation to Shay's wedding," she finally said. There was no chance to hide it from him anymore. "I don't want you to go."

His eyebrows rose. "Because…"

Would he understand? "Because we're sex buddies. Or possibly we're sex buddies—"

"About that." He moved in close again.

The heat of his body was all along the front of hers and she found herself holding her breath. If pressed, she'd have to admit she'd actually never done the sex buddies thing—the out-front, bodies-only, hormones-in-charge kind of relationship. But if she wanted Zan—and, oh, she did—that was the way it had to be. If she went in with shallow expectations, she figured when it was over she'd escape deep hurt.

Tough Mac, grown-up Mac, was smart enough to know that.

His head bent. But instead of touching his lips to hers, he found the skin at the side of her neck. She trembled. Okay, she was trembly, but tough. "Well…?"

"I'm game if that's what you want," he said, his breath hot on the thin skin over her pulse.

She trembled again, her body charged with anticipation, lust rushing through her veins, so that she felt on fire.

Then he tongued her flesh, sucked. She jolted in reaction, her body hitting that fancy desk next to her and causing something on top of it to slide to the floor with a thunk.

They both looked down at their feet.

She heard the harsh crinkle of paper as Zan's hand fisted around the invitation.

A heavy photo album sat on the floor, with an eight-by-ten color picture inserted in the plastic-covered slot on its front. The image was of a family posed on a beach. A mom, a dad, a boy, a girl, a smaller boy.

Chills ran down Mac's spine.

As if in slow motion, Zan bent and picked it up, set it back on the desk. Then he stared at the album as if it was spiders, snakes and alligators.

Mac knew his parents and siblings had died in a private airplane crash. He'd not been on the flight. Instead, he'd stayed home with a babysitter for the weekend because of an ear infection.

What she hadn't known until this very moment was that Zan's wounds from that loss still went to the core. As a boy, he'd never talked about it. As a teen, she'd never pressed.

As a woman, she recognized pain that scored to the marrow of one's bones. She saw it etched on his face now, the lines of it harder than normal, the bleak expression in his hazel eyes leaching the green and leaving only darkness behind.

And it turned out that Zan's pain…well, she couldn't deal with it, not now, no matter how tough she professed to be.

To keep from touching him, she fisted her hands at her sides. Another woman, or the Mac she'd been before, would want to comfort him, kiss him, talk to him about his loss. But then their relationship couldn't be merely shallow, merely surface. And getting close to him emotionally as well as physically…that would be her downfall.

She could be a friend or she could be a sex buddy, but not both.

Still, she felt craven as she slipped around him. "I'll leave now," she whispered, her chest burning, her throat tight.

He didn't try to stop her.

AT HIS NOW-FAVORITE stool drawn up to the bar at Mr. Frank's—it was on the end and in deep shadow—Zan acknowledged that coming back to the mountains had been a mistake. For years he'd managed to outrun his memories with a globe-trotting lifestyle that required he be both mentally and physically alert and always in the moment. But now, with former lovers and photo albums in his face, the past felt as if it was looming like a big-ass insect swatter poised to squash him like a bug.

So tonight he was planning on getting drunk and forgetting about everything but booze and whatever game was playing on the TV.

The young bartender was not much busier tonight than during Zan's last visit, but since he barely looked up from his beer when the guy tried to start a conversation, the man wandered away. Zan savored another long swallow of beer and his solitude. A buzz couldn't come soon enough.

It was just beginning to build when someone slid onto the stool beside his. Zan didn't glance over, not wanting to encourage any kind of exchange. He was an old hat at this, after years of long and short flights. If he kept his head down, he'd keep hold of his separateness.

Only when he signaled for another beer and a shot of tequila did the person beside him clear his throat.

"Going for it hard, huh?" Brett Walker asked.

Zan stifled his groan. "What? Are you my conscience now?"

"It would be like old times, then."

Not looking at his friend, Zan tipped back the shot glass and poured the tequila down his throat, embracing the burn. Then he coughed once. "I have a DD," he said, jerking his thumb in the direction of a small table where Ash Robbins was nursing a soda, his attention on the game showing on the overhead TV.

Brett turned his head, turned back. "How come you're not sitting with your designated driver?"

"Because I'm not feeling sociable." He glanced over at Brett to see if he got the point.

"I'm here to meet a client." The other man took a sip of his own draft. "But you could do your drinking at home if you truly wanted to avoid the huddled masses."

He wanted to avoid the empty house. That photo album. The memory of Mac saying, *Want to be sex buddies?*

"Is this any of your business, Brett?" he asked, completely aware of his testy tone.

"I guess not," the other man retorted, "since you never bothered to find out about *my* business during the last ten years."

He signaled for another shot. "I always said I was going down the hill. Never hid the fact that I wanted to get out of the mountains."

"You never explained that meant it would appear you fell off the face of the earth, either."

"That's not exactly true. I..." Zan didn't want to go there. Explaining he'd kept a kind-of contact with Mac would only lead to more questions.

"Yeah, I know what you did. Those effing postcards, no words on them and only signed with the letter *Z*. Quite the prolific correspondent you are."

Shit. "But—"

"I'm sure my sister appreciated keeping up with your travels. Maybe she would have liked to let you know what was going on with her life, but hey, like I said, you couldn't be bothered."

"I never knew my next mailing address," Zan muttered.

"Let me explain about this little thing called email. It moves from computer to computer, no stamps, no physical mailbox necessary."

Zan swallowed down half his beer. "Sarcasm doesn't become you."

"I'm not kidding about how pissed I am that you left the way you did."

"Jesus. I always said I was going to get out of here!"

"You never said that you'd leave your family behind like that. No real words from you, no way to keep in touch."

Family? His head started to pound as if he already had the hangover he anticipated for the next morning.

Then his mouth opened, and words came out of it without his permission. "How'd you get those scars?"

It wasn't that he hadn't wanted to know about them since his first glimpse of them at Oscar's. One bisected an eyebrow and another crossed the bridge of

Brett's nose, and anyone could see they weren't cat scratches. But, Christ, a man might be self-conscious and not want someone to pry…just as Zan didn't want to let anyone in on the scars he had, the ones on the inside.

"Forget I asked," he muttered, when Brett remained silent.

"Are we gonna get all touchy-feely now?" the other man said, his voice mild.

"Screw you—"

"I went into the army. Saw action in Afghanistan, followed up by doing hurricane relief effort work in Florida. It was there that a house fell on me."

"Like the Wicked Witch of the East?" Zan couldn't help but ask.

Brett snorted. "Didn't die, just lost some of my pretty looks."

Still, it gave Zan pause, not that he'd admit it out loud. "I bet the girls were worried."

"My sisters, yeah. But it turns out the scars actually seemed to attract women."

"Bet you hated that," Zan remarked drily.

"Of course I didn't. While I was enjoying my share of female company, I also earned a degree in landscape architecture and started a business up here that was mostly mow and blow and a little bit of design. Now I'm trying to flip that equation."

"Flip it?"

"Mostly design, a little less mow and blow."

Zan thought of that picture he'd seen on Brett's wife's phone—a rendering of the lodge he and Mac and Brett had dreamed of long ago. The lodge that belonged on Walker mountain.

Which they didn't own anymore, not one piece, including the cabins, because all of it now belonged to him.

Guilt had him throwing back the rest of his beer, and he considered sharing with his old friend the truth. But he'd made a promise.

Shit. A promise to Mac, who was just another problem he didn't want to contemplate right now. *Want to be sex buddies?*

She'd actually asked him that yesterday.

Seeing the bartender was occupied down at the other end, Zan reached over and grabbed up Brett's beer. "Hey," the other man snatched it back.

"I'm trying to do you a favor. I imagine that beautiful wife of yours wants you horny not sleepy when you get home tonight."

A slow grin overtook Brett's face.

Zan put on a disgusted expression and shook his head. "I never thought I'd see it, but you're totally gone." And he was glad for his friend.

"You said it, 'beautiful wife.'"

"Is that why you're doing more design now, and less mow and blow?"

Brett's expression turned serious. "If you're asking if Angelica is behind that, pushing for me to make more money or something, you've got it all wrong."

"Okay."

"That woman...what she wants is all she has already with my ring on her finger. A place to call home, a family—husband, sisters, a nephew, a niece—more of all that to come in the future."

"What she has is the Walkers."

"Yeah." Brett let that sit, and then he grinned again. "And my prowess in the sack, of course."

"Always so modest." Zan shook his head. "I'll tell her you said that."

His friend's expression turned smug. "She won't deny it."

Christ. "You're married, Brett. You're really married."

"Yep."

"Poppy and Shay minutes from walking down the aisle, too."

"We've all grown up."

With plans and futures they were making, while Zan didn't even have a clue where he was going to go next and what he would do when he got there.

In the mirror, his gaze caught on a new patron entering the bar. Mac.

He hunched around his beer, hoping she wouldn't spot him, even as he didn't take his eyes off her. She was dressed to socialize, in a pair of tight jeans, high-heeled boots and a sweater that clung to every curve. As she passed a booth, someone grabbed her arm and she turned, a smile breaking out for the woman who dragged her onto the seat beside her.

Want to be sex buddies?

"So what about you?" Brett said. "A steady woman been in your life?"

Mac, all those years ago. Zan shook his head to dislodge that thought. *Want to be sex buddies?*

What the hell was he going to do with that?

He felt Brett's attention on him. "What?" he demanded, without looking over.

"Christ, you're surly," Brett complained. "When was the last time you got laid?"

"Really? We're getting all touchy-feely now?" Zan said, echoing the other man's earlier words to avoid spilling how he'd almost gotten laid by the other man's sister. *Want to be sex buddies?*

Of course he wanted to have sex with Mac. There was no doubt about that. But *sex buddies*? Once she'd left him at the house, he'd had a clearer head to contemplate that proposition.

He'd been sex buddies with Simone. Mac was not Simone.

Then a man strode into the bar, in jeans, a snap-fronted shirt and cowboy boots. He glanced around, and then his gaze landed on Mac. At her name, she looked up, smiled at the newcomer, then slid out from beneath the table where she sat.

At the hug she gave the guy and the kiss he pressed to her cheek, Zan realized that Mac wasn't just at Mr. Frank's to socialize. She was here to have a *date*.

"Who the hell is that with your sister?" Zan said, lifting his chin to indicate the pair in the mirror.

Brett took a gander. "Friend of hers. Stuart Christianson."

"Should I remember him?"

"Used to often go around with Glory Hallett—she's married to someone else now."

"What the hell!" He watched Mac and Stuart Christianson seat themselves at a table for two. "Is this matrimony central, or what?"

"Time didn't stand still when you ran off, and we all didn't stand still, either."

Not for the first time, Zan wondered if that's what he'd expected. Everyone in the mountains staying the same, just waiting for the occasion of his return to re-animate and then start moving about their lives again.

Okay, that was self-centered.

"I thought about visiting before," he confessed to Brett. Uh-oh. Maybe getting shit-faced wasn't the right thing to do.

"So why didn't you?"

"I suppose I was waiting for the right moment."

"The right moment for what?"

How the hell did he know? The moment when he was settled enough within himself to come back to them, maybe. The moment when he'd be convinced the ghosts were gone from the mountains—which was ridiculous, because he'd carried them with him all this time.

The only thing he'd managed to do in ten years was to ignore their presence by immersing himself in new challenges, new sights, new people.

But always, just as surely as the ghosts rode his shoulders, there had lingered a thought in the back of his mind. A thought that there might come a day when he'd return and pick up where he'd left off with Mac, and…what?

Want to be sex buddies?

In the mirror, he found her again, leaning toward Stuart Christianson, who wore a smile on his face and kept his eyes on Mac's. A few couples were moving around the dance floor now, and as he watched, Stuart Christianson and Mac joined them. It was something slow and country, and Stuart Christianson took the opportunity to pull Mac in close. Too close, for a weeknight at Mr. Frank's, if you asked Zan.

And it was then he realized, with a pang, that though

he'd come out tonight to forget…he'd only been focused on regrets.

And at the top of that list would be losing out on Mac if he didn't do something about her. Tonight.

CHAPTER TEN

ASH SPOTTED TILDA the instant she walked into the bar. Though he'd been debating with himself about how much time he should let pass before asking her out again, now he didn't hesitate to vault from his chair. Her arrival had to be a sign that tonight he should make his move. Coming up behind her, he laid a hand on her shoulder.

She whirled, surprise shifting to a quick smile that she smothered too soon for his liking. "You."

He grinned. "Me." Again she was dressed in that too-thin jacket, which she wore over jeans, a long sweater and sneakers with a hole in one toe. "You look cold. Let me buy you something to warm you up."

"I…" She shook her head. "No, no, thanks." Her head twisted to take a look around the bar.

"Are you meeting someone?" That would be disappointing, since she was here, practically in his lap.

Which sounded very nice, by the way.

Her gaze still roamed the patrons of Mr. Frank's. "I'm looking for a friend."

"Come on, I'll get you that drink. You can sit with me until she arrives."

She threw a glance at him. "It's a he."

Shit. He should have sewed up the second date before he'd let the first one end! In the two days that had passed since they went out, some other guy had already moved into Ash's territory.

He winced at the proprietary thought. His parents had raised him to be more gentlemanly than that. A woman wasn't his property, of course. Backing off, he gave her his best polite smile. "Have a nice night."

"Thanks," Tilda said in an absent voice, then seemed to mutter to herself. "It was an off chance he'd be here, anyway."

That sounded as if she *didn't* have a date.

The fingers of Ash's right hand curled into his palm and he tapped it against his thigh in surreptitious victory. "A drink from me's a sure thing," he said.

"I need to find Lee."

Ash's gaze narrowed. "Lee's your mechanic friend."

"Um…yeah." She seemed surprised he remembered.

His teeth clenched, and then he tried to relax his jaw. "What's wrong?"

She shook her head. "I thought there were good things coming…" she murmured, the words trailed off on a shrug. "But never mind. It's no big deal."

"Is your car giving you trouble again?"

"It's no big deal."

"You keep saying that, but 'no big deal' is not what I'm seeing on your face, Tilda." It was true. Now that he knew there was a problem, he noticed the faint line of stress between her dark brows.

"I'm handling it."

Ash felt a burn kindle in his belly. Since he was a little kid, fuming on the soccer field because the other five-year-olds kept clumping around the ball and didn't get the concept of *pass*, he knew he had a temper. His father had talked to him about it for years, encouraging him to put a choke hold on the feeling when it arose. *Deep breaths, son. Nothing's worth losing control of yourself.*

So he hauled in a breath and did his best to channel John Robbins, and be the cool and calm customer his dad expected. "I can look at it again," he said. "Wouldn't be a problem."

"It's too dark to now. I left it in the market parking lot."

"Tomorrow, then," he said.

She acted as if she hadn't heard him and shoved the strap of her purse higher on her shoulder. "Well, uh, nice bumping into you."

"How are you getting home?"

"Um…" Her gaze darted around as if the answer might be written on the walls.

"Come on, let me give you a ride." He smiled. "My dad would never forgive me if I left a damsel in distress."

She stiffened. "Your dad," she began, then shook her head again. "I really need to go."

"With me," Ash said. "Are you ready to take off now, or would you like to have that drink or something to eat first?"

Her front teeth hit her full bottom lip, and she sucked it into her mouth. Stalling, he thought, and she had no idea how damn sexy he considered the move.

Even with his dick getting hard, his temper fired again. Why was she always so resistant? "Hell, Tilda, do you have to make this so effing hard?"

Her eyes narrowed. "Maybe things come too easy for you," she snapped back.

He liked the show of spirit, but her stubbornness wasn't going to win the day…or get her back to her place. "Done with this," he said and grabbed her hand. "Let's get out of here." Then he remembered why he was at Mr. Frank's, so instead of immediately heading toward the exit, he towed her over to Zan.

"I have someone else to drive home," he told the other man. "I'll be back."

Another guy sitting beside Zan glanced over his shoulder. "I can do it."

That was enough for Ash. Ignoring Tilda's sputters, he hauled her out of Mr. Frank's. Once the cold night air hit him, his temper cooled and his mood jumped from frustrated to feeling pretty damn happy. After all, he had Tilda's small hand in his. He was the one who was taking her home.

All good.

"You can be annoyingly arrogant, you know," she said when she slid into the passenger seat.

He shut her door and rounded to his side, smiling at the snotty tone of her voice. It meant he was getting to her, he decided.

Yeah, annoyingly arrogant.

But she was in his car and he was going to turn the heater on and make sure she was warm for the ride, too-thin coat or not.

"Directions?" he asked when he settled behind the wheel.

A new vibe entered the small space of the car. As he tried figuring it out, he started the engine, fiddled with the heater controls and adjusted the vents so they'd blow on her. That small hand had been near-freezing.

"Which way do I go?"

She was hesitating again, that bottom lip in her mouth.

Instead of getting mad this time, he softened his voice and smoothed his palm over her hair. "I can't get you there if you won't tell me."

"I suppose you're right," she said on a sigh. Then she told him how to get to her place.

It took a while on the dark roads that were unfamiliar to him. They passed the outskirts of the village and then wound through forested land. Instead of going up, this route took them beyond a tiny hamlet in the notch of two mountains. On the outskirts of that, they passed a couple of bared lots that held nothing but snow-clearing equipment.

Then they were at the mouth of an even narrower lane.

"You can drop me off right here," Tilda said.

He looked out his windshield at the dark night, the dark pavement ahead, the darker shadows created by the trees crowded alongside it. Then he turned his head to Tilda. "You've got to be kidding me."

She sighed. "It's about a quarter-mile along here." Her voice sounded resigned.

Ash thought it was the perfect setting for a teen horror movie. Up ahead, he could see a dilapidated two-story building of six units, the only lighting bare bulbs highlighting the apartment numbers. As his tires crunched on the gravel in the adjacent parking lot, he kept his eyes peeled for an ax murderer or even a rabid bear.

Continuing forward, he noted a bent and rusted screen over the door to the nearest apartment was flapping in an errant breeze, letting out a scratchy squeal each time it moved. Seriously creepy. Before he had a chance to turn off the ignition, she was half out of the car. "Thanks."

He caught her by the arm. "I'll walk you to the door."

"Totally unnecessary."

As if he would let her go without seeing her safely inside, if *safely* was a word that could be applied in any way, shape or form to this run-down set of apartments. "Again, I couldn't look my dad in the eye if I didn't."

She yanked her arm out of his hold. "Believe me. It's better this way."

Before he could blink, she was on the gravel and scurrying toward a set of rickety stairs to the second floor. Cursing under his breath, Ash followed. Though she had to hear his footsteps on the metal steps behind her, she didn't acknowledge him. Instead, she made her way to a door marked with a five. No light seeped from the curtain-covered window beside it.

With her keys in hand, she paused, though she didn't look at him. "Okay, your duty's done. You can leave now."

"Or you can ask me inside." He stepped up behind her, wanting her again so damn much. "We can talk." Bending his head, he touched his cheek to hers, then pulled her around to face him.

For a long moment, she only stared up at his face. Then he saw her lips move.

Had she mouthed "gorgeous"? Running a knuckle down her cheek, he smiled at her, hopeful again. "Or we can not talk. I'd be content just to spend time with you."

"Really?"

"Really." He lowered his voice. "Aren't you aware we're good together?"

Though she nodded, there was a battle going on inside her, he could see that.

Watching her, he touched her cheek again, his finger trailing down to stroke the side of her neck. At her full-body shudder, he gave up.

"You're cold," he said and began to move back. "Go inside."

Tilda grabbed his hand and pulled him close again. "I'm not cold," she said. "That's not why I'm shivering."

It was Ash's turn to still. "Then why not let me in?"

"Because..." She glanced over her shoulder, then back at him. "Right now it's because I don't want you to see this place. I don't want you to know how I live."

His heart felt twisted by her two small hands. "Tilda—"

"It's nothing like you're accustomed to."

He was accustomed to things being way too easy. She'd been right about that. But now it was his turn to make things easier for her. With his free fingers, he found her keys and plucked them from her.

She let them go and she also let him nudge her to the side so he could unlock the door. Pushing it open, he noted that while the place smelled like pine cleaner, the air was barely warmer than the outside temperature.

He pulled her inside and shut the door. A dim light was on, illuminating a tiny kitchen and a living room with a futon and a clunky TV on a metal stand. "Roommates home?" he asked, guessing that she had them.

"They waitress at one of the ski lodges. They won't be back until late."

"Can we get this place any warmer?" he asked, glancing around for a thermostat.

She remained by the door, as if second-guessing

her decision. "The heat hardly works. When it's cold like this, we hang in our bedrooms, under blankets."

"You share a room?"

He heard her swallow. "I have the single."

Crossing to her, he took her hand. "Take me there."

At her hesitation, he drew her against him, then softly kissed her mouth. She trembled in his arms and he could feel warmth rise to the surface of her skin. "Take me there," he said again.

Now she moved, guiding him along threadbare carpet into a short hallway. They passed a bedroom, a small bathroom, and then she opened a door. The space was tiny, almost dominated by a single bed heaped in blankets, a tiny stand beside it holding an even smaller lamp that was letting off a faint glow. Some plastic drawers were tucked in a corner and a curved metal rod—maybe formerly for a shower?—was bolted into a wall for hanging clothes.

"They made the closet into another bathroom," she said, pointing to another narrow door.

Inside was only a toilet and a tiny sink.

"It's awful," she whispered.

"It's cold." He crossed to the bed and pulled back the covers. "Come on. Slip off your shoes and get in here."

When she did as he asked, he unlaced his boots, slipped off his coat and crawled in beside her. She scooted to make room for him, but he pulled her against him, cuddling her close.

She went stiff in his arms. "I'm worried about this, Ash."

"We're only getting better acquainted," he said.

"You might not like what you learn about me."

"Not a chance." Because he felt as if all the questions had been asked and answered months ago, when he'd looked over at the table of young women and his gaze had lit upon her—the paper crown listing on her mane of hair, the sweet, pouting lower lip, the way her eyes had lit with pleasure when the server handed her the drink he'd sent over. Her head had turned his way, a smile tilting the corners of her mouth, and he'd known.

There you are, he'd thought.

His parents had been college sweethearts and he admired and wanted a relationship like theirs, so he'd expected to find his own sweetheart during those years. But while he'd enjoyed himself and admired plenty of girls and dated a few, not one had given him that instant sense of certainty.

There you are.

"I couldn't get you out of my head, the whole time I've been gone."

Tilda turned her face into his neck. "I wanted to forget you," she said, her mouth moving against his skin. "I wanted to forget everything about that night and especially about leaving you the next morning."

The first of that didn't sound promising. Only the last bit was slightly better. But Ash figured he couldn't be here, in this bed with her, if she really was serious about wanting to forget him.

Using his finger under her chin, he tilted her mouth toward his. Then he was kissing her, soft at first, and then with more heat and desire. Her body turned more deeply into his and then he felt her stubborn resistance finally fall away.

But when he broke the kiss he could tell she was still worrying too much by the way her gaze was anxious on his. God, all he wanted to do was make things simple and easy for her. Be her comfort instead of her concern.

"This place," she whispered, "is a dump. I still wish—"

He cut off the rest by pressing his fingers to her mouth. Then he touched his forehead to hers. "What I see is you," he said. "What I know is you."

What I want is forever with you.

There. It was said. Out in the open, at least in his own mind.

MAC SAT WITH her elbow on the table at Mr. Frank's, her chin in her hand, while Stuart went to the bar to get second drinks for them. She was thinking of how she could break it to him, and gently, that while he was welcome to attend Shay's wedding with her she didn't want him getting the wrong idea that it was a *date* date. Then fingers wrapped around her wrist and pulled her out of her chair.

Blinking, she looked up to see Zan. When had he arrived? "What?" His gaze was intense and she wondered if he might be a little drunk.

"Dance," he said.

Drunk seemed more definite. "You don't like to dance."

He hadn't attended his high school prom. Neither had Brett. Instead of tuxes and corsages, that night they and a knot of buddies had broken into the school's office and stolen all the caps and gowns, stored there in preparation for the upcoming graduation.

Upon detecting their absence, the administration had threatened to cancel the ceremony and then the missing items had been "mysteriously" returned, the whole plastic-wrapped lot of them crammed in the cafeteria's refrigerator.

Well, she didn't know for certain that Zan, Brett and their buddies had done such a thing, but it was exactly the kind of thing they *would* have done. She and everybody else assumed it had been their prank, with Zan the mastermind.

Without another word, he now towed her to the small dance floor and took her in his arms. The dance music was exclusively ballads on weeknights. On the weekends, there'd be a mix, including some line-dancing tunes, but tonight it was straight up love songs.

She sighed. "Lay Me Down" by Sam Smith. Great.

They had gone together to *her* high school prom. It had been held at the ritzy yacht club on Blue Arrow Lake. She'd worked for months making stars and moons out of tagboard covered with aluminum wrap. It had taken hours to hang them from the ceiling. Zan had helped her and the rest of the decorating committee, he'd brought her a gorgeous wrist corsage to match her dress—thanks to the hints dropped by her sisters—and he'd shown up wearing a black tuxedo that she knew for a fact he owned and hadn't rented.

Weeks before, she'd driven down the hill for prom dress shopping with her girlfriends, and the gown she'd found on sale had probably cost less than his socks.

But she'd felt beautiful.

When she was with Zan, everything was beautiful... until he left. At that thought, her spine stiffened and she moved to put more inches of space between them.

He tried pulling her closer. Though some traitorous part of her wanted to press her cheek to his chest and melt against him, the older and wiser Mac forced her head back to catch his gaze with hers. Something was up. "Explain the dancing," she demanded.

"If I sat at your table, your friend Stuart would join us and then we couldn't have a private conversation."

"A private conversation about what?"

"The other day."

She'd managed to almost wipe yesterday out of her memory banks. But now it flooded in, the uncertainty she'd felt about the Zan situation, the solution she'd come up with to deal with it. How the cards-on-the-table, bravado-laced discussion she'd imagined having on the subject of becoming sex buddies hadn't taken place because she'd knocked his family's photo album off the desk.

And then she'd taken off.

"Are you okay?" she couldn't help but ask, her voice low.

"I was fine. I am fine."

He said both sentences with a flat inflection and a blank-paper expression.

"Still," she said. "You could talk to Brett—"

"I never talk about that."

It was true. All that she knew about his family tragedy had come from other people. "The Walkers have suffered loss, too, Zan," she couldn't help but remind him.

"Yeah. But the Walkers still had their siblings and this whole place, the mountains and the lakes," he said.

She wanted to tell him he could have had them, too. The Walkers, the mountains and the lakes. Her. For always.

Danger!

"But like I said," he continued, "I don't want to talk

about that." Then he pulled her tight to him, so close their thighs brushed and she could feel his belt buckle against her middle. At that sensation, her breath caught and her skin tingled. A shiver rolled down her back.

Zan's voice went quieter. "I want to talk about you and me being sex buddies."

Her gaze jumped back to his. Sex buddies had been her mature solution to the problem that was the sparking and spitting chemistry that erupted whenever she and Zan were in the same airspace.

It was simmering between them now, their thigh-to-thigh and belt-buckle-to-belly friction kindling a full-body heat that made her breathe high in her throat. Just the thought of him brushing his lips against her sensitive skin made her want to whimper.

Her proposal was common sense, really, because she'd known that day, just as she knew right now, that it was inevitable they'd both get naked…and then things would really ignite.

But his ultimate leave-taking wouldn't break her as it had before if she gave it parameters, certain and rigid lines, designed entirely to keep the relationship a shallow one.

So…sex buddies.

A twinge of pleasure spasmed between her legs just saying the words in her head.

"If we do this thing," Zan continued, "it has to be exclusive."

Her jaw dropped. "Exclusive?" Did he think she was collecting sex buddies like pearls on a string?

"Yeah, exclusive. You'll have to get rid of Stu. Whoever else."

That heat in her belly now kindled to a fire that shot

through her blood. But this wasn't the sweet, pleasurable kind of fire. This was the kind of fire that was anger, that made a woman do drastic things like make a bonfire out of a collection of postcards or change her hair color or change her hair color *and* get one of those severe cuts with the pointy sideburns.

"Stu and whoever else," she repeated, between clenched teeth.

"Yeah."

Zan must be blind not to see the temper on her face. "Stu and whoever else," she said a third time. "You know what?"

His expression turned wary. Finally. "What?"

"Your mention of 'Stu and whoever else' is really rich coming from you, considering you left town but not before leaving a warning to all the males in my age group that I was off-limits *because I belonged to you.*"

It didn't seem he grasped the exact depth and breadth of her anger, because now the wariness fled and a small grin overtook his face. He looked more than a little pleased. "Hot damn. I remember you mentioning that the day I got sick. Did it really work?"

"Do you think that's funny? Giving out the idea that I'm taken or something? What did you think it might do to my ego if the men around here listened to you and nobody ever asked me out or expressed an interest?"

"You only had to look in the mirror to restore your ego, Mac," he said. "You've always been the most beautiful thing I've ever seen."

She wasn't going to let the compliment soften her up. Since learning of this little stunt of his a few months back, she'd been stewing about it. And he wasn't taking the offense seriously! "I'm done with you." Her hand tried sliding out of his.

His clasped it tighter. "We're not done."

That's when she realized he'd somehow dance-shuffled her out of the bar portion of Mr. Frank's and had dance-shuffled her down a dim hallway that led to an empty events room. Part of her was happy about this, because she was sure the patrons had been noticing the heavy conversation between she and Zan and that would cause rumors racing up hill and down dale. Another part of her felt bad due to the fact there was an entirely different man she'd made arrangements to meet that night.

"I have a date who has to be wondering where I am," she said.

"And you'll get back to him just as soon as we finish working this out." He'd quit moving because he'd backed her into a wall, and now one of his hands was planted against it and the other was cupping the side of her face. "Sex buddies. Exclusive. Until I head down the hill."

While she was happy he didn't want to go around the mountains being indiscriminate sex buddies with other women while being sex buddies with her, this whole thing was getting too clinical by the moment.

Isn't that the way you wanted it? a little voice asked. *Devoid of emotion and drama? Merely shallow and surface?*

"I think I've changed my mind about this whole thing. I'm not comfortable with it."

Zan studied her face, his gaze roaming over it as if he was puzzling something out. "Mackenzie Marie," he finally said. "How many sex buddies have you ever had? More specifically, when was the last time…"

Her body stiffened, anger spiking again. Could it be, could he truly be insinuating that she hadn't had a lover…*maybe since he'd left ten years before*?

Talk about ego…how about *egotistical*!

He continued, his voice contrite, an expression of concern on his face. "Sweetheart, I really would feel bad if—"

"Don't even finish that sentence, you jerk!"

"So you haven't been pining—"

"Do not say that word!" It was the word she feared that everyone she knew used when it came to her and how she felt about Zan. It was the reason why she'd asked three different men to be her date to three different weddings in the space of a few weeks. She did not *pine*.

"Okay. So you haven't—"

"No. I definitely haven't spent the last ten years inconsolable over the loss of you." She tore free of him and slammed her hands to her hips. "As a matter of fact, Zan, I've been engaged."

His eyes widened in surprise.

"That's right," she said. "Engaged to be married. *Three times*, to *three separate men*."

CHAPTER ELEVEN

LATE AFTERNOON SUNDAY, Zan knotted and unknotted his tie half a dozen times, considering and reconsidering whether to attend Shay Walker's wedding. When it was either leave or be inexcusably late, he adjusted it for a final time, grabbed his suit jacket and left his grandfather's house. Mac might not want to see him, but he'd told her sister he'd see her married.

A promise was a promise.

Mac didn't seem to feel that way. She'd texted excuses about coming to his grandfather's all week, but given the upcoming important day, he'd let that go.

Maybe he'd have to let go of everything that concerned Mac.

Shoving that thought from his head for now, he made his way to a swank ski lodge higher up the mountains. He shuffled behind a large throng filing into the place, realizing it was going to be quite a crowd. Shay Walker must have emptied every home in the area for the evening.

While he didn't mind being alone, he wasn't a fan of feeling like an outsider, so he told himself he'd do the bare minimum in attendance time and then book. Once back at his grandfather's, perhaps he'd even start packing up himself, something he'd left untouched since Mac's defection.

Shay looked lovely in a white satin gown, the only embellishment some beading around the hem. The bridesmaids wore a similar shiny fabric, but in silver. Their dresses were sleeveless, with beading around the neckline and with intricately tied sashes that left most of their backs bare. The Walker sisters stood up with Shay, along with her almost-stepdaughter and Brett's wife, Angelica.

As a group, they were all beautiful. He didn't allow his gaze to linger on anyone but the bride.

During the ceremony, the bride and groom stood centered before a huge glass window that offered incredible mountain views. After the vows were exchanged, the guests moved into another room set with round tables. A bar was open at one end, and already servers were moving about with trays of hot hors d'oeuvres.

Zan asked for a beer, then stood before another window to enjoy the stupendous vista it offered, snagging a few of the appetizers as they passed by. When it was time to take a seat to be served dinner, he found his designated place. Guests had taken to theirs before him and he discovered the two at his left were still empty. That gave him the idea to sneak off, back to his car, but then the person who had the place to his right—a young, very pretty woman—introduced herself.

Tilda Smith, he discovered, who worked for Mac.

Zan decided to stay for the meal.

After telling her his name, he discovered that while Tilda Smith might be a new person in his acquaintance, she knew more than a couple of things about him. "At the high school, the theft of the caps and gowns is still talked about every year before graduation," she shared.

"The administration now locks them up in the room with all the expensive music equipment."

Zan knew how to break into that room, but he didn't share it with Tilda.

"And the prank on the ski lift—"

"That was dangerous," he hastened to say. "I hope nobody ever tries to do that again." Just recalling the incident made him want to go over to the head table at the other end of the expansive room and thank Brett for saving his life.

But the two of them weren't on particularly good terms and he was the outsider, so he stayed where he was.

That didn't mean he couldn't get some inside scoop. "Do you like working for Mac?" he asked, forking up some prime rib.

Tilda's brows rose. Her plate held chicken in some good-smelling wine sauce and she paused in cutting a bite. "I'm studying for a degree in biology."

"You're probably getting a good learning experience in bacteria and molds then, as one of the Maids by Mac."

Her mouth curved in a smile, so pretty and bright he bet she'd been breaking hearts since she was five. "I'm going to think of it exactly like that," she said. "As part of my education."

"But what I actually was asking about was, uh, how you like your boss." He told himself not to let his gaze drift Mac's way. "She can be kind of...prickly."

Tilda's gaze slid to her plate, then slid back to him, obviously considering. Then a small smile curled her lips. "In her left bottom desk drawer is a pile of postcards from all over the world."

Before he could process why she'd told him that and how he felt about the fact Mac held on to them, a woman with short blond hair was tugging at his arm. "Zan Elliott!" It took him a minute.

"Glory? Glory Hallett?"

The man at her side he found out was her man, and he wasn't from the mountains, so Zan didn't have to feel bad about not recognizing him. Then the pair took the empty seats beside his and their plates were served.

"We ran into traffic," Glory explained, "so we missed the ceremony." She craned her neck to take a gander at the head table. "Was it wonderful?"

"Sure," Zan said, smiling at her enthusiasm.

"Shay had plans to get married at those cabins the Walkers own, but Jace didn't want to wait for warmer weather," the woman said. "So she caved and agreed to a winter wedding."

Zan hung on to his smile, even though guilt tugged at the corners of his mouth. Thank God for the date adjustment. By summer Shay would have known those weren't the Walker cabins any longer. He would have been happy for her to have the wedding there, of course, but something told him there would have been a change in venue.

Then Glory's spine snapped straight. "Oh, my God." Her eyes widened. "Mac's here with Stuart?"

This time, Zan couldn't keep the smile. *I've been engaged. Three times, to three separate men.*

Since the night at Mr. Frank's bar he'd been avoiding thinking of that statement and why Mac had never married. As Glory babbled on about the portent of that particular pair attending the wedding together as well as the possibilities of a Mac-Stuart bright future, Zan felt for his keys. *Time to go.*

Then Tilda, on his other side, leaned close. "Stuart's just a friend," she whispered, then went on. "And she has that drawer full of postcards and those sweet little Russian nesting dolls lined up on her desk during the day. Every night, she nests them again and takes them home."

Zan stared at her.

Tilda's cheeks turned pink. "Oops," she said. "Maybe too much information? Definitely too much champagne. And the fact that this wedding has made me feel a little bubbly, too."

He remembered now that he'd seen her hand in hand with Ash at Mr. Frank's the other night. Maybe the girl had romance on the brain.

He felt for his keys once more and started to rise.

"What the hell!" a new voice boomed out. "Zan Elliott. Prodigal son of the mountains. I thought you were the adopted king of some native tribe in Antarctica!"

The voice, it turned out, belonged to Skylar, aka Skeeter Jenks, a satellite member of Zan and Brett's teenage posse. Long on brawn, short on brains, Zan had thought then, and didn't see a need to revise his opinion now.

"And Bitcoin," Skeeter said. "You invented that, too, right?"

Heads had turned at the man's loud voice, and after that, Zan learned there were more than a few people in the room who remembered him, all endeavoring to postpone his escape. Old acquaintances arrived to greet him. Glory dragged him to another table, where he exchanged a few friendly words with her parents and some of their contemporaries.

He was forced to set the record straight about not being the king of anything, the founder of Bitcoin, nor the star of a circus act. Very weird.

"There are some strange stories circulating around here," he murmured to Tilda when he retook his seat. But before she could comment, a distinguished-looking gentleman arrived at his elbow. "Mr. Chen," Zan said, fighting an old urge to slink down in his chair. "Good to see you, sir."

Then he shook hands with his former high school principal, who not only welcomed him back, but who talked to him on a variety of topics: Zan's late grandfather, the upcoming documentary that Zan worked on and the education foundation that supported the local K–12 students. Recalling the cap-and-gown incident and a handful of other misadventures from his formative years, Zan ended up pledging a substantial donation in his grandfather's name.

Mr. Chen beamed and told Zan it was a pleasure to see him again.

When the older man went back to his seat, he found Glory smiling at him. "What?" he asked.

"I've got a life down the hill now," she said, "but I can see this is a happy homecoming for you."

Happy? Homecoming? "I just got squeezed by our old high school principal," he said. Then he glanced around the room and noted the many people he'd interrupted his meal to speak to. "And I made an appointment with Skeeter for a complete car wash and detailing, I have a complimentary half-dozen doughnuts card from Olivia Tiller at the bakery, and your mom wants me to stop by the hardware store to check out some hand-painted frames she has for sale by the front register."

Glory's smile widened. "She takes classes."

"I don't need hand-painted frames. I'm trying to get rid of frames."

"They're folding you in," Glory said. "And who doesn't like doughnuts?"

Zan had just decided again it was time to take his leave when an older woman across the room caught his eye. She elbowed the lady next to her, and they both waved. Not knowing what else to do, he waved back at the woman who used to cut his hair and the librarian who had shushed him every time he made a visit to the stacks in order to "study."

Despite doughnuts and friendly waves, "folding in" wasn't going to happen. He wouldn't be around long enough for that, but it was...nice not being anonymous, either, he decided, as an unanticipated yet comfortable warmth rolled through him. Usually it was the new places, new people, new challenges that quieted the ghosts on his shoulder, but now it seemed familiarity could do the same.

The thought was interrupted by someone standing up to a mic and beginning the usual wedding reception toasts. Those were followed by the obligatory bride and groom first dance. With that good feeling still running through him, Zan leaned back in his chair and watched little Shay Walker, all grown up on her big day.

Then the general dancing began, and he saw Stuart Christianson pull Mac onto the floor. When Glory gave out a delighted squeal at the sight, Zan's pleasant feelings evaporated and his gut knotted. This was not his place. These were not his people.

He might as well have been alone on an ice floe.

As the song wound down, he found himself standing up.

"Where are you going?" Glory asked.

Zan ignored the question and stalked across the room, his eyes on Mac, who was returning to the head table. It was time to start wrapping up his time in the mountains, and the way to do that was to get Mac to follow through on the contract they'd made.

He didn't question the near-desperate need to address that now; he only knew he had to get Mac back into his grandfather's house so he could get out of the mountains ASAP.

Steeling himself for her reaction to his presence, he came up behind her. Her hair was softly bundled at the back of her neck, with just a few tendrils allowed to curl against her cheeks. The style allowed him an unfettered opportunity to touch one of her bare shoulders. She spun, her eyes going wide.

Then she grabbed his hand, her fingers biting hard, and she went up on her toes to stage-whisper in his ear. "Get me out of here, quick!"

His head jerked back. "What?"

"Are you my friend?" she demanded.

"Uh...yes?" What the hell?

"Then you'll save me, like, right now." With that, she strode off, taking him along with her. Four feet into her escape, she linked her arm in his and gave another order. "Put an expression on your face that says we have pressing business that *cannot wait*."

Fighting to hold off a sudden grin, he did his best

to comply. He glanced over at Mac, enjoying the hell out of getting a glimpse of the old her. A Mac who was fiery but not flinty, a Mac with determination, not wariness in her eyes.

They found an alcove off the lodge's foyer. It held a pay phone and a house phone and a couch was concealed by a half wall and a big potted plant. Mac dropped onto the cushions.

Zan followed suit. "What's all this about?"

"They're changing up the schedule, and I think Stuart's in on it." Her eyes flashed. The silver color of her dress made their pale blue stand out like frosty jewels.

"Um...schedule?"

"I have refused to go along with the bouquet toss, so they're trying to sneak it in so I can't sneak out before it happens."

"You don't want flowers?"

"I don't want to participate in a tradition that makes me look desperate for a husband, and my sisters find it 'high-larious' fun—to use Poppy's ridiculous term—to trick me into it."

"Maybe they just want to see you happy like they are, Mac."

"Via marriage? Pfft." She waved one hand in clear disgust. "Not counting on that."

I've been engaged. Three times, to three separate men.

And because he didn't want to consider that any longer, nor the reasons behind her clear aversion to marriage, Zan bowed to impulse and the desire for her that always dogged him. He snatched Mac close to slam his mouth against hers. It was the most direct route he knew to not thinking, and it worked like a charm. There was a quick stiffening of surprise, and then she moved into him, practically crawling into his lap.

He speared his tongue into the hot sweetness of her mouth and ran his hands over the warm, silky, bare flesh of her back. Her fingers went to his head, and she forked her fingers in his hair, held on.

His head slanted, hers followed, and the kiss went harder, deeper, wetter. He felt the rush of thick blood to his cock and the tremor of Mac's slim body. His lips moved to her jaw, her neck, and then he needed more mouth to mouth. Her tongue tangled with his, and something new overcame him, with the familiarity of her taste in his mouth. The tightness in his gut loosened, and even though his heart pounded hard against his ribs, it wasn't pain he was feeling…but ease.

This was all so easy. Hot and erotic, but…*easy.*

Natural.

He continued kissing her until he figured they both needed air. Tearing his mouth from Mac's, he looked down into the dazzled and dazzling depths of her eyes. Her mouth was swollen and her cheeks were pink and her chest moved up and down in the same ragged time as his.

Finally, she whispered to him. "What do we call this, Zan?"

A word resonated inside him, at first a murmur, then a whisper, then in a tone low and sure. Belonging, it said. Belonging, *belonging.*

"Lust," he replied, lying to her. Then he came at her with the truth.

"And we're going to do something about it, finally, tonight."

MAC CLIMBED THE steps to Zan's grandfather's house in her bridesmaid dress, coatless, hatless, scarfless, one hand behind her back.

She didn't feel the cold.

Some of that had to do with the amount of champagne she'd imbibed. Most of it had to do with the anticipation fluttering in her belly as she took in the glow coming from the windows and the lights burning on either side of the double entry doors. She'd been mad at him that night at Mr. Frank's, at his presumptions and assumptions, but now there wasn't room inside her for any emotion but one.

Lust. And we're going to do something about it, finally, tonight.

Bowing to the inevitability of that—okay, thrilled by the inevitability of that—she pressed a trembling finger to the bell. The door almost immediately swung open.

Her palm went to her jittery belly. *Wow. Oh, wow.*

Zan stood in bare feet, his dark wool slacks and his dress shirt untucked and unbuttoned. His tie was gone and his hand was wrapped around a rocks glass with a couple of inches of amber liquid at the bottom.

He looked sexy and sophisticated, an ad for all things expensive and potentially dangerous: luxury liquor, fast cars, private jets.

It was Zan Elliott, all grown up, all man, and Mac suddenly felt shy and awkward and as if she should have reconsidered draining that last flute of champagne.

"Sheesh, girl," he said and grabbed the wrist not tucked at the small of her back to pull her inside. "It's freezing out." Peering over her shoulder and into the night, he frowned. "How did you get here? I don't see your car."

"Poppy and Ryan dropped me off."

One of his brows winged up as he shut the door behind her. Then he led her to a parlor off the foyer, where logs were snapping and popping in the fireplace. "You told them—"

"That I owed you an hour of packing up."

Now he looked even more skeptical. "They believed you were coming here to pack boxes after a family wedding and in your tissue-thin bridesmaid dress?"

"Don't forget tipsy," she informed him.

His smile grew slowly. "You're saying they believed a tipsy woman came here to pack boxes after a family wedding, wearing her tissue-thin bridesmaid dress."

She shrugged. "They didn't dare question anything, not after they noted my displeasure upon catching *this*." She whipped her hand from behind her back to display the ridiculous spray of flowers that made up the replica bridal bouquet. The one that Shay had thrown to the gaggle of women that Mac had been forced to join.

Zan grinned.

"I kept my hands down and my eyes closed, I swear. But once again, just like at Brett and Angelica's, it hit me square in the face. I actually ate rose petals."

He leaned down and sniffed her cheek. "You smell like roses." His mouth touched hers. "You taste like roses."

The light kiss made her head spin and her belly squeeze, so she stepped back, determined to be as sophisticated as he looked. That was the way to survive this, she was sure. "You should have saved me. From the bouquet and from drinking too much champagne."

He shrugged. "You had to stay and I had to go before throwing you over my shoulder and carting you off to my cave."

Her eyes rounded because the idea of Caveman Zan was even sexier than Classy Zan. But she forced herself to breathe and sauntered over to the love seat before the fire. Tossing the bouquet on a side table, she dropped onto the cushions. "My feet are killing me."

Zan followed and then stood over her, watching as she hiked up her long skirt to expose her ankle and the buckles of her strappy sandals. Her hands stilled as she stared up at him, backlit by the flames.

Danger, she thought again. Demon. *He'll make you burn.*

"Need help, baby?"

Oh, yeah, she needed help. Because she was going to combust, and who was going to gather the pieces of her back together if that happened? Popping up from the cushions, she dashed to the bar set up in the corner of the room. Glass, ice, water.

"That's vodka, baby," he said, coming up behind her. "A tipsy woman should try this." His fingers brushed a bottle of water she'd overlooked.

"Yeah. Hah. Thirsty."

Ice clinked in the glass as Zan drew one finger down her spine, bared by the dress. Why hadn't Shay opted for outfits of burlap? With long sleeves and monk hoods, please.

His mouth brushed along the slope of her shoulder. Her naked shoulder.

"Oh, God," she whispered to the water as she brought it to her mouth. She was way, way too turned on.

"Hey, sweetheart?" he called, that fingertip now drawing intricate patterns on her back.

Closing her eyes tight, she tried not to think of Adult Zan stroking her skin. She tried to remember Boy Zan, who used those hands to make grass-blade whistles, mud castles and snowballs.

It wasn't working.

"Sweetheart?"

"Um, yes, Zan?"

"I told myself I wasn't going to ask…"

"Go ahead, ask." Anything to give her a moment to get a handle on this simmering need for him. Another second and she'd take him down to that fancy rug and tear off his clothes, just like the rowdy mountain girl she was at heart.

"I was wondering about those three engagements."

Cold flooded her bloodstream. She jerked away, muscles going taut, then moved fast to put space between herself and Zan.

"Honey…" His tone held quiet concern. "Sorry. Just forget—"

"No!" She tempered her volume. "I mean, no, not a problem." She was a mature woman, one who could handle the question. "What do you want to know?"

"You have three dresses, three engagement rings?"

"I never made it to the dress-buying stage," she confessed. "The rings I returned, of course."

Her gaze on her bare hands, she hoped this was the end of the interrogation.

It wasn't.

"Did…did they break it off?"

She shook her head.

"Then what caused you to run?"

She bristled. "I didn't *run*. I'm still here, aren't I?"

"You didn't make it to the altar. Three times."

"I couldn't marry them because…" Her throbbing head made it hard to think. Perhaps it was a prehangover, perhaps the pins from the updo were digging into her scalp. She fished for the little metal buggers, taking them out one by one so that her hair fell around her shoulders. "You remember my dad left my mom and us for a time."

"You were pretty young."

"Still." She dropped the handful of pins beside the bouquet and fluffed the ends of her hair. "I remember the tension when they were fighting. My mom's sadness when he was gone."

"So you're saying you couldn't marry three different guys because you were convinced all three of them would ultimately leave you?"

"Something like that," she said, trying to make light of it. She couldn't bring herself to point out that *he'd* left. "Trust issues."

"You couldn't marry them because you thought you couldn't count on them?"

No, I couldn't marry them because not one of them was you!

The words poured into her consciousness before she could feel them coming. Before she could call them back. Before she could build a dam to keep them out.

"Trust issues," she said again, whispering, because it *couldn't* be Zan who had prevented her from saying "I do." Zan had left the mountains and he'd left her, and she'd had no hint that he'd ever come back or that he'd ever want to.

Not one of the 117 postcards had carried the message "Wait for me."

"Trust issues," he echoed, coming closer. He cupped her jaw in one big hand and traced her lips with his thumb. "So are you going to trust me with you tonight?"

She couldn't take the way he was looking at her, tender and warm, the same way he'd looked at her that first day, right before that first kiss when he'd gone from being her friend to her first love. She'd been crushing on him for years, of course, getting his attention in any way she could, knowing he was handsome and funny and *her* Zan. But not until she'd felt his lips on hers had the seed blossomed in her heart, a wildflower blooming inside a wild mountain girl.

She'd been so happy…until she'd been so unhappy.

Zan's thumb moved over her mouth again. "What's going on in that head of yours?"

And because she didn't want him aware of what was roaming around in there, she went on her tiptoes and kissed him.

Until they were breathless.

Until he was clutching her behind and she was gripping his shoulders.

Until she knew the inevitable was going to happen that night, the explosion, the flames, the burn, and she had to find a way to take the serious edge off it or she wouldn't outlive the experience. So, after breaking the kiss for air, she gathered in oxygen and gathered her guts and recalled that playful girl she'd once been.

"Want to play strip hide-and-seek?" she asked, throwing him a cheeky grin.

If she had to do it all over again, she would have come up with the idea when she had on more clothes.

See, the rules she established gave the hider to a count of one hundred. The seeker got to two hundred.

If the hider was found by the seeker before the final number was spoken, he or she had to remove an item of clothing.

They took turns doing the hiding and seeking.

Lucky she'd never gotten around to removing her sandals, because they gave her some extra opportunities. But, finally, he was standing there, a smirk on his face, his arms folded over his bare chest, and he said, "Strip," because he'd found her wedged in the broom closet in the butler's pantry.

And he knew she'd taken off everything but the tissue-thin bridesmaid dress—while he still had on his pants and whatever was under them.

Note to self, Mac thought, *next time don't suggest strip hide-and-seek in an unfamiliar house to the person who'd once lived there.*

"Strip," Zan said again.

Eeek. The childish game brought out the child in her, it appeared, because Mac gathered the skirt of her dress in her hands and—

Took off at a run.

Her bare feet on the stairs made hardly a sound and his were not much louder, but she could feel him following and a bubble of glee rose up her throat. Eagerness pinwheeled through her body, every part of her buzzing with excitement and a smidge of belly-curling fear, like a person felt when the roller-coaster car was tick-tick-ticking up the big hill.

On the second-floor landing she didn't pause, but her mind didn't have much of a plan, because she fled into the dimly lit master bedroom and found herself without a place to go from there. Pulse thrumming, she stood on the middle of the rug and could only heave in great gulps of air as he passed through the door, all muscles, smooth flesh and those dark pants.

"That's fine about the dress, baby," he said, prowling closer. "I'd rather take it off you myself."

Then he bypassed her entirely and went to the fireplace opposite the big bed. It was gas-powered, she remembered, and the flames went *whoosh* and the room went from dimly lit to romantic, so Mac's insides went *whoosh*, too. She twisted her fingers together at her waist and wondered again how best to handle this.

Then, as he turned to her, she was taken back in time. It seemed uncomplicated then, so simple, to step inside her teenage skin, and be the person who didn't worry much about tomorrows, who could be playful instead of watchful, who reached out without fear because Zan had been her playmate for so many years and now they merely had a new field for that play.

Perhaps he read that on her face. As he stepped toward her, he smiled, and it only widened as she met him halfway. "Hello, there," he said, his voice low.

"Hello," she said and ran her palms from his solid, rippled abs to his chest. His nipples were hard points against the soft cups of her hands, and she brushed them with the edge of her thumbs before leaning in to taste one with the tip of her tongue.

His fingers clutched her waist as she took him between her lips and sucked, and she loved the helplessness of his low groan.

She continued to suck and nibble as his fingers searched for entry into her dress. It was a complicated setup—a fastening at the neck and a hidden zipper along one hip—and she lifted her head to grin at him. "Ten points if you can figure it out."

His brow quirked, and he looked as calm and in control as before despite the flag of color along each cheekbone. "We're keeping score?"

I already won, she thought and circled her tongue around one areola.

Then Zan found the snaps at the nape of her neck, and he popped them open so the bodice fell to her waist. He filled his hands with her breasts and she froze, her body giving one big shiver of delight. His thumbs brushed her erect nipples and they tightened to hard, achy points, and in retaliation she cupped his sex, with her palm and fingers forming the shape of it over the thin wool.

Zan pinched the beaded points of her breasts. "Game on, baby," he said, then found the hidden zipper.

The rest of her dress slithered to her ankles. She'd lost her panties during hide-and-seek, and he stared at her bare body until her legs were restless and the center of her was pulsing and wet. Then he went down on his knees, opened her with this thumbs and feasted.

She tried holding back needy, urgent sounds, but it was good, *so good.* Heat and arousal flashed through her as his mouth on that soft flesh made her feel both vulnerable and cherished.

The climax was twisting inside her already, and she gripped his hair to pull him away. He glanced up, his mouth gleaming in the firelight, slick with her juices, and another shudder rolled down her back. "Too soon," she whispered to him.

But he ignored her warning and leaned back in to lavish her with long, broad strokes of his tongue. One hand gripped her hip, and from every point of contact more ribbons of heat and sensation curled around her until she was wrapped in insistent desire.

She looked down to see if that need was marked on her flesh—she felt as if it must be—only to see him glance up again. Their gazes met, and then his eyelids lowered to half-mast and he took that bundle of nerves at the top of her sex between his lips and sucked, soft, and then harder, and then without mercy.

She shook with sensation. Mac's orgasm burned along the paths of those ribbons and she was aware of him watching her face until her own lashes dropped and she could only tremble with the waves and then the aftershocks of delirious pleasure.

Girl Mac had thought orgasms were the most amazing invention on earth, not at all minding those seconds of handing control to Zan and the pure demands of her body. Adult Mac had become more circumspect, always holding something of herself back by her silence, a strategic piece of clothing, the need for alone time immediately after climax.

But she was still in her throbbing, hypersensitive teenage skin, so when Zan picked her up to take her toward the bed, she threw her arms around his neck and her legs around his waist. Her wet, throbbing center met his hard abs and she ground against them, without shame or decorum, and he said, "God, Mac," and fastened his mouth to hers.

Once he was naked, they rolled around on the sheets like rambunctious puppies, fighting for the top, bucking up when on the bottom, finally turning so they could tease each other's sex with their mouths. Mac fondled Zan's balls as she took him deep between her lips and he licked her again—so delicate and tender this time that the climb to orgasm was in delicious, excruciating tiny steps. When it finally shuddered through her, he spun her back so her head was to the pillows and he rolled on top of her.

This time, she didn't fight for the dominant position, she only opened her thighs and opened her arms, and as the climax continued to pulse through her, she welcomed Zan into her body.

She welcomed him home.

CHAPTER TWELVE

ZAN CAME AWAKE SLOWLY, his body heavy, his mind muzzy. Sleep had often been sought and caught in fits and starts as he traveled the world, but now he knew he was swimming out of a deep, long sleep. Well-being was as present as the blankets covering his naked body.

Turning his head, he dragged a second pillow close and buried his face there.

It smelled like Mac. Rose petals and winter and her glowing skin.

Memory returned, and his eyes opened, taking in the master bedroom at his grandfather's house. The empty place in the big bed. The light coming through the windows that said it was midmorning.

Shit.

She'd left him without a goodbye. Buried in layers of somnolence, he'd lost his opportunity to say something about their night together.

Thank you. You're blow-my-mind sexy. More, please.

He'd held her for a night, but he suspected, like a snowflake caught in his warm bare hand, she'd already slipped through his fingers.

Shit!

Then he heard noise come from the floor above. He lifted his gaze to the ceiling. Either raccoons had invaded, or a person was moving around up there.

Jackknifing up, he glanced around the rooms. There were his slacks, carefully slung over a chair. His boxer briefs folded onto the seat.

Mac.

But there was no sign of her dress, the only thing she'd been wearing when they'd reached his room.

Strip hide-and-seek, he thought, smiling to himself as he left the bed and pulled on jeans and a sweatshirt. Only that girl.

She was wrapping knickknacks in newspaper in one of the small third-floor rooms that held a table piled with a variety of items he'd gathered from other spaces. Leaning on the jamb, he let his lazy gaze drink her in. She wore a pair of derelict jeans, sneakers and a faded navy sweatshirt with a sagging sleeve due to the rip where it attached at the shoulder.

The slice of skin revealed there made his dick twitch.

He'd tasted the bare flesh there…and everywhere. Roses and winter. Clean and pure and velvety and hot.

Mac. His Mac.

More, please.

But he didn't dare say it out loud, because the new Mac was also skittish and prickly and suspicious. *Trust issues.*

Though she hadn't seemed to hold anything back the night before.

"Your eyeballs are going to dry out if you don't blink," she said, her voice teasing, her gaze on the porcelain bird she was enclosing in paper. Then she looked up, smiled.

He grinned at her warm, open expression. Maybe

the old Mac was back. "Sorry, just glad to find you here. I woke up and thought I'd missed you."

"We have a deal, don't we? You're paying me to help you pack."

"Where'd you get the clothes?" he asked, strolling into the room, needing to get closer.

"I had one of my employees drop off a few things I keep at the office. It's a nosy part of the world we live in. Nobody needs to know I didn't go home last night."

He was near enough to smell her now, and one breath brought it all back to him. His skin rippled and he felt his dick twitch again.

She'd been magnificent. Open and uninhibited and as demanding as he was. Natural, he thought again. Free.

He liked to think it was because he made her feel safe. Because he made her forget her "trust issues."

"Mac," he said, his voice low.

She looked up. "Hmm?"

"Just Mac." He sifted his fingers through her hair, watched her smile. That was open, too. "I like to say your name."

"You used to tease me I had a boy's name," she said.

His thumb ran along the edge of her delicate ear and he watched pink color wash over her cheeks. "I was loathsome."

"I loved it," she confessed. "Any bit of attention you would give me."

Leaning in, he kissed her ear, then tugged on the lobe with his teeth. "What could I do to convince you to let me give you more than a bit of attention right now?"

One hand clutched his T-shirt at his side and she

pressed her forehead to his chest. "Tilda's picking me up any minute. It's Monday, I have houses to clean."

He hoped that was regret he heard in her voice.

As if on cue, the doorbell rang below. Mac moved away, heading in the direction of downstairs. Before she reached the hallway, she paused. "By the way, I finished boxing up your 'Keep' pile. It took twelve cartons."

He groaned. "What the hell am I going to do with all that? I've got to get things cleared out for the home to sell, but I don't want to drive around with those boxes in the back of my car."

She wrapped one hand around the doorjamb. "There's a public storage building just outside of the village. You could rent some space."

"Naah. I'll have to find some place to store them, but I'm not staying around here long enough to make it worth that—since I won't be coming back." Rubbing the back of his neck, he stared up at the ceiling. "You think maybe Brett might temporarily help out a friend?"

When she didn't respond, he aimed his gaze her way. She still stood in the doorway, unmoving.

"Mac?" An icy sensation slipped down his spine. "What's wrong?"

A second sounding of the doorbell goosed her into moving. "Have to go!"

He followed her fleeing form. "See you later?"

The slam of the front door was the unsatisfactory answer. He'd wanted an affirmative. He'd wanted to nail her down to more—more of them together—before she left.

Fine, he thought, wandering in the direction of the

kitchen and coffee. He had the rest of the day to figure out how exactly to make that happen. She wasn't going to retreat behind her thorny shell again.

Later, going through his pants pockets reminded him he had things of his own to do. So after coffee he headed into the village of Blue Arrow Lake. Skeeter Jenks had a garage with a two-car bay off a side street from which he conducted his car cleaning business. Zan found the man inside a tiny office and he broke into a grin when the bells on the door rang out.

"You made it!" Skeeter said, holding out both arms, then reaching forward for a handshake.

"With a forty percent discount, why would you doubt it?" Zan asked.

"I don't know. Big wedding last night. Thought you might forget."

"Nope." He glanced around. "Good deal you have going here, Skeeter."

He beamed. "It was actually my mom's idea, since she made me clean her car every Saturday. She said I was good at it, which might be the only thing she said I was ever good at besides causing her grief." His smile didn't dim.

"Cool," Zan said.

"Yep. Drivers can drop their cars here in town, but I also send out guys for a mobile detailing service. That's popular in the summer. We drive to the big estates and can take care of a few cars at a time."

"That's smart."

Skeeter shrugged. "It's what we do around here. Find ways to make a buck off you rich dudes. No offense."

"None taken. I understand."

"You would. It's the same kind of thing that Brett

Walker does. Mac, too. She sure looked pretty last night." Skeeter wiggled his brows.

"Can't disagree."

"Gave folks a start, I'd say, to see you two with your heads together again. Like old times."

Like how Zan wanted it to be in present times, but he couldn't shake the feeling that he'd lost an opportunity back at the house this morning. *Trust issues.*

"Speaking of weddings..." Zan cleared his throat. "What do you know about Mac's, uh, engagements?"

"Three of 'em," Skeeter said, nodding.

"Do you know why they ended?"

"Not me," Skeeter said. "Maybe if she ever asked me to clean her car, I would. People leave the most telltale things. I found a pair of extra-small panties in a guy's car when his wife was definitely a size large. Underneath a married lady's seat I pulled out a love note signed by her boss."

Had those men cheated on Mac? Who would be stupid enough to do that?

I don't know, genius, an inner voice answered. *You left her for an on-and-off case of dysentery and ten years of itinerant travel.*

He couldn't have stayed, damn it. Every day had made him want to wrap himself tighter in someone else's family, someone else's birthright, while his had been lost so long ago. It had been self-preservation against any more loss.

Pushing that thought away, he left his car with Skeeter and walked into the village proper to collect his half-dozen doughnuts. A smattering of people were seated at the small bistro tables in the bakery and there was a short line at the counter. He occupied himself by staring at the glass display cases filled with croissants and crullers and cupcakes until it was his turn to greet the counter lady and present her with his coupon.

She hailed the baker, who came to the counter from the back, her apron dusted with flour. "Zan! I hoped you'd stop by."

He smiled. "You knew I would. Doughnuts are my favorite, Mrs. Tiller."

Reaching for a white bag, she smiled at him. "It's nice to know some things don't change. I saw you talking to Mac Walker at the wedding."

She clearly wanted to know the way the wind blew on that front.

He had his own intelligence to gather.

I've been engaged. Three times, to three separate men.

Trust issues.

"It's been great catching up with all the Walkers," he said. "I've been out of touch for a long time."

Mrs. Tiller got a gleam in her eye. "Long enough for that girl to get engaged three times."

Bingo.

"Yeah. About that." He made a big show of opening the bag she handed to him and lifting it to his nose for an appreciative inhale. "I'm not learning too much on that score. I hope my old friend didn't get entangled with bad guys."

Actually, the more he thought about it, he hoped they were permanently incarcerated for petty crimes and misdemeanors. He pictured them with missing teeth, lanky hair and aunts he couldn't tell apart from the uncles. Growing up, they'd kept skunks as pets. Now locked up, they'd never bother Mac again.

"Every girl loves herself at least one bad boy," Mrs. Tiller said.

Um...*he'd* been Mac's bad boy! He had the pranks and the speeding tickets and the scars to prove it.

But you left her, genius, that taunting inner voice piped up. *Remember?*

His fist crumpled the top of the paper sack. "So they..."

"Are perfectly nice young men who were devoted to her," the baker said with a wave of her hand. "Don't worry on that score."

Shit. He didn't like the sound of that, either, as he pictured medals on burly chests, ticker tape parades, solutions to world hunger.

"But she never married one of them."

"Yes, that's true." She smiled. "Maybe they were intimidated by the Mac and Zan legend and didn't try hard enough to keep her."

You didn't try at all, unless postcards count.

It shamed him to admit now, that while he'd thought of her 117 times when mailing off his missives, and while he'd commissioned that doll with her image in mind, he'd not thought about her finding someone else. Not seriously. Not until he'd seen her that night at Brett's wedding reception had he let himself consider her growing older and even more beautiful.

Selfish asshole that he was, he'd always held close that image of her as the girl she'd been. *His* girl.

Munching on doughnuts, he wandered out of the bakery and along the village's main street. The day was cold, but the sky was a bright, optimistic blue. Still, it felt strange to be stopped several times—just as he'd been at the wedding—and greeted like a long-missed relative.

Unlike at the wedding, the "folding in" didn't make him worry today. Not even when a couple of others managed to work into conversation the Mac and Zan legend.

He started to like that they were remembered that way. That he was remembered as one half of something with her.

After lunch at the deli, he visited almost every shop, steering clear of only the girlie places. At the drugstore, he perused the rack of postcards and on a whim bought one that showed a summer view of Blue Arrow Lake. He'd keep it for himself, he decided, as he'd be gone by that season.

He'd be gone before spring.

His stomach churned and he decided doughnuts and pastrami were not a good mix.

Finally, he wandered back to Skeeter's and picked up his car. The guy's mom was right, he did good work. The thing was pristine inside and out. Even though it was a rental, Zan was glad he'd gone for the wash and detailing and handed over a massive tip. Then, on his way back to his grandfather's, another whim prompted him to drive by the Maids by Mac office.

He didn't expect to see her there. She'd said she had houses to clean.

But as he crawled past, he saw movement through the window. Without even thinking about it, he knifed into a parking space and headed for the door, *more, please* at the forefront of his mind.

He walked into an empty space that smelled like burned coffee. The door made a sound as it closed behind him, and Mac must have heard it, because through a doorway in the rear he heard her call out.

"Be there in just a minute! I forgot and left an inch of coffee on the burner again," she said, in a way he knew it must be a frequent occurrence.

He smiled, shaking his head a little. It was still hard to accept that Mac Walker had become a coffee drinker.

She came into view, a clear but dripping carafe in her hands. Upon seeing him, her feet stuttered to a halt.

So did his heart.

Weird, because they hadn't parted that many hours ago. But it came to him like a full-body slam, her sweet curves, even in something simple like jeans and a T-shirt, the shining fall of her dark hair, those dark lashes that surrounded her pale blue eyes. Suddenly he regretted not turning all the lights on in his bedroom the night before. He should have done that. Then he could have absorbed that face and those eyes as he slid inside her. He could have read all that she felt when the two of them were joined.

"What are you doing here?" she asked, moving to the coffee machine on a back table.

He noted the Russian dolls he'd brought her sat in a line on the battered desk by her computer. His heart started beating again, even though he didn't like that odd, wooden expression on her face.

She didn't look happy to see him, while she'd stopped his heart.

Hell.

He approached the counter separating them. "How's your day going?" Maybe something had gone wrong and that look on her face had nothing to do with him at all.

"Fine," she said, glancing toward her desk. "Paperwork for hours."

His brows shot up. "I thought you left this morning because you needed to clean houses."

A flush turned her cheeks pink. "Houses, paperwork. All the same. I needed to work."

Or get away from me.

But she'd smiled at him this morning, damn it, when he'd found her on the third floor. She hadn't been this stiff automaton who couldn't even look him in the eye. There'd not been a hint of morning-after remorse.

Fiddling with a stack of papers on her desk now, she threw him a quick glance. "Uh, what did you do?"

"Hung out in the village for quite a while," he said. "But now that I'm here, I'm hoping I can convince you to go to dinner with me tonight."

"I don't think so, Zan."

All right, now he was certain something was off with her. Not because she refused him, but because she did it as if she had a poker up her ass and was sucking on a lemon.

And still, she looked beautiful.

Inhaling a deep breath, he leaned his elbows on the counter. "Do you have other plans?"

He could see her thinking over her answer.

"Dinner, sweetheart," he said. "I feel like steak, okay? We'll go to that place with all the antler chandeliers and the old boating stuff hanging on the walls."

Her mouth twitched and she darted another look at him. "That describes, like, fifteen places around here."

Her near-smile cheered him. “Then we won’t have any trouble finding it.”

Pursing her lips, she ran a hand through her hair. He decided to change the subject before she found a way to say no. “I heard a lot about the wedding from people today.”

She met his gaze, clearly interested in that subject. “Yeah?”

“Verdict is, Shay was gorgeous, her husband handsome and the entire wedding party glamorous.”

“We were kind of glamorous,” Mac said, appearing pleased.

“I’ll say.” He kept his gaze on her face. “I heard a lot of talk about us, too.”

Her eyes widened. “Us?”

“Remember when you grabbed me and towed me away from the reception?”

“Oh. Yeah.”

“People noticed. Now the grapevine is buzzing about the Mac and Zan legend.” He shook his head. “It surprises me how they’re still attached to that.”

“A good reason not to go out for dinner together,” she said quickly.

Shit. He’d stepped right into that, hadn’t he?

“I don’t care what people say. I care about taking you to dinner. I care about letting you know how much I enjoyed last night. How much I want more nights just like it.”

She’d gone stiff again, her gaze trained on the stack of papers.

“Wouldn’t that be nice, Mac, honey?” He lightened his voice to a teasing tone. “We can formalize our sex buddies agreement over a pair of good steaks.”

"No," she said. "I was wrong about suggesting we start that up. It wasn't a smart idea."

Fine, he thought, telling himself he did not feel disappointment. Calling it a sex buddies thing was stupid anyway and hadn't sat well with him from the start. He just wanted a meal with her, damn it. "Steaks, Mac. That's all."

"No."

He remembered now, how she could be as obstinate as a jackass. One time, when she was about eleven years old, she'd climbed a tree and gotten stuck, then refused his help to get her down. For hours, she'd stayed up there, her cheeks tear-streaked but her will inflexible.

She was wearing the I'm-staying-on-this-branch-forever face.

He sighed. "I just don't see why we can't—"

"Think, Zan." She seemed impatient.

"Think what?"

"You wouldn't want me to get too attached, would you?"

It was his turn to freeze. Her blue-crystal eyes were on him and under their cool power, there was no way he could bluff.

Yeah, she had him there. He didn't want her to get too attached.

He didn't want either one of them to get too attached. That was exactly why he'd left ten years before. He hadn't wanted to risk losing something he wanted so very much.

TILDA AGREED WHEN Mac wanted to catch a bite to eat after their workday was done. While the wedding had been a success, the Monday after apparently hadn't gone so well for her boss and friend. When five o'clock rolled around, Mac suggested the two of them try the new café in town, thinking it might not be too busy so early in the evening.

There was no reason for Tilda to refuse, not even because she didn't have the money. Mac offered to buy as payback for Tilda driving out in her car—Ash had fixed it the morning after their night together—and bringing her clothes, then later picking her up at the Elliott place that morning. Providing company over a slice of quiche or some crepes and cups of hot tea was what friends were for.

Not to mention it also gave her a reason not to go home right away. Tilda had a bad feeling that Ash might try to track her down there if she continued to leave his calls and texts unanswered. Yes, she was avoiding him, despite her big talk to Mac about good things coming. Her good thing with Ash hadn't survived twenty-four hours.

The café was a far cry from the dark, paneled Mr. Frank's, where you could get bar food half-off every night between four and seven, making nachos or wings a cheap meal. It wasn't a large space, but it felt big with the floor-to-ceiling windows overlooking the lake. In the summer, the outdoor deck would be a beautiful place to dine. In winter, it was still pretty and cozy with a fire crackling in a stone corner fireplace. It wasn't yet crowded, but looking around at the other patrons and what they were wearing, Tilda could see it had already caught on with the affluent part-timers to the community. She crossed the sole of one sneaker over the hole on the toe of the other and was glad the pair of jeans she wore were in good condition and that she'd borrowed a nice sweater that Mac had in her car.

Fragrant tea was in delicate cups and an almost-full pot sat on their table. Salads with vinaigrette and candied pecans and crumbled blue cheese over field greens had been served. Tilda didn't often have an opportunity to eat like this—as in never, unless at the end of a catering gig—but her appetite wasn't as keen as it should be, and Mac, too, appeared to be only toying with the torn leaves on her plate.

Yep. The boss was definitely not having a great day.

Tilda cleared her throat. "The wedding was really beautiful. Jace had the smuggest expression on his face when he and Shay were pronounced man and wife."

"Yeah," Mac said absently. "He's a goner when it comes to my sister."

Tilda treaded cautiously next. "I don't know if you were aware, but at the reception I was seated beside Zan Elliott."

Mac's fork froze. "Yeah?"

"He's nice. Very handsome." And very into Mac, that was clear. Tilda wasn't sure she should have spilled about those postcards in the bottom drawer, but champagne had been her downfall before. And the fact was, the other woman had gone to him at the end of the reception, Tilda knew, since she'd been standing right there when the arrangements were made. "Um... did you two have a nice night after Poppy and Ryan dropped you off?"

Mac looked up. "I owed Zan some packing time. That's why I went over there."

Tilda widened her eyes. "You were in a bridesmaid dress."

"And tipsy," Mac added.

"Tipsy, in a bridesmaid dress, you went to do some packing."

"That's my story, and I'm sticking to it." A smile flickered over her mouth, but it didn't appear a happy one.

Tilda sucked in a breath, thinking she should give her friend another opportunity to share, in case that's what she needed. "Everybody knows about you two, and you've told me—"

"What we had was ages ago. And then he left. He's leaving again."

What was there to say to that?

Mac stabbed a piece of lettuce. "We know to be careful of short-timers, right?"

"Right." Smart girls figured that out early, when you lived in a vacation destination. There was a local mantra about it, even. "Never trust your heart to a guy who shows up in town with a suitcase."

Lifting her head, Mac eyed Tilda. "I wasn't going to pry, but since that just came out of your mouth... what's up with you and Ash Robbins? I've heard things myself—"

"Nothing's up with us," Tilda said quickly, then couldn't hold on to the lie. "We slept together."

Mac blinked. "Okay."

"I mean, we *slept* together." Her face went hot. "I told you I met him last May. What I didn't tell you was that night we had sex. Then he came back to town recently and we kept running into each other and then the other night we *slept*."

Cuddled together under heaps of blankets with their clothes still on. At first, they'd whispered in the dark about everything and nothing: books they'd read as kids, first crushes, his upcoming job in London, her determination to get her degree in biology. Finally, they'd fallen asleep, tangled in each other.

"The next morning, he helped me fix my car again… something about the rotor this time. I don't know."

"Handy guy."

Scary guy. Because she'd felt so close to him after those hours cozied up in the dark. He'd seen her terrible apartment and not run away screaming. He'd heard her voice her dream about obtaining a college degree and hadn't expressed a single doubt that she'd achieve it—even if she'd ultimately have to find a way to put in hours at a lab as well as at her computer. *You want that*, he'd said, *you'll get it*.

With his arms around her, his warm voice in her ear, it had seemed totally reachable. Actually doable, for the first time.

"And then?" Mac prompted. "Since fixing your car again?"

"Since then I've been avoiding him."

"Uh…why?" Mac studied her face. "Because you should never trust your heart to a guy who shows up in town with a suitcase?"

Remembering that wasn't what had put her gears into reverse. It happened when they were standing by her car in the cold morning air. Smiling, he'd told her the tip of her nose was pink, and then he'd kissed her there, his warm breath bathing her cool skin.

Following that, his expression had sobered. *Tilda*, he'd said, his gaze intent on hers, *this feels so fucking real.*

Flushing hot all over, she'd looked everywhere but

at him and mumbled her response. *How would you know what real is like?*

My parents, he'd replied. *I see what they have. It looks like this feels.*

She'd gone from hot to frozen over in an instant. But if she was honest with herself, that last sentence wasn't what had put her into full retreat, either. What had made her withdraw was her own certain sense—that she had, for no good reason she could name—that what was going on between her and Ash Robbins was very real, too.

Mac was staring off into the distance now, a strange expression on her face. Then her eyes cut to Tilda. "You probably made the right decision."

Tilda frowned as something small but ugly skittered down her spine. A premonition. A bad omen. "Why?" she whispered.

Her friend's gaze flicked over Tilda's shoulder again. "John and Veronica Robbins just came in. Ash is with them, and with *him*…"

This time, the feeling crawled *up* her spine. Tilda shuddered and slid down in her chair. Then she glanced over her shoulder. At the opposite side of the café, Ash's mother waited while her husband pulled out her chair. He was tall and straight, a good-looking middle-aged man whose face could sell stocks and bonds, political deals, pretty lies. He didn't look like a cheater, but did any of them?

Ash had his back to Tilda, and she could only see the profile of the blonde, glossy-haired young woman who stood beside him. From the side she was perfect, and perfect for him. Tilda's soul let out a raw cry as she watched him solicitously help slide off Perfect Girl's gorgeous, fitted wool coat that was a striking and deep sunny yellow with big black buttons running down the back.

To get completely free of it, the young woman had to transfer the big leather purse in her left hand to her right. A designer purse, Tilda was certain, the kind that cost two times more than her car. For all she knew, it cost four times more than her car. Five.

Then Ash pulled out her chair and the girl gracefully folded her slim self, dressed in a form-fitting black dress, black tights and high-heeled black boots, onto the seat. She turned her head toward Ash, looking up as he drew out his own chair, and this side of her face was just as flawless as the other.

Perfect Girl would have an impeccable manicure, unmarred by cleansers and unchipped by hauling a cumbersome vacuum around. Not one pair of holey shoes. And the perfume she wore wouldn't be something that had been given to her mother by her mother's married lover.

Tilda couldn't sit in the same room with them. "Mac," she said, agonized.

Her friend covered her cold hand with a warm one. "If you have to go, go." There was sympathy in her eyes.

For the stupid girl who had almost fallen for the rich short-timer who came to town with a suitcase.

Tilda nodded. "Thanks." She just had to make it to the exit without Ash being any the wiser.

Slipping her own cheap pleather bag over her shoulder, she scanned her surroundings, trying to figure out how best to get out unseen. Instead of the direct route, she'd skirt around a couple of tables behind where they sat, pass the kitchen door, then hug the front wall and duck outside.

Best laid plans and all that…

Because as she walked past the kitchen access, a man came barreling out with a tray of plates held at shoulder level. Tilda tried avoiding the collision, but she'd been hurrying herself. So woman met waiter and the dishes flew, only to land in a spectacular crash of noise.

The heads of the nearest patrons in the place swiveled their way.

Tilda went deer-in-headlights when she saw Ash glance around, too. His father, thank God, hadn't turned toward the sound, but she saw the instant his son decided to move. Mac was there already, however, murmuring, "I've got this," and Tilda woke from her spooked trance and escaped.

Back at home, she barricaded herself in her apartment—that was to say, she turned the little round lock in the middle of the knob, the kind of lock that was usually on bedroom or bathroom doors. She wasn't too worried about its flimsiness. Ash had to know his gig now was up.

The girl he'd had fun slumming with knew he had one of his own kind on his arm.

Tilda's roommates had night shifts again and it was still as cold as the dark side of the moon in the place, so Tilda retreated to her room. There, she threw off her clothes, then went to the hall bathroom that had a stall shower. At least the hot water was plentiful and the pressure strong, so she was able to wash away the day, the cold and the tears that persisted in running down her cheeks.

Stupid, too, those tears.

In her pajamas—a pair of old, soft sweatpants and a man's flannel shirt that had been around forever—Tilda crawled under her thick stack of blankets. With her bedside lamp on, she picked up the tattered copy of *Pride and Prejudice* that was her first choice in comfort reads. There was homework for one of her courses due soon, but she wanted to lose herself and it would be in Lizzy Bennet's world, not in the details of cell specialization.

In a different season, it would be a night for a gallon of ice cream and copious tears, followed by a bitch session with her roomies that included plenty of trash talk about a particular guy, then all guys in general. They'd vow to become nuns, or, if not that, to have each other's backs when they were eighty and needed help recovering from broken hips.

But it was too cold to do that tonight and her roommates were making good tips up at the ski lodge, and in reality, they would not have each other's backs when they were eighty. Her roommates were sisters, so they would have each other's backs, and they had boyfriends who were ski instructors whom the two would likely marry.

It was Tilda who would end up alone. So if it was any season but winter, she would have gone to bed with an ice cream headache and another ache in her throat from trying to hold back more tears. Once in her room, she would have let them flow, just as they would tonight after she had her fill of Lizzy and Mr. Darcy.

The book fell open to a favorite spot and she was just settling in when she heard her front door pop open.

Bolting upright, she held the covers to her throat. Had one of her roommates gotten off work early? But that popping sound wasn't of a door being unlocked—it was the sound of a locked door being opened with a shoulder, not a key. And her cell phone was in her purse, which she'd left in the front room.

"Danni?" she called out, clutching her paperback as if she might use it as a weapon. "Cheryl?"

Then Ash Robbins breached her doorway.

Fear morphed into anger. "You scared me!"

He eyed her coolly. "It took me three seconds to get from the front door to this one. You survived."

Tilda gritted her teeth. "Remember annoyingly arrogant?"

"How about we talk about you instead? Would we say chain yanker? Game player? You run sweet, Tilda, and then you run mean."

Mean? Her? The back of her eyes went hot. "I don't know what you're talking about."

"How many of my messages have you ignored, Tilda? Texts?"

"I don't see how you had time to send them, considering you have another girl—your type of girl—that requires your attention." How hadn't she realized right away that he was a philanderer like his father?

"I don't have another girl. I wish I could think I had you."

Her copy of *Pride and Prejudice* was so soft from being read a million times, it would probably land like a kiss if she threw it in his face. "Go away."

His jaw tightened. "You misread the situation."

"Oh, are you going to tell me that…that person is your *sister*?"

"She's my cousin."

Tilda's eyes flared wide. "What?"

"Okay, I lied about that. Amber's the daughter of family friends. But she might as well be my cousin."

"Baloney."

He stalked closer to the bed. "I'm not interested in Amber, Tilda. I'm interested in *you*. Tonight, I would have taken you out if you would have responded to one of my calls, voice messages or texts. Since you didn't, I got roped into going out with her and my parents."

It sounded true, she supposed. It could be true.

But regardless, she reminded herself, there could be nothing between them. It would never work for reasons that went beyond the Ambers of the world. *Way* beyond.

Maybe Ash saw all that on her face, because suddenly he was at her skinny bed, sitting on the edge of the mattress so their faces were close. "Tilda. Damn it." He slipped the paperback from her grasp, glanced at it, then paused.

"Pride and Prejudice." He quirked a brow at her. "Sound familiar?"

"You think you're Darcy?"

"I've never looked down at you. But you've been prejudiced against me from the start."

He didn't know how very right he was. And she could never tell him why.

"What do you want, Ash?" she asked.

Leaning closer, he framed her face with his hands. "You, of course."

Her heart hurt. Her temples throbbed. She was so tired of fighting to get through every day, worrying about money and school and whether her car would start. Running from Ash took energy she did not have.

Especially when surrendering sounded so much nicer.

Couldn't a hardworking girl get a break once in a while?

Okay, so they wouldn't last, no matter how real it might feel to them, but she could have right now. Another night. Maybe another few.

She swallowed. "I mean, what do you want right now?"

"Cuddling with you was the best night I ever had." His thumbs brushed her cheeks. "I'll settle for more of that."

But she didn't want to *settle*, not tonight, not when golden-haired Ash Robbins was on her bed and she was allowing herself to have more "amusement." More "recreation." Now she let herself acknowledge the way the jolt of adrenaline from his break-in had morphed into an entirely different kind of excitement. She was breathing fast, almost panting, and under all the blankets she was getting very hot.

Tilda pushed her thighs together, trying to address the growing ache there. She was super aware of all things Ash, the subtle, so appealing scent of him, the point where his hip pressed against hers, the tracks his fingertips had made into her hair. He studied her face with his intense blue eyes, his attention solely on her, and it was...heady. Exciting.

A surge of want rose from her toes, up her legs, to make her breasts swell and her nipples tighten. Nothing had changed. He was still out of her league. He was still moving to London. She was still her mother's daughter and he was still the son of his father.

But she wouldn't think about that again. Not tonight.

Pulling away from the stacked pillows, she slid her arms around his neck. Ash took a sharp intake of breath, and it gave Tilda the confidence to bring her mouth to his.

She touched lightly. Brushed back and forth.

His body went harder, all his muscles tightening. He was letting her run the show, and that made her want him even more.

With a flick of her tongue, she bathed his bottom lip. He gasped again, and she took that as an invitation to push inside. Oh, God. He tasted so good, mint and heat, and she ran her tongue over his slick, perfect teeth.

He groaned. "What is this?" he said, tearing his mouth free to draw in a ragged breath.

"This is me, giving you pleasure," she said, almost drunk on his taste. They could exchange that, couldn't they? Pleasure shouldn't be something to be wary of, right? "Pleasure," she repeated against his mouth.

This time Ash took over the kiss. It was his tongue in her mouth. But she did her part by threading her fingers into his hair and holding on tight as he showed her what his lips could do.

Then they were on a tour of her: her ears, her jaw, her neck. He tossed the covers back to her waist and then he was following his fingers with his mouth as they unbuttoned the flannel shirt.

Her skin goose-bumped, but she wasn't cold. She went to pure flame when he exposed her breasts and bent his head over them. He cupped one with his hand and held it plumped for his mouth. Tilda shivered at the first touch of wetness against her nipple and she squirmed against the sheets.

Then he sucked it, hard, and her hips arched off the bed. "Ash," she said, her short fingernails digging into his scalp.

He looked up, his eyes soft, his mouth still pulling hard.

Uh-oh, Tilda thought, as heated sensation rolled through her, a wave of it that surged against her heart, turned it over. Then he kissed a path to her other nipple and she could only think, *Ooooh.*

That night in the hotel room, months ago, it had been a hot bump-and-grind, with groping hands and greedy, fast kisses. Now, though, now Ash seemed determined to take his time, his touch gentle and his mouth on a mission to map out all her sensitive places.

He was still dressed as he drew her pajama bottoms and panties over her ankles and feet. Then he widened her thighs and pushed up her knees to crawl between them.

Though lust curled deliciously through her body, Tilda looked at him with some alarm when he positioned himself at the hot, wet apex of her legs. "What are you doing?" She'd had exactly two sexual partners in her life, the boyfriend she'd had at nineteen, and then Ash, that one time.

This had never been on the menu with the first guy, and not the night of her twenty-first birthday, either.

She swallowed, torn between anticipation and mortification. "Ash?"

His gaze didn't leave the soft flesh he parted with knowing fingers. "This is me, giving you pleasure."

Her body went rigid at the first delicate touch of his

tongue. Then bliss darted through her, set her blood aflame, took away her need for air. He played there with a tenderness that destroyed every defense she could throw up. She might think it was merely a generous act, but he was groaning as he licked and thrust, making clear he was enjoying himself.

So Tilda let herself go and just let him drive her up and up and up, toward an ultimate delight that caused her muscles to spasm, her toes to curl, her notion of sensual enjoyment to expand.

She couldn't *wait* to reciprocate.

As she came down, Ash threw off his clothes. Then they were skin to skin, his pinning weight already setting a match to her sated senses. "You are so beautiful," he whispered. "Everywhere."

Grasping his hair, she took his mouth now, tasting herself on his tongue, drawing in the flavor that was the two of them together. Finding strength she didn't know she had, she flipped their positions, so she was on top, his erection against her belly, her sensitive nipples against his hard chest.

He smiled, and she saw welcome and happiness and…a future in his eyes. Something she'd never fully believed in—maybe even for herself.

Certainly never for the two of them. But, oh, she could almost feel her fingers around it now.

Smiling back, she felt a burning pressure gather in her eyes.

Ash blinked, one hand trailing to her bottom, the other brushing away the single tear she'd blinked free. "What's this?"

"This is me, giving you me," she whispered, and banishing worry from her heart, Tilda proceeded to show him exactly what that meant.

CHAPTER THIRTEEN

MAC WAS AN indulgent aunt. Since her little sister Poppy had given birth as a single mom to Mason, Mac had enjoyed lavishing the little guy with all her love and attention. He was a precocious kid, funny and smart, who would get weird ideas in his head that he'd refuse to give up.

Stubbornness was a Walker family trait.

Consider how she'd managed to keep her relationship with Zan strictly business since the morning after Shay and Jace's wedding. The morning he'd made clear he was once again preparing for a clean break with the mountains in no uncertain words: *I won't be coming back.*

That assertion shouldn't matter. Her whole sex buddies proposal was predicated on the fact that they were going to have a short-term fling, after all. But following the night in his arms, flesh to flesh, she'd woken up humming. Happy. A happiness that had dropped like a rock in the bottom of a barrel when he'd said those five words.

I won't be coming back.

So she'd vowed right then and there to insulate herself from another painful farewell by shutting down anything intimate between them.

No matter how he'd wheedled for a steak dinner.

No matter how much she wanted to roll around with him naked again.

It was how she'd save herself from getting too attached...again.

Yep, the Walkers were an obstinate lot, as evidenced by Mason not taking no for an answer the dozen times she'd said the word since she'd arrived at her sister's house to babysit for the evening.

Standing in the spacious Hamilton kitchen, he looked up at her now, his adorable face cherubic, his hands clasped beneath his chin. "Please, Auntie Mac."

She pretended to glare at him. "Do you practice that look in the mirror?"

"Uh..." His eyes slid to the side.

"You do practice that look in the mirror!" She tried not to laugh.

"Duke's teaching me how to act."

Mac shook her head. "Duke" was what her nephew called his stepfather-to-be, Ryan Hamilton, former child actor and action star. Actually, Ryan was the boy's father-to-be, because an adoption was following fast on the heels of the wedding. "I'm telling your mother. She needs to brace herself."

Mason's brows shot together. "Don't tell Mom anything, okay? Duke told me we don't want to worry her right now. No stress, Duke says. It's not good for her."

"I'm kidding, sweetie," she said, glad Ryan was looking out for Poppy. She was the beating—and bleeding—heart of the family and with the wedding so close keeping her calm was best.

It was why Mac had made Zan promise to hold on to the fact of the true ownership of the cabins. She grimaced, knowing that wouldn't be a secret for much longer.

"Auntie Mac," Mason said, tugging on her sleeve. "You have a sad face."

"Yeah, I do." She pulled him to her for a quick hug, finishing with a brisk hair ruffle.

He squirmed away, gave her entreating eyes again. "I know how to make you feel better."

"I just bet you do." She sighed. "But I'm just as sure you shouldn't be putting on your tuxedo before the wedding."

"I want to show you what it looks like on."

"It looks awesome," she told the boy. "I don't have to see it to believe it."

"But I *need* to wear it when I practice my toast."

It was going to be the cutest thing ever, when Mason acted as best man at his mother and almost-father's wedding. Not only would he stand beside Ryan during the ceremony, he'd also memorized a short speech to give at the reception.

The boy was certain it wouldn't go well unless he practiced while wearing the mini Armani tuxedo that had been purchased for the event.

She sighed. "I really don't think it's necessary—"

"Haven't you heard of a dress rehearsal?"

See, this was when his five-going-on-twenty-five side defeated her. How did he even know what a dress rehearsal was? Ryan again, she supposed. Mason hung on every word of every story the man recounted.

Which was so damn touching she suddenly wanted the toast to be perfect, too.

"Are you clean?" she asked.

"Showered before you came."

"Let me see your hands."

He held them out.

Mac bit her lip. "What about Grimm? If he gets dog hair on that suit, we're sunk. Your mom will know."

Mason pointed to his big dog, flopped on his bed in the corner of the room, dead to the world.

"Oh, all right," she said, capitulating. "We need to make it snappy, though. You have bedtime in an hour."

She convinced him to don only the slacks and jacket, knowing Poppy would notice the tiniest crease in the starched white shirt. After he was dressed to almost the nines, they went into the family room, where a fire was burning. It was a big but cozy room, and Mac propped herself in a corner of the comfy couch. "You look so completely handsome, I wish I'd asked you to be my date for the wedding."

Mason grinned. He claimed to have a loose tooth or two, but for now they were all in there.

Mac gestured. "Okay. Go ahead and wow me."

"As soon as my second 'pinion gets here."

There he went again. So funny sometimes. "Do you mean a second *opinion*?"

"Yeah. I need a guy. Mommy let me call him before you came."

"Uncle Brett's coming over?" She'd thought he had plans for tonight.

Mason shook his head. "Zan."

She was still sputtering—and promising to find some adequate retribution for her sister, who'd left without any warning about this—when the doorbell rang. Mason ran off to answer its call. Both boy and man were in the family room before she could blink, and then her only thought was of the awkwardness of the situation. Cozy setting, no other adults around, Zan looking so tempting and so part of her world in scruffy boots, an old pair of jeans and a long-sleeved, green-brown thermal the exact color of his eyes. She forced herself to remember his words. *I won't be coming back.*

"How come you're here?" she demanded, knowing of no better defense than a shrill offense.

Zan narrowed his eyes. "I didn't know you would be, actually. My man—" he gestured to Mason "—phoned and I had to help a bud out."

She couldn't exactly complain about that and she didn't have a chance to before her little nephew reminded them he only had until his bedtime at eight-thirty. Shooting her an unreadable look, Zan took to the other corner of the couch.

They spent the next forty-five minutes watching Mason strut around the room, giving various highly amusing inflections to the words of his toast. Mac struggled to keep a straight face and didn't dare look at Zan, who occasionally made noises that she figured were choked-off laughter.

Finally, she checked the clock and told Mace the practice session was over. "Pajamas, kid," she decreed.

The boy decreed right back. Story time with both Mac and Zan.

She never could say no to him.

Mason climbed into bed wearing striped flannel. The dog, Grimm, hauled himself from the kitchen and up the stairs, then flopped down at the foot of the mattress with a loud groan. Not unfamiliar with the routine, Mac waited patiently while her nephew sifted through the stack of books on the bedside table.

His choice: a story about a cat and a bull, told in

alternating viewpoints. He insisted that Mac and Zan alternate reading as well, with appropriate voices. Zan snickered when Mason assigned her the part of the bull.

She said a soft "Meoow" when he was called upon to be LaToya the tabby.

In the end, they did a credible job, if she did have to say so herself.

Once Mason dropped off, they tiptoed out of the room to the tune of Grimm's snores and shared a celebratory grin. Mac elbowed Zan at the bottom of the stairs. "Good job, LaToya."

"Back at you, Rolando." He rolled the *R*, just as the tabby had, something that had tickled Mason's funny bone over and over again.

It was impossible in this moment not to feel charitable toward the man. She even smiled at him. "Can I get you one of Poppy and Ryan's beers?"

"Sure."

Minutes later they were back on the family room couch, both sets of feet propped on a shared ottoman, cold bottles of microbrew in hand. Relaxed, Mac smiled at the blazing fire and was totally unprepared for the thoughts that popped into her head next.

That could have been our kid.

That's what it would be like if we were parents.

She stiffened, and Zan must have noticed. She felt his glance.

"Okay, Mac?"

It seemed unlikely he'd guess the train of her thoughts, but she didn't want to give him a chance at it. "Sure, fine. Just wondering if they should take Grimm in for a sleep apnea test."

Zan glanced toward the stairs. "Yeah. Good God.

I can hear him from here." Then he shook his head. "Little Poppy Walker, having it all. Son, marriage, big noisy dog."

All the things Mac had dreamed of for her life with Zan.

Maybe he really could read her thoughts, because then he said, "You want all that?" His gaze was focused on her, she could feel it. "Kids, pets and et cetera?"

Her mouth opened and, surprising herself, the truth poured out. "I thought I did. Remember? Three engagements." And before that, too.

"Were they…recent? Or years ago?"

"Years ago. I told Josh I'd marry him about six months after you went down the hill." Of course she didn't share why. She wouldn't give him the satisfaction of knowing she'd been desperate to find a replacement for him in her heart. It wasn't her best, most honorable move, but she'd been that young and that broken. In the following three years she'd tried making that same substitution two more times until finally she'd managed to harden the organ in her chest so that no man could find his way in.

Zan was silent a long moment. "Six months? So soon?"

"'So soon'?" She bristled. "It's not as if you told me you were coming back. As a matter of fact, you explicitly told me you had no plans to return." The same as he'd said the other morning.

"Take it easy, wildcat," Zan replied, his tone mild. "I was just commenting."

Holding tight to her beer, she scowled at the fire. "Whatever," she muttered.

"Josh," he said after a few minutes of silence.

"Yes." She poured some beer down her throat. "And Adam and Jeff."

"I heard they were nice guys."

"Probably nicer than I deserved," she said, muttering again.

"Mac." Zan took her beer out of her hand and set it aside with his. Then he shifted on the couch so he was facing her instead of the flames. "What are you talking about?"

"Three times, Zan." She glanced over at him. His face, washed by the firelight, showed no judgment. "Three engagements to be married. Who *does* that?"

"An optimist?"

She laughed, but it was a bitter sound. "I think an optimist would go through with at least one of those weddings."

"What kind of events did you plan?"

Groaning, she let her head fall to the back of the cushions. "Can we not go there? It only reminds me that I hurt three good men."

"How so?"

"I made promises I couldn't keep."

"It would be worse to keep a promise that wouldn't make you happy."

"I suppose." Taking a breath, she moved to face him. "Is that why you left here, because I didn't make you happy?"

"You made me happy." He looked away. "I just always said I was going to leave the mountains. I had to follow through on that."

"But you left right *then*, when we were together." She wanted her beer back. "Tight together."

"I wanted to leave when it was all good," he said.

"Huh?" She stared at him. "That makes no sense."

"Went out on a high." Turning his head, he met her gaze. "That way I was able to take beautiful memories with me."

She tried to reason this out. "So if you'd waited until we were in a fight, it would have meant—"

"Sour memories."

There was no making sense of this. "That's man-logic. And I don't mean that as a compliment, in case you're wondering. I need my beer."

Zan handed it over and then took up his own for a swig. "If I'd left after we broke up—"

Something tore inside her chest. "We were going to break up?"

He stilled, and then his gaze shifted away again. "Everything ends, doesn't it?"

MAC STARED INTO Poppy and Ryan's refrigerator, supposedly on a second-beer retrieval mission, but not really seeing a thing in the gargantuan space. She could only hear Zan's matter-of-fact voice. *Everything ends, doesn't it?*

Those words moved through her again, each syllable slow and precise, each one another rip. What he'd shared with her before should have made her mad—he'd actually planned to leave when they were on a relationship high!—but instead she just felt…turned inside out, as if her vulnerable, wounded insides were now showing.

Everything ends, doesn't it?

Her sisters would say she was the master of happy-ever-after cynicism—and they didn't hesitate to give her digs about it now that they'd found their men—but she didn't think she'd ever expressed her doubts about finding and keeping "the one" as baldly as that.

Everything ends, doesn't it?

She must have been ruminating on that for a while, because now Zan sauntered into the room. "You okay? Or have you been forced to mash your own hops?"

Yanking out two more beers, she shot him a look, trying to dredge up some anger at him. He was a jerk! He'd broken her young heart! On the way out of town he'd warned other guys off! Not that the warning had completely worked, obviously, but still!

But still…

He'd left when things were wonderful between them because he wanted to take with him beautiful memories.

The idea of it made her bleed.

"Mac…" His expression turned concerned and he approached, taking the beers out of her hands and placing them on the nearby countertop. Then he cupped her face in his palms, tilting it toward him. "What's the matter?"

"I don't know," she said, sounding way too young and uncertain. Mac Walker never sounded uncertain. Mac Walker's soul had aged as old as the mountains when her first love walked away from her so he could go out *on a high.*

She should hate him. Really.

"Don't," Zan murmured. "Don't."

Had she said that out loud?

His mouth lowered toward hers. In a panic, she squirmed out of his hold. "Then you don't do that."

With her back to him and staring out the dark windows into the night, she considered her options. While she had babysitting duty, there was nothing keeping

Zan there. She could insist that he go. With only the one beer, he was fine to drive. But that would leave her with that raw feeling. And that imbalance of power between them.

"What about you?" she said, turning to swipe up a cold bottle and handing it to him along with the opener.

"What about me, what?"

"Give me something. I told you about Josh and Adam and Jeff."

Smirking, he handed her the open beer, reached for the other. "I've never been engaged to one dude, let alone three."

"Hardy-har-har." She slugged back the cold brew, then narrowed her eyes at him. "A regret. Tell me one of yours."

He took his own long pull, tipping back his head so she couldn't help but admire the strong column of his throat. She wanted to bite it.

Once he'd swallowed, he still didn't answer her. Mac pursed her lips, tapped a toe. "Hello? A regret?"

He appeared to consider as he took another swallow of his beer. Then he eyed the half-empty bottle. "That I didn't eat something before coming over here tonight."

She rolled her eyes. "Nice try at deflection."

But then his stomach rumbled. Loudly.

"Oh, for goodness' sake." She sat her beer on the counter and pulled open the refrigerator door again. Not that she was giving up on getting what she wanted from him—it was just that everybody knew a hungry man was even less likely to share than a sated one. "What sounds good?"

"You cook now, Mac?"

"It's too expensive to eat out all the time. Do you

feel like an omelet?" She opened a produce bin. "Poppy has some cold baked potatoes. I can make you my famous Spuds à la Mackenzie."

"I'm willing."

"You say that as if it could be a sacrifice." She began pulling items out of the refrigerator. "I've come a long way from the days when my only culinary achievement was chocolate chip cookies."

"You've changed," Zan said.

Mac glanced over her shoulder at him. "Of course I've changed. It's been ten years."

He was frowning at his bottle of beer. "I'm not sure I have."

"Yeah? Well, you're a man. Your gender matures much more slowly."

He laughed. "So prickly, Mac. That's new, too."

"Let's get back to you," she said, arranging the potatoes, onion, bell pepper and avocado on the cutting board. "While I'm preparing to appease your hunger, I'm still waiting on a regret."

"My grandfather."

Whoa. She kept her attention on the knife and the cubes of potato she was creating. "What about your grandfather?"

"I saw him on occasion over the last ten years. But I wish then…and when I lived here in the mountains, that I'd been more…appreciative."

"Because he took you in?"

"Yes, that, and because I now see how that must have been difficult to suddenly have a kid thrust upon you when you're in your senior years."

"I only saw him around town on the rare occasion,"

Mac said, while on the cutting board she tossed together the onion, potato and bell pepper.

"He kept to himself. He liked a quiet, orderly life."

"Good thing you kept the Walkers out of his house, then."

Zan laughed again. "Yeah. Granddad was from a different generation. Men didn't have much hands-on contact with kids. Children should be seen and not heard. That kind of thing."

"Yikes," Mac said, distributing the food between two microwave-safe bowls and covering the chopped pieces with grated cheddar cheese. "Whoops. Almost forgot the bacon."

"There's bacon with that?" He sounded overjoyed.

Curse her for finding it cute.

"Yep. Crumbled on top. When they're out of the microwave, I'll top the bowls with slices of avocado."

"I love you, Mac," he said, his tone fervent.

She froze. Just for a second. Then she forced herself to move again. "You must be starving."

"No kidding. And I'm watching like a hawk to see how you make Spuds à la Mackenzie. I hope it's not a secret recipe."

And she hoped he hadn't seen her reaction to the *L* word, she thought, popping the bowls into the microwave. "It's nothing special, and you're welcome to it. You can make it for your kids someday. Wow them with what yummy goodness Dad can whip up." It all came out before she realized it might sound as if she was fishing.

Okay, so she was fishing.

"No, Mac," Zan said quietly. "I'm no family man."

"You were great with Mason." The words tumbled

free, again without her permission. "He's a good judge of character." Why was she wanting to argue with Zan about that?

"That's one little kid a couple of times. A full-time father? I wouldn't know the first thing. I don't remember much about my dad—how would I go about being one?"

The microwave dinged, giving Mac something to do besides gape at him. She brought out the steaming bowls full of cheesy-potato-bacon goodness and topped them with the avocado. Then she placed them on the bar, indicated that Zan should sit.

He dug in once she handed him a fork and a napkin.

Maybe he'd hate the thrown-together snack so that she could begin building up an animosity toward him that would turn her right side out or at least toughen her tender skin. Glancing at him out of the corner of her eye, her mind floated away from that thought as she marveled at the fact it was Zan beside her again. Zan, with his breathtaking face. Zan, whose big hands and long fingers had run all over her body the other night, causing her senses to riot, causing pleasure to break out all over her like a raging fever. The orgasm had been—

"Best I've ever had, Mackenzie Marie."

She started. "W-what?"

"Best spuds I've ever eaten."

A laugh erupted from her and it sounded a lot breathless and a little bit hysterical.

He turned his head to look at her. "Are you all right?"

"Sure." She poked a piece of cheesy potato with her fork and tried desperately to remember where their conversation had left off. "The, uh, family thing. You really never considered going there with anyone in the last ten years?"

Her swift glance at him didn't tell her anything except he was serious about her food, so she found herself pressing further. "Not even with, um, Simone?"

Fork midway to his mouth, Zan sent her a questioning look. "Now, why would you bring her up?"

Yeah, Mac, why would you bring her up? She shrugged. "I don't know." *Because I can't forget you calling her name in the night. Because I'm insanely, irrationally jealous of some dead woman because you thought of her instead of me in your sleep.*

Yep, insane and irrational. *Get a grip, Mac.* This was the guy who walked away only to send her crumbs for ten years, crumbs in the form of 117 postcards that meant she could never wholly forget about him.

That was a stinkin' low move, no two ways around it.

So she chewed, stewing on that in silence. Nursing her resentment, a safe emotion for a woman to feel for the man who was never planning to stay.

His offer to do the dishes once they'd consumed the food didn't alleviate her welcome rancor toward him. In more silence, she helped him take the dishes to the sink and watched him push up the sleeves of his thermal—trying not to notice the corded strength of his forearms—then squirt liquid into a bowl and commence the cleanup.

As much as she found it surprising that he could do dishes, she didn't say a word about it. The process wasn't rocket science. It didn't make him special.

Except that feeling was creeping into her as he

handed her the washed plates and cutlery to dry. She should have told him to put the items into the dishwasher, she thought. But instead they were standing together at the sink, as a team, taking care of domestic business.

And thoughts began winding themselves in her head again, unbidden thoughts. Unsafe thoughts. *This could have been my life. This could have been us, together. With a kid, kids, sleeping just a hall away.*

Mac and Zan.

A legend.

Her hand holding the dish towel was going around and around the inside of a bowl as she was lost in those painful impossibilities.

"Hey, Mac."

She came back to the present, her gaze shifting to Zan.

"LaToya got your tongue?" he asked. Then, when she blinked, he smiled. "Cat, baby. LaToya? Cat?"

Her good sense was hijacked by that smile, the humor in his eyes, the muscled length of him so close to her. She thought of going on tiptoe and kissing that smile right off his face, to see if it would transfer to her own. She thought of sliding her hand under his thermal at the small of his back to feel the heat of his sleek skin. She thought of him backing her into the counter and surrounding her with his scent and everything else that was Zan.

"I think you should do something to really annoy me right now," she told him.

His smile widened into a grin. "Is that so?"

Even remembering those 117 postcards, she wanted to once again be in his arms.

"This is bad," she said, serious.

He lost the grin. "Mac—"

"Just finish the dishes." She half turned away from him. "Please."

For another long minute he didn't move, and then he reached into the soapy water. "Fuck!" He yanked his hand from the suds.

Blood dripped from his fingers. "What did you do?" she cried.

"Cut my hand on the knife. It's no big deal." He fumbled for a paper towel.

Mac ripped a couple off for him, passed them over, then headed for the bathroom. "I'll get the first-aid kit."

"It's okay," he called after her. "No big deal."

She returned with antiseptic and elastic bandages to find Zan staring down at his bleeding hand. The tension she could feel coming off his body didn't make sense. Blood didn't bother him. She'd seen him with much worse wounds than that one.

Unsure what to make of it, she briskly went about squeezing the antiseptic on the cuts and then covering them. "Do you need a sucker, young man?" she asked, as she gathered up the towels and wrappings to throw away. "You were a very good patient."

When he didn't say anything, she glanced at him over her shoulder. "Shall Nurse pull your emergency contact card to find someone to drive you home?"

His head shot up and she went still, struck by his anguished expression. "What is it?"

"It doesn't matter," he muttered.

"Come on," she prodded. "What's bothering you?"

"It's just… It's just the emergency contact thing." He pushed his uninjured hand through his hair. "I was just remembering… Simone didn't have one. After the accident, we tried to find a family member or a friend to notify. But there wasn't any name listed on her employment records. There wasn't any contacts outside the documentary crew on her phone or on her laptop."

"She was all alone in the world." Mac's belly hollowed. And then ice gathered in that empty space. "What about you? Who is your emergency person? Who is on your contact line?"

When he hesitated, the cold in her center washed over her entire body, followed quickly by a flash of fire. She stepped close. "You put my name there, Zan Elliott," she demanded, knowing she could never truly hate him. He'd been her first love. "For the rest of your life, you put my name on that line."

CHAPTER FOURTEEN

ZAN PUSHED OPEN the door to the small office he'd located by means of his smartphone. He had a vague awareness of colored renditions of home landscapes on the walls, a pair of filing cabinets and a table covered in papers. But the woman behind the desk consumed most of his attention.

He grinned at Angelica Walker. "You really are ridiculously beautiful." Her coloring was warm and exotic, her features in perfect symmetry, but Zan decided it was her air of happiness that cinched the deal.

She reminded him of Poppy in that way. All sunshine and soft-furred puppies. By contrast, Mac was a cool mountain creek edged in snow, with unexpected deep pools and shallows that still held mystery.

Angelica smiled back at him. "That's a lovely compliment for a winter afternoon. What can I do for you?"

He hesitated. "Is Brett around?"

The man in question came through a rear door that likely led to some kind of storeroom. He wore a flannel shirt and a pair of jeans. "Yes. And I heard you flirting with my wife."

Zan held up his hands. "Harmless, I promise."

"What did you want?"

Angelica shot her husband a disapproving look.

"That's not very friendly." She sent Zan another smile. "We have coffee in the back. Would you like some?"

"No, no." He glanced around, taking a longer look at the framed drawings of distinctive homes surrounded by trees, shrubbery and flowers. "These are really good."

"Brett's work," Angelica said, getting close enough to link her arm through her husband's.

"Your idea to frame them." He brushed a kiss to her forehead. Then he addressed Zan again. "She's also tackling my paperwork mess on her afternoons off, praise be. I can't deny I inherited my father's lack of organization in that area."

Zan hid his inner wince. Talk of the Walker dad reminded him of the promise he'd made to Mac—though staying quiet about the cabin property he'd inherited continued to bother him. The only thing that kept his mouth shut was his knowledge that it wouldn't be for much longer. "I didn't stop by to take up your time."

"You stopped by to…" Brett prompted.

Zan was restless and his crappy mood didn't help. This much inactivity gave him too much time to think. "I thought maybe you could direct me to a good local gym. I'm in need of a tough workout."

Brett's eyebrows rose. "Yeah? You want to do that workout indoors?"

"There's an alternative you'd suggest?"

The other man glanced at his wife, who gave him a nod. "I was thinking," Brett said, "about a workout on one of the local mountains."

"I don't know—"

"Afraid I'll best your ass on a board as usual?"

"You'd go?" Zan asked, surprised.

"I could use a run or two or three."

Zan glanced down at what he was wearing. "I have a jacket, gloves and hat in the car, but I'm in jeans."

"So you're planning on falling?"

"Asshole," Zan said, grinning. "About equipment—"

"We'll rent what you need."

"And you'll come back for dinner at our house," Angelica put in. She glanced up at her husband. "Have fun."

Brett's gaze softened. "Thanks, sweetheart." Then his head dipped to give her a thorough kiss on the mouth. "There you go."

Angelica blushed, then slid Zan a look. "I read somewhere that a man who always kisses his wife goodbye improves his life span by five years."

Brett was smiling. "She's always looking out for me."

A team, Zan thought, as he followed his old friend out to his SUV. Not just a couple, but a team.

Something heavy moved into his gut and he supposed it was envy.

The afternoon on the slopes was the tough workout he'd requested...and the exercise nearly killed him, in a good way. The last time he'd played on snow had been long ago—and somewhere in the Alps if he recalled correctly—and his screaming thigh muscles let him know all about it.

But the pain was countered by exhilaration, and as he stood at the top of one run and looked down over the wide white highway before him, he felt as if he could fly for miles. Take off on snow and then soar over the pines that looked sugar-dipped, passing above suburbs and city only to land on soft golden sand beside the Pacific, surprising some flatland beach bunny.

Southern California had everything.

"Great, huh?" Brett said, pausing beside him.

"Yeah."

"Had enough? Good food's waiting at my place."

The only thing that sounded better than breathing in more clean cold air was doing something about the hunger gnawing at his belly. But Zan glanced at his old buddy and hesitated, his mountain high deflating. They weren't exactly on friendly terms. "Are you sure you want me there?"

"I'll hear it from my wife if I show up without you."

Not exactly an enthusiastic welcome, but the idea of returning to his grandfather's house alone didn't appeal at all.

"We have to make a stop first, then," he said to Brett. "I can't show up on your doorstep without flowers and a bottle of wine for Angelica."

Brett smirked. "Such good manners."

"I have hopes I'll convince her to run off with me."

"Your ego always was outsize," Brett said, then took off downhill, leaving Zan smiling behind him.

Damn, he'd missed that kind of trash talk.

His smile died. He'd missed that friendship.

If Brett still held some reserve toward Zan, during dinner his wife made up for it with her bright smile, easy chatter and excellent meal of meatloaf and mashed potatoes. She managed Hallett Hardware in the village and seemed to have a close acquaintance with everyone in the area. By the time dinner was over, Zan almost imagined he'd never left the place.

He'd learned about illnesses, changes in occupation

and the intimate relationships of a host of people he'd forgotten he knew. His head was reeling by the time he and Brett had walked the dishes to the kitchen counter and Angelica shooed the men back to the family room, where she'd serve dessert.

"She loves it here," Zan said to Brett.

"No doubt. She didn't have anyone in her corner for years. Now..."

Zan thought of his nine-year-old self. "Walkers came to the rescue?"

"We found out she was living out of her car." Brett shook his head at the memory. "I made sure she had a real roof over her head. Mac gave her some hours to tide her through until she was needed full-time at the hardware store."

"The Walkers came to the rescue."

"In reality, she rescued me," Brett said. "I was stuck in my head, letting the past keep me from a future."

Troubled by the confession, Zan prowled the room. One wall was filled with framed family photos. At the center was Angelica and Brett in an obvious wedding shot; though the bride and groom were in jeans, she held a huge bouquet of flowers and there were new rings on their left hands.

"Vegas wedding," Brett said, coming up beside him. "I couldn't wait and she was willing."

Surrounding that shot were many framed Walker family moments. Their parents, Dell and Lorna Walker, mugged for the camera, smiling faces close together. Zan could see some of their children in both their features.

"Your mom and dad were great people," he murmured.

"Yeah. Not perfect, and neither was their relationship, but I think they taught us not to let go or give up on each other." He paused. "Or other people."

Without comment, Zan moved to stand in front of yet another photo. It was recent and showed the four Walker siblings, arms slung around each other, at the reception in honor of Brett and Angelica's marriage. A solid group, yet another team, their confident smiles saying "We have the whole world because we have one another."

They'd been so easy to care about from the very beginning.

So fucking hard to lose.

And then he heard himself telling Brett about another loss. "I had a sister, you know. Jana. She was five years older and taught me how to jump rope."

The atmosphere in the room changed. Zan didn't turn to look at the other man, but he could feel Brett's sharp gaze on the back of his neck.

Zan rubbed his palm there, aware he'd never talked about this stuff with the other man—even when they were kids. They'd known his family was dead, but not any further details. "I also had a brother."

"You had a brother," Brett repeated.

"Yeah. His name was Damon. I called him Dragon, for some reason I don't remember. He was three years older than me."

Zan closed his eyes but couldn't dredge up his sister's or his brother's faces. There were photos in the album back at his grandfather's that would help him remember, he supposed, but he couldn't bring himself to look through those pages. They would take him back to the sharp pain of his parents' and his siblings' deaths. Of the bewilderment he'd felt, of the sense of being untethered from everything and anyone.

He'd felt as if he was facing a long, dark tunnel.

The first light he'd glimpsed was the day Brett Walker spoke to him after school.

"Cool nickname," Brett said now. "Dragon. I bet he loved that."

Zan's brows rose. "Yeah. You're right. Cool." It almost made him smile. "So, thinking on that—" he gestured toward the photos "—you've got it all. Right there."

"It's missing someone, that wall," Brett said slowly, then hesitated. "I once had a brother, too."

Surprised, Zan turned. This was the first he'd heard of it. "I didn't know."

"Yes, you did," Brett said.

When Zan continued to just stare, the other man crossed his arms over his chest. "Damn it, dumbshit. I'm talking about you."

"I…" He had no idea what to say.

"Yeah." Brett nodded. "Think on *that*. I could have used my brother more than once over the last ten years."

When Brett lost his mom. When he'd gotten mired in events that prevented him from moving on from the past, whatever those events were. Maybe when Zan's own cousin was causing trouble for his friend and the woman he loved.

Fuck. Fuck. *Fuck.* When he'd left, he'd let his oldest friend down. The one who'd considered him a *brother.*

His mood, temporarily lifted by those hours on the mountain and the good food at Angelica and Brett's table took a sharp nosedive. He scrubbed his hands over his face. When planning to get out of the mountains those many years ago, all thoughts had been about himself and about getting away. He'd considered very little what his absence would do to those he left behind.

His focus had been on protecting himself. He'd not foreseen how in doing so he neglected those who'd considered him part of their family. Those who'd helped him get through the agony of extreme grief.

Selfish asshole.

Go now, he told himself. *Get the hell out of this cozy house. Get gone to some other place on some other continent where no one gives a shit about who you are. Travel light and loose, making sure that you don't get attached to anyone and they don't get attached to you. Where you won't mess up again.*

Then Mac's voice came into his head, unbidden, talking about being his emergency contact. *For the rest of your life, you put my name on that line.*

His chest filled with cement.

"Shit," Brett said now, sounding disgusted. "Angelica will kill me if I make you cry."

"I'm not going to—" The glint of humor in the other man's eyes made him pause, then lightened the dense weight encasing his lungs. "Shut your ugly mug."

"Prettier than yours."

"You wish," Zan said automatically, then scrubbed his face again. "Hell, Brett. What can I say? I'm sorry. I'm so sorry."

The other man held his gaze a long moment, then sighed. "Lucky for you, I'm lousy at holding a grudge."

"Yeah?"

"Yeah." Brett reached out. "And I learned that lesson about not letting go or giving up."

Zan gripped his friend's hand, squeezing. Messages

were sent along that connection in a silent language forged in boyhood and tempered by the hard-earned wisdom of adult mistakes.

Angelica came into the room, bearing a tray of chocolate cake slices and cups of coffee. "Is everything okay here?" she asked, looking between the two men.

"We're good, sweetheart," Brett assured her, moving forward to take her burden. "All good."

Zan nodded in agreement. Maybe the best he'd been since his return.

ZAN SUSPECTED BRETT had passed a word around the Walkers about their reconciliation, because the very next day he was texted an invitation—which came off more like a summons—from Shay's stepdaughter, London. The family was getting together at Shay and Jace's to prepare a welcome home for the honeymooning couple. Zan didn't even pretend to himself he wasn't damn happy to be included. His old friend had offered absolution, and he was going to prove he deserved it during the time he remained at Blue Arrow Lake.

As for the future…he wasn't contemplating that just yet. His only goal was to keep—and enjoy—this current peace.

He found himself on a ladder stringing up a banner in the foyer of the house that was built along the lines of a steamship. "This place is…different," he murmured for Brett's ears only.

"Jace bought it sight unseen, and he and Shay both thought it butt-ugly at first. Now they say it's grown on them."

The lake views were spectacular, Zan would give them that. And the teenager London brightened the place with her excited chatter and bouncy energy. She'd been staying with a friend while her parents were gone and clearly she was looking forward to their return.

Zan was ordered to bring in groceries from Poppy's car that she'd bought to stock the fridge. He mock-saluted her, then opened the door to the garage, only to find Mac standing there, juggling an armful of market totes.

They stared at each other.

He'd been avoiding her since that night they'd traded regrets. To earn her eternal gratitude, when she arrived to work at his grandfather's house, he would leave and only return once she was gone.

The words she'd said in her sister's kitchen were in an endless loop in his mind. *I think you should do something to really annoy me.* It was because of that attraction, he knew, the chemistry that burned and spit like solar flares whenever they were together.

She scowled at him now. "What are you doing here?"

So much for eternal gratitude.

Still he stepped forward. "Let me take those from you," he said, reaching for the groceries.

"I've got them," she said, as she made to step around him.

But she misjudged the distance or her hold on the bags was tenuous, because just as she moved past his body her elbow brushed his arm and all the groceries came crashing down, cans rolling, chip bags scattering, oranges and apples taking off for parts unknown. She stared at the mess, her expression so crestfallen it looked as if she'd lost her pet kitten.

"Mac." Zan touched her back, and she jerked away from him, kneeling to gather the items again.

He mirrored her movements.

"I've got this," she mumbled.

"Are you okay?"

"Just peachy." She glanced up at him. "I didn't expect to see you today."

"London somehow got my number. I was invited to the welcome party." He hesitated. "Would you rather I leave?"

She shrugged a shoulder and tossed a stack of bagels into a bag. "Do what you like. I can't stay long, anyway. Big date later."

That set him back on his heels. Literally. Stupid, really, that the news would bother him so. "Anyone I know?" he asked, hoping it sounded polite instead of prying.

"No," she said.

He winced. It must have sounded as if he was prying. "Well, you look very nice," he said, taking in her outfit as she rose to her feet. She wore a sweater and a short skirt. Patterned tights covered her legs until meeting her ankle-length boots. Some guy was going to be happy to be out with her that night.

Some other guy.

"Thank you," she said, stepping close to swipe up an orange that had rolled near his foot.

He caught her wrist before she could move away.

"What?" Her frosty blue eyes widened.

"What" was that he couldn't help but play with fire. Without letting go of her, he got to his feet. He could smell her perfume now, a fragrance that she'd stroked or sprayed onto her skin for *some other guy.*

"Look nice. Smell nice," he muttered, then bent his head, getting his mouth close to hers.

She didn't jolt away this time. Instead, her gaze stayed glued to his. "I…" He saw her swallow. "What's this about?"

Jealousy, maybe. Need. Possession. Or perhaps it was something less tempestuous, just the desire to make peace with her, the last Walker who carried a chip on her shoulder when it came to him.

Yeah, as if making peace with Mac would include kissing the hell out of her.

"I thought we decided," she said, a thread of uncertainty in her voice.

"You decided," he countered. "While I—"

"Hey, Zan." Brett came around the corner, catching his hand on the wall to stop his movement as he caught sight of them close together. "Oh, shit," he said, eyes moving from one to the other.

Zan instantly released Mac's wrist.

She stepped back. "'Oh, shit' is right," she said, gesturing toward the remainder of the spilled groceries. "Come help pick these up, would you?"

When Brett bent to grab a couple of cans, Zan mumbled some excuse and made himself scarce. He supposed the other man's forgiveness wouldn't extend to being thrilled Zan was starting something up with Mac again when his intentions weren't the least bit honorable…or lasting.

His attendance at the event wasn't lasting, either—he didn't stay much beyond the moment the happy honeymooners arrived home.

His next chance to bask in the family's company arrived the following evening, when Poppy asked him to her place. The first time Brett had brought Zan home to the Walkers, their big brother referred to Poppy and Shay as the "ankle biters." But the little girls had smiled and charmed their way into his affections, and he'd always gone marshmallow around Poppy in particular. From an early age, that girl's sunniness had been beyond engaging.

When a beaming Poppy ushered him in he thanked her for the invitation.

Her expression turned serious. "We all missed you, Zan. A lot." Then she put her hand on his sleeve. "Did you know Ryan lost a son?"

He nodded. "I did. It was tragic."

"My lesson from that is not to take for granted having the people I love in my life. I try to enjoy every moment they're with me." Her smile returned. "So now I'm enjoying you."

He thought of how he'd left this wise soul and the rest of her family behind. His chest ached. "Pop…"

"And maybe I have an ulterior motive, too," she said, smile turning to a grin. Rubbing her palms together, she winked at him. "A master plan."

He frowned in mild alarm. *"Pop..."* But she was already dashing farther into the house, forcing him to follow behind.

In the kitchen, Shay, London and Angelica sat at the kitchen table surrounded by twine and pieces of tagboard and tiny bottles of sand lined up like soldiers. They smiled and waved.

Their pleasure at seeing him wrapped him like a hug. *I might not deserve this*, he thought, *but I'm taking it, anyway.*

"We're making place cards for the reception," Poppy explained.

"Is this part of your master plan? I'm not very crafty," he warned.

She wouldn't meet his gaze. "The master plan is something else altogether. Tonight your job is Mason-wrangler."

On cue, the boy came racing into the kitchen in his stocking feet. He slid the last bit of distance, causing Zan to catch him by the shoulders to prevent a tackle. "Zan!"

"Mace!" he echoed, in the same enthused tone. "What's up?"

"Duke's down the hill for the night, so Mom promised you'd play cards with me."

Now Poppy gave Zan hopeful eyes. "Please?"

A goner, he tugged on the ends of her hair. "If I can line up a single lady or two, is strip poker okay?"

"Don't be bad," she said, pushing at his chest just as Mac strolled into the room.

Her jeans were tight, her long-sleeved V-neck T-shirt clung to her curves. The color of the thin material, something between cotton candy and berry, matched her lush mouth.

He wanted a taste of it. Desperately.

Don't be bad. At the echo of those words in his head, he felt a gaze on him and glanced over to see Poppy watching him with satisfaction in her gaze.

He frowned again, but then Mason's voice drew his attention away.

"Auntie Mac's a single lady," the boy said, indicating the new arrival.

Her brows came together. "Uh, yeah. What's this about?"

"A new card game. You wanna play strap poker with me 'n' Zan?"

"*Strip* poker," Shay corrected.

"Strip poker," Mason repeated, obligingly.

Mac lifted both hands, pointing one index finger at Poppy and one at Zan. "Handle this," she ordered, then flounced over to the table and took a free chair.

Zan shot another look at Poppy, then slung an arm around the boy's neck. "Let's go talk appropriate card games in the other room."

Zan would be better off away from the temptation that was Mac, that was sure. *Keep the peace*, he reminded himself. *Keep away from Mac.*

If he got her alone, he'd likely do inappropriate things like demand to know about her date. How it ended. If she'd stripped.

Shit.

Keeping his distance meant keeping Mason entertained with card games, then a kid version of dominoes, and then they played another game that involved dismantling a tower of wooden blocks. "You Walkers," Zan said in disgust when his latest movement caused the whole thing to come tumbling down. "Your uncle Brett beat me at this every time, too."

Mason grinned, looking so much like his mother that Zan just had to ruffle his hair. "Good going, kid."

"Let's play ag—"

"Nope," Poppy said, poking her head into the room. "It's time for Mason to go to bed and Zan to have a well-deserved beer."

He didn't protest, though Mason did. It took a few

minutes to get the kid up the stairs, and then Zan was fridge-bound. In the kitchen, he didn't see Mac with the others, and he told himself it was just as well that she'd slipped away before he was free.

Yeah, since he was still picturing all the ways her date could have ended, it was better for her to be gone if he wasn't going to jeopardize his standing with the Walker clan.

Beer in hand, he was directed by Shay to find himself some chips in the separate pantry around the corner. It was a tidy room, holding shelves of foodstuffs… and Mac.

She whirled when he walked in. He could see she'd just stowed a box of finished place cards in an open space. Inhaling a breath, he took in a hint of her perfume and his chest tightened.

Her tongue came out to lick her lips.

Zan took another step closer.

"These place cards," she said, talking as if that might keep him from her. "I told Poppy to pay a professional to make the damn things. Ryan couldn't care less about the expense. But she keeps saying she wants their event to have a personal touch and I keep saying not one guest is going to give a hoot whether we tied that stupid twine or someone else did."

"Give a hoot?" he questioned, when the toes of his boots were an inch away from the toes of her sneakers.

"It's an expression," she said, hunching her shoulders and then tucking her hands under her arms as if to make herself smaller…or to stop herself from touching him.

Because her eyes were eating him up.

Their chemistry sizzled and hissed.

Or maybe that was Mac.

Still, Zan set his beer on the shelf above her head.

Mac's eyes were their usual frosty blue, but her body was hot. He could feel her heat reaching out to him. He could see the flush on her cheeks and the rapid beat of her pulse in her throat.

"Mac…" he began, thinking of how to ask this. *How was your date? How did it end? Did you strip?*

And then he said none of those things, because he went completely nonverbal as his mouth slammed down on hers.

She instantly moved in, going on tiptoe to make the fit tighter. Deeper. Better. Her hands moved to grip the sides of his shirt.

He slid his hand around her waist, then down to her ass, tilting it to bring her belly against the jut of his hardening sex. Then, with her pressed tight to him, he slid his fingertips beneath the low-slung waist of her jeans to cup his palm over one round cheek.

She moaned against his tongue.

"Hey, Mac," London yelled from the other room, not more than four feet away.

Zan froze as Mac went stiff in his arms. *Fuck.*

"Where'd you hide the scissors?"

The moment was lost. The mood broken. Mac tore out of his arms, sent him an unreadable look, then rushed away. "Coming," she called.

Releasing his frustration, he breathed out a sigh of relief instead. To keep in Walker good graces meant keeping things cool with Mac.

A vow that was challenged again a few days later when he made his way to Walker mountain to join the family. It had snowed the day before, the flakes drifting down slow and thick like winter fairies parachuting from the sky. The Walkers, en masse, were planning on an afternoon of snow play, using one of the cabins for rest and warm-up. To Zan, who'd been knocking around a huge house that felt emptier than his heart, the invitation was impossible to refuse.

Second thoughts settled in when he got there to find the group in a spirited discussion about the future of their property. Voices were excited. Poppy bragged about the website she'd been working on with the help of a friend and teenager London.

Damn. He was really beginning to hate keeping that secret. He'd been thinking on it, trying to come up with ways to handle the situation that would appease Mac as well as himself. As soon as she gave him the go-ahead, he was going to present the papers and facts to Brett and the others and together they'd find a solution.

But in the meantime he'd made that promise to the girl with the dark hair and frosty eyes...

Inside the cozy bungalow where a fire was blazing, Zan's gaze sought Mac. But her attention was directed out the window and when he strolled toward her—maybe he could persuade her to tell all now—she zipped up her jacket and stepped outside. By the time he reached the porch she was already trudging up the hill with Mason, a sled under her arm.

Avoiding him.

Which she did the rest of the afternoon—and he told himself he was glad about it—slipping away to the snow or back into the cottage whenever he appeared anywhere nearby. Despite the secret he was really getting antsy about keeping, he ended up having a good time during the moments he could forget his subterfuge.

The snow was powdery. The selection of food and drink they laid out delicious and designed to take out the chill. He almost felt like a kid again when he captained one snow war team and Jace the other. Years of experience with the Walkers let him know the best picks for his team. Shay had a trick for packing a mean snowball. Poppy's sweet disposition made the opposing team members feel like bullies if they picked on her, so she went about her business virtually unscathed. He took a chance on Ryan, and London turned out to be both stealthy and ruthless.

It might have been years since he laughed so hard when the whole lot of them turned on Brett at the same time and buried him in snowballs.

But as everyone began piling into cars to head home, he finally gave in to the clamor inside him and managed to corral one certain unsuspecting Walker. As she headed out the door toward her vehicle, he caught her by the back of her hood and towed her inside the cabin. Though the fire was almost out, the interior remained warm. With his foot, he shut them in.

"Someone will see!" she hissed.

"They're leaving. I told Poppy you and I would lock up."

"They'll...they'll *think* something!"

"They'll be wrong unless they think we're going to be discussing telling the truth." That was all he was after, he promised himself. Didn't it weigh on her as much as it did him?

"We shouldn't be alone together," Mac insisted. "We

don't want anyone imagining Zan and Mac as a couple again."

"But this isn't about Zan and Mac. This is about Zan and Mac and being honest."

"Not right now—"

"Don't you think the sooner the better? Then we can put our heads together and come up with something acceptable to all."

"There isn't anything acceptable beyond accepting the situation, don't you get that?"

He put his hands on her shoulders. "I could—"

"No." Her body was rigid in his grip. "We *can't* take from you. We *won't* take from you."

He rolled his eyes skyward. "Mac, don't you see I took from all of you for years? You were my friends and as close to family as I had."

"We don't expect payback." Her color was high and her eyes burned with icy fire. "Please tell me you get that."

Letting her go, he ran his fingers through his hair. "Why are you so damn stubborn?"

She turned her back on him and made for the fireplace. Staring into the burning embers, she braced one hand on the mantel. "Brett is settled now. Shay secure with Jace and London. Please let me make sure Poppy has the day of her dreams before you do anything to shake up what she sees as her future."

"What is this?" Zan said, coming up behind her. "I've never seen this mama bear side of you."

"In the years you've been gone, I've become the head female in this family," she said, her voice quiet.

Oh, Mac. Was that some of the reason she'd been engaged three times? Her effort to ensure the stability of the family? “Poppy’s stronger than you think,” he said, even as he thought, *And you’re more vulnerable than I knew.*

“Something’s off with her, I can tell,” Mac said. “She looks tired. And I…”

“You…what?”

“I can’t have anything endangering her happiness. At least not until she’s safely committed in marriage to Ryan and sheltered in his arms.”

Who is there to shelter you, Mac? With all the Walker siblings paired off, who was going to be her buffer against the cold? “Mac…” Zan took hold of her shoulders again, but he lost the thread of his thoughts when she looked up into his face, her eyes big, her expression anxious.

“Please, Zan.”

“Sweetheart.” Tightening his grip, he lowered his forehead to hers, no longer concerned with keeping distance. “What’s going on with you?”

“I think… I think Poppy holds all my hope. I think if we can keep her buoyant and bright, then I might eventually be that way, too.”

He closed his eyes. “There’s honesty for you,” he muttered. The killing kind, because he wanted buoyancy and brightness for Mac, too. She used to be so assured, so easy with herself. And sometime in the past ten years she’d taken on the weight of the world—and built up a thick armor to help her hold it steady.

“What am I going to do with you?” he asked, opening his eyes.

She hesitated a long moment. Then her mouth opened. “Hold me?” she whispered. “For just a minute, can you hold me?”

Oh, Mac. No scruple could hold strong against that request. Drawing her close, he pressed his face to her hair. It smelled of snow and smoke and this winter interlude that he'd never forget. Her arms went around him and she fit her body to his.

His cock hardened, even though he told it not to, and then she pushed her face into his neck and breathed him in and there was no hope to stem his sexual reaction. No hope in the universe, when she pressed an openmouthed kiss there.

"Mac." He groaned her name. "You've got to feel what you're doing to me."

"I *want* to do it to you." Her body trembled against his. "I want to do it *with* you."

She was willing to be honest about this, at least.

"Yeah?" He brought his lips to her ear and drew her more tightly against him so he could feel her every breath. "Right now? Right here? Are we going to do it in the cabin?"

Because, God, he was no longer capable of holding out.

"You're so easy," she murmured in a teasing voice that might have been forced, and then she kissed him again, running her mouth along his jaw. "Do we need to discuss this? Have some rationale? Give it a name—"

"Not sex buddies," he said, vehement about it.

"Not sex buddies," she agreed. "For old times' sake, then?"

Zan held her away a little, just so he could look into her eyes. "Not for the sake of old times, sweetheart. But because this Mac, the present you, is beautiful and complicated and a smart-ass and… Oh, screw it. I just want to fuck you."

Her laugh rang out, natural and easy like the girl she used to be. But the look in her eyes was mature and sultry and his dick went impossibly hard. He slid one hand into her hair at the back of her head and let the other follow the line of her spine until he breached the waistband of her jeans. There, he didn't hesitate to slide below it so he cupped her fine ass.

"God, you feel good," he said, and took her mouth.

Consumed her with his kiss. He sunk his tongue deep inside and hers tangled with him there, her hands exploring, too, one under his flannel shirt at his back, the other crawling up his belly. His muscles twitched beneath her touch—then he took her down to the rug beside the hearth.

Mac lay on her back and he ranged over her, elbows on either side of her face. Her cheeks were flushed, her mouth already reddened by his kiss.

"We have a hell of a lot of clothes on," he said.

She nodded. "Layers."

"Socks and boots. Long underwear."

"I still have on my jacket."

Then he smiled at her. Slow. "I've got an idea. We'll race. First one naked gets—"

She already had pushed him over and was throwing off her clothes.

He had to laugh until his fingers were tangled in the laces of his snow boots. Then he was cursing and she was laughing, and then she was nude and Zan gave up on his shoes and just stared at her in the orange and gold light from the fire's dying embers.

He pulled her into his lap and began kissing her again, and it was unbelievable, all her soft, warm skin available to his touch after days of keeping his distance.

Bending his head, he sucked in one of her nipples, deep, and she made a hungry sound and arched her back, pushing it farther into his mouth.

He thought the top of his head might blow.

The top of the other head, too, as she wiggled against the denim covering his dick. "I can't get enough of you," he said, moving his mouth to her other breast. Cupping it, he fed it between his lips. Mac arched again, and he ran his free hand between her legs until he found her slick folds.

He glided into her wet inner heat with one finger. Then two.

Her thighs fell apart and he looked down at the pretty pink flesh open for him. Mac, open for him. A special gift, he thought, instinct telling him being this exposed didn't come easy for her.

He inserted another finger in her, working it in slow, and her eyes closed. "I'm not going to be able to do without you," he said.

She made a noise somewhere between a moan and a whimper.

His fingers rotated, scissored, and she caught her lower lip with her teeth. "You hear me, baby?"

The sound she made was an affirmative one, then its note squeaked high as he dived deeper inside her. "Oh, God," she whispered.

Oh, God, he thought, *beautiful*. With his thumb he found her clit and she jerked in his arms at the first touch. "Yeah, not able to do without you," he said.

Her head dropped back as he circled the bundle of nerves and started thrusting inside her in a careful rhythm. Her inner muscles clamped hard on his fingers and beneath his flannel, a drop of sweat rolled down his spine.

"While I'm here, baby, you're in my bed." It wasn't smart, it wouldn't keep the peace, it went against the inner voice shouting warnings at him. He didn't care.

"What?" She buried her head into the side of his throat. Took hold of his skin with her teeth.

Christ, he was going to come in his jeans.

He grit his teeth, holding off the climax. "My bed. You. Me."

When she didn't reply, he pulled his hand free of her. They both groaned. She lifted her head, her gaze hazy, her breathing heavy.

"Mac—"

"Shut up and fuck me, Zan."

"Smart-ass," he said with a laugh, and then he was kissing her, and she was helping him shed his remaining clothes, and when they were both naked she took the condom he handed her and slowly rolled it over him.

He drew in a sharp breath through his teeth, barely holding on as she knelt at his side and slowly worked the latex down his aching shaft. Then she shifted over him and he groaned, falling back, letting her guide him into her wet heat.

Once inside, she dropped to his chest, and he closed her in his arms. Her hips canted up, then down, starting a rhythm that was going to take him there in too short a time. His mouth pressed a kiss at her throat, and he thought again, *Not able to do without you*, as he tightened his hold on her.

But even knowing he might be jeopardizing the peace, even knowing that he must, eventually, do without this luscious, sexy woman, he was able to lose himself and every further thought in the beauty of Mac. In the beauty of being her shelter, if only for this winter moment.

CHAPTER FIFTEEN

THIS IS ME, giving you me.

The moment Tilda said those words to Ash, they changed the course of his life. Well, not strictly true. His course was still the same, but now he was determined to bring a companion alongside him on the journey.

When he went to London, he wanted Tilda to be with him.

He was in love with her, and every sign suggested she felt the same toward him.

Life was good. Life was fucking good when you could see your future in bright relief.

That didn't mean he expected convincing her would be easy. But as he'd always been taught by his dad, he first used his head. After considering what objections she might have, he'd concocted a strategy.

First, he had to open her world.

Then he'd open her mind to what was on his.

As he'd expected, he found her at the local branch of the library. It was a light-filled, airy space, with windows providing spectacular mountain views. Tilda was taking them in, sitting at a long table in front of her laptop, chin in hand.

He took a moment to enjoy his view: the sweet oval of her face framed by her long brown hair, the curve of her brows, the lush bow of her mouth. Certainty washed over him, and he strode forward, eager to get on with this day and the rest of his life.

Her head came up when he was three strides away. She blinked in surprise and held out her hand to him in artless welcome. Grinning, he took hold of her fingers and slid into the chair beside hers.

"What are you doing here?" she whispered.

He kissed her mouth, then pressed another to her warm hair, taking in the scent of her shampoo. It was on her pillowcase at night, on the thin pillow they shared when they were wrapped around each other in sleep. "I couldn't stay away."

A blush turned her cheeks a soft pink. "We've only been apart a few hours."

Enough time for him to arrange their afternoon and enough time for her to study. "Did you get what you wanted done?" Attending an online college one or two courses at a time meant her degree would take her longer than his four years, but it worked perfectly into his plans.

"Well..."

"I saw you staring out the window instead of studying," he said. "So I won't feel guilty in the least for springing you now."

Her brows came together over her small straight nose. "Springing me how? Springing me why?"

"The why is that you work too hard. The how is my secret." He snapped shut her laptop.

"Hey—"

"Don't tell me conscientious Tilda Smith didn't save her work."

Her mouth twitched. "Okay, I saved it."

He grabbed her hand, pulled her to her feet. "We have places to go. Things to do."

"Places to go?"

If only she knew. Without another word, he ushered her into his car. From there, he took off for a mountain town twenty-five minutes away.

"This took some research, but I think I have a new experience for you," he said, pulling into the parking lot adjacent to a three-story cedar-shingled medical building with smoky windows and a sign reading Orthopedic Specialties.

Her expression was curious as he took her by the hand and led her toward the lobby. "Do you have some injury I'm not aware of?"

"Not me, but I think this place is in business thanks to falls while other people are skiing, boarding or climbing."

A reception desk sat front and center. "Hello," a young woman said. "Who are you here to see?"

Ash quickly scanned the board over the woman's head. "Uh…Dr. Szabo."

She nodded. "Third floor. The elevators are to the right."

He considered limping toward them but decided that was overkill. Instead, he led a wide-eyed Tilda in the indicated direction.

"Elevators?" she stage-whispered.

She'd told him, in a recent dark, late-night confession, that she'd never used one. He'd been disbelieving, until she'd pointed out that even the local hospital was one story. And he'd been unable to come up with a single building in the Blue Arrow Lake village that had an obvious need for something other than stairs to a second floor.

Some of the more luxury residences around the lake might have the convenience, but not one that he—and apparently, she—had visited.

"Press the button right there," he said, pointing toward the faux-paneled wall.

And with a small smile curling the corners of her mouth, she did.

They stepped inside when the doors slid open. "I can't believe you found this!" she said.

Ash pushed the button for the third floor.

Her eyes went wide. "We're really going to visit Dr. Szabo?"

"No, we're just going to ride this thing up and down until you've had enough or a half hour passes. Because *then* we have someplace else to go."

To his gratification, they went up and down for twenty minutes. When they were alone she wore a broad smile on her face. If other people stepped inside, she'd look down at her feet and, God, it was so cute because he could tell she was trying to play it cool, even on her twenty-fourth trip.

At the twenty-fifth, she said she was getting a little woozy, so they walked back through the lobby on legs that felt as if they'd been at sea.

Ensconced in his car again, she looked at him with alert expectation. "Next?"

"Another surprise."

He figured she got it when he made a turn at the sign indicating Airport. She twitched and her gaze slid his way. "Um…"

"You've never flown before, either, right?"

"Right." Her fingers clutched each other in her lap. "I'm not sure…"

"You'll like it," he said, hoping.

Her hand was cold as he guided her across the tarmac. "A helicopter?" she asked, as she saw the aircraft up ahead.

"For a bird's-eye view. They fly slow and low."

"How did you arrange this?" Her fingers squeezed his.

"It's a charter. This is their business. Tours."

Her eyes went wide. "It must cost so much. Too much!"

"Don't think about that. I don't want you worrying about anything."

Even the pilot could tell she felt apprehensive. He smiled and shook their hands with a sturdy grip. "Welcome aboard," he said. "Most everyone is nervous their first time on a bird."

"This is her first time in the air," Ash told him.

"Then I'll make sure our flight is smooth and extra special."

He helped Tilda climb into the backseat and put on a headset with a flexible attached mic. Ash settled in beside her and slipped on his own. Then he laced his fingers with hers and smiled. "Relax," he said. "I've done this before with my family. Wait until you see the view."

Her hold tightened on him as they took off and he elbowed her when he saw her eyes closed tight. "You shouldn't miss this, pretty girl."

With a deep breath, she opened them, and then they went wider as she took in the scenery. Below was the small-and-getting-smaller airport and its vicinity.

Around them were the mountains, draped in white and dotted by dark green trees. Their trip took them over several small lakes and above ski runs busy with tiny ant-like figures moving down the wide slopes. They saw narrow ravines and broader valleys and then they were above Blue Arrow Lake, the homes along its borders looking like Monopoly game pieces, the village something from a child's toy set.

They left that familiar setting for a sweep nearer the tallest peaks of the mountain range, where they spied a fire lookout but not any other sign of human life. The mountains were awe-inspiring from this vantage point. Unspoiled and unpopulated, they stood like sober, imposing sentinels.

"Beautiful," Tilda murmured.

"They're the walls of your world," Ash said, then pointed beyond to a sky so blue it almost hurt to look at it. "But there's more to see and do and discover outside the gates."

She gave him a strange look and slipped her hand from his hold to tuck it around her waist. He let her have her silence but not her hand, and taking it back, he cradled it firmly in both of his for the rest of the flight.

Back on the ground, she remained quiet as they returned to his car.

"What's on your mind?" he asked, worried about her mood.

Her mouth turned down. "I'm thinking how you're going to get on a plane and leave in a couple of weeks."

Relief nearly made him spill his plans. But it was too early for that, so he silenced them both by taking her into his arms and kissing her until her fingers clutched the back of his jacket and her face was flushed.

"Time to feed you," he said, opening the passenger door and gently pushing her inside.

She glared at him, an expression of thwarted passion on her face. He laughed and took in deep breaths as he made his way around the car. So far, so good.

If all the rest went as planned, next time he flew he'd be holding her close all the way across the Atlantic.

He found the fish-and-chips place he'd located not far from the airport. As he nosed into a parking space, she cast a curious look at him. He tried to hide his sudden nervousness with a smile. Had she guessed?

"Here they serve, uh, the favorite thing I ate in London." He had no idea if the restaurant was any good, but he'd thought it might be a fun way to bring up the topic. "Have you had fish-and-chips?"

"I've had fish sticks and French fries, does that count?"

"You'll have to tell me if you taste the difference," he said. His stupid nerves were doing something to his stomach and he hoped he could eat. As they walked across the parking lot, he reviewed his talking points.

His posting in London was for six months. She could stay with him there for that time with nothing more than a passport—which she could apply for at the Blue Arrow Lake post office.

He knew from experience that the generous stipend his company offered for living expenses would cover them both. She could continue with her online classes, and without having to pay for rent or food or gas for her car, she could afford tuition to take more of them if she'd like.

He'd be happy to cover that cost, too, but he didn't think she'd agree.

Most important of all, they'd be together. Together, building a life. Building a future.

Ash settled her into a booth, then went up to the counter to order a beer for each of them to enjoy while they studied the offerings. The place wasn't busy, it was just after five, but it smelled delicious, and if he could just get his jumpy belly under control he guessed the food would be great.

"Are you all right?" she asked, over her plastic-coated menu as he slid a beer her way.

He must look as apprehensive as he felt. "Terrific," he said, playing over in his head how he planned to begin. *I'm in love with you, Tilda. Come away with me. Trust me to create something good between us.*

They made their selections and Ash returned to the counter to place their orders. Glancing over his shoulder, he saw Tilda's back, her head bent over her phone.

"Son," a voice said.

Ash nearly leaped out of his skin. He glanced over, saw his father right beside him. The man wore his usual retirement-wear of khakis and a golf sweater, but the garment was buttoned wrong and there was what looked to be a coffee stain on one sleeve. "Jeez, Dad, I think I lost a life." He took in his father's grim expression. "Are you all right?"

His father didn't blink his bloodshot eyes. "What are you doing, Ash?"

"What are *you* doing? I thought you and Mom were staying at the Palm Springs house for another few days."

"I brought your mother back up here, but I've decided

to leave her the car and I'm taking a private flight back to the Springs place in about an hour."

Odd, that, as well as the tense set to the man's shoulders. "Is there a problem?"

His father's intensity didn't abate. "Son," he said again. "What are you doing?"

When Ash opened his mouth, his dad didn't give him a chance to speak.

"What are you doing," he continued, his gaze jumping past Ash, "with *her*?"

"You mean with Tilda?" Okay, he hadn't told his parents about her or about the progression of things between them. One, because his parents had been out of the mountains since the relationship ramped up, and two, because he wasn't thirteen years old with an eighth-grade crush. Ash glanced back, saw she was still in their booth, her back to the two of them.

"I'd like you to meet her—" he began.

"Not a good idea," his father replied.

Huh? "I'm seeing her, Dad, and it's serious."

Pain contorted his father's even features. "Shit, Ash."

His father rarely swore, and only while watching football.

"Shit, Ash, what?" He didn't understand this. "She's great. And I'm—"

"She's not the right kind of girl for you."

His eyes widened. "She's twenty-one. A woman. And what 'kind' is the right kind?" He couldn't believe his father was a snob.

"I misspoke, then," the other man ground out. "I only mean you shouldn't be with that woman."

Ash stared. This couldn't be the man who'd raised

him not to prejudge anyone. "You don't even know her," he pointed out. "How can you—"

Then his father interrupted him again, another surprise in itself. "Look, Ash, I'd like to save this for another time, but you've backed me into a corner here—"

"*I've* backed *you* into a corner?" He'd respected his father his entire life and always strove to earn his dad's respect in return. But this was nuts. What could he possibly have against Tilda?

"The fact is, I have a plane to catch." His father wiped his hand over his mouth and Ash noticed the gray cast to his skin. "And there isn't a good way to say this anyhow, I suppose."

"Say what?"

"Your mother told me I was the one who'd have to tell you," his father muttered. "And maybe I should wait, but seeing you with that young woman..."

Ash had never seen his father like this. Stressed-out and strung-tight. Something big had surely pushed him to the edge. "Tell me what?" Ash demanded. "What's going on, Dad?"

Then his father spoke, revealing information that rocked Ash's world. When the other man walked off, Ash felt angry, betrayed and literally ill. Standing there alone again, his only cohesive thought was that the designs for the life he'd been anticipating ten minutes before had completely evaporated.

Because how could he plan for a future when his past was a complete fraud?

TILDA HEARD ASH'S footsteps approach their booth and looked up. Everything inside her went colder than her apartment at midnight in midwinter. She put off questioning him for a moment, holding on to the day, the rightness of the two of them together for another fifteen seconds. The elevator experience had been funny and fun, the helicopter flight exhilarating, but the best part was, by Ash giving those to her, he'd told her something important.

That he'd seen her.

For months, she'd been the household help who cleaned up after other people, soundlessly, efficiently. Mac said their goal was to give homeowners the impression their houses were tended by magic and they did this by not leaving so much as a fingerprint on stainless steel or a footprint in a plush rug. If the homeowners were in residence, they put their phones on vibrate and returned calls away from the house so the sound of their voices wouldn't be in the air.

Working the catering gigs had been the same. She'd been paid to be a convenience in the life of the host, like an appliance or a piece of furniture.

With Ash, it was different. He'd seen her and heard her. Knew her.

They're the walls of your world, he'd said about the mountains. *But there's more to see and do and discover outside the gates.*

Thanks to him, she'd begun dreaming of that other world. She'd begun to truly believe she wasn't trapped by poverty and circumstance and that another life awaited her, all because he'd found value in her.

Now she knew if she had that life, it would be without him.

Because she could see, too, and that fact was written all over his face. Dread formed a lump in the pit of her stomach, joining the ever-present guilt that she'd been trying to ignore since he'd returned to her bed. "What's wrong?" she asked. She had to say something.

"Every fucking thing," he muttered. Then he drew in a deep breath. "I have to take you home."

Of course Tilda didn't protest. There was no point. Hadn't she always known, in her heart of hearts, that it would come to this? So the ride back was silent. When they reached her apartment's parking lot, she slid a look at him, committing to memory the classic handsomeness of his face, the burnished golden-brown of his hair.

The tires of the car crunched on the gravel, then all went silent as he braked. Ignoring the burn behind her eyes, Tilda gathered her belongings and reached for the door handle.

"Wait," he said. "I…I should explain."

"You don't—"

"I should. I have to." He lifted both hands, then slammed the heels of them against the steering wheel. "Fuck! This is all so fucked up."

"Ash…"

He turned his head and his tension was clear in the way his flesh seemed stretched over the elegant bones of his face. "I don't even know who the hell I am anymore."

Her temples pounded. "What happened?"

"What I know is I've been an ass."

"No—"

"Yes. I thought my life was so golden. I thought decent and deserving Ash has all this great stuff going for him."

"You are decent and deserving."

"I said I didn't look down on you, Tilda, but…shit, of course I did."

Directing her gaze to her lap, Tilda twined her fingers around each other there, meshing them so tight her knuckles turned white.

"Mr. Fucking Perfect was going to share with you all the good things he had because of the good people who had raised his fucking golden self. I was going to persuade you to go to Europe with me."

Her head came up. She stared at him.

"Yeah. Where you could have an opportunity to better yourself."

"You thought that?" she asked, her face going hot.

"Not in so many words. But boy, was I feeling magnanimous. Ready to share with you all the glory that was Ashton Robbins, son of John Fucking Robbins." His laugh was short and raw. "But in truth, John Robbins was fucking another woman. The man I've admired and wanted to emulate my entire life has been fooling around behind my mom's back for years. He confessed to her today, and then he told me."

"I…I'm sorry, Ash." What else could she say?

He stared out the windshield, his expression stony. "I feel dirty just knowing it. I feel stupid, too. Betrayed and bitter and fucking tainted by him, John Fucking Robbins."

"It's not your fault. It has nothing to do with you. It doesn't change *you*." All phrases she'd said to herself, over and over and over.

"Like hell it doesn't change me. Because you won't want to look at me again once I tell you…" He glanced away from her again, a muscle in his jaw ticking.

She swallowed. "Tell me what?"

His fingers curled into fists, and then he faced her again. "The woman my old man had an affair with—

an affair that began, by the way, when I was sixteen years old—was *your mother*."

Tilda recoiled. Not because the news was new, but hearing Ash's vitriol toward his father and the words *your mother* in the same tone stabbed deep. Guilt shot from her belly toward her throat, choking her.

Ash's eyes widened. "Shit. I shouldn't have said that. I shouldn't have said anything to you about it..."

She bolted from the car. It wasn't Ash or his apology or even her own misery she was trying to escape.

It was the glimpse of a shiny future she'd been given that had now been so cruelly snatched away.

THREE NIGHTS LATER, Ash took the stool at the end of the bar at Mr. Frank's. The man on the other side didn't even bother asking what he wanted. For the third night in a row he slid him a draft beer, one of the first Ash planned on drinking. Thank God there was a taxi service to take his drunk ass home.

The bartender had been making those calls on Ash's behalf. Yeah, so blotto his fingers wouldn't work on his phone.

He was doing his best to silence the thoughts that spun in his head like a carousel. A few beers and he hoped he wouldn't be plagued by the decision that had to be made.

His mom wanted him to continue with his plan to go to London.

They hadn't hashed over the details of his father's affair. She said she wanted to keep him out of the middle and that she didn't want to do or say anything that might damage his relationship with his dad.

Ash didn't know if they'd ever have a relationship

again. His father had been what Ash considered the model of integrity and loyalty and now he didn't think he could even look at his dad.

But then again, he couldn't look at himself.

Avoiding the mirror hanging over the back of the bar, he downed half the beer in one long swallow. Then a voice called his name and he closed his eyes, wishing he could avoid *her*, too.

"Go away, Tilda."

"I have some things I need to say."

The air around him moved and he knew she'd taken the empty stool beside his. Eyes still closed, he heard her ask the bartender for a Diet Coke.

"The evening's not going to get better if you stick with that, sweetheart," he murmured to her.

"How's all that beer working out for you?"

He opened one eye and rolled it her way.

She shrugged. "Mountain grapevine."

Instead of answering, he downed the rest of his beer, then indicated to the bartender he'd take another. "Tequila chaser." It was going to be that kind of night, unless Tilda took her pretty ass out of the place.

When her cola came, she settled more firmly onto her stool.

"I'm sorry," he said, keeping his gaze on the bar where his shot of blue agave–based alcohol should show up any second. He owed her that apology. "I can be a hothead, and I just spewed all that out without thinking about your feelings. Maybe if I'd given it a second thought, I would have broken things off more… gently. At least I would have found a better way to tell you the truth."

Her deep breath was audible. "Don't blame yourself

for that." She took in another. "That's why I'm here, to tell you things *you* should know."

That drew his complete attention. Those beautiful green eyes were big in her face. Her bottom lip looked swollen, as if she'd been worrying it. She looked as if she'd been worrying, period.

"Tilda," he said, "I messed up. *I* was messed up after what my father told me, then I messed up when we talked. None of this is on you."

"It's all on me," she whispered. "It's all on me… and more."

His shoulders cramped with tension, his muscles prepping his body for blows he could sense in the offing. "What? No, don't tell me." Hadn't he had enough crappy news? "I don't think we should talk about this."

She ignored him. "First, you need to know that you did share good things with me. You gave me pleasure and acceptance and you made me feel beautiful in my dollar shoes and discount clothes."

"You *are* beautiful."

"I thought you were out of my league, but you made me believe I could be a member of any one I want. You did that just by listening to me, Ash."

His head started pounding and a vise clamped down on the back of his neck. "Tilda—"

She held up a hand. "Let me have my say, please." Her fingers reached for her drink, curled around it. "My mother…"

Ash saw that his tequila shot had been delivered and he didn't hesitate to knock it back. "Let's not go there. I don't blame her—"

"She poured drinks at the yacht club on Tuesday and Thursday nights. That's where she met your father. I don't know if he lied to her about being married, but I can tell you she wouldn't have cared. He wasn't her first lover who was someone else's husband. She wanted attention—I guess to be seen in her own way—and she liked the presents and the cash she was given by men like your dad."

Ash frowned. "Wait—"

"She didn't have much of anything, including self-esteem, though that doesn't excuse her having an affair with your father. I…I'm ashamed of her."

"Are you…" He blinked. Blinked again. "Are you saying you knew?"

"And I'm ashamed of me, too. Deeply. I'm so, so sorry."

The tequila was moving in his belly like a fire-breathing monster. "You knew. When—" *Fuck.* Was it so? It had to be so. "You knew that night last May."

"You introduced yourself. I never met your father face-to-face… I tried to stay out of sight when he came to the apartment, but the walls were thin, and I heard him talk about his son on occasion. His son, Ash."

The walls were thin. Ash thought he might be sick. He pressed the heels of his hands to his temples. "Why the hell did you go back to the hotel with me?"

"Last spring my mother was getting too clingy with your dad. I heard it in her voice, I heard them argue. He broke things off and she…she stopped caring for herself as she should. She got sick and that sickness turned into an infection that caused her death."

Groaning, he let his head drop back.

"It wasn't your fault. It wasn't even your dad's fault. Not really. But that night… I wanted to punish someone and it turns out I did it to both you and to me."

"Yeah," he said, putting it all together now, the whole series of events coming into painful, nauseating focus. "No wonder you didn't want to see me again when I came back here. I thought we'd made a connection and you thought…" Christ, he didn't know. What the hell *had* she thought?

"I thought I was finding some way to ease my hurt and loneliness and… I don't know, Ash. I was grieving and upset."

"And I was a fool."

"No," she said quickly. "That night you were fun and game for dancing and I liked you, truly. You didn't deserve what I did."

"Fucked me so hard I passed out?" he asked bitterly.

"What I did after that."

His body went rigid again, bracing. "What did you do after?"

"I made there ever being an us impossible. This last week, I've been kidding myself that we could somehow get past everything, and that I could give you something as powerful as you've given me and we could… could go somewhere with that."

If he didn't feel the darkest of dark clouds hanging over his head, maybe he'd be gratified to know that the past week had been good for her, too. If he could believe her about that. If he could believe anyone about fucking anything.

His father was an adulterer.

His girl was a liar.

"Even while I was trying so hard to believe we could be something, guilt has been eating me up inside because…" She hauled in a breath. "Because I stole from you that first night, Ash."

His girl was a thief?

He turned his head and his whole body went cold. "What do you mean?" Because yeah, his belief in other people's honesty was gone, gone, gone.

"That money…the four hundred dollars you thought you'd tipped the room service person?" She didn't flinch from his gaze. "I took that before I left. I can't explain why. I've never stolen anything in my life. But it was sitting on the dresser and when I grabbed up my purse…I just grabbed the stack of twenties, too."

Her face turned red and he saw tears swimming in her eyes. "It was an absolutely despicable thing to do, and I regretted it instantly. You don't have to believe that, but it's true."

He felt sick again. "I don't believe a word you say."

The color drained from her cheeks, but she nodded. Then her hand went into the purse perched on her lap. She drew out a wad of bills. "The twenties are gone. But this is four hundred one-dollar bills. My roommates' tips."

His eyebrows flew up.

She shook her head. "I paid for them. I just wanted to have these four hundred pieces of paper to say four hundred times that—" She broke off, gave a quick shake of her head and began again. "So you'd know I'm being punished for what I did. I'm paying for everything I did wrong by never being able to have you." Then she shoved the money his way, slid off her stool and left the building.

Ash stared at the cash without seeing it. Instead, he saw himself that first night, sending over a drink to a tipsy birthday girl. He saw them dancing, her face bright with laughter.

He saw how hard she'd resisted him when he came back to the mountains and how he'd broken down that resistance. He saw the flush on her face when he'd gone down on her and the wonder in her eyes as they took flight in the helicopter.

He remembered the pitch of his belly up, then down, up, then down, when they'd ridden the elevator.

Her first time to be in one.

His first time to be in love.

Despite everything, he still wanted her.

Yet his philandering father had slept with Tilda's mother. Tilda's dead mother. And the affair was no longer a secret between his parents.

His mom said he shouldn't worry about their marriage, that it was up to her and his father to work out the repercussions of John Robbins's actions. *Adult life is complicated*, his mother had said. *It's better to learn that sooner than later.*

But could he look at Tilda without thinking of their cheating parents?

Could she look at him without remembering, too?

Could they really get past that and be an "us"?

At sixteen, no, he thought. But he was a grown-up now, by all measures. *Adult life is complicated.*

But Tilda had stolen from him!

Truth be told, though, it was his dignity that took the blow. He didn't miss the stupid four hundred dollars; the cocky asshat he'd been that night had flung cash around as if it meant nothing. With a fingertip, he nudged the pile she'd left behind and one bill curled free. Writing stood out on the green-and-white dollar, written in a dark pink felt-tipped pen.

I love you.

He nudged another bill free to find the same message. *I love you.*

Hands starting to shake, he flipped through the mass. *I love you. I love you. I love you.*

Four hundred times.

Tilda was in love with him, and she saw it as her punishment. *I'm paying for everything I did wrong by never being able to have you.*

She hadn't made a fool of him. Or if she had, she'd become the exact same kind of fool.

A fool in love.

And so? What kind of examples did either of them have of love? Her mother, who'd apparently had a string of married lovers?

But Tilda wasn't her mother.

Might Ash become like his father, though? A man who looked the right way and said the right things but who had flaws in his character that had finally come to light. Christ, he didn't want that for himself.

So don't become that. Even if your father is not the man you thought, that doesn't prevent you from becoming the man you want to be.

The man who should be reaching for his own life, future, love.

Ash jumped off his stool. Shoving the four hundred bills in his pocket, but dropping some of his own to pay his tab, he ran out of Mr. Frank's and into the night. In the dimly lit parking lot he spotted his car, then noticed Tilda's a few spaces away from his own.

She was nowhere in sight.

Piece of shit probably broke down on her again. Looking around, he thought he saw a slight figure in the distance, heading in the direction of the village. Without thinking, he tore after her.

The central part of the main street through the village was draped in fairy lights. They even crossed overhead. Ash slowed as Tilda came under their canopy. From half a block back, he called her name.

She stiffened, then glanced over her shoulder. Seeing him, her eyes widened and she turned to face him with the air of someone preparing to receive bad news. Cautious but resigned.

He wanted her smiling. And he knew he wanted her back. He was that annoyingly arrogant…and maybe that was a good thing his upbringing had given him. "Can we talk a minute?"

"I don't think that's a good idea." She began scuttling in reverse.

"We should talk a minute."

"No," she said and stepped into the street to cross to the other side.

Damn, she was moving fast.

"Tilda!"

As she glanced over her shoulder, he pulled a bill from his pocket. Not one of the four hundred, but another that he dangled over the grate in the gutter. Melted snow ran in a small river that would take the money in a flash to wherever melted street snow ended up. "We talk or I'll drop this."

She paused, her gaze glued to the money, fluttering at his fingertips. "That's wasteful."

He let it fall. Her gaze followed its quick journey down into the sewer. When her eyes shifted back to his face, he pulled out another bill.

Her expression turned aghast and she swung around to return to the sidewalk. "Ash, no."

It was a stupid stunt, but at least he'd halted her flight. Without looking away from her, he slowly approached, the cash still in his hand.

"We can get past this," he said.

She shook her head.

"We can. You said I made you believe, and I can make you believe this, too." He shoved the bill back in his pocket.

"It's such a mess—"

"Not our mess, not really." He was close enough to touch her, and he did that, stroking one fingertip over her cold cheek. His heart moved in his chest at that coolness. He wanted to pull her into him. Warm her forever.

"Your parents—"

"It's *their* mess." He tucked her hair behind her ear, certain now he was right about that. "What we have is a future to plan. Come with me to London for six months."

Tilda crossed her arms and tucked her hands in the crooks of her elbows. Because she wanted to touch him, too?

"I can't do that," she said.

"Of course you can." He pulled one of her hands free and laced his fingers with hers. "When the six months are over we can decide what comes next."

"Six months of you," she whispered. "After all this, you'd really give me that?"

"Six months of *us*. Maybe it will be happy-ever-after, maybe it will be happy-for-now. I think it's the former but I'll settle for the latter. Bottom line—I want happy…and every instinct I have tells me that's being with you."

The twinkling lights overhead revealed the sudden hope on her face. Then she shook her head. "No, no. I'm—"

"Too smart and too determined to throw away this chance."

She looked around. "I've never been anywhere else. The mountains…"

"We can come back if you want that. But for now, let them be your stepping stone, not your cage."

Her gaze returned to his face. "A stepping stone," she murmured. "Not a cage." Then she shook her head. "Ash, think about it. Really think about it. Our parents—"

"They shouldn't be a cage, either—your mother and my father and what they did. We're not them."

"Who are we, then?"

"I guess this is the time in life when we get to figure that out. We make our own choices. Become our own persons."

He saw her tremble. "I'm a strong, smart mountain woman."

"Then you'll make a strong, smart choice." He lowered his voice as his heart beat hard in his chest. "Please, Tilda, please. I'm in love with you. Give us a chance. Give us that chance at happy."

Her gaze studied his face. Then she released a small sigh. "O-okay."

Tentative relief sluiced through him. "Okay…what?"

She stepped into him and he wrapped his arms

around her as hers rose to circle his neck. “Okay, I want happy, too,” she said. “God, how much. And that’s with you.”

CHAPTER SIXTEEN

POPPY UNEXPECTEDLY STOPPED by Mac's office on Paperwork Day. From her place behind her computer, Mac scrutinized her sister and decided she hadn't been imagining things when she'd told Zan something was off.

"You look tired," she said to Poppy. "Aren't you sleeping well?"

"I'm sleeping great." Her little sister pushed through the swinging door cut into the front counter. Then she narrowed her eyes. "What about you?"

"Sleep? I get it." Not that she'd tell Poppy *where* she was getting that sleep. The deal she'd made with Zan was a private one, and simple. Until he left town, she slept in his bed. Though she hadn't initially agreed when he'd made the proposition that afternoon in the cabin, she'd discovered that fighting the man—and their potent attraction—was useless. She kept ending up with him between the sheets anyway, so she'd taken to just letting go and enjoying the spectacular sex.

And depending upon her well-defended heart not to let him in again.

Poppy tilted her head. "Why are there shadows beneath your eyes, then?"

Mac pretended great interest in the numbers running across her computer screen. "Probably because

I'm concerned I'm not going to fit into my bridesmaid dress for your wedding."

"I can fix that," Poppy said, then whipped a white bakery bag from behind her back. "I brought you a muffin from Oscar's and one of their big lattes."

"I didn't say the dress was going to be too loose," Mac replied, even as she snatched up the bag. "I've been eating too much."

Every night, cooking for Zan. When he'd mention wanting to take her out, she'd demur. They shouldn't be seen together. Not by her family. Not by the general public. She didn't want there to be any more talk about the legend of Mac and Zan, part two.

He was leaving, and when he was gone she didn't want family and friends pitying her.

Poppy settled on the corner of the desk, one foot swinging. "So what's up with you and Zan?"

Mac bobbled the muffin and it fell to the desktop. Picking it back up, she focused on peeling the waxy paper off the sides for a bite and wondered how to redirect the discussion. This conversation was already heading into dangerous territory. Sisters could be mind readers, but worse, sisters could leap to conclusions that would never be.

Poppy saw the world in rosy tones, which was lovely for Poppy, and Mac wanted that for Poppy for the rest of her life, but if she started coloring her sister's world in those same pinks, there would only be disappointment in the end.

"Mac?" her sister prompted. "You and Zan? Why'd he want to have that supersecret talk with you at the cabins the other day?"

She waved her free hand. "Just stuff about his

grandfather's house. You know I'm helping to pack it up and clean it so it can get on the market."

"I like that house. It's got the cool pool, and that library. Very nice."

Mac lifted her brows. "Want me to put in a word for you and Ryan? I'm sure he'd rather have you guys own it than strangers."

Poppy shook her head. "I think Zan should hold on to it."

"Why?"

"He doesn't need the money, does he?"

"I suppose not," Mac answered. All his grandfather's considerable wealth had gone to him and he hadn't been hurting before the old man died. "But he doesn't live in the mountains."

"Yes, but he could," Poppy said, her eyes going dreamy.

Mac didn't like that look on her sister's face. "Don't be painting that picture. He's going…somewhere, and soon."

Poppy's gaze sharpened and shifted to Mac's face. "You don't know where he's off to next?"

She shrugged. "He hasn't said." Not that she'd asked. If he was going, then it didn't matter to her where he went.

A dark moroseness moved through her and she set aside the muffin. There wasn't room for it with all the gloominess inside her.

"Even if he has a plan, that doesn't mean he should sell the house," Poppy declared. "It could be his home base. A place to rest between…whatever."

She aimed a smile at Mac. "Wouldn't that be great?

We'd get our other brother back. Our brother of the heart."

"Yeah, great," Mac muttered. "Our other brother."

Poppy's smile didn't die. "Of course he wasn't always a brother to *you*."

Something in the way she said that line had Mac shooting her sister a suspicious look. "You aren't spinning romantic fantasies now, are you, Pop?"

Her sister shook her head, all innocence. "I just got the impression he and Brett are tight again, and I like the idea of Zan being around. You know…at least some of the time. Don't you agree?"

Mac tried imagining Zan being around "some of the time." How would her life go on? Would it include constant bargaining with herself against driving past that house every day, checking for lights or cars or other signs of life?

If he lived here "some of the time," maybe one day he'd come to the mountains with a woman on his arm. The one who'd convinced him he could be a family man, after all.

Her stomach roiled and she pushed the muffin farther away.

"Mac," Poppy said. "What's wrong? Is it what I said? I'm sorry—"

"No." Mac shook her head. "I'm just in a weird mood. Let's talk about something else, something fun. Have you wheedled out of Ryan where he's taking you on your honeymoon?"

Her younger sister took the bait and they chatted about the possible destinations and her groom-to-be's stubbornness about keeping it a surprise, despite her best efforts at persuasion. "I'm beginning to think I've lost my feminine mojo," Poppy grumbled.

Maybe she should talk to Ryan, Mac thought, worrying again. That sense that something wasn't quite right just wouldn't go away. Of course, maybe it was due to her own preoccupation with Zan.

"Hey." She tipped her chin to her sister, suddenly inspired. "I have an idea. Why don't you break out a piece of your honeymoon nightwear early? Or go to Bon Nuit and buy something special to wow Ryan with tonight?" Bon Nuit was the expensive boutique in town that carried lovely lingerie as well as perfumed soaps and beautiful linens.

"Now, that sounds like a plan." Poppy's mouth curved.

"And I'll collect Mason and have a sleepover with him at my place. Tell him it's a dress rehearsal for when I have him while you two are gone." It would be her own rehearsal as well, practice at being alone in bed again.

Her sister was out-and-out smiling now. "He'd love that. But are you sure?"

"Heck, yeah. You know we have a great time together."

Poppy's smile died and her voice lowered. "You should have kids, Mac."

Not going to go there. Not going to go *there!* It had once been a dream and for a few weeks long ago a possibility both exhilarating and terrifying, but she tried not to think about it now. "I've got kids, Pop. Mason and London and whoever else might come down the pike thanks to my siblings getting rings on their fingers, all three of them."

"Mac…"

"Please, Pop. Can we drop it?" she said, squelching any note of desperation from her voice. Cool, calm, in control Mac Walker knew what her life held—and what it did not—and was fine with it.

"But—"

The office door burst open, cutting off her sister's next words. Yay. But then she half rose because Tilda walked in wearing an expression Mac had never seen on her before. Usually the girl was alert and tightly focused. Now her eyes seemed to be seeing things that were not the office with its blue-gray walls and long counter.

"Are you all right?" she asked her.

Tilda started, then blinked, as if coming awake to her surroundings. "Um, yeah," Tilda said.

"You're on board to do the Conover condo today?"

She nodded, then sucked in her bottom lip a moment. "But I can't do it the next time."

Mac's brows rose. "Okay, we can make a change to the schedule."

"It's going to have to be a permanent change." A smile broke over Tilda's face, like a bright, blazing dawn. "In two weeks I'm going to London for six months."

"Wow!" Poppy said. "How come? What will you do there? Where did this sudden decision come from?"

Mac knew—or at least she could guess. "Ash. Ash Robbins." She'd seen the way he'd torn after Tilda the night she'd run from the café.

The girl nodded. "We're sort of together."

Poppy was wide-eyed. "You don't run off to London with someone you're 'sort of' together with."

"I know. You're right." Tilda bounced on her heels,

something Mac had never seen her do, ever. It was an exuberant action, young, and at odds with the Tilda who'd seemed old beyond her years. Always serious. "It's just hard to think something so good would happen to me."

Mac knew that feeling. She remembered the glory of not needing food or water or air to survive, only the love of that other person. Seeing it on Tilda's face, it brought home to Mac how distant her memory of it was.

And with Zan temporarily back in town, how bittersweet.

With effort, she pushed all that aside—or tried to—as Poppy asked pertinent questions and Tilda spilled all about her plans and the absolute thrill she felt about going off with her young lover on an adventure.

Ash wanted her at his side.

Six months was too long to be apart.

Mac thought of a decade. Of 117 postcards.

"Ash makes me believe," Tilda confessed.

Poppy clapped her hands. "I *love* that!" she said. "Ryan tells me that all the time."

Apparently Mac hadn't made Zan believe. *Everything ends, doesn't it?*

Instead of stewing over that, she thought instead of what Tilda's leaving would mean to her business. Down an employee, she'd have to work that much harder. That would mean much less time to think of the man who would be leaving soon.

Finally, Tilda wound down and went about collecting what she needed to clean the condo as well as the keys to one of the Maids by Mac vehicles. She left for work with another blazing smile and a jaunty wave.

Poppy sighed as the door closed behind her. "Awesome, huh?"

"Yeah. She's had things hard. Maybe this is the beginning of easy for her."

Poppy was studying her face. "And for you? My supersonic sister sense is tingling, I tell you. Are things hard or easy for you right now?"

"I'm good." Of course she was. Cool, calm, in control Mac Walker knew what her life held—what her future held—and was fine with it.

She grinned at her little sister. "Life's good, right? Another wedding coming up. A night ahead with my favorite nephew. A honeymoon trip for you that I better hear about tomorrow morning *in detail*, since you're making a stop at Bon Nuit in order to cajole the destination out of Ryan."

Poppy wiggled her brows. "Oh, I can so do cajoling."

Mac laughed, loving the anticipation on her sister's face, the confidence she had. Her sister had always been optimistic, holding tight to those rose-colored glasses of hers. But with all she'd gone through to get a deeply wounded man to love her and cleave to her side, Mac thought Poppy's hold was no longer quite so tight. Now her sister just counted on them staying firmly on her nose.

Ryan had given her that assurance. As Poppy had given him belief in beautiful things and happiness after grief.

Mac's mood lightened more as she thought of how well things had turned out for her younger sister. She'd been right when she'd told Zan that she herself was invested in Poppy's happiness. *I think if we can keep her buoyant and bright, then I might eventually be that way, too.*

Her sister now came to her feet. "I should let you get back to work."

Mac nodded. "Yeah, and I need to get back to it. I want to finish early so I can dream up what Mason and I might do tonight."

"Ryan's teaching him to play chess."

Mac groaned. "I don't even remember which piece does what."

"He'll tell you," Poppy said on a grin. She slung her purse over her shoulder. "Off to shop."

At the door, she paused. "I think I'll see if there's something special for a pretty girl heading off to London with her guy."

Mac nodded. "I'll go halfsies."

Before she left for good, Poppy gave Mac one more smile, and Mac heard the echo of her own words again. *I think Poppy holds all my hope. I think if we can keep her buoyant and bright, then I might eventually be that way, too.*

Through the window, Mac watched her sister climb into her car. Yes, it was going to be all right. She didn't need any more than this: her mountains and her business. Her family, whole and happy.

She was deep in paperwork when her cell phone rang. Glancing at it, she saw that her brother was on the line. Picking up the device, she swiped to accept the call. "Yo."

There was silence on the other end.

"Hello?" Mac lifted the phone from her ear, stared at it, put it back to the side of her head. "Hello? Did you butt-dial me?"

Then something about the quiet on the line made the darkness gather inside her again, a heavy weight that made it hard to breathe. "Brett? Talk to me."

"Mac." Her brother's voice sounded rough. He cleared his throat. "Mac, there's been an accident."

"What?" Panic flowed, then froze, and her heart skated without control, as if across black ice. "Who?"

"It's Poppy, Mac. We need to get to the hospital, stat."

HOLD ON, HOLD ON, HOLD ON, Mac chanted, both to herself and her little sister. Brett had offered sparse detail over the phone. A car had crossed the midline on the highway and crashed head-on into Poppy's vehicle. That driver was okay. Her airbag had gone off. When Ryan called, Poppy was in the process of being evaluated.

So Mac was driving, her hands squeezing the steering wheel, bracing to do whatever was necessary to keep her family calm and contained. Her job was to minimize the drama, and so falling apart was not an option.

Brett was standing at the doors as she rushed into the emergency entrance at the small regional hospital. He caught her by the shoulders and studied her face as if assessing her status. "Okay," he said. "Here's the deal."

Mac continued her slow breathing as her brother explained they'd already put Poppy in an ambulance with Ryan to go down the hill to a larger facility. Shay, Jace and Angelica were already following behind. He'd waited for Mac so they could travel together.

"But why down the hill?" Mac asked, trying to keep fear out of her voice.

"You know this place is so small they practically send everything beyond splinters to a bigger hospital. But they said when there's the potential for soft tissue injury they particularly want a patient to be at a facility with more diagnostic equipment."

But she wished she could see her sister, *now*. "Do they have any idea exactly what's wrong?"

"We won't be certain until she's seen by the doctors there and had those tests," he said. "Now come on, let's go in my car."

It was a tense forty-minute drive. She asked only one question. "Is Ryan losing his mind?" The other man's ex and his little boy had died in a fire. Hospitals—and the thought of something happening to Poppy—were sure to wig him out.

Brett glanced over. "We're all losing our minds."

"I'm good," Mac said, instantly. "I'm holding it together."

Her legs were even steady as they rushed into the much bigger hospital. There, they had to follow a painted line to their destination, and the *Wizard of Oz*–ishness of it brought a hysterical bubble of laughter into Mac's throat. But she swallowed it down, and she was glad of it when she arrived in the waiting room.

Four pairs of eyes—Ryan, Jace, Angelica and Shay—swung to her.

"Hey, everybody," she said calmly. "How's our Pop? She's gonna be mad if anything gets in the way of the upcoming wedding."

"Nothing's getting in the way of the wedding," Ryan ground out. Even with his hair askew and his face already haggard, he looked determined…but beyond stressed.

Mac immediately walked over to him and enclosed him in her arms. His banded around her, tight enough to communicate his dread. "She wasn't making any sense during the ambulance ride."

"Well, you know Poppy," Mac said, trying to sound unalarmed. "She doesn't make sense a lot of the time."

"Yeah." Ryan pressed his cheek against the side of Mac's hair. "I couldn't talk her out of loving me, thank God."

"You and Mason are the best things in her life," Mac said, patting his back. "She'll be bossing you both around again in no time, you'll see."

Mac made the rounds of the others after Ryan retreated to a chair, a picture of abject anxiety with his head in his hands.

Angelica was wiping away tears with her palms, so Mac found her a box of tissues and squeezed her shoulder. Brett took a cushion beside his wife and slung an arm around her, looking more as if he was holding on than offering support. In return, Angelica curled herself into him, so they appeared to be a single unit.

Shay was pacing, Jace's concerned gaze on her.

Mac went to him first. "London's getting Mason from school?"

He didn't take his eyes off his wife. "Yeah, when it lets out. One of her friend's moms is going to take them both home, keep them there as long as necessary."

"Okay." She touched his forearm. "Walkers are tough, Jace."

"I don't think I am," Jace said. "Not when I can't fix things for her." He nodded at Shay.

"Let me see what I can do." She patted him one last time, then headed for her sister.

When she got near, Shay stopped her movement and addressed Mac in a voice of hoarse but muted outrage. "*Our* Pop!"

"Yeah, little sister," Mac said softly. Though Shay was younger than Poppy, like everyone else in the family, she had a deep protective streak when it came to that particular sibling. Poppy had never asked to be defended and was most likely insulted by their habitual need to shield her, but there it was.

Tears sprang into Shay's eyes, and Mac felt her own despair shudder through her. But she clamped down on it and kept her spine straight. "C'mon," she said to Shay, holding out her hand. "I know what will help."

Shay squeezed hard on her fingers as Mac led her toward Jace. "He needs to hold you, yeah?" she whispered. "Can you give that to him?"

Without answering, Shay slipped her hand from Mac's and walked right into her husband's arms, resting her forehead on his wide chest. Jace shut his eyes and seemed to be breathing again, as he closed her in his embrace.

Now that the two couples were united in support of each other, Mac returned to Ryan. He didn't look up, though, and she didn't try to reach him in the place where he'd retreated. Instead, leaving a chair between them, she took her own seat and settled in to wait.

It was hell to keep her knees from shaking and her expression free of the grinding dread carving a hole in her belly. She clasped her hands loosely in her lap and stared at a stack of bedraggled magazines, seeing a thousand images of her little sister.

Always smiling. Often laughing.

Crying over car commercials, for goodness' sake!

Kissing her son.

Looking at Ryan as if he'd hung the moon and the stars just for her.

She just had to be all right.

Poppy holds all my hope. I think if we can keep her buoyant and bright, then I might eventually be that way, too.

A doctor came through the door to the examining rooms. "Mr. Hamilton?"

The waiting area flooded with apprehension as Ryan jumped to his feet. The doctor gestured for him, and Ryan ate up the space with quick strides until he and the other man disappeared, the door swinging shut behind him.

Angelica released a soft sob that she tried smothering against Brett's shoulder. The sound sent Mac's dread on another forage through her belly. Shay must have been feeling much the same, because she said, "*Our* Pop," again in that same distressed and almost disbelieving tone.

Their Pop.

Then the door opened again and a nurse in pale pink scrubs looked at them. "Walker family?"

They stood.

"You can all come this way. Not for long…but come on back."

Mac was the last of their party to approach the room. Everyone huddled in the doorway, but no one was talking, so she had to peek around Brett's arm to see what was going on.

Poppy lay cocooned in the hospital bed, her head slightly elevated. There was a bandage on her forehead near her hairline, her face was pale, but her eyes were on Ryan. He sat on a chair beside her, one of her hands in two of his.

His head was bent and he'd brought her fingers to his mouth.

"Ryan," she heard Poppy say. She lifted her other hand—an IV needle in the back of it—to stroke his hair. "My love."

"I worried I might lose you." He'd whispered, but they could all hear him. Mac wondered if she should let him know the two of them had witnesses, but she figured Ryan wouldn't care about that at this moment.

Ryan only cared that Poppy was all right.

"I'm okay," she said now, confirming that. Her hand stroked his hair again as he once more kissed her knuckles. "See? One piece?"

"I want to get married," Ryan said.

Poppy smiled. "Well, good thing, since we have all those people coming to the yacht club on Saturday to witness that very event."

He looked up into her eyes. "I mean right now. We have a license. This place will have a chaplain."

"I'm wearing a hospital gown!" Her brows slammed together, and then she winced as if that hurt.

"Careful, baby." Ryan leaned in to drop a kiss on the bandage near her hair. "And I don't care what you're wearing. Let's get married."

Poppy squinched her eyes, then glanced past her fiancé's shoulder to catch Mac's gaze. "Tell him I'm not getting married in a hospital gown."

The tight grip fear had on Mac's heart loosened. "I don't know. Angelica got married in jeans."

"But she drew the line at sweatpants," Brett said,

grinning. "And I don't think Mace would be too happy to miss it, right?"

"Collect him when you collect the wedding license." Ryan didn't take his gaze off Poppy. "You'll do it, won't you, Mac?"

"Mac first wants to know the extent of Poppy's injuries," Mac said. "They told us we couldn't stay long."

"A concussion. Bruising from the seat belt," Ryan said. "I think they were worried about cracked ribs or a fractured sternum, but that turned out not to be the case."

"Ouch," Shay said sympathetically. "Does it hurt very bad, Pop?"

"Not too much. But it gives me an out from all those prewedding crunches I've been doing."

"That you've been *talking* about doing," Brett corrected, a smile in his voice. Then he turned serious. "You scared the shit out of us, Pop."

She shifted her gaze from Ryan to her big brother. "I know. Sorry."

"Is your head going to be okay?" he asked. "Because we all know it's already kind of soft."

"Oh, you." She stuck her tongue out at him.

"The air bag deploying caused the concussion," Ryan said. "Which I guess explains all that weird stuff she said in the ambulance on the way here."

"I didn't say weird stuff."

"You wanted me to tell the doctors about 'her.' You were quite insistent."

"Oh." Poppy made a face, then slid her gaze to the side. "Well…"

Mac narrowed her eyes. Something was going on, she'd known it for days. "Pop?"

Her sister looked up at the group still hovering in the doorway. "There's a reason I asked for all of you to be here. Somebody get their phone out to take a picture."

"I don't need a way to remember you being banged up in a hospital bed," Ryan groused. "I don't *want* a way to remember that."

"Angelica?" Poppy asked.

The other woman obligingly pulled out her phone.

"Now, honey," Poppy told Ryan. "Look into the camera—"

"Poppy," he said, sounding exasperated.

"*Look* into the camera." When he at last followed direction, she continued. "Because I want to have a photographic record of what the famous Ryan Hamilton looks like when I tell him I'm pregnant."

For a moment Ryan's face went blank, then it registered stunned amazement. He whipped his head from the direction of the camera toward his bride-to-be. "Poppy?" he whispered. "Yes, we decided to try, but so soon? Really?"

She beamed him the sweetest of smiles. "Surprise!"

In the five additional minutes they were allowed in her room, they found out that the news was to have been her wedding gift to Ryan—but she'd had to tell the doctors, so she wanted everyone to know. Oh, and that she wasn't actually sure it was a girl but had taken to calling the baby "her" in her mind. The infant wasn't due for another six-plus months.

And the last thing they learned was that Ryan Hamilton still looked movie-star handsome with tears of relief mingled with tears of joy running down his cheeks. The Walkers shuffled back into the hall as he pressed his face to the mattress beside his beloved while her tender smile beamed down at him, her gentle hand slowly sifting through his hair.

They trailed back toward the waiting room. First Brett and Angelica holding hands, then Jace and Shay, arms wound around each other. Mac followed on stiff legs. The emotional overload should have rendered her near-numb but as she thought of the pair behind her and gazed on the couples in front of her, a knife's edge of loneliness found its way inside her.

Silly, to hurt, when there was so much to celebrate.

But that pain was there, nearly agonizing, as she walked back into the waiting room…and saw Zan.

His gaze arrowed straight to her and his body followed, pushing past the other couples to reach her. His hands went to her shoulders and she looked up. "How'd you know to come here?" she asked.

"London called." He gazed into Mac's eyes and his fingers tightened on her. "Poppy?"

Mac mustered a smile. "Battered, but okay. And guess what else? She's pregnant."

His eyebrows winged up, and then he grinned. "Sweet," he said. "Auntie Mac times three."

Hold on, hold on, hold on, she ordered herself again. *Keep standing, don't lean in, keep your cool.* But how much she liked what he'd said—Auntie Mac times three. How much she liked that he knew to count London as well as Mason and now the new baby.

And she liked that he'd come directly to her. That his hands were on her.

That he was studying her face with such obvious concern. "*You* okay?" he asked now.

She widened her smile even while pain seared through her. "Absolutely!" she lied, because that knife she'd felt earlier had done it again, and worse. This time it shattered her armor to pierce straight through her heart.

Her previously well-defended heart.

It was breached now, and with that gentle "*You* okay?" Zan Elliott had unwittingly twisted the blade a total of three times.

One spin for each word that bubbled up in her consciousness. Three words that meant loneliness was a feeling she would have to learn to get used to, probably forever. Those dire, dreadful, impossible three words.

I. Love. You.

She was in love with Zan.

Again. Still.

Probably forever.

CHAPTER SEVENTEEN

As they traveled back to the mountains, Zan glanced over at Mac, noting her defensive posture hadn't changed. Though the passenger side of his SUV had plenty of room, her legs were bent so the heels of her sneakers were perched on the seat cushion. Her arms were wrapped around her knees.

In the thirty minutes since they'd left the hospital, she hadn't said a word or moved a muscle. On the outside, she looked rock-solid. On the inside…

"That had to be a scare," he said, flicking on his headlights. The dark was coming on. The Walkers had stuck around for more updates on their sister, then gone to lunch as a group, all of them much quieter than normal. After returning with food for Ryan, they'd received a final update on Poppy.

The hospital wanted to keep her overnight. Well, that's what the nurse said, but Zan wondered if the decision came at the behest of Ryan, who had the pretty face and the cash to get just about anything he wanted.

And he wanted his pregnant bride-to-be to have a night of rest and recuperation under professional supervision.

Zan understood the man's feelings. Mac was clearly holding tight to a bundle of emotional stress and he was going to do what he must to help her release that. He didn't like to see her hurting.

"Mac?" he said, trying again to get a response. "What do you say we go out for a nice dinner?"

She suddenly jolted, spine straightening, and even in the dim light he could see her anxious expression. "I'm supposed to take care of Mason tonight!"

"No, don't you remember? Shay and Jace are keeping him, since he's already with London."

"Oh, right." Her back relaxed into the seat, but she was still folded into a tight ball.

"So what do you say to dinner?" he asked again.

"Just take me home." She rested her cheek on the top of her knees, her face turned away from him. "I'm tired."

She had to give him directions. But he found her duplex off one of the narrow side streets near the village center. It was a no-frills white stucco box with a single-wide driveway and a solo garage on each end. "I left my car at the Blue Arrow hospital," she said, as he pulled in.

"I'll drive you to it tomorrow morning."

She cast a swift look at him but didn't say anything until he killed the car engine and made to exit the car. "You don't need to get out."

"I do if I'm going to rustle up some dinner for us," he said, trailing her toward her front door, illuminated by a small porch light and painted a deep green.

"Zan," she began as she shoved her key in the lock.

"Mac," he countered. "You've had a rough day. Let me do this."

Once they were inside, he saw the bathroom straight ahead, at the very end of a short hall. He made for it, then glanced around at the small tiled room. A relaxing bath was what she needed, but there was only a narrow stall shower. So he got that going, adjusting the temperature.

"What are you doing?" she said from behind him.

"Getting this just right so you can hop in and wash some of your stress down the drain."

Backing out, he had to turn sideways to let her pass. "By the time you're done, I'll have something for us to eat. Don't rush."

She shook her head at him but proceeded inside the steamy enclave and shut the door behind her.

That gave Zan a real chance to look around. It didn't take long. There was a good-size bedroom with a brass bed that looked as old as the mountains covered in a hand-stitched quilt. A small, painted dresser and a nightstand rounded out the furnishings. Another, smaller quilt hung on the open wall and opposite was a window framed by simple cotton curtains.

The living area was big enough for a comfortable-looking couch, covered in denim fabric with a crocheted blanket tossed over the top. A wooden chair with thick cushions on the seat and back was positioned at an angle to the couch and the flat-screen television sitting on a low table beneath the front window. The kitchen was an L-shaped countertop tiled in dark green and yellow with a small range and white-painted cabinets. All the rooms were—unsurprisingly—very clean and almost oddly tidy.

There were only two items stuck to the face of the fridge with plain round magnets: a crayon portrait with "Mason" scrawled beneath a round head with a big smile and a photo of London—probably her most recent school portrait.

It struck him, hard, that Mac should have more disorder in her life. There should be a bigger house with a man's hiking boots tumbled on the bedroom rug and his jacket hanging in the entry. She loved to read, so books should be left open on the couch—one a thriller and one a romance. A cookbook should be tossed on the countertop with take-out menus used as place marks.

Where were the flowers in a vase, the ones her guy brought to her every Friday afternoon? A beautiful bunch that would last a full seven days until he came home with the next one.

There should be more things stuck to her fridge. Ticket stubs, a pending invitation, a dozen photos. More signs of life.

Signs of a fuller life, in which Mac had a partner who appreciated her—a man who didn't mind brushing up against the occasional thorn because the honey beyond was so very sweet.

While Zan had been gone, he'd never imagined her having that life. For ten years he'd pictured her just as he'd left her, young and wild, though still rooted to her mountains. But in that decade, she should have made a match and built the kind of relationship her siblings had with their significant others.

But then...then Zan wouldn't have had this hiatus with her and it would be some other man's pleasure to provide her peace and solace after a long day. Instead, it was he who had the opportunity to give Mac the security and space to let out all the emotional turmoil bottled inside her.

To once again be her shelter.

So he got busy.

She wandered into the kitchen with her hair slicked back wet and wrapped in a long robe. Beneath it he could see flannel pajama pants and a T-shirt. Her slippers were puffy and most likely down.

"Just in time," he said, sending the wooden spoon in another circle around the saucepan. "There's a glass of wine waiting for you in the fridge."

"You're cooking?" she asked, coming closer to peer at what was sitting over the heat and to look into the bowls on the counter beside the range.

"My specialty. A recipe I learned from an old gypsy woman in Kiev."

"Hmm," Mac said. "It sure looks like the chicken soup with alphabet letters and the Goldfish crackers I keep on hand for Mason."

He glanced over his shoulder at her. "You mean the old gypsy woman lied to me?"

Her lips twitched, but then she turned away from him to head to the fridge, where she pulled out the wine.

The lip twitch he'd take. Mac had been strung so tight on the way back up the hill that he'd worried he'd never see her smile again.

"I've got nachos in the oven, too," he said. "Baked like you like 'em."

"Soup and nachos." She sipped at the wine he'd poured for her. "Gourmet."

"Your pantry, sweetheart. With a different set of ingredients I could have whipped up something more exotic that I learned on my global adventures."

There was a tiny two-top seating area to one side

of the room and he heard her pull out a chair there. Presumably, she sat. "Global adventures," she mused. "What were you looking for, exactly, when you went adventuring around the globe?"

He shrugged a shoulder, turned down the heat on the soup. "What every traveler wants. Beauty. Spectacular vistas. Sunrises that blow your mind. Full moons so close you feel like you can dip your fingertips in the green cheese."

"That was all here, Zan." She let a beat go by. "Are you sure instead of looking for beauty you weren't *escaping* something else?"

Zan wasn't touching that remark. Instead, he served up the food and took a seat at the small table with Mac. When his knees bumped hers, she swung her feet around to the other side of the chair, which caused her to half turn away from him.

She went quiet and tense again.

Shit.

But instead of pressing her for conversation, he let her play with her food—she didn't eat much, even though he thought the nachos were damn good—and then let her clean up her kitchen. She made it so pristine it was as if they'd never eaten there. It was as if Zan had never touched a thing in the place.

He wondered if that was the point.

Shit.

After that was done, he topped off her wine, swiped a beer for himself and turned off almost all the lights. In the shadowed living area, he sat on the couch and patted the cushion beside his. "Take a rest, babe."

"I think maybe I'm tired enough to go to bed now."

He stood up. “Sure. It looks big enough for both of us.”

Mac promptly sat down on the other end of the couch.

Zan narrowed his eyes. “Are you all right?”

“We’re not going to sleep together anymore,” she said, making it sound like a dare.

Okay, she was definitely wound up. Taking his seat again, he made another assessment of her. “Whatever you say, baby.”

She glanced over at him. “Whatever I say?”

“Whatever you say.”

“Please don’t make such a fuss about it,” she snapped in a snotty tone. “I hate to see you broken up like this, Zan.”

Definitely wound up.

“Hey, I understand you’re in a mood. You had a shock today. You were afraid you might lose someone you loved.” The person who held all Mac’s hope.

At that, she curled into herself again, her feet on the bottom cushion, her arms curled around her knees.

He gentled his voice. “You could talk about it, honey.”

“I don’t want to,” she whispered. “I want to put it from my mind.”

Too bad it wasn’t that easy. “It stays with you, Mac. You know that.”

“I don’t know that. I only know that I’ve got to stay strong. I’m Mac Walker, female head of the family, keeping it all together.” She said that last to her knees, with her forehead pressed to the caps of them. “Mac Walker, female head of the family, not thinking about all that might go wrong.”

"Mac..." He slid down the sofa, getting within touching distance.

"Don't," she croaked out when he reached a hand toward her. "Don't make me break."

At least that's what he thought she said, though it might have been "Don't make me weak." Shit.

She was the least fragile woman he knew, but right now he wanted to wrap her in cotton and rock her like a child. If he had the power, he'd make her universe filled with sunshine and smiles, clean snow and perfect sunsets.

It was a powerful yearning.

"How do you handle it?" She was still talking to her kneecaps.

"What?" he asked.

"You lost people you love. What's your coping mechanism? You never speak of it, of them."

She had that right. Mentioning his family by name to Brett the other day was one of the rare times he'd addressed the subject.

"What's your way to handle that loss?" Mac insisted. "It almost broke me, just thinking something had happened to Poppy."

"Babe, you wouldn't be able to handle it my way." She had too many people who loved her and counted on her, so she couldn't just cut herself off. "I'm not sorry about that—it's just true."

"What do you mean?"

She wasn't looking at him, which made it easier to explain. "Maybe because of when it happened to me—at such a young age—or how I lost them all at once, but I cope with my losses in a manner that can't be your manner." He'd never stated it so baldly. He'd never thought it through so clearly.

"What do you mean?"

"I cope by keeping separate. That's not an option for you. You can't keep distant from your family. They would never allow it."

"But you can keep distant?"

"I *do* keep distant, you know that. I don't have real family any longer and getting too close to other people is out for me because…because I just won't. I won't care deeply because I learned the danger of it young and avoiding that danger became ingrained early."

"You cared about us," she whispered. "You cared about me."

"Not enough, right?" He had to be truthful. "I left. I left you all." Before *he* could be left. "To me, loving means loss." It was always the end game. The fucking price.

That he didn't intend to pay ever again.

Something that he said got to Mac. One moment she was curled into that frozen ball, and the next her shoulders began to shake. Every part of her began to shake and seeing that knocked something loose inside Zan, too. He needed her in his arms.

"Sweetheart," he said, starting to move into her.

She swung toward him, too, crawling into his lap and clinging. He held her but her arms came around him, too, and her face was pressed to his neck as silent sobs racked her body.

"Mac…" he said, whispering it against her hair. Glad for the breakthrough that was releasing her from all that tension.

"Oh, God," she said, her lips moving on his skin.

And as he held her tighter it came to him. This was no true release. While she seemed to be crying, her eyes were actually dry.

"Oh, Zan," she said now.

And then he suspected something else—that these non-tears were not just for herself...but for him, too.

He hadn't the faintest idea what to do with that.

MAC MADE BREAKFAST in her kitchen, Zan doing his part with monitoring toast and watching the eggs and bacon while she poured juice and set the table. A few days ago, this domesticity might have made her heart ache just a little. This morning it was much more than a twinge because now she was absolutely, completely, a million percent convinced it was just an illusion.

Not that for any complete minute since his return had she really believed they could have something again, that he could be the man in her kitchen and in her bed and with her forever—because, duh, he'd *left* before, when he'd wanted to go out on a stinkin' *high*—but the night before he'd destroyed even the merest second of time when she might have fooled herself into playing with the possibility.

To me, loving means loss.

Her mini breakdown after he'd shared that hadn't been as cathartic as she might have wished. When she'd stopped shaking, they'd climbed into her bed and she could have sworn she'd drop right to sleep, worn out by everything she'd felt since Brett's initial call.

But she'd heard the echo of Zan's voice—*To me, loving means loss*—in her head, causing her to toss and turn until Zan had hauled her close to him and effectively stopped all her movement by throwing one thigh over hers and his arm across her belly. After that she'd fallen asleep, only to wake up to find herself wrapped around *him*—Zan on his back, her head on his shoulder, her legs tangled with his.

Angry at herself for her unconscious need to be close, she'd slid out of bed and headed straight for coffee, intent on waking herself up…and up to the fact that despite knowing she was in love with him, it didn't change a thing. As much as she wanted to wail and weep and even scream at the man for doing this to her again, she had to keep control of her emotions or else she'd find herself flying apart.

"You're quiet," Zan said, as she dished up the food. "Still worried about Poppy?"

Mac shook her head. "Ryan texted. She texted. Shay texted. London texted. Jace texted. The whole round-robin of assurances that Pop's on the mend and everyone else is feeling good about that fact."

You can't keep distant from your family. They would never allow it.

Truer words and all that, but being part of a family circle didn't give her the partner that her siblings had found. And she doubted she'd ever find that special person.

Because being in love with Zan felt like something she'd never, ever get over.

Damn it.

She set the plates down on the small kitchen table with a loud *thunk*, then yanked out her chair.

Zan's brows rose as he took his own seat. "Are you mad at me?"

"Of course not," she said from between her teeth.

"Why would I be mad at you?" *I loved you, you left me. I loved you again, you're leaving again.*

With another wary glance at her, he forked up some eggs, chewed. "I got a call from the real estate agent yesterday."

"Oh?"

"You were right. She thinks my grandfather's house will show better with the furniture that's in place. It's enough to have the personal stuff out. The pieces that are left keep it from being too cavernous."

"Awesome," Mac said, gaze on her plate. *Stay cool, stay cool, stay cool.*

"No more sorting and packing."

"Right."

He cleared his throat. "So there's really nothing left for me to do here—I can do all the rest remotely."

Her heart jolted and her fingers spasmed on her fork. "Soon, then?" she asked, staring at her food.

"Not until after Poppy and Ryan's wedding. I can't miss that."

"Okay." She tried to take in a full breath. "What's your plan when you leave?" she asked, hoping for a casual tone.

"I'm not sure."

That moved through her, pain joining the anger. If he had a purpose, she thought news of his leaving wouldn't hurt quite so much. But he was going just to…go.

Poking the tines of her fork in a fluff of scrambled eggs, she spoke again. "As long as you keep your promise."

"Mac, I'll wait until after the wedding, but I'm going to have to tell your family about the cabins."

"Not that promise."

"What other one is there?" He sounded puzzled.

Mac's head came up. "You know. The one about your emergency contact."

His gaze slid away from hers. Then he cleared his throat. "Oh, yeah. That."

Her face went hot from the burn rising from her belly. The anger tasted like smoke in her throat. "You lied?"

"I didn't lie," he said quickly. "I didn't respond and you came to your own conclusion."

Mac shot to her feet. "You don't get to do this again."

He eyed her cautiously. "Do what?"

"Go away without a forwarding address or some other way to reach you."

"I won't have a forwarding address, Mac." Now he stood and grabbed up their plates. "Calm down."

"Calm down?" She stalked behind him as he moved toward the sink and her voice rose. "Did you actually say, 'Calm down'?"

Zan slid the plates on the counter and then turned to face her. "What's the big deal? I'm not going to have an emergency, okay? No one will need to make contact on my behalf."

"This is not just about you," she hissed, her fingers balling into fists.

"Yeah?" He crossed his arms over his chest. "Explain to me who it's about, then."

Oh, he thought he was the king of cool. She wanted to slap that aloof expression off his face. "This is about those of us who consider you a brother of the heart."

"What the hell does that mean?" he asked, frowning.

Hah. She'd gotten to him, she could see, and it took

her ire down a notch. "Just yesterday Poppy was all keen on the idea of you keeping your grandfather's house. She thought it would be great to have you visit here on occasion, since you seemed to be getting tight with Brett again."

"Brett doesn't need me."

Zan's offhand manner set her temper to smoking again. "Maybe not today. But other times we've had… struggles that it might have helped to share."

His eyes narrowed. "What kind of struggles?"

She threw out an arm. "I don't know! Struggles!"

"Did *you* have struggles?"

Was he *trying* to be an idiot? "Hello? Three broken engagements!"

Zan continued to study her. "This is about something other than that. Something else. Something else about you."

Careful, careful, careful. She didn't want him guessing she was in love with him. "It doesn't matter what it's about." Turning away, she snatched up the egg pan and dropped it into the sink. "That's not the issue."

His hand clamped on her shoulder and he spun her toward him again. "What happened to you after I left? What would you have shared with me if I'd been here?"

My life, you stupid man. She tried breathing through the anger, but it was growing, ten years of banked fire now, finally, beginning to flame.

"Well?" he prompted.

Tectonic forces had built her beloved mountains. She felt the same kind of pressure inside her now, causing fractures in the rock guarding her most long-held, her most well-buried secret. As she tried to hold it back, her body began to shake.

"Mac?"

"You don't want to know." Her arms wrapped around herself.

"For God's sake," he said, sounding impatient. "Just tell me."

She managed to hold it in another second, but then the truth burst from her mouth. "I thought I was pregnant!"

He stared. "What?"

"You heard me." Her breath bellowed in and out of her lungs. "I thought I was going to have your baby and you weren't around to share in all that might have meant."

"Mac…" He looked stunned. "I didn't know."

"Of course you didn't know," she shot back. "I couldn't tell you. That's the whole damn point. I never heard from you unless you count 117 flipping flimsy pieces of paper."

He shook his head, then shoved his hands in his pockets. "What happened?"

"After you left, I missed two periods." Later, she'd concluded it must have been her body's response to her grief over losing him. "It turned out to be a scare, but that's what I was, Zan. Scared. Scared out of my mind."

He jerked back as if he'd been hit by a blow. Then his hands came up and he pressed the heels of them to his eyes. "Oh, fuck. Oh, fuck, fuck, fuck." His body collapsed against the counter. "I let you down."

"You did let me down." Hell no, she wouldn't sugarcoat it. Hell no, she wasn't going to try to make him feel any better. "But you know what? It turns out I learned from that."

"Learned what?"

To guard her heart. To be impenetrable and unsentimental. And though in the secret depths of her soul she'd found herself longing for that partner her siblings had found, during the past ten years another lesson had been taught.

"It turns out I learned I don't need any man to keep me up."

ZAN SLAMMED THE side of his fist against the door to Ryan Hamilton's house. Then he did it again. As he raised his hand a third time, the door swung open and Brett stood on the other side of the threshold, guarding it like a sentry.

"Hell, Zan," he said, brows climbing toward his hairline. "Trying to raise the dead?"

No, because they'd never gone to rest. They stood on his shoulders weighty and cruel, it seemed now, because their presence had caused him to desert Mac, his Mac, without a way to find him.

She'd thought she'd been pregnant. Eighteen years old. Pregnant.

And he'd been unavailable, no help to her at all, which meant that when it came to her "trust issues" they were largely on him.

Brett should beat the shit out of him.

Instead of inviting that, Zan pushed his way past the other man. "Everybody here?"

"Uh, yeah. Pop got home this morning. The rest of us are over for dinner."

He found Poppy ensconced on the couch in the family room, propped up on pillows and covered with a blanket. Her head lifted when he strode in. "Hey!" she said, and her smile added, "brother of the heart."

Zan took the pain of that, then presented her with the vase of flowers he'd picked up in the village. "For you."

She smiled again, then glanced around the room. "Look, everybody, for me."

Angelica came forward to help her place them on the coffee table next to a steaming cup of tea. Shay and Jace and Mason were gathered around a chessboard on a game table near the fireplace. London stood nearby, phone in hand.

Ryan wandered in from the kitchen with two beers, one of which he passed to Zan. The other he presented to Mac, who was sitting at the end of the couch near Poppy's feet and who appeared to be completely focused on the magazine in her lap. Her silky dark hair swirled around her shoulders and framed her face that looked too pale for his liking.

"Stay for dinner," Poppy said. "We have oodles."

"I've got things to fix," he told them, ignoring the invitation, unsure if they'd want him at the table when he was finished.

"Fix?" Brett asked, his expression puzzled.

"Say." He glanced at Mac, who still wasn't looking at him. That morning, she'd stopped speaking to him after her revelation, and, reeling, he'd climbed into his car.

For a visit with his grandfather's—well, now *his*—lawyer.

He pulled a handful of business cards out of his pocket. They belonged to his attorney, but Zan had added other numbers and two email addresses, an additional one he'd set up just that day. "This is how you can get ahold of me and/or my attorney, anytime of the day or night."

Making the rounds of the room, he handed a card to each and every one of the Walker clan, including London and Mason. The boy looked up with a grin. He must have just lost a tooth, because there was a gap on the top row.

And like that, Zan couldn't breathe as heavy emotion moved through his chest like a cement mixer. The knowledge hit him so hard, he went back on one foot.

He could have left Mac a single mother, like Poppy. He could have had a kid, a boy or a girl, cute like this, who needed a dad. He couldn't remember much about his father, but he for damn sure knew a man was supposed to be one if his lover had a baby.

The knowledge of that, of how he'd failed Mac—not been there in her moments of uncertainty and vulnerability—had finally driven him to ensure he'd always be available if this family needed him.

Feeling as if he was a million years old, he moved on to stand before Brett.

"Brother," he said.

The other man was fingering the business card, a thoughtful expression on his face. "Yeah?"

"I need to give you something else…as head of the Walker family." He glanced back at Mac, aware in her mind that he was going to pile on the unforgivable. "As the oldest."

"Give me what?"

"I'm giving it to all of you, actually," Zan said, sending his gaze around the room. The group was still, expectant, except for Mason, who was lining up the chess pieces on the board.

Mac rose from her seat, the magazine falling to the floor. "Don't," she said.

He ignored her. "I discovered a couple of weeks ago that my grandfather bought the mountaintop property from Victor Fremont."

The Walkers glanced at each other.

Zan took a deep breath. "And before that, he made a loan to your dad, with the lower piece of land as collateral. The money wasn't paid back, and through a series of events and unintended consequences, that land has now come to me."

"Zan!" Mac's hand flew to her throat. She was looking at Poppy, though, who appeared more surprised than anything else.

"Unintended consequences?" Brett asked.

Zan nodded. "I'll lay it all out for you as soon as you like. I have all the relevant paperwork and we can make an appointment with the estate lawyer as early as tomorrow."

Ryan moved forward. "You own the mountain, then? The whole mountain?"

And without waiting for a reply, both he and Jace said together, "I'll buy it from you."

Zan felt his faint grin. "Not necessary."

"Not going to happen," Mac said staunchly. "That's *Walker* land."

"It's Elliott land now, I guess," Poppy pointed out. She was looking at Zan with interest, as if she suspected he had something else up his sleeve.

Which he did.

"We're not letting flatlanders get involved in this," Mac said, her tone vehement.

Shay looked over. "Um, Mac, Ryan and Jace and Angelica have married or are marrying into this family. Can we cut them some flatlander slack?"

Appearing affronted, Mac slumped back onto the couch. "It's our Walker legacy."

Shay's face softened. "I know where you're coming from, but look. Now we have a chance, maybe, to get our legacy back, the whole thing, intact. That is, if Zan will consider a sale?" She turned to him.

"No." He waited a beat. "Because I'm already giving it to you."

"We can't take charity!"

Mac again. God, she was still fighting, but now he knew where at least some of that stubbornness was coming from. *I learned I don't need any man to keep me up.* That was the irony, of course. In failing her, he'd actually caused her to build those strong, high walls he found so very maddening.

"It's not charity. It's family." He angled to give Poppy a small smile. "Brother of the heart, right?"

Her gaze softened and she smiled back. "Brother of the heart."

"Poppy." Mac rolled her eyes. "Everyone knows you're squishy to your soul."

Zan turned to the oldest Walker. "What do *you* say, Brett? Can you accept something from your brother?"

"You're playing dirty," Mac said angrily.

Zan didn't take his eyes off his oldest friend. "Or am I playing fair? If you're my family, then I share with you. That seems reasonable to me."

Brett studied his face. "You staying?"

"You'll always know how to get in touch." That was all he and his ghosts were prepared to offer. "And if you want my opinion on what to do with the place, then build your dream. Make it Walker Mountain—a place for family and visitors alike."

Brett cocked his head. "Are you giving us a choice, Zan?"

"Not about the land. My attorney is already drawing up the papers. What you do with it and…and about the brother of the heart…not my call."

"I know what I want," Poppy piped up.

Then Mason did, too, and proved he was wise beyond his years. "Does this mean I have another uncle? Does this mean more Christmas and birthday presents?"

Most everybody laughed, loud enough to cover his mother's scolding.

"I like the sound of Uncle Zan," Zan said, looking toward Mason and London. The boy grinned. The girl uttered, "Cool," and went back to her phone, clearly this event on a scale of a mere one or two in the teenage drama department.

But to Zan, it was off the charts.

The room exploded with enthusiastic talk after that, as the assembled group discussed possibilities, timelines, and divvied up new responsibilities. The action moved from the family room to the kitchen. Poppy tried to bustle about, but Ryan took things into his own hands by sweeping her off her feet and holding her on his lap as everyone else prepared the meal.

Zan didn't do much, either, but he couldn't stop smiling, and he found himself early on ensconced in a chess game with Mason at one end of the granite island. Grimm wandered in and with a groan flopped at the feet of Ryan and Poppy's stool.

Zan was sucked back in time.

Happy voices, family voices, that included some squabbles and some teasing, but most of all communicated a pervading sense of security and contentment. It was what he'd experienced with his first family—his mother and father and siblings. It had been there those years with the Walkers, too, but he'd always stood on the edge of it…afraid of becoming too dependent on something he knew could be snatched away.

Breathing in, he realized the heaviness on his shoulders had eased some. His ghosts seemed lighter in weight and not so dark in spirit.

Or *he* wasn't so dark in spirit.

And he was able to hold on to that until they all gathered around Ryan and Poppy's dining table for the meal and he realized that one person was missing.

Mac was gone.

CHAPTER EIGHTEEN

WITH HER FULL backpack slung over her shoulder, Mac stomped toward Zan's front door. It was twenty-four hours since she'd left Poppy and Ryan's, stealing into the night as her siblings ramped up their enthusiasm for the Walker mountain and what they might create there.

They'd taken the news of the ownership in stride, unbothered by the implications, untroubled by the problems the situation wrought.

Because, she realized, it wasn't trouble or problems for *them*.

That ties between Zan and the Walkers would now never be severed didn't give them the tiniest pause—because not one of them had thought about what accepting that property might do to *her*.

In all fairness, she hadn't stopped to share that with them. She hadn't *wanted* to share that with them.

She'd wanted to maintain her poise and her dignity, sure the truth would only gain her their pity.

So she'd run off to lick her wounds and while doing so she'd come up with a plan she hoped would cut her own personal bonds with Zan.

The doorbell rang out its distinctive musical phrase. Luckily she didn't hang out with a crowd of classical music aficionados. Once Zan was gone, the likelihood of hearing this set of notes was so small she could count on not encountering anything that would prompt the unpleasant memory.

Before the last tone sounded, the porch light blazed on and Zan pulled open the door. She didn't hesitate to push her way inside, making for the parlor, where a low fire was once again burning. There, she slipped off her coat and slung her backpack onto the coffee table.

"Mac?"

Turning, she took him in from head to toe. She'd seen him in suit-type clothes and she'd seen him in mountain clothes, looking either *GQ* magazine-suave or as if he'd walked straight out of a Patagonia catalog. These garments were something entirely new—well, not new at all. He wore a ratty white T-shirt advertising a marathon in San Diego from twenty years before and a pair of sweatpants that had been washed to a bleached-out blue. The ragged hems trailed threads that brushed the floor.

Because the shirt clung to his shoulders and the waistband of the pants hung sexily at his hip bones, he looked good, of course. But still a surprise.

One of her brows rose.

He must have understood the question in the gesture and his jaw worked for a moment. "Stuff of my dad's."

Okay, sucker punch to the gut. Because now she was seeing Zan's dad, a tall, lean man who dressed like that when he was rolling around with his kids before the fire or when tucking them into their beds upstairs. After story time, he'd sit on that couch, and fitting his wife to his side, watch the flames and dream about their future.

Zan, dressed in his dad's old clothes, was not Wanderer Zan, but Domesticated Zan, a side that rounded out Classy Zan and Caveman Zan in a manner that she wished she didn't know.

Unless he was still your *Zan*, a little voice said.

Breathing in deep, she squelched the thought and reminded herself of the purpose of the visit.

"Well—" she began.

"Are you here about the land?"

She glared at him, remembering all over again that not only had he broken his promise by telling early, but he'd actually given the land away. "Would it matter if I was?"

He rubbed his hand over his face. "I guess not. Mac—"

"I know why you did it." The anger leached out of her, leaving only a dull sadness behind. She sighed. "And I know why they agreed so readily."

Her sibs thought accepting Zan's property would keep him joined to the place and to them. They expected him to return regularly and be the brother they had missed and wanted once again in their lives.

She knew better.

Zan had arranged to transfer that property for exactly the opposite reason. It was his way to pay back the Walkers for what they'd given him when he was young. Now with that debt wiped clean, he could go on without another thought to them.

"So then what brings you here?" Zan asked.

"These," she said, and her hand snagged the straps of the backpack to yank it open. Upending the canvas, she dumped 117 postcards onto the rug in front of the hearth. The firelight played over the glossy, colorful images from faraway places, highlighting those that had landed on their faces so their white underbellies showed, only marked by the distinctive *Z*.

She started to fume all over again. "Why did you do it?" she demanded. "Why did you send them?"

She could only see the top of Zan's head as he stared down at the heap. "To let you know I was thinking of you, I suppose," he said slowly.

"One hundred seventeen times?"

"A hundred times that. A thousand. Ten thousand."

The quiet admission didn't do anything to quell her temper. "Ten *years*, Zan. You rambled about for ten years, yet you still felt compelled to…to keep the knot tied with postcards. Why did you do that when it was you who left?" She nudged the pile with her foot, setting those on top sliding. One slithered all the way to Zan's bare toes.

Bending, he picked it up. A snowy mountain range. The Andes? She couldn't remember. "Yes, I did leave." His long fingers ran over the postcard's edges, and then he folded it into a crude airplane. It was a poor design, because when he let it go, instead of sailing it spiraled to the ground, nose first.

"And that leaving…" he began, staring down at the ground. Then he looked up, his gaze direct on hers. "My parents and brother and sister were on their way here."

"What?" Mac blinked and her stomach pitched. "Here?"

"A ski weekend. It was hardly more than a couple of driving hours from our house at the beach, but they had a friend with a private plane."

God! "I…I didn't know, Zan." *God.*

"Turns out, I'm the only one of the family who made it to Blue Arrow Lake that winter."

Mac's legs folded as both her indignation and her strength ebbed. She dropped to the rug, right beside the hill of postcards. Pressing her hands to her eyes, she thought about the boy that was Zan, arriving at the place that had been the destination his loved ones had died trying to reach. "No wonder you always were bent on going away from here."

"Yeah." He sat on the rug now, too, 117 postcards between them. "You were right when you wondered if I was trying to escape by leaving this place. I thought I could leave the ghosts of them behind. Turns out, they came with me. All over the fucking world."

Mac closed her eyes at the bitter pain in his voice. "They wouldn't want to be a burden. They would never want to hold you down."

He went on as if he didn't hear her. "They weren't the only thing I was running from. It was all of you, too, of course."

"I don't understand why," she whispered.

"Because I was a Walker hanger-on, obviously. A pretender."

Her eyes popped open and her head came around to stare at him. "What do you mean? Did you only pretend to…to care for me?"

"Fuck, no, Mac." He pushed both hands through his hair. "But it was only a matter of time, right? Sure, I was your first lover, but you'd move on. Shay and Poppy and Brett, their lives would move on, too, and ultimately away from me. You'd have each other forever. Me, I would have no one if I stayed."

Everything ends.

"Zan—"

"It was easier for me to go away than for me to be left behind again."

God! She drew up her knees and dropped her forehead to them. It made so much sense in a twisted, miserable sort of way.

"So, Mac…the postcards?"

Her plan. Remember the plan! Lifting her head, she glanced down at the small souvenirs of his travels. "It's time to get rid of them."

He was staring into the fire, his face expressionless. "I feel a symbolic annihilation coming on."

"I thought about the shredder in my office, but they'd dull the blades," she said. "I don't have a fireplace, but—"

"I do."

And it had seemed fitting, that their destruction should be witnessed by them both. He wanted to burn the bridges between them, and he would watch while she did that, too.

Climbing to his feet, Zan reached for a log in the holder on the hearth. "We'll get the flames roaring, then." He tossed it in, then used the poker to stir up the embers and resettle the wood.

After a few minutes the fire was leaping and snapping and putting off so much heat that Mac scooted back a couple of inches. She swallowed. "I guess it's ready."

He settled back on the rug. "Looks like it."

She stole another glance at him, his handsome profile limned by gold and red light, another memory she'd have to eradicate after the 117 that would go up in smoke tonight. Blindly, she reached for a postcard.

Her fingers closed over the nearest, then froze. Her entire arm couldn't move.

Zan's head turned to look at her. "Do you need help?"

"Um…maybe." She was still clutching the postcard she'd selected in a rigid grasp.

"How about I do the first?"

Her fingers tightened as did every muscle in her body. "Okay."

Then she watched him reach for a card. As his fingers closed over tagboard, her muscles snapped, releasing her body from its prison. She lunged. "Not that one."

He glanced at her, eyebrows raised, but let her pluck it from his hold.

"I like that one," she said, retaking her place without looking at it. "I'll…I'll save it for last."

"Then why don't you choose? Tell me which one and I'll toss it in."

Toss it in? That sounded so casual. So cavalier. This was her past he was conferring to the fire. Her secret pain and her secret dreams that had been triggered every time the mail carrier arrived.

They were about to burn the 117 reasons she'd never married anyone else—the reasons that had to be destroyed or she'd never be free.

She darted another look at Zan, then at the pile of cards. Could she destroy them? Did she really *want* to be free?

Maybe not. Maybe not this way. Burning the postcards would mean she was attempting to also forget those precious, joyous moments of her youth.

No way did she want to lose the memory of their first kiss after that silly, teenage tussle.

Or the first time he'd taken her to the movies and instead of being one of a group of Walkers and Zan, arguing over who got the seats with the rail in front, it was just Mac and Zan, and they'd climbed to the top row, making it *their* place.

She didn't want to extinguish her recollection of the day they'd first made love and she'd been so excited she'd bit her hand to stop her cries until he'd pried it away from her mouth and encouraged her to make all the noise she wanted.

All those Mac and Zan memories.

She didn't want to forget their legend, not one single second of it.

"Mac."

Her head turned, and he was staring at her. "Yes?"

"You're not moving."

"I guess… I guess I don't want to burn the postcards anymore."

"What do you want?" he asked, his torso turning toward her so that his left shoulder and left biceps—both hard and buff—were outlined in that golden light. Her heart yearned, but so did other parts of her.

"Mac, baby, what do you want?"

Him. Forever. But she could never let him know that because without her pride, her mere bones wouldn't keep her standing.

So creating another memory of them together would have to do. A final memory. The idea of it tightened her throat and made her eyes burn, but she managed to pin on a sassy smile. "I don't know. If you can rustle up a deck of cards, maybe we can play that strip poker you mentioned the other night."

His spine went rigid and he didn't smile back. Her effort at sassiness petered out in an instant and for a long moment he just looked at her. Then he scooted closer and cupped her face in his hand. "No games this time, Mac. Okay?"

"Okay," she whispered, turning her head to kiss his palm. "No games."

But he still let it be her show and she crawled over the postcards to him. They scattered across the carpet as she moved, scenes of all the places he'd been, crushed beneath her knees and then their bodies as she undressed him. With her hand, she shoved him down so he was on his back and she let her hair curtain them both as she kissed him, kissed him deep and deeper, wet and wetter. His hand clutched her hip as she rolled her lips over his stubbled chin and down his neck.

Then he was pushing up her shirt as she continued to explore his naked chest with her mouth. She tossed it away, and then he one-handedly worked at the hooks of her bra. It fell away, too, as she licked a trail down his belly.

His hand fisted in her hair, drawing it to one side so he could watch her take him into her mouth. She lavished her attention there, pulling him in, memorizing the taste of him on her tongue.

Glancing up, she saw his gaze fixed on her. She sucked harder, giving the performance of her life, her final performance, and she got into it, because this wasn't a play or a game, of course, but a wordless demonstration of all she felt for him.

He groaned, his fist tightening on her hair, and then

he was drawing her away from him. She tried resisting and persuading, drawing her tongue along the hard shaft, but he kept tugging her upward and then he had turned the tables, his body on hers.

The postcards dug into her naked back, but she forgot about them as he drew off her jeans and panties. Zan crawled between her spread thighs and she looked into his face, committing the tenderness there to memory.

With an old wrestling move taught to her by her brother, Mac flipped Zan once again. She hovered over him, knees straddling his hips, her hands caressing his chest. Then she reached down, circled his hard and damp cock with her fingers and fit it to the pulsing groove between her legs.

Zan's hand clamped on her wrist. "Mac, baby, condom."

She froze. God, right.

"Upstairs—" he began.

"No," she said, refusing to interrupt their connection, even for a second. Instead, she rolled them to their sides, so they were face-to-face. Then she took him in hand again. "Remember this?" She caressed up, then down, lightly, then with more force.

Zan groaned again as his fingers traced down her belly to toy with the folds between her legs. "Sweet, baby," he said, his voice rough. "Wet."

She shuddered at the words, his touch, both calling back other times. Maybe this was better than intercourse, she thought, because this act wasn't one of taking and surrender. This wasn't pleasure created by him inside her, but pleasure being stoked *between* their bodies, each of them having a hand in it, so to speak.

"Why are you smiling?" he whispered.

"Just feeling good."

His other hand came up to play with her nipples, and her back arched as goose bumps broke out over her skin. "Oh, Zan," she said.

They'd both had practice, in those weeks and months before they'd experienced full-blown sex with each other. She was getting close now, her hips moving into his caresses, and he slid fingers inside her. Mac's hand tightened on Zan's cock and she worked him in the short, almost harsh strokes she knew he liked.

They both were breathing hard.

His gaze was fixed on hers, and as she looked into that familiar face, her favorite in the world, she found herself letting every last game go. All subterfuge dropped. The last piece of armor around her heart fell and even her pride couldn't hold her back in this intimate moment of connection. If this was their last time to be together, then honesty was more important than preserving her ego. "You know what this is, right?" *I love you.*

His hand jerked, and she gasped. "God, Mac," he said.

"You know," she insisted, saying the words through her ragged pants. "You know."

He closed his eyes a moment and she could sense his body tightening, all his muscles contracting in preparation for release. "I know." Then his lashes lifted and his thumb pressed her clit as his fingers drove deep, triggering her orgasm.

She rode it out, her hand moving in time with her waves of pleasure, and then he was coming, too, his head dipping to shove his face against her throat. It was beautiful. Painfully tender. Unforgettable.

As their breathing evened out, he spoke against her skin. “I’ll say I’m sorry if you want,” he whispered.

“No.” She tipped her chin to rub her cheek against his hair, no longer fighting as she’d been doing for so long—from the moment he’d returned—but instead accepting. Her newly revealed heart might feel tender and defenseless, but she also felt oddly happier now. More like herself—that arms-flung-wide, bring-it-all-on girl that she’d once been. A kind of peace settled over her. “I’m not.”

Her gaze caught on the sky outside one of the windows. Snow was falling, the soft kind, and the flakes were driven by the wind to hit the glass, where they slid down in fat, wet tears. She couldn’t stop the snow or the wind any more than she could stop the seasons of the year or the seasons of a life.

You couldn’t stop loving someone.

So you might as well not regret the feeling.

THE PROPERTY TRANSFER papers were boxed up and wrapped in white with a big silver bow. Zan had taken them into the village and the fancy stationery boutique had done the packaging for him. He carried it under one arm and under the other was a different gift. This one was a blowup of a shot he’d found when clearing out his grandfather’s house.

He didn’t remember who had taken the photo, but it showed the Walker kids and him, aged about ten down. They were bundled in snow gear and the two youngest girls wore pink knitted beanies with pom-poms on top. He and Brett and Mac had crazier hats: Zan’s had plush Viking horns atop his, Brett's was shaped like a joker's headgear and Mac's was helmet-styled with two thick, yellow yarn braids hanging from the sides. Zan had put the photo in a heavy antique silver frame he'd found in one of the other shops along the main street.

Like at Shay and Jace's wedding, he followed a long line of people from the parking lot to the event, many townspeople—including Olivia the baker and Lewis the postal carrier whom Zan also remembered from his youth—and others arriving in sleeker cars and wearing fancier clothes that he supposed were part of Ryan's Hollywood crowd. He and Poppy were holding the reception at the yacht club on Blue Arrow Lake. Guests checked in at a small building that held a welcome desk and also a small souvenir area. At the rear of that space was another door that opened onto a long gangplank—today, covered by a waterproof tunnel-type structure because of the weather—that led over the water to the octagonal-shaped clubhouse with its glass walls offering nearly 360-degree views of the lake.

Once inside the larger building, Zan placed his two gifts on a table piled with many others. Then he glanced around, orienting himself. Round tables were set around a dance floor, each white tablecloth decorated with a profusion of flowers in white and lavender and those place cards he'd watched the Walker women make one night.

French doors opened to a deck on the water and above these were great swags of the same flowers. The bride and groom were slated to come through those to join the reception.

Instead of getting married in a church or at the reception venue, the wedding rites were an immediate family–only event on a boat that toured the lake at sunset. By the time Poppy and Ryan entered the yacht club, they would already have been pronounced man and wife.

Not long after Zan arrived, the pair and their attendants did, too. A great cheer went up, and he clapped as loudly as anyone. Ryan looked like a movie star and Poppy so damn happy Zan felt his throat tighten. No nerves for that mountain girl and no sign of her recent accident. She was ready for her close-up.

Then the wedding party got swallowed up by the crowd. Zan hit the bar for a beer and propped himself in one corner. Tilda Smith found him there, and she was hand in hand with Ash Robbins.

More glow.

Tilda smiled. "Hey!"

Zan and Ash shook hands. "We're off to London soon," the young man said. "The both of us."

Tilda smiled up at her companion. "You could light the night," Zan told her.

"She lights up my world," Ash said.

Then their gazes met in a way Zan recognized. Young love, as fresh and bright as a new fall of snow.

He'd walked away from that.

Dinner was announced and guests moved about to their places. Zan found he wasn't hungry, so instead of taking his designated chair, he returned to the bar and drew up a stool, settling with his back to the rest of the room. The bartenders were busy, so no one paid him any attention and he remained apart from the ensuing frivolity, though he spared a smile when he heard best man Mason give his well-practiced toast.

Uncle Zan, the kid had called him.

He was walking away from that, too.

The dancing began, and he got up rather than be tempted to turn and see Mac in the arms of some of the slick Hollywood guests. His tour took him along the room's glass walls, and he directed his attention to the views of the lake. It was dark outside, but there was enough light from the clubhouse and the houses ringing the shore to illuminate the thick clouds hanging low on the water. It was supposed to snow.

He was staring at the far shore when the hem of his coat was tugged. He glanced down. A little old lady stood there, somewhere in the octogenarian years, he guessed. Her silver hair was braided at the top of her head. It took him a minute to place a name to her face.

"Mrs. Lind!" he said. "You look great."

"Thank you, young man." She shook a finger at him. "Have you cleaned up your bad boy ways?"

He had to smile. "Uh…no?"

She placed her palm on his sternum, tried to push. "Oh, you." Then she sipped from the champagne glass in her hand. "How's your grandfather?"

"I'm sorry to tell you," he said, sobering. "But he passed some months ago."

Her expression registered confusion, then it cleared. "That's right. I was sorry to hear that."

"Thank you."

"And your parents? How are they?"

He took a breath. "I lost them, too."

Her silvery brows came together a long moment, and then she blinked again. "Well, of course you didn't *lose* them." Her hand rose to his chest once more, and her fingertips brushed the center of his tie. "They're right here."

She moved away before he could come up with anything to say. That was good, because he wasn't certain he could speak. His hand rose to tug at the silk wound around his neck. It was strangling him.

They're right here, Mrs. Lind had said, touching his heart.

Except he knew they were on his shoulders, his mother and father and Jana and Dragon. A weighty yoke, no matter that they'd loved him and he'd loved them back. Grief had a way of solidifying, a sharp, dark ache becoming a heavy, crushing load.

They would never want to hold you down, Mac had said.

Of course not. He didn't blame them. No one was to blame for the tragedy. But a smart man learned from it.

A stupid one let it become an excuse, a voice said. A stupid one let staying detached to avoid pain become a habit that needed to be broken.

Okay, yes. The grief had shackled him. He'd resisted not holding on to a new family—the Walkers. He'd turned away from a future with Mac because…

Not because he'd been smart, he thought now.

Movement from the corner of his eye had him turning, to see Poppy and Ryan on the dance floor, wrapped in each other's arms. The man had survived losing a child…and he'd managed to wade out of his sadness to hitch himself to Poppy's brilliant star.

Shay was dancing with Jace, their foreheads touching as they spoke quietly to each other. The youngest Walker had found a single father who came with a challenging teenage daughter he didn't know, but Shay hadn't hesitated to take them both on.

Angelica was dragging a reluctant Brett to join the

others. Her husband was grinning, and Zan could tell that his unwillingness was all for show when he swept her close for a lavish dip. Her laugh floated above the crowd and he heard Brett's lighthearted response. His old friend was not dragging his feet any longer.

His brother and sisters of the heart each had what he'd been avoiding for ten years.

Because he'd been too cowardly to take that risk.

Love means loss.

But hell, look how much he'd missed out on. So damn much.

Years.

His eye traveled over the happy couples again, and his gaze caught on someone standing at the edge of the dance floor, all alone. Mac. Her dress was the palest purple lace and strapless. It clung to her figure until it flared at the knees, with some sort of white netting peeking out from beneath that made her look as if she was standing in the froth of an incoming wave. Her hair curled around her face and was held back on one side by a tiny lavender rose pinned above her ear.

He'd walked away from her, that woman he'd loved.

And then he'd tried to bind her to him anyway, 117 times.

What a dick move.

And yet she still loved him. That was the message she'd given him the other night in front of the fire. She was in love with him.

He felt himself freeze. His heart stopped beating, his blood no longer ran through his veins, his breath stalled in his lungs.

Everything ends, he'd said, believing it.

But not Mac's love for him.

Not Mac's love.

Everything didn't end, did it? She'd proved that.

"My man!"

A voice boomed in his ear and made Zan jump. He looked over. "Hey, Skeeter."

The guy clapped a meaty hand on his back. "Great to see you again. Heard you were leaving soon, so I'm glad I have a chance to say goodbye."

"Yeah."

"What are you doing here, standing by yourself?" Skeeter asked. "Gotta join in. Be part of the group. We'll get one of the photographers to take a picture of us, what do you say?"

Without waiting for an answer, he dragged Zan in the direction of a man strapped under a couple of cameras.

"Right here!" Skeeter said, waving to get his attention. "You gotta get me 'n' Zan!"

Guests were staring. The photographer obligingly turned to aim one of his lenses at them. For a moment, Zan wished to change places. For the past ten years, that had been him, the observer, standing back from the show.

Standing back from the beauty of real life and real emotion.

A tickle pricked the back of his neck and he glanced around. There was Mac still across the dance floor, now looking at him. *His Mac.* Her lips curved in a small smile and then…it happened. His heart moved in his chest, expanding, as if the ghosts that Mrs. Lind claimed were in there were elbowing each other, creating space, making room.

More room in Zan's heart for all those he loved.

A euphoria like champagne bubbles invaded him,

and his spirits soared. He had to do something, he thought, suddenly impatient. He had to make moves, tie knots, set down roots, latch on to that future he suddenly saw. The future he wanted so very much.

"You're staring at our sister."

Glancing around, he saw that the bride and Shay had arrived at his elbow. "Poppy. Shay." His mind was reeling, so he spouted the cliché. "You, um, both look beautiful."

"You look poleaxed," Poppy said, sharing a swift glance with Shay. "Something wrong?"

"Something's right…or at least I want to make it that way." His gaze searched for Mac again. Her slender body was moving away and his gut clenched, now not wanting to lose her even for a second in the crowd.

"He's in love with her, Shay," Poppy pronounced.

"Well, of course he is. He always has been."

He turned his head to stare at the women.

Shay shrugged. "It's legend."

"And I think you should add to it," Poppy said, her eyes sparkling like the diamond on her ring finger. "Tonight. Right now."

"Um…" Zan felt his heart lurch, the thing in full agreement. "No. It's your day. Another time, tomorrow, when we can have a private moment, I'll tell her how I feel. What I want." *A future together.*

Poppy frowned. "We don't want that happening in a private moment, do we, Shay?"

"Uh-oh, Zan," her sister said, but she was smiling. "You're in for it now. If Poppy wants something, Poppy gets that thing."

The bride's expression turned wheedling and she wrapped her small hands around his forearm.

"Uh-oh," Zan echoed. Poppy Walker had never been easy to refuse, especially when she took on that coaxing tone. Under its influence, he'd rescued baby birds and even played pretend tea party on more than one occasion.

"Zan," she said now, "remember how I told you I had a master plan? It's a master plan for my perfect day. And seeing Mac happy with you would cap that off."

He groaned. "Poppy—"

"She's always done so much for all of us…for me." Her big gray eyes were trained on his face. "You could have her in your arms forever, starting tonight. Starting right now."

During this impassioned declaration, Ryan had come up behind his bride. Zan met his gaze. "You heard her," the other man said, grinning. "Give me some peace. Cap off my wife's perfect day."

Zan's pulse pounded. How much he wanted to begin his perfect night. "Are you sure?"

"Of course I'm sure!" Poppy said, her excitement contagious. "Do you need help?"

A smile grew on Zan's face and he shook his head. "I already have an idea…" It would mean taking a public risk and, worse, putting everything on the line for that emotion he'd been trying to escape for ten years, but Zan wasn't walking away any longer. This time he was running toward what he wanted. Who he needed.

CHAPTER NINETEEN

MAC'S FACE HURT from all the smiles she'd been doling out that evening. She was tired, but also tired of responding to the same comments and questions she'd fielded at the past two Walker marital events.

Though it was easy to agree that the bride was beautiful and the groom looked doting.

Effortless to nod along when Mason—her date for the evening as the other had gotten sick—was effusively complimented for his toasting abilities.

But she was out of clever or evasive responses to some of the other things that had been said, and she was tempted to respond less graciously to the next round of queries.

Did she know when it was going to be her turn? Likely never.

Didn't she want kids before she was too old to have them? Twenty-eight was hardly over-the-hill.

Was it lonely to be the only Walker sibling without a partner? Yes, so she already had her multi-cat adoption papers turned in.

Why was a beautiful girl like her unmarried? Because she was in love with a man who didn't love her back—the one who'd better stop looking at her or she'd be inspired to nab him with a flying tackle, thus humiliating herself and adding to that wretched legend she'd be hearing about for the rest of her life.

That would be the clunker of all conversational clunkers, wouldn't it?

So she turned and headed for a destination unknown, intent on avoiding guests with unthinking remarks to make as well as Zan Elliott, whose gaze she continued to feel upon her.

As she strode past the table displaying the wedding cake surrounded by the bridesmaids' flowers, she set her jaw and added another item to her evasion agenda. No way, no how, would she be forced into one more embarrassing round of catch-the-bridal-bouquet. The instant she sensed it in the offing, she was going to retreat to the kitchen and hide among the ladles and chafing dishes.

Then Mason popped up at her side, and she smiled at her small and welcome distraction. After her arranged date had been forced to cancel because of an unfortunate chronic sinus problem, her nephew had declared himself to be her escort for the evening. She didn't mind at all. He was funny and smart and didn't make this weird whirring-clicking noise in the back of his throat due to postnasal drip.

Now he wanted her to show him to the restrooms. His business finished there, he next asked her to accompany him to the deck over the lake. The temperature was freezing outside and she could smell snow, but she accepted the goose bumps and took the opportunity to clear her head.

This was her new normal and it was time to accept it. Her brother and sisters were married and the

Walker family clan would continue on, paired up and with more pregnancies to follow, she supposed, but she could deal. Even if none of those pairings were hers, even if none of the children to come would call her "Mommy."

Mason was playing airplane all over the deck, his arms out as he surfed the wind in his little tuxedo. What a guy. Her guy, at least for the evening—and for Poppy and Ryan's honeymoon, too. Yes, that was something to smile about.

"I love you, Mace," she called out.

The Mason Walker Hamilton flying machine made a sharp turn and buzzed her way. When he reached her side, he grinned, exposing the gap in his top row of teeth. "The Tooth Fairy left me a dollar," he said.

"Coolio," she answered, unsure why he shared that news now.

"London gave me five."

Mac's eyes widened. The teenager was paying for baby teeth? What was that all about? If she still dressed as she had when she first came to the mountains—in all black, her hair dyed to match, her eye makeup scary dark—Mac might have worried she wanted one for some kind of weird ritual or odd jewelry idea, but London wasn't like that anymore. "Why'd she pay you the money, Mace?"

Instead of answering, he slid a cell phone out of his front pocket. "She gave me this for the night, too." He held it up.

It was the girl's distinctive pink-on-purple device.

"Uh…that was nice?"

Mason sent her a quick grin and slid it away. "I'm waiting for a signal."

"Um..." Mac narrowed her eyes. "I think we should go back inside." There, she'd track down the teenager and find out what was what.

Her nephew paused, then pulled out the phone again. "Okay," he said, glancing at the screen. "We can go in now."

She pushed open the French doors just as the DJ played a raucous fanfare. A spotlight started roaming the darkened room. "Time for the bouquet toss!" he said into the mic. "We need all you single ladies onto the dance floor." Beyoncé's song started up, just as the light found Mac's face.

Her body froze, her gaze slid to her nephew. "Did you have something to do with this?" she hissed, seeing London coming toward her, the girl's face filled with glee.

"Five dollars is five dollars," he said, unrepentant.

Crap, what could she say? He was a true Walker.

The crowd applauded as her niece tugged her onto the dance floor. Mac considered making a break for it, but that would only be more embarrassing. And after three broken engagements and ten years of listening to the legend of Mac and Zan, she should be used to mortification.

Still, she wished the floor would open, swallow her up and take her straight down to the bottom of the lake.

Someone was going to pay for this.

As the lights came up a little and more women

joined her and London, Poppy caught Mac's eye and gave an apologetic shrug.

Mood only lower, she crossed her arms over her chest and waited for the stupid ritual to begin. London jostled her with an elbow. "I cooked up this plan with Mason so you wouldn't miss this. Isn't it fun?"

Mac only snorted, then uttered her sister's favorite word in the most sarcastic way possible. "High-larious."

Twenty or so women had joined them when the lights went down again and that stupid spotlight turned them all into washed-out deer.

"All right, everyone," the DJ said. "We're about to—"

"Hold it," a familiar voice called out. Then Zan strolled onto the dance floor to stop right by her side.

Oh, yes, let's just rub salt in the wounds. "Go away, Zan."

He bent toward her ear. "I tried to get this done earlier. But the DJ is on a schedule and Skeeter was slow getting back from the souvenir shop. Not to mention that at first I couldn't find Lewis—"

"What?" Lewis the mail carrier?

"And just for the record," Zan added, "this has Poppy and Ryan's full approval."

"What?" she said again. But then another voice rang through the room.

"Special delivery for Miss Mackenzie Marie Walker!"

She swung toward the sound of her name. What was going on?

Lewis pushed through the crowd. Middle-aged and smiling, he had kids about the same age as the Walker clan. With a flourish, the man handed Mac a postcard.

She stared down at the glossy image. It was a highly colorized shot of Blue Arrow Lake in spring, daffodils circling the shoreline. Baffled, she stared at it.

"Turn it over," Zan whispered.

In his handwriting, that she knew so well, was one word. *Will.*

She only had a chance to send him a confused look before Lewis stepped forward again, with another card.

Summer at Blue Arrow Lake. It was written in script across the bottom of an aerial photo showing blue water, boats, water-skiers. And on the other side, it read *You.*

Mac began to tremble. The chill her skin had taken outside was washed away in a flush of heat.

Lewis was grinning as he gave her yet another postcard.

In this one, there were yellow aspens. Pumpkins were lined on a fence and the lake glistened in the distance. Mac stared down at the photo and it shook in her fingers as hope made it hard to breathe. She was afraid to turn it over.

Zan's hand came in her line of sight and did it for her.

The word wavered. She blinked, blinked again. *Marry.* It most definitely read *Marry.* In Zan's handwriting.

Then he was in front of her, holding a fourth postcard at eye level. A snowy scene. Blue Arrow Lake in winter. This very season.

His gaze on her, he slowly flipped it over so she could see the two letters that would change her life.

"Me," he said aloud as she traced the word with her eyes. "Mac Walker, will you marry me?"

The DJ cut the music and a hush came over the room.

Her head lifted and she looked into Zan's eyes. They were crinkled at the corners in a way that Boy Zan's hadn't done… They were the eyes of a man who'd seen the world.

"This is not just so I can get out of the dumb bouquet toss, is it?"

He shook his head. "It's so that I can begin a life with the woman I love. The woman I have loved for so, so long."

Her heartbeat was going so hard, so fast, the whole room must have been able to hear it. "You love me?"

"So much, Mac." He smiled. "I think you knew."

"One hundred seventeen times, I knew," she said, or at least that's what she'd always wished the white spaces around the letter *Z* meant. A pressure built behind her nose and a burning at the back of her eyes. "I thought *you* would never figure it out." She'd thought he'd run from the risk of it forever.

"It took me ten years to learn to live with my ghosts. And ten years to win the battle against letting people in because I was afraid of losing them. You showed me how to do that the other night."

When she'd told him she loved him, despite the fact that he'd been bent on leaving her again. He tucked a tendril of hair behind her ear. The tender touch sent tingles all over her body. "That decade hurt you, and I'm sorry for it."

"You don't have to be," she whispered, understanding now the profound effects his tragedy had wrought on him. It made this decision of his just that more precious. "Maybe we needed to let our love age."

"Then I guess it's ripe now." He grinned and leaned close. "That sounds kind of salacious. Not to mention delicious."

His mouth was close enough to kiss, but she couldn't do it quite yet. "Is this really happening to me?" she wondered aloud. Was this her very own grand gesture?

Zan began to answer, but his words were lost when a bouquet of flowers hit him square in the face, then fell into Mac's arms. She looked down at it, then glared at her sister, who stood a dozen feet away, laughing like a loon.

"Hey, it's not supposed to be this way," Mac groused. "I'm off the market now."

"We haven't heard a 'yes' yet," Poppy called out, her smile unrepentant.

Mac's gaze shifted to Zan. His expression sobered and he studied her face as if wanting to memorize this moment. "Marry me, Mac. I'll make those ten years apart up to you. I'll make the next seventy-five the best ever. The legend deserves a happy ending."

"*We* deserve a happy ending," she said, because she'd been brave enough to open her heart again and because that had inspired him to admit his own feelings for her. "Zan and Mac. So yes, I'll marry you. Yes. One hundred seventeen times yes."

The crowd broke into loud applause and she leaped into his arms, crushing the flowers between them so the scent of roses and lavender filled the air as they kissed. Then Mac Walker, cool, controlled, unsentimental Mac

Walker, now feeling as buoyant and bright as only happiness and hope for the future could make a person, buried her face in her beloved's throat and burst into tears.

EPILOGUE

Five years later...

WINTER AT THE Walker Lodge was nearly over. The last patches of snow on the ground were shrinking by the day, but they had bookings for their famous Lovers' Weekends that they advertised during the transitional periods between seasons to keep the visitors coming up the hill.

Mac Walker Elliott cleaned one of the great room's stackable set of doors that led to the large veranda where they served meals in summer. Soon the daffodils would be poking their brave heads out of the cold earth, but now it seemed all was quiet waiting for spring.

Once back in their hands, the Walkers and their spouses had worked hard to make this land a beautiful place for themselves, friends and visitors. They often thought of Zan's grandfather, the man who had made it all possible, and wondered if he'd had a secret agenda all along. Zan himself was sure of it, that the old man had been paving the way for his grandson to have a family again and a place that he'd finally know was home.

She put her hand over her belly as she felt the gentle kick of her and Zan's second child.

In the distance a little one was fussing, but her mother's

trained ear knew it wasn't their Damon—better known as Dragon. When he got going he lived up to his name, all fire and smoke. She'd mentioned just yesterday that she couldn't figure out where his temper came from, and everyone in the Walker-Hamilton-Jennings-Elliott clan laughed.

They were all *so* going to pay for that.

Poppy showed up to wrest the window cleaner and bunched newspaper from her hands. "I thought you were going to put your feet up."

Her sister's dark-haired daughter, age four, skipped into the room. "Hi, Auntie Mac!"

"Hi, Melly." The girl had her mother's gray eyes and light heart. "Where's Mason? He said he was going to play chess with me."

"Here I am," a boy's voice answered.

She glanced over her shoulder as her nephew walked into the room holding the hand of one of Shay's tow-headed twins. Mac's youngest sister followed next, the other twin draped over her shoulder, out like a light.

Cassie and Tommy were never asleep at the same time. The family had come to—wearily—accept this.

"I thought you were going to put your feet up," Shay said.

Mac rolled her eyes and then headed for one of several couches in the huge room. She made a big show of seating herself and crossing her ankles on an ottoman. Grimacing, she noticed they were swollen.

Then Brett wandered from the back room behind the check-in desk. His three-year-old, Susannah, nicknamed Sweetness because she'd been born with her mother's disposition, was on one hip. She sucked her thumb with her head against her daddy's shoulder. A baby lay in the crook of his other arm.

"Let me take Dorrie," Poppy said, hurrying to scoop up the infant. She blinked at her aunt, completely accepting that another person loved her and wanted her close. Together, the two of them plopped down to share Mac's couch.

Brett and Sweetness took to an adjacent love seat. Shay and Cassie joined them there.

Mac glanced around at her siblings. "Are we having a family meeting or something?" The baby rolled in her belly and she rubbed at its rump, which was poking up at her right side.

"I suppose we could," Brett said. "What do we need to talk about?"

They all stared at each other.

"Um…" Poppy seemed to be searching her mind.

Shay tilted her head. "Well…"

"I got nothing," Mac finally said. "I think that means everything's good."

Sweetness's thumb popped out of her mouth. "Happy," she said.

The Walker siblings stilled, then met one another's gazes and, sharing smiles, let that be the last word.

* * * * *

If you loved Mac and Zan's story, turn the page for a peek at how it all began with Poppy and Ryan in TAKE MY BREATH AWAY!

POPPY PUSHED OPEN the door of Johnson's Grocery, her mind on the list of ingredients she needed per her brief stop at the Blue Arrow Lake branch library. Johnson's Grocery was located on the same street, so she thought she'd start there.

Someone hailed her from the back of the store, where a butcher's case held fancy cuts of grass-fed beef, stuffed breasts of duck and free-range chicken, as well as fillets of salmon prepared for grilling. The store was small—real estate in the mountain resort area went at princely rates—but the narrow aisles were packed with gourmet foods, expensive liquor and fancy wines. Everything and anything a filthy rich Los Angeleno couldn't do without during a getaway to what was known as "Hollywood on High."

Cheaper merchandise could be had if she'd driven to a larger community, but that would have cost her in time and gas money, so Johnson's was her go-to market.

The endcap nearest the entrance displayed a selection of expensive children's toys, everything from miniature fishing rods to expansive LEGO sets for snowbound weekends. Gazing on them, Poppy's heart squeezed, sending a rush of tender longing through her veins. *Mason*, she thought, picturing her towheaded boy, who right now was on his way to a vacation filled with such delights as whirling in teacups and flying with Dumbo. *Mason, I miss you so much.*

"Poppy."

At the sound of her name, she glanced over, smiled. "Hey, Bill." Bill Anders was a scarecrow of a man and wore a bibbed, crisp cotton apron with the store's name stitched on the front, most likely by his wife. She had an embroidery business in addition to the day care she ran. Like many people who lived in the mountains year-round, the Anderses cobbled together a living out of more than one line of work.

"Heard Mason went to Walt Disney World with your cousin James."

"That's right. James and Deanne wanted company for their own little guy on a visit to Deanne's parents. When Mason heard the magic words *Mickey Mouse*, I could hardly say no."

"Heard, too, that you got laid off from Inn Klein until the remodel's complete. Sorry for it."

"Thanks," she said, hiding her grimace by stepping past the shopkeeper on her way to the fresh fruits and vegetables. Of course, news traveled fast when you lived in a tight community like this one. She knew how this worked, didn't she? People had been in the Walkers' business—and they in everyone else's, she supposed—since the logging family's arrival in the mountains.

But Poppy had felt her friends' and neighbors' interest in a more up close and personal fashion. Collective eyebrows had lifted and noses had twitched when she'd found herself pregnant by a summer visitor who'd skedaddled back to his moneyed family in Beverly Hills the minute she'd informed him of the test results. Though the truth was, Poppy minded less people gossiping about her sex life than them knowing she'd been dumb enough to fall for a rich and careless man.

Her mother had made a similar mistake before Poppy. Though she couldn't wish her half sister, Shay, had never been born.

Nor did Poppy regret one moment with Mason.

Mason... She mouthed his name, her heart starting to hurt all over again.

Then she shook off the melancholy. *Think of something else*, she commanded herself, as she stepped up to the tiered rows of produce, glistening from a recent misting. *Think of making something of the cabins. Think of getting rid of that stupid curse.*

"Sage," she murmured to herself, inspecting the selection of fresh herbs. Pulling a bunch of the gray-green leaves from the stack, she frowned at the price. There wouldn't be a paycheck from the inn until it reopened July Fourth, and the aromatic was expensive. As a rational woman, Poppy didn't, of course, completely buy in to the idea she could eradicate any negative energy at the cabins. But...

She was determined. And desperate.

Wincing at the mental admission, she dumped the herb into her basket and started her hunt for rock salt. Despite the dire predictions of her older brother, Brett, her older sister, Mackenzie, and her younger sister, Shay, Poppy hoped that by summer the dwellings would be available as weekly vacation rentals. Cabin two—if you didn't count the dubious state of the roof—was already in decent shape, and with a fingers-crossed kind of optimism, she'd placed notices on the community bulletin boards around town, including the one here at Johnson's.

Despite the point of view of her pessimistic sibs, Poppy would prove to them that the Walker albatross could be turned into an eagle, after all.

The cowbell tied to the store's front door clattered, interrupting Poppy's train of thought. She glanced toward the door.

Her guard instantly jerked up. From twenty paces she recognized the man standing on the mat. She didn't know his identity—that was well-hidden by a watch cap pulled low on his forehead, the fancy Wayfarers that covered his eyes and the dark scarf wrapped around his neck that almost completely obscured his mouth—but she knew his type.

Rich guy.

She'd bet the scarf was cashmere and that those sun specs retailed for five hundred bucks or more. The waterproof jacket and boots came from a high-end store that catered to "outdoorsmen" who spent their summer days sipping martinis on the terraces of their lakeside mansions while watching their fancy boats bob up and down at private docks. They whiled away winter nights beside fires built by other hands, eating meals prepared by personal chefs brought up from LA. The wine in their glasses would cost more than Poppy's monthly paycheck from running the front desk at Inn Klein.

"Can I help you, sir?" A round-faced teen, all perky ponytail and freckled nose, appeared at his elbow.

"Just stopping in for a few things," the man said. His voice was low but carried easily. Maybe one of the new moguls that had taken up residence at what was now known as "Silicon Beach," LA's own hotbed of tech industry that was rivaling the famed valley in Northern California. While she stared, his head turned her way. His hand lifted, tipping up his sunglasses.

Their gazes met. Poppy's heart jolted. His eyes were a scorching shade of blue, the color that edged the blades of magical swords in fantasy novels or that you could find at the innermost core of fire. Her temperature climbed, heat radiating from the center of her chest and reaching upward to warm her face. It was embarrassing, she thought, still unable to look away. Because it probably appeared to him she was ogling instead of… instead of passing judgment.

Sue her, she didn't trust men like this. Didn't want to be around them more than she could help in a region that catered to the over-the-top affluent.

That thought got her feet moving again. She gave her back to the stranger, only half listening as the teenage clerk chattered to him about the store specials—veal cutlets and cheesecake baked by the kid's own talented mother—and the big March storm the weather service was predicting.

Poppy smirked at that as she added the rock salt and a small bunch of daisies to her basket. The only thing predictable about spring weather in the mountains was its changeability. Her brother said it was like a cranky woman deprived of chocolate, but since he'd been short-tempered himself since returning from his service with the 10th Mountain Infantry Division, she and her sisters just rolled their eyes at him.

Behind his back.

Looking for candles, she turned a corner, almost plowing into the stranger. She drew back to avoid contact, swaying on her feet. He reached to steady her, but she took a staggering step to the rear, instantly sure to her bones she shouldn't be touched by him.

His hand dropped and he muttered something under his breath. Ducking her head, Poppy scooted past him, then glanced over her shoulder. She couldn't help it.

He was a big man, six-two, maybe, to her five foot four inches. When she'd whipped by, she'd caught his scent. That was expensive, too, but not cologne, no. This was a clean, not cloying smell. Handmade soap, she guessed, triple-milled, and with a mild but lingering note of sandalwood. As she continued to watch him peruse the contents of the shelves, a knot gathered in her belly. Her nerve endings seemed to lift to the surface of her skin, tickling the nape of her neck and sending prickling goose bumps cascading down her spine and racing across her ribs.

Startled by her visceral response, she stood another moment, rooted to the floor. Then she saw him stiffen and knew, just knew, he could feel her regard and was an eyelash away from catching her staring again.

Don't let him catch you at anything! her instincts warned.

And Poppy, suddenly a tiny bit spooked, broke free of her paralysis. She hurried away from the stranger, finished her shopping and rushed to the checkout stand.

With her selections paid for and bagged, she paused outside the store, breathing in the cold, piney air. She lifted her gaze to the snow-covered peaks and felt her pulse settle. Inhaling more calming breaths, she picked her way toward her beat-up four-wheel drive, avoiding potholes and patches of icy-looking pavement.

As she neared her car, something made her glance around.

And there he was, the stranger, emerging from the grocery. Now, even from behind those dark glasses, she knew *he* was staring at *her*.

That primal alarm inside of her went off again. Her nerves leaped, her feet tangled on themselves, her arms windmilled and her goods scattered as she fell on her butt—for the second time that day—into a deep, cold puddle.

Damn! Mortified, and aware that color was rising from her neck to her face, she scrambled for her fallen purchases and crammed them into their plastic bag. Then she gathered her feet underneath her, preparing to rise with as much grace as possible.

"Here," that deep voice said.

She allowed her gaze to lift. It snagged on his hand, its wide palm and long fingers outstretched to help her up.

Eyeing it like a dangerous viper, Poppy shook her head and placed a palm on the cold, gritty pavement, pushing off to a stand in one quick move. She relied on herself.

And the only hand she intended to ever reach for, to ever hold, belonged to the little man who also had sole claim to her heart. Mason, who was at this moment probably daydreaming about riding the carousel or chasing down Goofy.

Without a word to the stranger she jumped into her car and drove off, sighing with relief when the grocery store was no longer in her rearview mirror.

Thank God, Poppy thought on another sigh. Though she might still feel the smothering weight of that family curse, right now she had the distinct sense she'd just dodged a bullet.

NINETY MINUTES LATER, Poppy was in an even better mood as she stood in the clearing outside her home. With Grimm once again at her side, she'd accomplished nearly every step of the energy-cleansing exercise. Rock salt had been scattered near each cabin entrance—these five as well as the seven located deeper in the trees. At each door, she'd clapped loudly, startling Grimm and hopefully any negative energy that resided there.

Now she bent over the makeshift altar she'd established. Earlier, she'd carried a flat-topped rock to the center of the open area. Upon it she'd strewn petals from the daisies she'd bought. A white pillar candle was already flickering and beside it lay the bunch of sage she'd selected at Johnson's. She'd turned it into a smudge stick by wrapping the leaves around a brittle handful of slender pine twigs and tying them in place with twine. The whole thing was supposed to be dried for a week, but she figured if she waited that long she'd feel too silly to go through with the ritual. Though she was considered the whimsical Walker by her siblings, as a single mother she had developed a decidedly sensible side.

She picked up the aromatic bundle. Her final cleansing act was to light the stick and wave the smoke around while thinking positive thoughts. The dry pieces of pine caught easily on the candle's flame and she held it away from her body as the fire licked toward the first of the sage leaves. Smoke curled into the cool air and she moved her arm slowly. "I now release old stuck energy," she said out loud. "I now attract new beginnings and new opportunity to this place."

Grimm stayed close to her side as she turned, leaving her back to the steep drive that led up to the cabins from the road below. "I now release old stuck energy," she said again. "I now attract new beginnings and new opportunity to my life."

The scent of pine and sage rose and a sense of peace settled over her. Poppy closed her eyes, inhaling deeply. Wow, she thought. It works. For good measure, she repeated her last words, even louder this time. "I now attract new beginnings and new opportunity to my life."

Grimm's sudden bark scared the smudge stick out of her hand and shot her heart to her throat. It was his "stranger's coming" bark, and Poppy whirled to see a monster SUV with tinted windows climbing the drive, crunching over the slushy snow.

Her dog barked again, the hair on his neck bristling. He was a very effective, although faux, bodyguard. The fact was, Grimm wouldn't hurt a fly, but he had a deep voice and a brawny chest that gave him a belligerent demeanor. So, curious rather than alarmed, Poppy curled her fingers around his collar and watched the vehicle come to a stop.

Her jaw dropped when the door opened and a long leg in a familiar expensive boot emerged, followed by the rest of the rich stranger from Johnson's Grocery.

Once again, her skin rippled in apprehension and her stomach knotted. Grimm let out another bark, the harsh sound more welcoming than Poppy felt. To disguise her trepidation, she shoved her hands in the pockets of the jacket she was wearing—her brother's castoff—and leaned back on her heels. "What do you want?"

She couldn't see his expression, as he was swathed in that scarf, sunglasses and brow-skimming cap. Shutting the driver's door, he waved a flyer in his other hand. "A cabin to rent."

Her mouth fell open again. Narrowing her eyes, she recognized one of the half sheets of paper she'd pinned around town in hopes of enticing summer visitors. *Summer* being the operative word, she realized now...and the exact one she'd neglected to include on the advertising. Knucklehead!

"Sorry," Poppy said, commanding herself to stand her ground as the stranger moved from his vehicle and across the snow-covered clearing. "We're not accepting guests right now."

"Is that right?" He glanced around. "The coven using all the cabins?"

"The cov—" She broke off as he nodded toward the small altar and the smudge stick at her feet. Though it had extinguished upon landing in the snow, the pungent scent still lingered in the air. She inhaled a deep breath of it, trying to regain her earlier peaceful feeling.

For whatever reason, this man rattled her.

Deciding to ignore the coven remark, she took her hands from her pockets and crossed her arms over her chest as she tried pasting on a pleasant expression. "As I said, I'm sorry. We're simply not ready."

He glanced around again. Smoke rose from her cabin's chimney, but three of the others ringing the clearing were obviously vacant, not to mention inhospitable-looking with their peeling doors and dirty windows. The one nearest hers she'd decided to work on first, and it looked much better with its new paint and sparkling glass. From here, the iffy state of the roof was not readily apparent, though she'd have to come up with the money to replace it sooner than later.

"I'll pay you twice the going rate," the man said, as if he'd read her mind. His gaze shifted to the flyer grasped in his left hand. "I'll take the two-bedroom 'nestled in the woods.'"

"Sorry again, not available." Squirrels had made a home in the chimney and it smelled like something had died in the second bedroom. It was the farthest from the clearing and the last on her list to refurbish, though she'd foolishly—she realized now—advertised it, anyway. As her father's daughter, she should have realized that unchecked optimism could come back to bite her on the butt.

Speaking of bites, she glanced down at Grimm, who stood relaxed at her side. Usually he took cues about strangers from her reaction and body language. Odd that he wasn't picking up on that now...in which case he would be showing a lot of teeth and emitting one of his best "back off" growls.

The long-legged man followed her gaze. "Nice dog."

"If you like death-by-canine," she said. "We call him Grimm, as in the Grim Reaper." A little white lie. Her brother had chosen the name after some famous NFL player he admired.

The stranger patted his thigh. "Hey, Grimm."

Her dog raced forward, his jaw stretched in a toothy smile.

The man ran his hand over her pet's head. "Like I said, nice dog. And I'll pay you triple for whatever place you have available."

Triple? Triple? Poppy thought of her recent layoff, the cost of Mason's plane tickets to Florida and back, the extra dollars she'd given James to dole out on her son's behalf.

"Quadruple, then."

A fool and his money... Poppy mused, tempted despite her jittery nerves and knotted stomach. Mountain people were wary of everything about the rich flatlanders who came up the hill for alpine delights—everything except the money they flung about so freely. It was hard for average Joes and Joannas to make do in a place where real estate and gasoline and foodstuffs were sold at luxury resort prices. But people like the Walkers and the other descendants of early settlers were stubborn about staying among their beloved peaks and pines. Maybe Poppy had once dreamed of oceans and palms and big city streets, but then Mason had come along and sticking to what was familiar had made more sense.

The stranger crossed his arms over the chest of his posh squall jacket, mimicking Poppy's own pose. She couldn't see his eyes behind the dark lenses of his glasses, but she felt them narrow. "Quintuple," he said. "Final offer."

And greed overrode caution. "Done," she answered.

Second thoughts popped up the instant the word left her mouth. "Wait—you realize we're pretty far from civilization. The entrance to the highway is four miles from here."

"I realize. I got lost looking for the turnoff."

Poppy had the sense he was pleased by the fact.

Taking a step back, he tilted his head toward the steep slopes to the north of the cabins and woods. Snow covered the surface that was dotted with a few of the pines that grew densely on the other surrounding hillsides. "What is this place? Can you ski up there?"

"If you want to hike up carrying your equipment. The elevation of the nearest town—Blue Arrow Lake—is a little over five thousand feet but here we're at seventy-two hundred, which means plenty of snow in a good winter. My family had a nice ski business on the mountain, but a wildfire took down the lodge, the rope tow and the chairlifts thirteen years ago."

"You didn't rebuild?"

Poppy shrugged. "Not enough insurance money. And a bad financial deal with a certain arch-villain."

He looked back at her then. "Arch-villain? Like Lex Luthor or Two-Face?"

"Like Victor Fremont." Without thinking, she spat in the snow, ground the spot with the toe of her boot then crossed her heart with the tip of her forefinger.

Only when she felt his stare did she realize what she'd done. "Uh, sorry. Walker family habit." The physical manifestation of their vow to never forget or forgive how the old man had ruined their father's livelihood and health was something Brett had come up with long ago. "But, uh, let me show you the cabin."

Maybe he wouldn't like it, she thought, almost hoping that would be true, despite quintuple the going rate. Something was off about him. Or her. Or her around him.

As she dug the keys from her coat pocket, she walked toward the one-bedroom. There were three wooden steps leading to the narrow porch. Inside, it was cold, but warmer than the outside temperature. He walked past her through the small living area to peer into the room that held a queen-size bed and a Shaker-style dresser.

"The bathroom only has a shower," she warned, "and the kitchen…"

With his back to her, he scraped off his hat. His hair was glossy, nearly black, and when he rubbed his palm over it, the strands settled into lines that screamed "This cut cost a mint!" She saw him finger off the sunglasses. As he stuck them into his coat pocket, she wondered if she'd imagined the surreal shade of his irises back at the grocery store. Perhaps they'd be ordinary on second take. Duller, like the color of a faded cotton patio umbrella. Or with gray overtones, like shadows cast on snow.

He turned.

Poppy nearly staggered back. Her mind hadn't oversold them. His eyes were a hot electric blue that seemed lit from within. They were compelling. Mesmerizing. The eyes of a magician or a mystic or some supernatural being. Again, an acute wariness shot through her.

Grimm whined and she quickly shifted her attention to the dog, needing to look away before she confessed her sins or offered up her life savings. God. Her pulse was racing and there was a queasy feeling in her stomach.

"And the kitchen…?" he prompted, in that deep voice that carried to the corners of the cabin and maybe to the corners of her heart.

God.

"The kitchen." She focused on the velvety golden hair between Grimm's floppy ears and made a vague gesture. "It's over there."

His footsteps sounded against the hardwood floor before finding the living room's braided area rug. From the corner of her eye, she saw his big hand and those lean fingers curled around the scarf he'd had at his neck. *If you look now, you'll see his whole face*, Poppy thought. Then she heard a rustle of sound that indicated he was removing his coat. *If you look now, you'll see his whole body, too.*

It shocked her how much she wanted to check out both, despite how anxious the man made her.

She was a mother, for God's sake! A Walker, focused on creating something of the family legacy.

A woman who had proven herself an idiot when it came to romance, so had sworn off it altogether.

None of which meant it would hurt to take a peek.

That was the inner optimist in her, always trying to find sunshine on a cloudy day.

It might even be good for you!

Ignoring her little voice, she worked the cabin's key off the ring. "If you're still interested—"

"I want the cabin. Until the end of the month."

Quintuple the rate until the end of the month! Poppy focused on that, and only that, as she slid the key onto the small table next to the sofa. "You'll need to plug in the fridge. The heater should keep you warm enough, but there's wood for the fireplace. I'll make sure to keep some piled on the porch. Oh—and I should warn you. There's no internet and there's no TV."

"No TV?" he asked.

"Don't plan to put 'em in the cabins. We Walkers grew up without television—our mom's idea—and I've never picked up the habit."

"So what do you do for entertainment?"

"I read, and I—" She almost said she played with her little boy, but for some reason she didn't want Mason's name in this room, where she was responding so strongly and strangely to this man's masculine charisma. Those blue eyes had done something to her internal wiring, heating her blood and making it buzz as it raced through her system. "I have a good imagination."

Oh, jeez. Why had she said that? Yet another time, embarrassed heat crawled up her neck.

"We have something in common, then. I have an active fantasy life, too." The sudden note of humor in his voice made her chin jerk up.

Their gazes met.

But there wasn't a sign of laughter on his face. There were just planes and angles—strong cheekbones, a clean jawline—that made her instantly think of elegant European men stepping into low-slung sports coupes and spectacular parties where people in evening clothes ended up jumping into swimming pools while a band dressed in white dinner jackets played Cole Porter tunes. He was classically, memorably handsome and his features, coupled with those spectacular eyes, put him at the absolute top of her list of the most beautiful—yet still so male—men she'd ever seen.

Her skin was tingling, her stomach was pitching and her palms were probably sweating, but she couldn't tell because her fingers were curled into tight fists. Everything inside her was reacting to him, but in confusing ways. While some of her was going soft and languid, a sense of melting low in her belly, at the same time her defenses were rushing into place and she felt hyperalert and poised to fight her way out of…out of…

Danger.

Silly, she told herself. Stop being so silly.

Still, she backed up, keeping her gaze on him as she retreated toward the door. He remained where he was, though she thought she detected tension in the lean muscles revealed by the thermal Henley clinging to his powerful torso.

Those magnetic eyes swept over her. "I don't know your name," he said, his voice soft now, the near-whisper of that seductive snake in the Garden of Eden.

She shook her head to dispel the image. "Poppy," she replied, trying to sound businesslike and brisk. "Poppy Walker."

He was strolling toward her now and she retreated farther, until her shoulder blades met the wood of the door. Before she could find her way through it, the man had her hand in his. Heat ran like fire ants up her arm. "Ryan Harris," he said, his gaze fixed on her face.

The words barely registered as the burning touch overwhelmed all her other senses. His palm was warm and strong, its size enveloping hers—making her feel small and feminine. That's when she understood. That's when she could finally put a name to what he'd been able to do to her from that first glimpse.

After more than five years, Ryan Harris reminded her of what it was to be a woman.

"I have to go," she said, ordering herself to step away.

"You do," he agreed, nodding. Then he replaced the warmth of his skin with a bundle of bills. "Rent."

Squeezing her fingers around it, she hustled out the door and into the cold sunlight.

The scent of sage lingered in the air. She thought perhaps her ritual had worked. Maybe the negative energy was gone. That would be good.

And bad. Because it had apparently left a vacuum in its place, allowing in an entirely different sort of energy—one that Poppy was much too uneasy to name.

Don't miss a single story in
USA TODAY *bestselling author*
Christie Ridgway's CABIN FEVER *series:*
TAKE MY BREATH AWAY
MAKE ME LOSE CONTROL
CAN'T FIGHT THIS FEELING
KEEP ON LOVING YOU

CHRISTIE RIDGWAY

78003	CAN'T FIGHT THIS FEELING	___$7.99 U.S.	___$8.99 CAN.
77871	MAKE ME LOSE CONTROL	___$7.99 U.S.	___$8.99 CAN.

(limited quantities available)

TOTAL AMOUNT	$______
POSTAGE & HANDLING	$______
($1.00 FOR 1 BOOK, 50¢ for each additional)	
APPLICABLE TAXES*	$______
TOTAL PAYABLE	$______

(check or money order—please do not send cash)

To order, complete this form and send it, along with a check or money order for the total above, payable to HQN Books, to: **In the U.S.:** 3010 Walden Avenue, P.O. Box 9077, Buffalo, NY 14269-9077; **In Canada:** P.O. Box 636, Fort Erie, Ontario, L2A 5X3.

Name: ______________________________
Address: ____________________ City: ____________
State/Prov.: ________________ Zip/Postal Code: ________
Account Number (if applicable): ____________________

075 CSAS

*New York residents remit applicable sales taxes.
*Canadian residents remit applicable GST and provincial taxes.

www.HQNBooks.com

PHCR0216BL